BURIED!

The only sound is the wind howling down through man-made canyons.

The snow is piled four and five stories high. The city seems totally dead now . . .

Yet there is life . . .

Under the leadership of a woman, a meager band struggles to survive in the city . . .

Packs of wild dogs roam through the blinding white snow . . . circling the survivors.

The trick is not to kill the savage beasts, but to catch them, tame and train them to pull the dog sleds you have built so painfully.

Do whatever you can to exist . . . to live another day.

D1637411

ICE!

ARNOLD FEDERBUSH

BANTAM BOOKS
TORONTO · NEW YORK · LONDON

ICE!

A Bantam Book | December 1978

ISBN 0–553–12151–0

Published simultaneously in the United States and Canada

Bantam Books are published by Bantam Books, Inc. Its trademark, consisting of the words "Bantam Books" and the por-
trayal of a bantam, is Registered in U.S. Patent and Trademark
Office and in other countries. Marca Registrada. Bantam
Books, Inc., 666 Fifth Avenue, New York, New York 10019.

PRINTED IN THE UNITED STATES OF AMERICA

ICE!

The latest of the weather satellites was by far the most complex—and the most successful—of a series that began in 1960 with Tiros I. It orbited from pole to pole at right angles to the Earth's rotation, so timed as to daily scan the whole of the planet as it passed beneath.

It tracked the currents of air and water working their slow, sinuous paths from equator to poles, but watched with eyes far more varied and subtle than human ones. Certain senses were attuned to invisible segments of the spectrum. Others were turned toward space and noted the emissions of sun and stars and space itself. All the known influences upon weather and climate were recorded and transmitted openly and freely to radio receivers about the Earth.

With its solar batteries supplying unending power and its orbit perfectly balanced, there was every reason for technicians to boast it would function in the protective vacuum of outer space for thousands of years, even if unneeded or superseded, endlessly transmitting its complexity of data without worry or wonder if it had an audience.

At night, it shone by intercepted sunlight, an apparent star except for its great speed and a path clearly different from other stars. A primitive tribesman contemplating the night sky might eventually take note of this curious light, and ponder.

GREENLAND, 35 MILES S.W. HUMBOLDT GLACIER:

The Eskimo village lay at the foot of the mountains, shielded from the Arctic winds, and so the night was quiet. Outside the igloos, the only sounds were the heavy breathings of the sled dogs, with occasional muted snarls as they dreamt of the hunt.

One wakened, and its sleepy attention was drawn to the igloo, opalescent from the oil lamp glowing inside. The shifting shadows indicated that someone was awake and prowling about, but this was of little interest to the dog. It closed its eyes and returned to its dreams.

Inside, the old woman finished sewing her clothes. It had been a long and arduous task, for not only were her tools primitive, a sharpened bone for a needle, seal sinew for thread, but her fingers were stiff, her eyes dim, the teeth with which she softened the fur worn to the gums—those teeth that she still had. But the love of her labor lessened the pain, for these were her finest clothes, her final clothes, richly embroidered, soft, thick, and comfortable beyond all others, for in these clothes she was to die.

Suddenly, the stillness was shattered by a sound like an immense gun that echoed across the valley.

The old woman stiffened and listened.

There was a sharp splintering, but pitched so deeply she could feel it inside her. Then came a series of gunshots and splinterings, sometimes alternating sometimes combining into rolling thunder that was answered before the echoes died, and even the ground shuddered.

She looked about her at the sleeping family. They stirred, rolled over, but did not awaken. The sounds, though awesomely loud, were presently irrelevant to them, and so were ignored, just as a sleeping mother shuts out noises outside her window, but springs awake to an irregularity in her child's breathing. For the old woman, the sounds held great and immediate meaning.

She looked at her son and daughter-in-law, strong

and well, and at her grandchildren who were ably cared for. She watched lovingly as they gradually settled back and slept on comfortably. She remembered her own mother, how she too had dressed in her last and best clothes when the tribe had moved on to better hunting, while she stayed behind, waiting to starve to death, or to meet the great white bear should he come first.

It was all quite right and natural that the person who could no longer hunt nor sew nor contribute to the survival of the family, be left to die. And though the occasion was joyous, though that person knew he or she would soon be bound up in the Spirit of All Being, and be reunited with those who had died, there was still sadness at taking leave from the living.

Generation after generation it had been this way, until it had come at last to this unworthy woman herself, but with a great difference. Her death would be of far greater magnitude. She would be taken into the ice itself into the Spirit of All Being. She would see her own parents and grandparents again, and would no longer know the pain of old age.

She smiled at the thought, and then she realized the sounds had stilled, and the night was quiet again. Lovingly, she folded her clothes, and put them carefully away.

Soon, soon, she would wear them.

NEW YORK CITY:

"Jesus, I'm too old for battles," sighed Guzman, wiping his forehead in the heat.

The staff glanced at each other, and knew the news couldn't be good.

"Gentlemen, I want you to know I fought for us. I really did. I did everything but get down on my hands and knees and sing 'Mammy.' . . . Unfortunately . . ."

They looked glumly at their notes or the carvings on the table. Mark Haney looked at the patterns of peeling paint, and in a rare flight of fancy thought he could make out tufted altocumulus.

"So we got shafted again?"

"Look, these're lousy times for everybody. New York's one big basket case, I don't have to tell you, and it hits the school no harder than anybody else."

"Well, it sure as hell's hitting the department harder than anybody else."

"Look, I gave 'em the usual routine: meteorologists are in demand, it's an open field, there's lots of weather to go around, we're not running out of it . . ."

"Yeah, the usual. Maybe they don't hear us when we're down in the basement."

"They will if you make some noise, Haney."

"Well, I'm doing it."

"I don't mean at me, and I don't mean to the board. I mean a paper, a project, a something. Get your name in lights."

"Fine, get me some light bulbs."

"Very funny."

"I mean equipment, stuff I can work with. Biz Ad gets the computer and we don't even get time on it."

"There's a difference. Biz Ad is sexy."

"Geology upstairs, they're getting grants like crazy, plus equipment. Since when's geology sexy?"

"Since the energy shortage. Same for geography, oceanography, everybody upstairs."

"Where the air conditioning is."

Lew Fink interjected. "Mark, if you did something about the weather instead of just talking about it . . ."

"Yeah," said Professor Guzman. "There's that new satellite they sent up, and you've got your radio receiver. Give a listen."

"What good's listening? Without a printer, it's just a lot of dit-da-dit."

"Well, you built the radio. Build a printer. Improvise. Make do. Pull a rabbit out of a hat."

"First I need the hat."

"Ah, now we come to it. I've been saving the *good* news." Guzman reached under the table for a well-wrapped package. "I did get money out of them for one new piece of equipment. And I asked, who should get it? Who's the young genius likeliest to come up with that great paper that'll put us all on the map?"

All faces turned to Mark, with obvious jealousy.

"I'm glad you all agree. So here it is, Mark, all yours. I trust you'll give us some time on it."

Mark was already tearing open the wrappings.

"The way I understand it," said Guzman as Mark placed it on the table for all to see, "is that when the weather looks good, the Hansel and Gretel come out. And when things go bad, then it's the witch."

"Well, what's the prognosis?" asked Fink, stifling a giggle.

Mark looked morosely at the little house. The witch was already on her way out.

"Wow, is that real, Dad?"

"That's real, all right. You seen 'em in the movies. One of those big things comes alive, goes crashing down Times Square, knocking down buildings. Yeah, you betcha it's real."

The boy looked at the immense skeleton, the monster lifted on its powerful hind legs, balanced by its heavy tail, its grinning jaw with dozens of great, sharp teeth, towering almost too high to see. "Well, I mean could it happen?"

"No, it couldn't happen. They're dead. Those're bones, just bones. They ain't gonna come alive."

"You said they're real."

"They are real, but they're dead. They been dead I don't know how many years. A lotta years."

The boy struggled with the difference between "not real" and "dead." He looked up again at the awesome skeletons, two and three stories high, creatures that had ruled the earth. Even his father, whom the boy once thought a giant, looked small and puny alongside them.

But if such powerful creatures died, then why not his father? Why not the boy himself?

The boy began to cry.

"What the hell's the matter with you now?"

"They died."

"You're goddamn right they died. I don't want something like that around Times Square."

"Why'd they die?"

"I don't know why. Look, ain't you glad they died? You wanna have one of them crashing into your room, grabbing you out of bed with those teeth?"

The boy yelled in terror. "No-o-o."

"Then ain't you glad they died?"

The boy stopped short, and for a moment the father thought he had effectively quieted his son, but then the boy asked, "Dad, are we gonna die?"

The father was stunned for a moment. He had never been asked that question, but he knew his answer would be important, might affect the boy for years to come.

"Nobody's gonna die," he said finally. "Not like them, anyway."

KANKAKEE, WEST VIRGINIA:

The carefully rigged dynamite blasted away a whole hillside to get at the rich seams of coal lying beneath. It blasted away forest and farmland, topsoil and bottom, for something more important to an energy-starved nation.

An immense steam shovel tore out a whole boxcar of coal and earth. As it swung its awesome load to the waiting railroad car, the wind lifted plumes of the uprooted dirt and swept them up out of sight. No one noticed.

Twelve thousand miles above, the satellite circled, delicate gyro mechanisms keeping its eyes constantly oriented toward the ground. At this height it saw quite plainly what escaped human eyes, the dirt and dust traveling up to higher winds, finally joining the major air streams that traveled from equator to poles.

The satellite circled on, coming upon the great palls of smoke and soot that hung over the world's cities. Down there, factories and plants created new wonders of metals, plastics, and fibers that necessitated dumping ever stranger wastes into the atmosphere. Cars, trucks, furnaces burned fuels that formed complex oxides and sulfides, some noxious, some not, but all of them altering the processes of nature.

Even the most innocuous action, uncapping a soda bottle, uncorking champagne, emitting only the tiniest bits of carbon dioxide, still upset atmospheric proportions that had held constant for millenia.

Weighed down on one side, the balance simultaneously lightened on the other. In the country, forests were cleared away in the interests of growth, crops slash-burned for easier farming. In the oceans, wastes were discharged and fuels spilled, choking marine plants, and so dismantling mechanisms that might have restored the balance.

And while the satellite might not have seen each individual alteration or destruction, it could certainly measure the summations and effects. It noted the increase in temperature, the shifts in the light, and even analyzed the contents of particulates, the kinds of dust and pollutants that drifted about the planet, caught up in the great air currents.

Without the slightest interest, it recorded and transmitted the vast store of data, leaving others to make sense of it all.

The signal was broadcast on 136.89 megacycles, calling for an antenna specifically trimmed to that frequency.

It was hot, very hot, on the roof as Mark worked on the adjustments. Even the roofing tar grew soft beneath his feet, and every time he moved he had to wrench his shoes free, only to take pieces of tar with them.

His legs felt like lead, and when he looked up to the sky to orient the antenna, the sun seemed bigger than he could have imagined. He felt dizzy with the heat, and for a moment it seemed the sun was growing, coming closer to earth, falling on top of him.

He shook his head to clear his vision, and looked down. He saw the grim old buildings of the school, and the students clinging to the walls for some shade.

When he dragged himself across the tar back to the welcome shelter of the stairwell, he felt very old and weary. His task suddenly seemed pointless, the whole afternoon wasted time.

The soles of his shoes continued sticking to the floor as he made his way downstairs, and he grumbled over the trouble he'd have cleaning them.

And what was it all for, he wondered, as he pulled in the antenna line dangling outside the window, and attached it to the receiver. Yes, now he could receive that signal, but so could any receiver that could tune to that frequency.

At first there was only hiss and static, but then, at precisely 3:08 p.m., there was another sound, barely heard but growing steadily stronger until it stood alone. It sounded like some electronic music, minus a melody. Mark would hear it for perhaps three minutes, and then it would fade, passing on to broadcast somewhere else, to another university and another meteorology department perhaps better equipped than his. They would have one of those printout machines he so desperately wanted. They would work up their own theories, disentangle the knots, get their own names in lights, while Mark would be forever stuck in this decrepit college in the middle of a city slum, making do with odds and ends. Eventually, he would be as old as old man Guzman, tired and burnt out, with nothing to show.

The signal faded as the satellite passed on.

Pull a rabbit out of a hat. Improvise. Make do. Shit!

The silence hung heavy in the room, then the intercom buzzed. He flipped the lever.

"Haney."

"Mark," said Lew Fink, "there's a visiting expert here, a Daniel Magnusson. You know him?"

"Can't say I do."

"You ain't been around. He's VIP. I'd say, *V*VIP."

"I don't know him, but that doesn't mean . . ."

"Well, pretend you do. He's got a project going, looking for collaboration. I think this is right up your alley."

"Could be."

"*Could* be, you asshole, it is! What would you say to a guy with connections?"

"Major connections?"

"Federal. In fact, he's in uniform."

"Jesus! What rank?"

"I can't read these things, but it looks pretty high. I figure he's got the inside track on government contracts, foundation money, all that stuff."

"Damned right, he will. But the military's a stickler for protocol. Whyn't he call in advance?"

"You want me to kick him out?"

"No, no, but Christ, what'll I show him, the little doll house?"

"Hardware he's got. He's after brains. You wanna see him?"

"Yeah, sure."

"Jesus, Marcus, I should hope so."

There was a muffled conversation, and the intercom clicked off. As Mark waited, he wondered what such a VIP. was doing here. Then he wondered why none of the other guys had grabbed him first.

Daniel Magnusson entered the room. The description was mostly accurate. He was in uniform, all right, though it was ill-fitting. He was not quite as big as Fink made him out to be, however. About two feet shorter, in fact.

Mark recognized the decorations. They included the Bobcat and Wolf badges sloppily sewn on his left pocket, while the shoulder patches identified his local den and pack. His curly hair strayed out beneath his beanie cap.

"Professor Haney? I'm Daniel Magnusson. They said you'd help me," he said, very seriously, pushing his glasses back up his nose.

Mark was on the intercom in an instant. "Hey, this your idea of . . . ?" He stopped as he heard long, loud laughter. "Yeah, guess it is," he said, sheepishly, and clicked off.

He turned to the little Cub Scout. "Okay, kid, I had it coming. You can tell 'em I fell for it."

The boy did not smile. "I don't know what you mean. They said you'd help me."

"I meant, thanks, the joke was funny, and I'll tell it on myself next class. I'm sorry I can't do more, but you caught me in the middle of some tricky work."

"I'd like to see your work," said the boy, still very serious. He looked, in fact, as if he had never laughed in his life. Despite his scout uniform, he seemed the oldest ten-year-old Mark had ever seen. He was pale and thin, as if he had never had an adequate meal, or a moment of play out of doors. Mark briefly wondered about the boy's parents.

"I'm sorry. It'll have to be some other time."

"When?"

"I don't know when. Look, kid, it was very funny. You can go back and tell them the laugh's on me. I'd give you a lollipop if I had one, but . . ." He reached into his pocket. "Look, here's something. Buy yourself one, okay?"

"Don't insult me," said the boy in an amazingly adult tone, and he turned silently on his heel and walked out.

Mark felt a stab of guilt, as if something long buried had been touched. For a moment he hesitated, and pressed the intercom button.

The gales of laughter had still not let up, and suddenly his colleagues seemed more childish than his visitor.

He stepped out into the hallway. "Hey, kid . . . uh . . . what's your name again?"

The boy didn't look back.

"Daniel . . . Look, Danny . . ."

The boy turned around.

"I apologize. Come here, and we'll talk a while. What was it you needed?"

The boy hesitated. "I need an advisor for my elective. In meteorology."

"In meteorology? Why not something respectable
—like tying knots?"

The boy was obviously wounded, and turned
away. Mark gently turned him back. "Okay, you tell
me."

"Well . . ." Danny hesitated. "When I was a kid,
I asked all the questions kids ask, including why the
sky was blue."

Mark nodded.

"Well, people . . . didn't have time to answer, so
I read about it, all about refraction and water vapor.
But then I had questions about that, and when I went
and found out those answers, there were still more
questions. At first, I was upset, because I wanted
answers, not questions. I wanted . . . well, I wanted
the final answer that answered everything, y'know?
Then, finally, I grew up, and I realized that there's
never a final answer. The fun is in the questions, and
finding out, and it's like a long, long mystery story that
gets more mysterious as you go on, and it never stops."

Mark was deeply moved. "You still get lost in the
woods?"

He nodded.

"So do I, Danny, so do I. But don't change. You've
got a lot to offer. Now, how can I help you?"

"I need somebody to look over my weather station, and sign a paper. But only if you like it."

"I'm sure I'll like it. I hope you like what I
built." And he gave Danny a better tour than he would
have given a VIP. with a Federal affiliation.

After Danny left, and Mark had made an appoint-
ment to see Danny's station, he felt a curious combination of elation and emptiness. He thought back to his
own beginnings, when a child's wonder at the blue sky
led to answers that only brought out more questions,
and the world unfolded before him, complex, enig-
matic, and exciting. Challenge and opportunity were
united, and unlimited. He could spend a lifetime, endless lifetimes, just finding out answers that opened
more questions. That world had taunted, teased, and
finally seduced him, and he knew he would devote

himself to answering the most trivial, and most important, question on Earth: What's the weather going to be?

But then something had gotten lost along the way. Nowadays, when the latest issue of the journal arrived, he would read the authors' names before the titles, just to see who was getting ahead. Nature was no longer his greatest adversary. Other scientists were.

But now, once again, he was wondering about the awesome, infinite mystery of it.

Mark looked up at the little doll house. The witch was out.

MALI, WEST AFRICA:

"Politics as usual," muttered Dr. Schumer bitterly, as he watched the soldiers pulling the natives off the truck. They screamed their protests but the soldiers ignored them, which was probably why they had been assigned the job.

The government had simply declared the drought was over. There was no arguing with a fact, nor an order. The farmers were to go back to their land and start farming.

Dr. Schumer watched one native pick up the dirt, hold it out to the soldier, and let it dribble between his fingers in a manner common to farmers all over the world, showing it to be more sand than dirt.

The doctor knew some of the background for that government order, but that didn't make it any more tolerable. The Bambara tribe, the farmers, had quite simply become a pain in the central Mali neck. For generations they had tended green farms at the edge of the great Sahara desert, but in recent years the droughts had worsened, and the Bambara had watched the desert gradually grow and begin creeping outward like a living organism. They had fled to neighboring territories, to the still rich pastures of the Tuareg tribes who were mainly sheepherders.

It had been the American Old West all over again, the same range wars endangering a whole emerging nation, until finally, by a declaration of the drought's end and military force, the farmers were shipped back to their old territories and told to stay there.

At least medical volunteers were not being turned away as yet. But if there were no emergency, the reasoning would go, there was certainly no need for emergency workers. Their presence would only be an embarrassment.

Dr. Schumer knew what would happen. The drought would go on, and he would be overwhelmed by the coming disaster. Still, he couldn't leave.

He kicked at the ground in disgust, and sent up a small plume of dust, Sahara dust that didn't exist the year before.

The wind took the tiny cloud and quickly dissipated it, but the tiny grains were not lost. Eventually, they would float up to drift in the higher currents.

RANIER PARK, WASHINGTON:

"Doesn't look like much now, does it? Kind of tame, almost like a little pet, but it was once the monster that conquered the world."

The park guide waited for the tourists to pull out their cameras and start clicking. Ranged about them were the beautiful ridges and white-capped crests of the Cascade range. A blue-green haze hovered over the rounded peak of the tallest, Mt. Ranier. Below, deer grazed among the Douglas firs. Avalanche lilies bloomed at their feet.

They were surrounded by beauty, but they were most fascinated with the little glaciers strewn among the hills like so many gemstones.

"Only about twelve thousand years ago, a little before Babylon, the ice covered the continent a mile thick. It ground down whole mountains, scooped out the Great Lakes, and wherever it wasn't, it still made itself felt."

"That?"

"You better believe it." The particular glacier

above them looked almost sad, covered with debris, the ground poking through in spots like the stuffing in a worn-out couch.

"All melted back to these, and a few others around the country, not much bigger. They're all retreating in this heat, melting away and dying out like the dinosaurs. Now it's an endangered species, and we park people feel rather protective toward them."

The tourists stepped gingerly over the ice. One picked up a rock, and used it to chip off a piece.

"Don't do that, mister. It'll remember, and someday it'll come for you."

ZANESVILLE, OHIO:

"Holy Christ, what're those?" The hired hand gaped in astonishment.

"New to the county?"

"New to Ohio. Just passin' through when I heard you guys were hirin' like mad."

"Damned right," said Farmer Bjork, shouting to be heard without slowing the tractor. "Plowin' and plantin' this year right up to the river edge. That's why I don't like those rocks."

"Mister, those ain't rocks. Those're—hell—god-damn monuments."

"Goddamn nuisances, you mean. We call 'em haystack boulders. Gotta plow around 'em. Can't move 'em, can't even dynamite 'em."

The boulders were spectacular anomalies on the flat plain. They were as big as houses, though there were no mountains nor rock deposits in the region to have produced them, only the soft, deep earth stretching flat to the horizon. But there the boulders were, very real and yet as out of place as if they had dropped from the sky.

The hired hand felt dizzy. He wasn't certain if it was from the heat or the disorienting sight. "Well, then, what got 'em here?"

Farmer Bjork was annoyed at a question he had long since set behind him unanswered. "All sorts of stories around. Old Indian legend about some god dropping 'em. Some of these hippie freaks talk about a race that used mind power or something. Had a college professor out here years ago, hammered off a few pieces and went away happy. He must've known something, but I didn't wanna know."

"Why's that?"

"Mister, whoever or whatever brought those big rocks here, I don't ever wanna meet up with it."

THEBA, ARIZONA:

For long moments as they drove across Interstate 10, the Wilsons watched the brown puffball in the distance. Though there was no sure way of judging its size, it seemed too small to worry about. Certainly, other cars seemed to take no notice.

Yet, it was new in their experience, and therefore disquieting.

"Maybe it's a tornado," said Mrs. Wilson, and she had a brief flash of being carried off to Oz.

"I don't think they'd get 'em out here. Anyway, they're not shaped like that."

But Mr. Wilson couldn't be altogether certain. They were strangers here. They had come from New England, where Mrs. Wilson had developed her sinusitis, and her doctor had suggested she try Arizona or Southern California.

Mr. Wilson was about to say there was nothing to worry about, that perhaps it was a cloud kicked up by some dune buggy or herd of animals, when the words died in his throat. The cloud was growing visibly larger as it approached, and they could hear a howling from within it, like some giant vacuum cleaner.

Yet worse, they didn't know what to do, whether to stop the car or speed up, to close the windows or open them, race the engine or cut it off.

Tentatively, Mr. Wilson slowed the car, and his wife started shutting the windows. By then the cloud towered above them and shut out the sky. The next moment, it fell upon them with an astonishing shriek-ing.

The sand came whipping in through open win-dows and vents. Mr. Wilson coughed and hacked, while his wife gasped for breath. In moments, sand fairly flooded the interior. They could hear the engine grind and scrape in its own agony, then die as sand caught in the bearings.

At last they got windows and vents completely shut, but as if in anger, the sand continued to tear at the car, blasting off the paint layer by layer until the raw steel lay exposed and shiny beneath. Then the sight vanished before their eyes as the sand turned to the windows, pitting them to dense frost.

If they couldn't see, they could hear only too well the sand piling up outside, threatening to cover the car completely.

They thought of being entombed, of being com-pletely submerged, with their bodies never even dis-covered.

Desperately, Mr. Wilson shoved at the door, but the sand came blasting into his face, nearly blinding him, and he shut it again quickly.

They held onto each other, weeping, and waited for a death they could not understand.

Then, as quickly as it had come, the storm was gone, and all was quiet.

Cautious and trembling, Mr. Wilson tried open-ing the door. It didn't budge. He shoved harder, and at last it squealed open with a grating that sent shivers down his spine.

He peered out. Sand covered the highway in great drifts, and he could see a number of cars similarly swamped, like colored rocks half poking above the desert floor.

When Mrs. Wilson's coughs and wheezes finally subsided, they waded together through the drifts to the nearest car. The driver was sitting in a state that might have been calm acceptance or total shock. Mr. Wilson asked tentatively, "Uh . . . this sort of thing happen often here?"

The building had been recently renamed Planetary Sciences, a sleek and modernistic title that didn't hide the ancient architecture some called Early Dracula.

Under that umbrella were grouped a number of departments, their spaces illogically and unjustly apportioned. Meteorology, with its eyes on the sky, was down in the basement, while Geology had to examine the ground from the top floor.

A student might move freely from one department to another in his class schedule, but professors never spoke, regarding their departments as fiefdoms, and teachers outside as suspicious aliens.

There was one room, however, that was shared, and so contact of some sort occasionally occurred.

The man from archaeology was using one urinal when the geology professor came in. There was a bare nod, and then the uneasy silence that is honored ritual in such circumstances, each man with his eyes set straight ahead, eyes level with the obscene graffiti.

Geology finished first, and tried washing his hands. There was no hot water, and the cold-water faucet rattled alarmingly. The soap-dispenser valve was rusted so he couldn't get any soap. There were no more paper towels, so he had to dry his hands gingerly on his clothes. At last he spoke the first words to have passed between the two departments in years.

"It's the end of civilization."

"Hm?" Archaeology looked up.

"When your bathrooms go to hell, that's it. A thousand years from now, somebody in your department's gonna dig down and find this room, and then they'll say, 'Yep, here's where they fell apart.' "

"Make a great paper. Deliver it at the convention on Mars."

Silence again for some moments, and then Archaeology added tentatively, not knowing if the other teacher was really interested, "Y'know, that's what we're hassling out right now, what made a civilization fall apart."

Geology nodded, showing he was indeed inter-

ested, so Archaeology continued, "You can see it in
the artwork. As nearly as we can date 'em, with the
ratty radiocarbon equipment we got, there's a dividing
line. One year you're civilized, the next year you're
not. 'Course, up to that point, the art we deal with's a
little classier than that," and he gestured toward the
graffiti. "Mesopotamian. Nice while it lasted."

"Heard of 'em, but where were they?"

"Iraq, nowadays."

Now Geology was very much interested.
"Y'know, we've got some corings from there. We hustled a grant from Aramco on an oil hunt."

"What do you mean, corings?"

"Special drills, hollow inside. You pull out a long
core of strata and you can date 'em. You get not only
the geologic record, but the plant life, the climatology,
the water table . . ."

"Earthquakes? Floods?"

"That'd show. You think that's what happened?"

"Well, if the civilization goes, you figure something sure as hell happened, and probably on that kind
of scale. Just some major disaster."

Geology bit his lip thoughtfully. "Let's have a
look."

When they entered Geology's lab, Archaeology
was most reminded of a parchment library, such as the
ancient Egyptians must have had. Long, large
cardboard rolls were stacked floor to ceiling, each roll
with detailed identification. The coring from Iraq was
buried near the bottom, and Geology almost started a
small avalanche pulling it out.

There were markings along the length of the roll,
denoting the years. Archaeology could put his finger
on the point of the American Revolution, or the Black
Plague, or the Magna Carta. Back in time he went as
his finger moved along the roll, and then he found the
right era.

"Here, right here!"

Geology cut through the cardboard with a coping
saw, and the ancient earth was revealed.

He tested it for strata displacement, but there was none. "No earthquake."

He tested the water table. "No flood. A little drier, if anything."

He worked his whole battery of tests, and finally concluded," I'd say it's a big zero. Nothing geologic Maybe something meteorologic, some more dust settling, and got a few degrees warmer."

"Dust? They got buried?"

"Not like Pompeii. If the country was allergic, they might've sneezed to death."

"That's it?"

"That's it."

"Well," said Archaeology after some silence, "it was almost a great paper."

"Improvise . . ."

All at once, it seemed a challenge rather than a stumbling block. Mark thought how excited little Danny had been by every little device, book, and convoluted scrawl on the blackboard, and most of all by the all-wave receiver fashioned from parts of abandoned radios and TV sets.

The printout machine would be comparatively simple, Mark realized. He had come upon an abandoned washing machine outside one of the numerous empty slum buildings. He rescued the motor and gearings, and was soon soldering and fashioning, with an excitement and sense of wonder he hadn't known in several years.

It was 3:08 again, and Mark turned on the radio just in time to hear its signal grow loud as the satellite passed overhead. Its electronic chirpings never seemed so tantalizing, and Mark felt some of the child in him returning. Then it faded, leaving only the steady hiss that marked the absence of signal.

Suddenly, he felt earthbound and lonely. He stared at the receiver and realized he had never turned the dial outside that narrow sliver of a very wide band.

He rotated it slowly. The hiss changed in pitch,

grew intermittent, and then the receiver was crammed with signals, voices, codes, music.

The voices, even when speaking English, were nearly incomprehensible, with their own specialized jargons, but the world was alive, complex, and communicating, crowding the whole radio spectrum. Momentarily, he would catch broadcasts of the major governments, Vatican Radio at 9645, Radio Japan at 9505, Radio Sweden at 5990, Radio Mali at 4834.

There were dramas, lectures, operas, propaganda, news, and of course, weather reports. All was well, or at least, normal.

There were policemen and fire-fighters, journalists, utility and construction workers, farmers, physicians, cab drivers, the intricacies and complexities of civilization tied in a communications web.

Fascinated, he continued turning, and a new band came into focus.

"Hello, CQ, CQ, CQ, CQ, calling any forty-meter band. This is TL8XNT, Tango Lima Eight X-Ray November Tango, calling from Mali, in Africa, and standing by. Hello, CQ, CQ, CQ, CQ . . ."

At first Mark was intrigued at the gobbledygook, but grew bored rather quickly as the sentence was repeated over and over. He was about to change to something more cultural, or at least more varied, but then something stopped him, the tone of voice, the litany growing more imploring.

"Please answer . . . Will talk to anyone . . . CQ, CQ . . . Please, anyone. . . "

At last the call was answered, another combination of letters and numbers, followed by, "You're coming in fine business in the Aleutian Islands. Hey, we've a spell of nice clear weather like we can't remember, and it's good to be alive . . ."

"Sorry to interrupt idle chitchat, Aleutians, but we need help here. We've continued drought, monsoon long overdue, grain withered, cattle dying by hundreds, water holes drying. Relay my CQ. My name is Henry Schumer, I'm a doctor. Need food, water, medical supplies . . ."

"QRS, Mali. QRS. Your signal fading. Say again . . ."

Again Dr. Schumer repeated his call, describing the drought, the general starvation, predicting many deaths.

This time there was no answer from the Aleutians. The signal had totally faded. Dr. Schumer tried raising him again, until in clear exasperation he reverted to, "Hello, CQ, CQ, CQ, CQ, calling any forty-meter band . . ."

Mark listened until an obviously distraught Dr. Schumer gave up, and announced he would transmit again on that same frequency in twenty-four hours. Then the radio faded into that same empty hiss.

A puzzled Mark dug out his charts. The monsoons were as regular as the motions of the Earth. They were tied to the jet streams, the great air currents that circled the globe, carrying the ocean's moisture, watering half the crops of mankind. They had been known, on rare occasion, to be slightly late, days or a week or two, but apparently the country had been bypassed altogether.

Then Mark remembered the caller from the Aleutians spoke of good weather. The islands lay directly in the storm tracks, where bad weather was almost continuous. Mark saw the beginnings of a mystery.

Then he remembered Mali's own government station. He turned the dial back to 4834. The Mali announcer was playing African folk music, his slightly British accented voice brisk and cheerful. Obviously nothing was wrong.

Well, thought Mark, switching off the radio, anybody can say anything into a microphone, including indulging a fantasy, or practicing acting lessons.

For a while, it was a great paper.

Across the hall, the geologist stared gloomily at the Iraqi coring. He could not dismiss it so readily without a long, long second look. Indeed, if Hideo Kashihara's ancestors hadn't done as much, they'd have died out on their meager Pacific archipelago.

Again he focused the microscope on the sample. Nothing of interest. Just dust, and a few ordinary seed grains. Nothing important.

Then it struck him. If they were ordinary, they were crucially important.

He lined up the Polaroid camera and snapped a photo. Then he did something he would never have done before. He looked up the room number of the Botany Department, and was a little startled to find it occupied his building.

He wondered how much he should say, and how little. He certainly didn't want anyone else in on that paper. He decided to act nonchalant, to ask everything and say nothing. "The academic way," he chortled.

He marched downstairs, introduced himself, and casually handed Botany the photo. "What's that look like?"

"Don't you know?"

"How should I know?"

"You're Japanese, aren't you?"

"And you're Polish. Now what're those grains?"

"Rice."

"Rice!"

"Something important?"

"No, just curious. Little detail in a paper."

"Do I get a footnote?"

"Rice isn't important; only oil's important in my department. But if you've got a minute, tell me about rice."

"Well, it's an annual, two to six feet long, long pointed leaves . . ."

"Is it delicate?"

"Well, it's no orchid."

"Suppose you get marginal increases in dust, marginal decrease in rainfall, and a couple of degrees warmer?"

"You just lost half your crop."

"*Half?* I thought it wasn't delicate."

"Look, it still needs warmth, moisture, irrigation ditches and a lot of tender loving care."

"Okay, now suppose a culture that's rice-centered loses half its crop, what then?"

"Not my department."

"Whose?"

"Try geography. They talk about societies and ecology and all that. What about my footnote?"

"I'll let you know," said Hideo, as he dashed out.

The biologist stared after him. "I think I've just been hustled," he muttered.

"Let me put a case to you. A rice-centered culture loses half its crop. What happens to the culture?"

"Let me put a case right back," said Geography. "Personal one. Remember something called Project Noah?"

"If it's not geology, sex, or baseball, it's not my department."

"Well, I remember it because I worked on it in my more idealistic days. They were flooding an African valley with a new dam site. There were a lot of animals to be rescued, lions, rhinos, elephants. I volunteered. We broke some animals' necks, we broke some of our own necks, but by God, we rescued the whole arkful."

"Congratulations."

"Not yet. We had to put 'em somewheres, don't forget. So, now what happens where once there were two lions living, and you come along and dump in two more?"

"Well, you've probably got some angry lions."

"More than that. You've got four lions starving. In fact, you've got everything starving. We devastated the ecology, and it still hasn't recuperated."

"That's pretty dumb for someone in your department."

"What do you think got me into this department? All right, reverse the situation. Instead of doubling the population, you cut the rice supply in half. What happens?"

Hideo tried picturing a society with half its food gone, with granaries half-filled, with government and church equally impotent. He felt a cold fear grabbing at him, just when he should be feeling an elation at solving a mystery.

Finally he said, "All right, I could see it happening to a jungle, but this was a civilization."

"Before or after?"

NORTH ATLANTIC, 1,500 MILES N.E. AZORES:

"Captain . . . it's a . . . I don't know what it is."

"Directions, man, directions!"

"Off the port side . . . It's a squall, I think."

The captain looked. It indeed seemed like an approaching squall, but it was colored a brownish yellow, and was somehow opaque, like a slowly unwinding puffball that grew until it was greater than the ship. Then, moments later, the ship was completely immersed, but not in rain.

The scorching dust was everywhere, on the deck, in the hold, in the crews' mouths and nostrils. The sun was darkened and diffused to a milky glow that seemed now to come from within the storm, a part of the storm itself. There were flashes of sheet lightning answered by strange rolls of thunder like a pounding surf heard from inside a giant cave.

Then the storm was gone, leaving layers of dust all over the exterior, and in little heaps inside closed portholes.

When the captain finally cleared the dust from his throat, he was able to ask the mate, "God, you ever hear of anything like that?"

The mate nodded. "Oklahoma."

Mark reread his notes. "Jesus, that can't be right."

It was hard to believe there once was a time he could take down Morse code at thirty words per minute, but a number of muscles had grown soft since his Air Force days. Now he had to get back in shape to get his ham transmitter license, and listening to just such code transmissions was his exercise.

Most were uneventful, but this transmission was very strange indeed. "C'mon, gimme confirmation," he said to the unhearing radio.

For Danny, Mark's voice had come exploding out of a total silence. Mark was wearing headphones, and didn't know how loud he spoke.

"Yep, that's what they said," muttered Mark as he heard the standard confirmation.

Danny watched as Mark noted down the details, time, latitude, longitude, and other conditions in the meteorological shorthand, and at last he set down the phones and turned to Danny.

"Y'know, if I can't believe their stuff, how're people going to believe mine?"

"I'll believe you."

Mark ruffled Danny's hair. "Thanks. Y'know what you are?"

"What?" asked Danny, self-conscious and half afraid.

"My colleague."

Danny blushed, and Mark thought it was the first bit of color he had ever seen in Danny's pale face. He wondered about the care Danny was getting.

"Danny, tell me about your family."

Danny shrugged. "Nothing to tell."

"Try me."

"No, you tell me about what you heard on the radio."

"You tell me about your family."

"I'll trade you one for one."

Mark sighed. "You're making it hard. Okay, you first."

"You first."

Mark raised his hand in mock anger. "You're lookin' to get hit, kid."

Danny backed away in a terror so immediate and overwhelming, it frightened even Mark himself. "F'r God's sake, I was only kidding. C'mere . . ."

Danny still hesitated, and it was several moments before he gingerly received Mark's gentle hand of reassurance.

"All right, all right," soothed Mark, "I'll tell you something first." He took a breath. "First of all, I was just practicing up my Morse code 'cause you need that for a transmitting license."

"Why do you want a transmitting license?"

"Because listening isn't enough. There are some questions I want to ask about what I've been hearing."

"What've you been hearing?"

"I'll hold you in suspense. Now it's my turn. Tell me about your father."

Danny hesitated. "My father's dead," he said without visible emotion.

"I'm sorry to hear that. When'd it happen?"

"It's my turn. What were you hearing?"

"I was practicing listening to Morse code, and I was picking up ship-to-shore weather reports. There are no weather bureaus out at sea, so every ship that gets weather information also sends back its observations. It was normal for a while, until I just heard what I heard."

"What'd you hear?"

"Oh no, my turn. What about your mother?"

"She's alive. What'd you hear?"

"You're not giving me much."

"I know. What'd you hear?"

"They had a dust storm at sea."

"A . . . that's impossible."

Mark nodded.

"So?"

"So tell me about your mother. She good to you? She take care of you? She feed you?"

Danny shrugged. "I get along."

"Do you and she get along?"

"How do you get a dust storm at sea?"

"Because we're pumping dust into the air. It floats up to the jet streams, and it circles the Earth. So it could come down anywheres, and stir up a storm."

"Why hasn't it done so before?"

"I don't know. Maybe the patterns of the currents are changing."

"What's it mean?"

"I don't know. Why won't you tell me more about your mother?"

"I don't know either. Can I listen to the satellite when it comes over?"

Mark sighed, and tuned the receiver to the satellite's frequency. They waited for its sound, and said nothing more.

SUITLAND, MARYLAND:

As if underlining its commitment to the government that had funded the entire project, the world's largest computer was housed in a six-story building within easy commuting distance of the nation's capital.

It was devoted to the most formidable mathematical task imaginable, forecasting the weather, and even with the latest advances of microcircuitry, the machine still took up most of the building.

The amount of data was so great that were the Earth's entire population all trained mathematicians, each assigned to its processing, they would be overwhelmed by the task.

The computer contained the whole planet's atmosphere: an abstraction in a mathematical model. The scientists had set up the world's weather as it existed on a winter day at one point in time and programmed all the factors known to generate and affect it. Then they started the planet rotating.

If they could bring it down to the present day, with an exact reproduction of the day-by-day conditions, the computer would accurately project into the future, days, weeks, even years.

The model held, as December 23 became December 24, and on the cathode tube a weather map unfolded with isobars and isotherms bending and twisting exactly as they had on the official Weather Service charts for those days.

But as December 24 wound on to Christmas Day, and then the day after, the technicians' cheers faded to groans. It rained where they knew in actuality there had been a drought. Temperatures plummeted in a place they had risen. The model was breaking down.

"Well," said one, "there's just not enough data. When we get the satellite hooked in . . ."

"Sure. Meanwhile, I'll donate my arthritic knee. It's been acting up lately."

"This is the hygrometer," said Danny with absolute seriousness.

Mark made an effort to keep his face serious.

"Very impressive."

The instrument was as ingenious as any of Mark's improvisations. The hygrometer measured humidity with the cheapest material available, a strand of hair. An attached string winding around a dial amplified and measured the hair's shrinking or expanding.

An anemometer spun, measuring the wind's velocity. It was made from kitchen funnels, and turned around on a broomstick.

Mark nodded, and gave learned "Um-hm's" inwardly delighted with the boy's ingenuity. But his joy was tempered by his disturbance at Danny himself, still pale, still secretive. It was evident that Danny had chosen a time to show off his weather station when his mother would not be home.

"I approve," said Mark. "I'll bet this goes over great with your brother scouts."

"I . . . wouldn't know."

"What do they say?"

"I don't know. I'm always here."

"Don't you have any friends?"

"It's . . . nice here. There's always something happening."

"Do you ever go out?"

"Sure. Direct observation is important."

"Doesn't your mother care? Is she a good friend, someone to talk to?"

There was a silence. "Would you like to see the weather chart I drew today?"

Mark eased off. "Sure."

"I draw them in the dining room because it's got the biggest table," said Danny, leading him through the apartment. The rooms were large, typical of the once elegant, now blighted apartments in the neighborhood. Evidently, the space was needed for Danny's equipment, and for something else, as Mark discovered when he opened the door.

The room was dirty, and cluttered with strange, primitive artifacts. There were carvings in ivory and stone of animals such as seals and whales, an object resembling an overlarge ashtray, animal furs, drums, a harpoon, and, prominently displayed, a whip with an immense cord.

"My mother's," said Danny, finally.

"Jesus," was all Mark could answer. He knew he'd have a great deal more to say, and perhaps some things to do.

CAMPECHE, MEXICO:

Sr. Avila never used ocean charts, but he knew the winds and currents as well as he had to.

Of all these signs, the most obvious was the path of the Gulf Stream, a green river that flowed within the blue ocean. While no chart ever told him of its immensity, he had learned this narrow section intimately. The richest fishing lay in these green waters.

He had his favorite spot, which he found by lining up certain landmarks, confirmed by the shape of the waves, the direction of the wind, and a number of other signs he recognized so instinctively he didn't even think about them, as someone knows the route to his own house without being able to give a friend directions.

Which was why Avila now felt so uneasy without being able to see why. Things were not in their proper places. It was almost as if the Gulf Stream had

shifted. That was preposterous! The green river had
not changed its course in living memory, or the memory of his father, for that matter. He did not understand and he was deeply concerned. The whole village
was dependent on the fishing for its survival.

Soon, though, he forgot about it because the nets
were heavy with a new kind of fish.

"Ay, Dios!"

They were large, and their flesh was thick. He
guessed they must have migrated from some northern
spot, where their flesh provided protection against the
colder waters. The day was turning out nicely after all.

The Gulf Stream meandered on beneath him, a
green river in a blue ocean.

MT. ROBSON, ALBERTA, CANADA:

Flying the mail had always been dull for Bouchard, especially with the same routes traveled over
and over. It didn't matter that he was traveling over
some of the most spectacular scenery in the world. All
he could hope for was that this trip would go quicker
than usual. Flying had turned into hours of boredom,
with terror at the beginning and end, a tiring, enervating combination. It was bound to give him an ulcer one
of these days.

The tower had given reassurance the weather
would be clear, with no clouds except for some wispy
cirrus, fair-weather clouds. A monkey could have
flown the plane (Bouchard had a passing fantasy of
coming to work one day and finding a simian in leather jacket and cap replacing him).

The nastiest part of the flight was coming up,
the climb by Mt. Robson, but even this would be
dull.

As he approached, the cirrus clouds hugging the
peak no longer seemed quite so familiar. Though fair-weather white, they seemed to boil and churn like
storm clouds.

He shuddered, and glanced briefly at the weather
charts. No local turbulence was listed, and his instru-

ments confirmed all was stable. His alarm subsided and he moved in closer to examine the strange phenomenon, still holding to his general course over the mountain.

Suddenly, the plane seemed to drop beneath him. He gasped, and pulled back on the stick. It scarcely budged.

Now it was as if a giant hand had grabbed the plane and was playing with it, sending it spinning crazily, tail over head, as the engine howled. Then, just as suddenly, the hand let go. The ship righted itself, and the engine settled.

"Merde!"

He flipped open his switch. "Prince George Approach Control. Prince George Approach Control, this is Cessna three-eight-one Bravo, holding southeast Mt. Robson."

He had to repeat it several times before he got his answer, and even then it was peculiarly weak and bathed in static. "Cessna three-eight-one Bravo, this is Prince George. Your signal breaking up, your radio defective."

"Negative, Prince George, my radio fine. Something the hell's wrong." He described what had happened, only to get the answer that there was no turbulence and nothing in the charts. Something had to be wrong with his plane. They further advised he return to his departure point.

"Past point of no return, Prince George. Everything clear now. Maybe engine just choked on a bone. Will test controls."

Cautiously, he worked them one by one. They all responded neatly.

He looked out at the mountain. Those same strange clouds were there, but there was no sign of anything else amiss.

He thought he might try climbing higher for even safer clearance. He radioed the airport his intent, and the signal was sharp and clear again. He was reassured, but still he watched the altimeter carefully, doubling his usual margin.

The altimeter needle rose comfortably, indicating the support of gentle updrafts for his climb, but his peripheral vision indicated something was wrong.

He looked up, and nearly froze. His instruments were wrong. He was not going to clear the mountain.

He barely had time to reach for the stick when suddenly the same giant hand seemed to grab the plane again, spinning him end over end. The mountain gyrated crazily as he heard a screaming that came either from the plane or from him.

"Prince George, Prince George, it's happening again! I'm fighting for control . . ."

He kept up a running commentary as if it could focus his actions, but he could not wait for answers.

With his instruments spinning as crazily as his plane, he tried to center on the horizon but saw to his horror that he was being pulled into the mountain!

It was an air-pocket unlike any he had ever experienced, some giant whirlpool. He fought for altitude as the plane was buffeted so badly he thought the very rivets would pull apart.

He decided to ride with the current instead of fighting it, and pushed the stick forward. The plane zoomed straight down while he twisted to avoid the mountain, but now he felt it rolling one way, then another, almost too quickly for him to trim, tossed between currents and counter-currents.

Something was familiar about that sensation, and then he remembered white-water canoeing on one of the wild rivers down in those mountains. His only hope lay in that split second when this strange air current hit bottom and settled into smooth running, if it didn't crash him to the ground first, or sweep him in some backwash into the mountain.

The altimeter showed plenty of room to maneuver, and he took the few seconds to tell Approach Control his intention, remembering the instrument's treachery too late.

The last thing he saw was the ground and trees rushing up toward him.

The signal on Mark's radio suddenly went dead. Only the empty hiss remained, echoing like a distant rainstorm in the empty office.

He had almost tuned past it at the beginning. It seemed to be a typical aircraft communication, until he realized that some strange atmospheric skipping let him clearly hear a pilot in Alberta, Canada. But curiosity rapidly became horror as he listened helplessly to the pilot die.

He knew the cause of the turbulence. It was a mountain wave, a manifestation of the jet stream momentarily washing down a mountainside like some great waterfall. He had heard of the phenomenon in the Air Force, and he knew of pilots whom it had killed. The freak current disrupted instruments and radios as it sucked planes into deadly whirlpools.

But the phenomenon, rare in any case, occurred only in the jet stream's path. It had no business being up in Canada.

He yearned for the reassurance there was still normal life outside. He turned the dial, and suddenly his room was filled with boisterous visitors.

"Break two, break two."

"Yeah, breaker, go ahead."

"Thank you much, eighteen-wheeler. This here's one T-Bone Tyson. What's your handle?"

"Mobile John, T-Bone."

"Ten four, ten four, ol' buddy. I like that. You seen any Smokey Bears?"

"For shore, forshore. Smoke's thick at Red Hook Junction, ol' buddy . . ."

Mark listened to a number of conversations on the Citizens Band: to truckers informing each other of highway patrol stakeouts, to teenagers strutting their sexuality behind anonymity, to shut-ins keeping in touch with the outside, to self-considered comedians and singers.

He turned further, from the local hops of the brash CB'ers, to the world-wide leaps of the polite and deferential hams. A familiar voice stopped him short. This time the voice was bitter.

"Let me describe it, then, for you bastards who aren't interested, or don't care, just what a drought means. The earth itself cracks open, like a thousand small earthquakes. The topsoil blows away like dust. And all over, the cattle dying. They lie in the sun, their bodies blackening, their tongues and stomachs swollen, coated with flies they're too weak to brush away. The flesh sags down from the bones, and it's cracked open like the earth, with pus running.

"The land is flat, so you can see it over and over and over, all the way out to the horizon. And what's happening to the cattle, that'll happen to the children. There's already gastroenteritis, pneumonia, cholera, dysentery. I need supplies, you bastards, medicine, food, water. But most of all, I need you to get the news out. Anybody, anybody on this CQ. TL8XNT in Mali, West Africa. Will QSO again usual time. Pulling plugs."

The signal vanished.

Mark sat numb for a good while, listening to the empty hiss. At last he turned from the radio to the phone, picked it up, and started to dial the *Times*.

"Ah, I'd sound like a goddamn fool. They must know what's going on." He hung up.

He picked up the phone again, and dialed. He felt his blood pounding as he waited.

"Hello?"

"Is this Danny's mother?"

There was a pause. "Who are you?" she asked suspiciously, and then anxiously, "Is anything wrong? Has something happened to Danny?"

"Danny's in the library. I mean, the book collection. It isn't big enough for a library."

"Excuse me. Who *is* this?"

Mark sighed. Of course she wouldn't know what he was talking about. "I'm sorry. My name's Mark Haney. I'm a teacher . . ."

"Oh." She breathed a sigh of relief. "He talks about you a lot."

"I . . . uh . . . guess he does. Look, Mrs. Magnusson, it's Danny I want to talk about."

"Yes?"

He heard the suspicion in her answer.

"Uh . . . look, this isn't easy. I've become Danny's friend, a close friend, and I know how he lives . . ."

"Well?"

Her obvious impatience provoked him into blurting out the rest. "Frankly, Mrs. Magnusson, it strikes me that you're not taking close enough care of Danny."

"I see." There was a pause. "Not that it's any of your business, but I don't intend to, Mr. Haney."

"What . . . what's that mean?"

"Exactly what it says. If he wants to run around naked, shoot dope, rob banks, or hang around libraries, that's his business."

Mark was stunned. "You're his mother, and as nearly as I can determine, his sole parent . . ."

"Yes, and as his *sole* parent, I have the right to bring him up exactly as I see fit. Now I think, Mr. Haney, if you've said everything you have to say . . ."

"No, I haven't, not by a long shot. What you're telling me only confirms what I was afraid of . . ."

"I don't really care what you're afraid of . . ."

"I think you ought to care. I have serious doubts about your fitness as a parent . . ."

"Fitness! Well, who the hell . . . ?"

"I can report it to Child Welfare."

"What? You . . ."

"Let them come down and look your place over, and draw their own conclusions."

"Look, I'm not responsible to you or any Welfare goons or whatever. I raise my child how I see fit . . ."

"Fine, you tell them your ideas on not taking care of Danny. You'll see what 'Welfare goons' can do."

"It's a free country, Mr. Haney."

"I'm not going to argue government with you, Mrs. Magnusson. With Danny, there's not only a human life but a very precious mind at stake. You can rant all you want, but they can take you to court and see that Danny gets a proper home."

"He *has* a proper home! He . . . You wouldn't do that."

"I would, Mrs. Magnusson. I know what's at stake here, even if you don't seem to."

"At stake . . . I . . . What kind of country is this? What are you all after me for? What do you all want from me? It's a goddamn fucking conspiracy, isn't it? *Isn't it?*"

He didn't answer, and when she spoke again, it was with a very different tone, unnervingly cool, almost calculating. "Mr. Haney, where's Danny?"

"I told you, he's in the library."

"You . . . you haven't done anything yet, have you?"

"I wanted to talk to you first, Mrs. Magnusson. Frankly, I'm not too happy with what I'm hearing."

Her panic began returning. "We ought to talk . . . We've got to talk further . . . You've no right to . . ."

She sounded as if she were about to lose her temper again, and then she caught herself. "We ought to at least talk . . . You won't do anything until we talk, Mr. Haney . . ."

"Fine."

"Could you come over here?"

Mark had a sudden vision of being alone with an hysterical paranoid with that huge whip at hand, and no witnesses.

Quickly his mind raced. He wanted a public place, where the presence of others could provide a damper, and there would be someone to help if she flew off the handle. Someplace casual, of course.

"All right, the college cafeteria."

"That . . . that's a strange place to talk."

"No, it isn't, Mrs. Magnusson. Believe me, it isn't."

Twelve thousand miles above, electrical contacts closed, and an alternating current was generated. Special arrangements of antennas and amplifiers focused and strengthened the signal and beamed it earthward. Locked within were billions of bits of intelligence, observations of a weather machine so immense it could accommodate sixty thousand thunderstorms in a day, and yet so sensitive that the most minor disruption, the fall of a leaf in Australia, the jump of a grasshopper in China, disturbed atoms that disturbed other atoms, eventually working its way about the globe to alter the weather in America.

As the satellite circled southward in its path from pole to pole, it went on past New York City, and crossed the nation's capital.

The radio signal cut across a complex arrangement of rods and bars, delicately attuned to respond to that signal and no other. Vibrating in sympathy millions of times per second, the antennas generated their own corresponding signal, and this was held, nurtured, reshaped and amplified, then sent by other line-of-sight antennas across Chesapeake Bay to a waiting receiver, and finally patched in to the world's largest computer.

All of these mechanisms acted obediently and flawlessly. None could evaluate this data nor make any more sense of it than the birds that flew unaffected across the beam.

The satellite's signal told of the growing atmospheric aberrations of the planet, the increases in dust, carbon dioxide, heat, the shifts of jet stream and Gulf Stream, ice retreating in Washington, desert advancing in Mali. It carried news of the astronomical influences, the shifts in orbit and the emanations from outer space, all with a clarity and completeness denied earthbound observers. This was integrated with the data already in the computer's possession, filling in gaps, redefining processes, sharpening definitions.

With new understanding, both men and machine set up the weather of the world as it existed on a winter's day in recent history, and again set the Earth rotating. This time, as the green lines on the electronic weather chart writhed and coiled, they matched perfectly the actual charts. Days passed in minutes on the screen, January moved into February, and then into March.

"It's holding!"

Seasons changed, storms came and went, all in their proper place, and as each month passed with the computer's accuracy intact, a new cheer went up.

At last it came down to the present, and it showed the weather that was actually outside.

"Goddamn, hot and dry on the button!" There was a new cheer.

"Okay, kids, here we go."

The computer crossed the border into the future, into the unknown.

"Hey, there's a break coming up," said someone, as the computer predicted the end of the heat wave.

"About time." There were smiles all around.

Then their grins faded as the markings took an unexpected course, as summer ground on into autumn and then winter. All they could do was stare dumbfounded until someone broke the silence with an involuntary exclamation at the computer screen.

"My God!"

They'd recheck the process as a matter of course, but even then they'd have to make field trips, take measurements directly at the scene. Verification was particularly crucial here, but no one really doubted the horrifying implications of the changing green lines.

Weather information had long been the most international of languages, the most accessible and open of government information. At the height of the cold war, the Russian, American, Chinese, Indian, and French governments still sent their weather data back and forth over their high walls. No information was so unpolitical or so crucial.

But this was different.

It was too important for the men in the room to decide, said some, or any scientist, said others, or any politician, said the rest. It was too important to be kept secret and far too terrible to reveal.

But every man and woman in the room knew the decision would soon be taken out of their hands.

Forecasts as such would continue, of course. The satellite would beam its images to all who could receive them, though in degraded and incomplete form. But the projection of the data, the long-range prediction of the weather would remain secret until courses of action were decided.

The truth would eventually be evident to the rest of the world, but by then its fate would have been sealed.

The cafeteria was noisy and crowded. It was air conditioned, but the city engineers apparently hadn't included the heat of the crowd in their cooling-power calculations. It would have been far cooler with the windows left open. Of course, the windows were now sealed.

Mark weighed his approaches, from reasonable to imperious, pleading to demanding. It would have to depend, of course, on the woman with whom he was dealing.

He was looking for someone big, rawboned and hard-faced. He wouldn't have noticed the slight, pale girl in the cafeteria line, except for her rather odd behavior.

She waited just that extra moment before advancing to close up a space. The student behind her gave her a slight shove and, instead of moving, she surprised him by giving way very readily.

It struck Mark that a cafeteria line typified society, with its delicate balance between knowing when to push ahead, and when to defer. The girl seemed to have been suddenly thrust here from some other time and place, unable to cope in an alien environment.

The process was repeated several more times, and as people in line grew more aggressive in working their way around her, she gave way more readily, increasingly confused. It seemed she might stay in her place forever, and starve.

Finally, Mark walked up to her, and took her gently by the arm.

"Maybe I can help. What would you like?"

She turned gratefully to him. "Just anything cold. Very cold."

He guided her to the cold-drink section, looking at her carefully as she picked out a cold drink. She had the drink in her hand when he said, "You can't even push your way through a line. I don't see how you expected to push Mark Haney around."

She nearly dropped the drink. He steadied her, saying "It's all right. Let's just sit down."

"You're . . ."

"Let's just sit down. By the air conditioner, if you want."

She nodded, and followed him to the table, sitting down directly in the draft.

There was a silence until she finished the drink, and sighed deeply. "My God." She shook her head. "I'm terribly sorry . . . I . . . would've liked to put up a good impression . . . I . . . I'm afraid . . . I'm not doing a very good job."

"Believe me, it's better than I expected."

There was a long, awkward pause, and Mark finally decided it was up to him to speak first. "I want you to know, I'm only looking out for Danny's good."

She was indignant. "Well, what do you think I'm doing?"

"That's the trouble. I don't know. Look, Danny's a brilliant kid with a brilliant mind, but he's fragile. He could fly apart at any time."

She nodded. "I know. Dear God, I know."

He looked at her closely. "I don't know how to add this up. You were hysterical on the phone, you admit you neglect him . . ."

"No, no. You don't understand . . ."

"Didn't you say you just didn't care what happens to him?"

She was absolutely open-mouthed.

"Psychology's not my department, but Danny acts like somebody who's been beaten. And there's that whip with all your other weird stuff. But you don't look strong enough to beat an egg."

". . . You mean you think I . . . ?"

"What am I supposed to think?"

She leaned her head on her hand, and moaned. "Another time and place, this would have been funny." She paused, and looked back at Mark. "The people I lived with, they never hit, or spanked, or touched a child except in love. They don't discipline them. They don't order them about. They don't even tell them when it's time to eat or go to bed. They believe children are innately good and wise. They give them love, but they let them find their own way. And they grow up to be the most beautiful, the most gentle people on God's earth."

"Eskimos?"

She nodded. "Whatever a child does, it's his choice, and it'll be the right choice."

"Even shooting dope or robbing banks?"

"None of them have yet."

"Then why has Danny turned out the way he did?"

She shrugged sadly. "I wasn't with Danny. I guess if you have to find the worst sin I committed, that was it. I wasn't his mother."

"Then who was?"

"For the past year, the orphanage. I don't know what went on there. He doesn't talk about it, and I won't prod him."

Mark waited. It was a slow unwinding, but once started, she seemed only too anxious to share her burden. She had been an anthropology student, enamored both with the Eskimo culture, and her teacher. Eventually, they took their field trip to Greenland together. Soon after they were married, and she had Danny, he was already taking up with a new co-ed.

"Anthropology's sexy," grunted Mark.

"He knew a lot about the Eskimos, but he never really learned it. Everything was still pushing, hustling, stepping on your neighbor. Before I knew it, he had the paper we worked on published under his own name, he had his new wife, and he had Danny.

"I was devastated. I just lost my head and ran. I

ran all the way back to Greenland. The Eskimos were my consolation. I learned all over again what was truly important, and I found a kind of happiness and . . ."

"I'd still call that running away."

She shrugged wearily. "You're not the first."

"Who, Danny?"

She nodded. "You can't get visiting rights from Greenland. And who could handle him, or even understand him? His father was hustling for his career, his stepmother was a groupie, and I had deserted him."

Mark thought about Danny looking to science for love. He wondered if he should ever tell Danny how much it demanded, and how little it returned.

"So then what?"

"His father died."

"How?"

"Of getting ahead . . ." She smiled in self-reproach. "No, of course not. The usual. Heart attack. And a pubescent widow who certainly couldn't handle a child prodigy, so they looked for me. It took four months to find me, and six to get back."

"Wow. You sure took your time."

She tensed. "I was in one of the remotest parts of Greenland. By the time they found me, the thaw had set in, and we couldn't cross the ice. Dog sleds aren't jets. But if you didn't understand it just now, you can imagine what Danny thought, trapped in that orphanage. It was all happening at once. Culture shock, the legal complications, trying to make a living and be a mother to Danny, and then your phone call."

"I'm sorry. I couldn't have known . . . all this. I was just concerned about Danny. God knows what he could be if it goes right with him."

She sighed. "I just wish he could be a child."

TUCSON, ARIZONA:

Ruth Cooper had taken her third-grade class on a nature trip to the desert. The child pointed out the large, weasel-like animal darting by.

"Why, that's a . . . uh . . . I don't know. We'll look it up when we get back to the room."

The animal encyclopedia provided the answer. "Pennant's marten. Habitat, northern United States, especially Washington." Curious, Mrs. Cooper called the desert museum. Pennant's marten had no business in the desert. It must have escaped from a zoo or some private collector.

Interesting, said the curator. He knew of no missing animals, but a number of northern-based creatures had been spotted in the desert lately. He couldn't say why.

"Listen, you bastards, I don't care who's tuned in, and I haven't got time for my call letters and that bullshit. I watched a child die today. Her belly was bloated, but everywhere else her bones showed right through the skin. She didn't cry. These people don't. But her pain must've been beyond belief. She was leaking fluids she couldn't afford. She needed plasma, she needed antibiotics, she needed food and water. Hell, she needed someone who cared. There's a thousand more in this camp alone that're going to die like her, and the government's not waking up. They don't give a damn, and neither do any of you out there. Or maybe they're just trying to cover up the stupidest blunder in history. They're going to let a hundred thousand die like her before they wake up. If that's what you bastards want, a hundred thousand corpses, you'll have them. Believe me, you'll have them."

There was a pause, and when he spoke again, his voice was tired and numb. "This is TL8XNT, Mali, West Africa. Will QSO again, usual time. Going off, and pulling plugs."

The signal disappeared, leaving only the familiar hiss.

Mark turned from the loudspeaker to Danny. The boy was starting to look healthier, color coming into his face.

Mark looked out the window. Children were playing stickball, or dousing themselves in the water pouring wastefully out of the hydrant. Some were munching ice-cream bars from the Good Humor vendor.

At last Mark picked up the phone and called *The New York Times*. After being switched to several reporters, and a callback to confirm he was indeed a teacher at the university, Mark talked with a writer at the foreign news desk.

"The reports we've been getting from Mali have been highly contradictory," said the man. "It's an unstable country. There was a revolution, and the new government is just feeling its way. Communication has always been slow, and now it's just about nonexistent. As far as a drought or mass starvation goes, they're denying everything. They say the drought is over, the situation is in hand, and in the cities it's business as usual. Or what's usual for them."

"Well, when you're talking about drought, you're in my department. And I say it isn't over."

"Yeah, well, we all know how governments cover up, but look at it this way. If somebody walked into our office and told us they'd seen what you're telling me, we might think he had a story but we'd certainly want verification."

"But he's in Mali, not your office. He's an eyewitness."

"Not as far as we're concerned. He's a disembodied voice, and we can't find out *who* he is."

"I'll give you the frequency. Talk to him yourself."

"No good. I mean, like just now I called the university to make sure you were who you claimed to be. Who do I call there? Verification's the name of the game, and right now the evidence goes the other way. As far as I'm concerned, or as far as I have to be concerned, he's a crackpot, whether he calls on the phone down the block, or the ham radio halfway around the world."

"So you won't follow up?"

"Look, we'll keep an eye out till some evidence comes filtering out from there, but . . ."

"Yeah . . . I got you." Mark was ready to slam down the phone when the newsman spoke.

"Look, you're a meteorologist. Aren't you?"

"So?"

"And you say something's happening with the weather there?"

"You mean, are there significant changes in the climate?"

"That's the right idea. What does this mean? Is there still a drought, is it going to continue, what else is in store? If you come up with something, and get the faculty behind you, we might have a story."

"Isn't that a piece for a science editor?"

There was a pause. "Yeah, but . . ."

Mark smiled. ". . . But then *we* wouldn't have something."

"*We* would like to have something, wouldn't we?"

"I hear you, but there're a few problems. The faculty for one . . . or more."

"You can't get them together?"

"Yeah, at the Pope's wedding. Even if I do come up with a notion of what's happening, I've got to go through channels. There's the Journal of Meteorology. First you send them the rough article, then it goes out to experts. They check it out, you argue, they argue, you write a new one, it goes out again. Finally, if it survives, you get published, and then every meteorologist is down on your theory. If it survives all that, then they—not me, *they*—give it to the newspapers."

"If every story went through that, we'd still be reporting on the War of 1812."

"Yeah, well, that's the way it's done."

"You can short-circuit all that. We're built to take the heat."

"But I'm not. I'll go through channels."

"Okay. Just remember you've got a platform if you want it."

They exchanged good-byes, and Mark hung up. He turned to see Danny looking at him in awe.

"You could've gotten into the newspaper."

"Yeah, into the newspaper, and out of a career."

"Why?"

"Because you don't do things that way. Because the truth comes out of a grinding process. Because it takes time."

"A long time?"

"Most of us never make it. In fact, most of us never even try."

"You're trying, aren't you?"

Mark looked at his makeshift equipment, and thought about the struggle to make sense out of data that had stumped computers. "I guess so. Maybe it isn't worth it."

There was a silence. Finally Danny said, "Will any more people die?"

Mark looked at him. "We'd better get started finding out, hadn't we?"

He began at the library, pulling out current and back issues of newspapers from cities around the country, and compiling tables of their weather records. He soon expanded his research to cities around the world, and ever further back in time. He watched for news stories of freakish weather disturbances. He pored through almanacs, personal journals, and accounts of activities from agriculture to zoology, any field affected by the weather.

"What're you looking for?" asked Danny.

"Min and Max and Norm."

Danny looked puzzled for a moment, then brightened. "Minimum, maximum, and normal. Temperature and rainfall, I'll bet."

Mark smiled his approval. "I'm looking for patterns, and then deviations from them. Assuming there is a pattern at all."

"Lemme look some." Danny went poring through old records and newspapers with childike eagerness but also with an amazingly mature attentiveness.

They were soon submerged in numbers, looking for the key in larger chunks of data. The more information they accumulated, the more Mark realized he needed a far broader perspective than written history could provide.

Hideo was working on the Iraqi coring when Mark came in. Concerned about plagiarism, the geologist quickly threw a cover over his work, trying to be casual.

After the brief introductions the two scientists talked about the sad state of the city in general, and the college in particular.

"Your geology records tell you anything about climate?" Mark asked.

"They could." Hideo shifted a little uncomfortably. "What do you want to know?"

"I'm looking for a pattern, certain elements coming together at the same time."

"Yeah?"

"Unusual warmth, increase in atmospheric dust, a change in rainfall either way."

Hideo swallowed. "I . . . uh . . . might have something like that. It seems . . . a little familiar, somehow."

"Is that all you're going to say?"

There was an uncomfortable silence. Finally, Hideo said, "What's in it for me?"

The high winds of the ferocious thunderstorm roared across the flat Ohio land, almost tearing the wheat from its roots. Farmer Bjork had to shout his orders so as to be heard above the noise as they struggled to get the reaper out and working.

For one fleeting moment he was grateful for the haystack boulders as one of them now gave him brief shelter from the wind. But that only allowed him a better look at the horror of his heavy crop being destroyed. He shook his head numbly as he watched the rain drop in almost solid sheets. Bjork couldn't tell if the wetness on his face was the rain or his tears.

Though filtered by the radio signal, Mark could still hear his voice was hoarse and tired.

"God . . . You see death and dying, and it's nothing new if you're a doctor . . . But I'm watching a people . . . a nation die . . . all for lack of rain . . .

"There was this one waterhole . . . It was animals and people fighting . . . They stepped on *infants* to get at the water . . . more mud than water . . . They filled their mouths with it, they killed for mud . . . The troops are worse . . . There's no government, there's no law. I try and stay out of their way . . . I do what I can, but . . . I'm afraid of getting killed myself. Supplies are almost gone . . . The plains are littered with corpses . . . cattle and people . . . No one knows how many . . . A hundred thousand, maybe two . . . The dust is everywhere . . ." He managed a bitter laugh. "I can't care anymore. Maybe . . . I'll work this frequency usual time . . . if I'm alive . . . TL8XNT, going off . . . pulling the plug."

"Christ," said Mark. "The U.N. sends experts out to get details, and there are no details. They ask, 'What do you need?' and Mali says, 'Nothing. We're fine.' They take a look around, and there's nothing wrong. If a plane crashes, we know about it. You can't cover up two hundred thousand people dead. He's a crackpot, a crackpot who can operate a ham radio. Maybe he's not even in Mali. Maybe he's in Brooklyn, or Bellevue, more likely."

"I think he's telling the truth," Danny said.

"So do I," said Mark. "So now what?" He turned his attention back to the optical printer, oiling parts and making adjustments. He tuned the radio to the satellite's frequency, and waited.

"The old three oh eight, on time as usual," he said, as the beeping and chirps came over the loudspeaker.

Danny watched closely as Mark set the drum rolling. The old washing-machine motor squealed as the photosensitive paper turned in the drum and absorbed the signal.

Danny followed Mark into the darkroom. He held his breath as Mark slid the photo paper into the development tray. The image of the planet seen from outer space, slowly appearing out of whiteness, was almost magical.

Mark was less enthralled. The identifying numerals were clear, but the picture was weak and snowy, as if the earth were seen through a haze.

He hung the print on the wall, stepped back and stared in silence. Danny joined him.

Mark picked up a crayon and circled the most interesting patterns of clouds and haze. At last he said, "The storm tracks are shifting, the jet stream, the Gulf Stream . . . but what's it mean?"

Danny tried to answer.

Mark laughed and ruffled Danny's hair. "Don't. You'll burst."

He started working out some calculations on the blackboard, but threw down the chalk in disgust. He picked up the phone and dialed Business Administration.

"This is Haney in Meteorology. I need some time on the computer. It's important."

"Look, Haney, Biz Ad is important. Our guys go out in the cruel world and bring back the bacon. What do you do?"

"Tell you if the bacon will get wet!" said Mark, slamming down the phone.

He turned back to Danny. "Now I have to pull a rabbit out of a hat, but first they have to allocate me the hat."

"Huh?"

"I can't get the computer for a mathematical model, so I have to get a model model," he said, and rolled an allocation-request form through the typewriter.

"This is quite a shopping list," said Guzman.

"I need it, sir . . . badly. I've gotten it down as cheaply as I can, but I'll sweep up the place, buy my own chalk, wash dishes, whatever you want, to get this equipment."

"What kind of paper are you doing?"

"I really can't say as yet."

"Can't or won't?"

"Both."

"But you think it's big?"

Mark nodded.

"I can see the look. Your one big chance. If you make it, you're a hero. Blow it, and you're stuck here forever." He leaned back and stared at the ceiling. "Isaac Newton invented calculus at twenty-eight. Einstein published Relativity at twenty-six. This is a young man's game." He let out a deep sigh. "It goes pretty quick."

Guzman brought his attention back to the list.

CHICAGO, ILLINOIS:

To the inexperienced, the scene seemed one of chaos, men waving fingers and hands, screaming across the room to no one in particular. Yet orders to buy found their match with orders to sell, while prices asked and prices offered were marked by frantic men at the blackboard.

The action was normally much faster on the grain-futures market than on the floor of the stock exchange, and today it seemed to run totally amok.

As the speculators watched, the prices jumped ten, then twenty, fifty, one hundred percent.

The combination of severe droughts and storms was taking its toll on the grain supplies. The effects would soon work their way through the economic system, the first tremors of the coming grand quake.

"What's it for?"
"To demonstrate the Haney Effect."
"What's that?"
"I don't know."

Danny listened without expression to Mark's explanations. Dry ice represented the North and South Poles. There was water for oceans, fans for air currents, a light bulb for the sun. Various obstructions represented the Earth's topography that interrupted and deflected the currents.

Usually the forces of nature stayed in balance, the heat from the sun radiating to the equator matching the heat flowing out at the poles. Now the shifting currents in the satellite photo, the evidence of changes in the atmosphere, indicated the balance was being disturbed. But in what way, to what degree, and to what end, were questions the model might answer.

Mark turned on the light bulb, started the fans, and injected a neutral white smoke, the better to see the currents' paths. Heated by the light bulb, the smoke rose; cooled by the ice, it fell. The fans sent it in wayward paths about the obstructions. Sensors measured air flow, opacity, temperature, humidity, and as many relevant aspects as could be squeezed into the tank. Mark noted the readings, then added the recent anomalies. He increased the light's intensity for the added heat, injected dust, sand, carbon dioxide, and pollutants. The white smoke darkened, paths shifted, and the gauges jiggled. Mark noted the new settings.

At last Danny became bored, and yawned.

"Getting sleepy?"

Danny shook his head. "It's all right."

"Tell you what. We'll take shifts. You can check in the morning and take the readings, okay?"

Danny nodded vigorously, and Mark handed him the key.

"Do I get a footnote in your paper?"

"At least."

Danny's mouth came close to a smile. "That's nice." He shook hands good night.

Mark looked at his watch, and again noted the readings. He pictured the title page. "The Haney Effect . . ." It had a nice ring to it.

Time passed slowly. The smoke spun in strange spirals and the dials jiggled. Some had increased, some decreased, but none significantly.

"The Haney Syndrome . . ." But there was no clear syndrome.

The swirls of smoke and the fans' noise were hypnotic. Again Mark took the readings. The ones that had increased now decreased, and those that had decreased now increased.

"The Haney Paradox . . ." Not as good as an effect or a syndrome. It left too many question marks, invited too many others to do the extra work, and the last person with the immediate practical result got the credit. Edison was at the tail end of God knows how many researchers and theorists, but he was the one to get his name in lights, and the franchise for the power to light them.

He looked again. The model was equalizing, running down, like all the processes of nature, like life itself, like old man Guzman, like the city, like Mark Haney . . . Lots of motion, but nobody and nothing was going anywhere.

"The Haney Bullshit . . ."

That summed it up. He would be at this crummy college forever. He had been wasting his life just as he had wasted his time on this.

He thought back on the particular stupidity of climbing to the roof in the middle of a heat wave just to mount an antenna. It had never seemed so hot, and his feet stuck in the melting tar. He could look down over the roof edge and see the dreariness of the school, the Early Dracula buildings and the slums beyond, his whole world. He was stuck here as surely as his feet were stuck in that tar.

The air was stifling and still, and the sun hung huge and white in the sky. It had never seemed so close. As he stared, it came closer, growing ever more gigantic and hot.

He looked about frantically for shelter or shade, but there was none. He tried to scream, but the heat drained all energy from him, and he was alone, his feet glued solidly in the tar. He could only stare, paralyzed, watching the sun fill the sky as it plummeted to earth.

Then came the collision. The sun shattered into a million lights of myriad colors. He had never realized death was so cool and beautiful. At last he had been brought from pain.

Suddenly, he saw all the laws of life and death and matter. He had all knowledge in his grasp, but too late . . . too late . . . He watched his life flow away into the whitness. He had never been so cold...

Suddenly, he was awake and shivering.

It took a few moments to orient himself. He was in his room, in the quiet early morning. The fans in the model still spun on with their steady rushing noise.

He took a deep breath. The dream still nagged at him with a sense of excitement.

As he thought back on it, calculations, laws, equations, all started falling into a pattern. He saw now where those swirls of smoke were going, and he knew he had a bigger paper than he could have imagined.

There was a click at the door, and Danny came in.

"Still here?"

"Uh-huh."

"Something happen?"

"Plenty," said Mark, and told his theory.

Danny stood stunned for a moment. "You . . . you're sure?"

"Not completely. I'll have to cross into other fields, and get some other teachers involved."

"Will they want to?"

"Danny, one thing about scientists. When there's a subject that's bigger than they are, that's really important, petty jealousies just fall by the wayside. Then it's the team that counts. Wait till you see them together, Danny. You'll see true science in action."

The single piece of art only made the conference room more depressing. It was a WPA mural from the '30's, giving the history of Earth Sciences, as it was called back then. It went from dinosaurs to oil wells in five panels. Not only was the artwork poor, but the artist had managed to mix up his ages rather thoroughly, and giant reptiles from the Jurassic era gobbled up mammals from the Paleocene.

Despite the open windows, the air hung hot and heavy. Looking out, Mark could see the slum buildings, with the tenants escaping the heat on the front stoops, and children showering in the open hydrants.

Danny sat quietly in a corner reading another meteorology book, getting up every several seconds to laboriously check through the unabridged dictionary.

Fink walked in. "Hey Mark, who's the midget professor?"

"You don't recognize him out of uniform."

"Oh Jesus, the Cub Scout." He turned to Danny. "Look, kid, this is grown-up stuff. Why don't you play outside until we . . . ?"

"He stays."

Fink was taken aback at Mark's intensity. "I hear you're going to publish in the *Scout Digest*. You're calling it, 'I Am a Raindrop.' "

Guzman came in, looking at his watch. "I hope this won't take long."

"I think it'll be worth it, sir."

Guzman gestured to Danny. "The child yours?"

Danny looked up. "I can be addressed directly."

"My God," said Fink, "he *is* a midget."

"Mark, you bastard," whispered Archaeology, furtively grabbing Mark aside, "what the hell is this? There's a guy here I owe money to I've been trying to avoid all year."

"Haney," said Astronomy, even more furtively, "who's the chick?"

"The 'chick' is an old friend from the History Department."

"You ever make it with her?"

"She's here to contribute."

"I'll bet. Well, if you don't mind, I'll try for a contribution." He sat down next to her, and struck up a conversation.

Others were less cordial, feeling like participants in the mystery story where strangers are brought together in some lonely mansion. Most did not even notice Danny, or perhaps they regarded him as simply one more oddity in an odd meeting.

"All right, people, I'd like to get started," said Mark.

Fink mimicked, "I suppose you're wondering why I called you here today."

"Yeah, I suppose you are. Well, it'll become obvious. I don't want to bore you with a whole meteorology lesson . . ."

"Nah, Mark, you were always good for laughs."

"I'll leave those to you," answered Mark patiently. "There are a few peculiar things happening with the weather."

"Only a few?"

"All right, too many. There are always too many, and the problem is picking out the pattern. The world's biggest computer is down in Maryland, and that'll do it, supposedly, if they ever get the bugs out."

"You're drifting."

"Sorry. Meanwhile what I've got is serious enough." He went over to the world map and sketched in the other anomalies that he knew about. "It may not look like a consistent pattern, but it is. I built a mechanical model, complete with all the relevant factors: heat, carbon dioxide, dirt, dust. The results weren't too encouraging. In fact, I'd say they were downright devastating."

Mark paused, and enjoyed their rapt attention.

"What're you doing, Mark, pausing for a commercial? Just give us the facts."

"All right, first let me tell you why it's so hot." He took out one of the satellite photos. "This is an infra-red photo; it records by heat instead of light. Major cities, you'll notice, are hot spots."

"They sure are, baby, they sure are."

Mark glared at Fink and continued. "In fact, cities are, on an average, six degrees hotter than the surrounding country."

"There's a reason for that," said Fink. "There are more colleges in the city."

"How's that relevant?"

"The more colleges, the more degrees."

"Look, Fink, if you've got nothing substantial to contribute . . ."

Fink threw up his hands. "Just trying to lighten the lesson."

"I'll carry it without you, thanks."

Fink pantomimed zipping his lip, folded his hands angelically, and Mark finally went on.

"Apart from industry and people, who are great heat machines, all the pollutions we pour out are warming up the oceans. In addition, we're stripping whole forests and killing off the ocean plankton, which would have kept down the carbon dioxide."

"What's that got to do with it?"

"It's called the Greenhouse Effect. The CO_2 traps sunlight as heat, just like a greenhouse. Not to mention all the CO_2 we're adding every time we uncork a soda, or use an aerosol."

"So with all that, you mean it's just going to get hotter and hotter?"

"No, it'll turn around, unfortunately."

"Why, unfortunately?"

"You'll see." Mark turned to Hideo. "It starts with you."

"Right. I had rock corings from 4500 BC, Mesopotamia."

"What'd it show?"

"Unusual heat, high CO_2 content, volcanic dust, drought."

"When you came down a few decades, what happened?"

"Cooled off noticeably."

"Hey, hold on!" erupted Archaeology. "Whyn't you tell me you were picking up the research?"

"You never asked me. Look, if a paper came out of it, I'd've mentioned you."

"Thanks for the footnote. I'll plant a footnote on your fat ass, you . . ."

"Hey kids . . ." interrupted Mark, "can we pretend we're professionals?"

History asked, "When you say it cooled off 'noticeably' . . ."

"Enough to be noted. Couple of degrees, on the average."

"Is that important?"

Archaeology took the opportunity to touch her

on the shoulder. "You see, that's just about the time the society fell apart."

"I don't go back that far. Why'd it happen?"

Archaeology basked in her attention. "The record is skimpy because the record-keeping is almost non-existent. But there was a change of government, riots, general malaise . . ."

"But nothing about it getting cooler."

"That's why I didn't think of it. Mesopotamia was a rice-centered economy, so if the rice crop fails, everything else follows. You get starvation, food riots, and the whole society collapses . . . Yeah, I get the picture." He turned to glare at Hideo. "I get the picture very well."

Fink shook his head sadly. "I sure miss that Mesopotamian rice."

"C'mon," said History, with a nasty edge. "Gibbon took volumes to tell why the Roman Empire fell, and I still don't think he got the whole story. You're giving it to me in a temperature drop?"

"Why not?"

"Because it's simplistic. Societies aren't simple. You can do papers a foot thick on the complexities of some little tribe somewhere."

"Societies *are* simple. They're supposed to provide you with a bed to sleep in, some square meals, and sexual access."

"Sounds nice," said Fink. "You know of any?"

"You know, as long as we're into this," said Archaeology, "there was one coincidence I never gave much thought to. Around 2000 BC, there were two very classy civilizations, Egypt, and the Indus valley in India. They seemed to disintegrate about the same time."

"They had some things in common," said Hideo. "Drought, heat, dust, high CO_2 content, followed by cooling."

"How come you know my territory?"

"I got curious and dug out one of your books."

"Without me?"

"I didn't need you."

"You bastard!"

The two men were on their feet, fists clenched. They were persuaded with difficulty to sit, and order of a sort was restored. There was a strained silence. Archaeology and Geology stared in opposite directions.

Mark sighed, and turned to Botany. "What've you got?"

"Tree rings."

"Very nasty," said Fink. "I know a doctor who can cure that."

"We can judge rainfall and temperature by the width of the rings, narrow for bad years, wide for good, and we've got records back to 1000 AD."

"What do the rings show?"

"Up to 1400, it was very warm."

"Well, it's pretty far-fetched, but as long as I'm here . . ." said History. "The Vikings did their explorations before then. Also the time of Christianity's spread throughout Europe, and the biggest time of cathedral-building, which beats the pyramids, as far as I'm concerned. All in all, it was an age of social explosion."

"Then it turned cold. That lasted till the nineteenth century."

"When was it worst?"

"I'd say late sixteenth to early seventeenth."

"That's quite a coincidence. There was a famine in the 1690s in Great Britain. It was more devastating than the Black Plague. It ruined independence for Scotland. The Scandinavian colonies in Iceland were wiped out, and they never became colonial powers."

"Well, shit," said Astronomy. "Sunspot minimum."

Mark turned to him. "A new corner heard from. Can you explain yourself?"

"Sunspots are storms on the sun. We know they affect radio transmission; the other effects are arguable. The records on them begin at . . ."

"Don't tell me," said Fink. "They begin just at the time you interrupted."

"Right, 1690. By then they had telescopes, and started watching sunspots. Minimum sunspots means minimum solar energy, and minimum solar energy means . . . well, whatever you want it to mean. They also saw that the storms ran in cycles."

"How long?"

"Eleven years up, eleven down."

"Interesting," said Botany. "There's a regular twenty-two-year rhythm to the tree rings."

"Y'mean, eleven good years and eleven bad?"

"Not quite. Just a regular subtle rhythm within the larger ones. Now, if you want a point where they came together, 1816 was a really bad year for tree rings."

"Yeah," said Fink, "you can't hardly get a good 1816 tree ring these days."

"1816," said History. "They called it the Year Without a Summer. New York harbor froze, so shipping fell apart. Upstate in June it was below freezing, so we lost the crops. We were trying to get out from under after the War of 1812, and because of that one season, we nearly didn't. The whole country nearly collapsed."

"How about that?" said Astronomy. "1816, another sunspot minimum."

"Ah, we got dust," exclaimed Hideo, rejoining the group. "The year before, there was a major volcanic explosion in Indonesia. Pumped dust around the world. And it certainly affected the weather, because it brought on whirlwinds."

"It warmed up quite a bit after 1865," said Botany.

"1865: opening of the American West, the rise of the Industrial Age, era of imperialism, the whole burgeoning of modern civilization."

"Okay," said Mark, "which brings us down to the present. Same factors, heat, dust, drought, high CO_2. We're on the way down again . . . significantly."

History asked, "Is 'significantly' more or less than 'substantially'?"

"Let me explain," said Fink. "Substantially is horseshit, and significantly is bullshit."

Mark asked pleasantly, through clenched teeth, "And why do you think that?"

"Because it doesn't matter. We're not Mesopotamia, or India, or Vikings. We aren't even what we were in 1816. We are civilized as hell, and if it cools off, all we have to do is turn up the thermostat, and civilization is saved."

"And where's the fuel going to come from?" asked Geography. "We're into a fuel shortage as it is."

"If you ask me, that fuel shortage is ninety-five percent politics."

"So what do you think civilization is?"

"Bed, meals, sex."

"Well, I hope you have the bed and sex, because you won't have the meals," said Geography. "A one-degree drop in the temperature shortens the growing season by two weeks. Just about all the arable land is already tilled. We may be civilized, but we're on a precarious balance."

At that, History asked again, with a slight edge of fright, "How significantly, Mark?"

"You really want an answer?" Mark turned to Geology. "How many Ice Ages have we had?"

"Count keeps increasing. Last count, about twenty."

"How much time between them?"

"Roughly ten thousand years."

"And how long since the last one?"

"About ten thousand years."

Mark looked about the room. "I guess I have everybody's attention." He turned back to Geology. "What do the rock cores show at the ends of the warm periods?"

Geology bit his lip. "High carbon dioxide content, increasing heat, change of precipitation, large amounts of dust."

There was a silence, broken by Astronomy's cheery voice, "In case anyone's interested, we're in a period of sunspot minimum. Furthermore, what you're talking about, those conditions existed on planet Venus, clouds, dust, CO_2. Called the Super Greenhouse Effect."

"And now?"

"Near as we can make out, it's all ice now."

Mark nodded. There was a silence, and then the room erupted into shouting, and finally Archaeology grabbed the floor. "You mean we're coming into a full-scale Ice Age?"

"Looks that way."

"You mean there'll be polar bears outside the window?"

"Eventually."

"Oh Jesus," moaned Fink, "and all that bearshit in the streets."

"I don't think it'll be a laughing matter."

"I suppose we'll have mastodons and sabre-tooth tigers too."

"When you're extinct, you're extinct."

"Ah, bullshit, Haney. You're talking like the Ice Age is arriving next Tuesday. It must've taken thousands of years."

"Y'know," said Hideo thoughtfully, "they occasionally find mastodons and mammoths buried in the ice, perfectly preserved. Some thoughtless explorers even carved out a few mastodon steaks for themselves."

"I know," said Fink, "we had 'em in the cafeteria last week. So what?"

"So this. How come if there's so much time to get out of the way, we find them with food in their mouths?"

"That sounds pretty logical to me."

"Think about it, you bubblehead. If you die with your mouth full, you die suddenly. It means they were trapped."

"Whatever it was, we are not mastodons. We are

intelligent human beings who are masters of nature."
Fink turned to Mark. "You yourself said we're altering the weather."

"Inadvertently."

"Then we can make it advertent."

"Maybe, in time."

"Well, we have got time, haven't we?"

"I don't know."

"You don't know much."

"Right, I don't."

"You're a great one for straight lines, Marcus.
Is that your qualification for group leader?"

"Look, Fink, we're doing things to our planet
that have never been done, and the old rules have
been thrown out the window. I do know the factors
have come together with a far greater degree of con-
gruence than ever before. This time it's going to happen a lot faster."

"How fast is 'faster?' Five thousand years? Five
hundred? One hundred? An hour and a half?"

"I don't know how long the cycle will take to
complete, but it's already started."

Astronomy said, "You sure could fool me."

"You see how we're freezing already," said Fink,
mopping his brow.

Mark tacked a series of satellite photos on the
board. "These are a little dim because my equipment
isn't too great. Look. The Gulf Stream has drifted,
which is going to bring cold air down with it. There's
already increasing cloud cover and fog around Newfoundland. The storm tracks are shifting, which means
the countries that got the monsoons are not getting
them, while we're getting the storms the Aleutians
used to get."

"Well, at least we're keeping it in the family. It's
not like we're getting what's on Venus."

"You know Ranier Park, in Washington. We
wouldn't be too happy with their climate."

"Why not? It makes for great skiing."

"Small wonder. They had eighty feet of snow in
one season."

"Go on, Mark. Make me unhappy."

Mark held a few photos in his hand. "These are all of the Humboldt Glacier in Greenland. Watch . . ." He flipped them, and a white patch in the photos seemed to come to life and creep slowly outward.

"Animals are already reacting. Wolves have been coming down from higher latitudes. Martens, lemmings, musk oxen have all been migrating further south. Some have been found as far south as the Arizona desert."

He put up a series of graphs. "Here are the temperature means of some cities around the world. Take 'em every ten years and you see they've been climbing together, but now notice the sudden shift down, all at the same time."

He looked at them. "You all with me?"

Archaeology said, "Don't take it personally . . ."

"This isn't the time to take anything personally."

"Fine. The government must have more information than you."

"That's what they're always telling us."

"Well, they've got the best brains, the best equipment. They must know what's going on."

"I don't doubt it."

"Why haven't they said anything?"

Mark shrugged. "You tell me."

"They must run their meetings like we do," Fink said.

"Yeah," said Archaeology, "but sooner or later . . ."

"Sooner or later, we'll all know it. Only then it'll be too late."

"C'mon, Mark, you don't think they'll just let us all die, do you?"

"Look, they declare wars, and they *send* us out to die. I don't care to wait and find out what the government has. I say we go public on this. Now. Skip the conventions: the review committees, the trade journals. I made a contact on the *Times*. We can hold a press conference, let them know where we stand . . ."

"*We?* What do you mean, we?"

"This is a very short neck, Haney. I don't stick it out often."

"We're in science, not show business, Marcus."

"Damn it," said Mark, "there's a juggernaut coming down on us."

"Hardly. Your Ice Age may not happen for a thousand years. You yourself said you don't know."

Mark nodded. "It doesn't have to arrive all at once. Just the beginning is enough. You heard we're on a precarious balance. A drop of a degree or two and we start toppling like those other societies. I've been listening to it happen right now, a country in West Africa." He stopped. ". . . and there'll be others. And eventually us, 'civilized' or not."

The silence was suddenly oppressive. Outside they could hear the children playing stickball, and as the silence within the room grew deeper, they heard beyond the street to the roar of the city itself.

"Hold on a minute, Mark."

Guzman had the graphs and satellite photos in his hand, and was regarding them thoughtfully. They had forgotten he was even in the room. Now that he had everyone's attention, he seemed a little ashamed and very self-conscious. Finally he asked shyly, "Uh . . . Mark, you know the Canadian red fox?"

Mark blinked, puzzled. "Not personally."

"Well, it's not a very important animal, so I'm not surprised, and it's not your department anyway. But . . . uh . . . it used to be down near Saskatchewan. Now they've been finding it further and further north, even up near the Arctic Circle, supposedly because it's been getting warmer."

He paused. The others held their breaths, and the tension was almost palpable.

"Well," said Mark, almost struggling to get the word out as he realized his throat had gone dry. "One animal can always be eccentric."

"Oh, several animals can be eccentric. You're the one looking for patterns."

"What about *my* department?" asked History. "I

wouldn't have thought so before, but now there does seem to be a pattern."

"Well, your department isn't mine, but you said it turned cold . . . when?"

"Starting 1400, and it affected social vitality."

"Wasn't there something called the Renaissance starting up about then?" He turned to Geology. "You said there was a volcanic explosion in 1815?"

"Sumbawa Island, Indonesia. One of the biggest in history. Pumped dust around the world."

"When was Krakatoa?"

"1883."

"Well, geology isn't my department either. But Krakatoa was the biggest baby of them all, and I don't remember any cold spell afterward."

Hideo nodded slowly. *"Touche,* but what about the interglacial coming to an end? Once upon a time we did, after all, have Greenland's climate, and it could happen again."

"Well, it's certainly been colder, but you've seen corings from up north. Has it always been that cold up there?"

"Hell, no. In Alaskan corings, you can spot remains of fig trees and magnolias. And Spitzbergen had palm trees."

"So it's certainly been warmer, too. Now, I'm not smart enough to know which way it's going, but I don't think anybody else does."

"What about . . . the graphs?" asked Mark.

"Yes, I was looking at them here." Guzman brandished them. "They're good graphs, and I know it's standard to take every ten years for your norm, but just for the hell of it I took twelve years, and drew my own lines. And, well, there's no downturn. In fact, I don't see any pattern at all." He passed the graphs around.

"Which brings me to my point. I don't see any pattern anywhere, and I don't think anybody can. We can forecast accurately twenty-four hours, and stretch it thin to forty-eight. One week ahead, you're certainly taking chances, and maybe someday, not my lifetime but maybe yours, we might forecast two weeks ahead. But that's about it."

Mark couldn't talk at all as he held up the satellite photos of Greenland.

"Oh yes, the glacier. I admit, that's the weather factory, and if that glacier's expanding we're in trouble. The glacier's what really counts."

Mark nodded.

"Mark, how fast would you say a glacier moves?"

"Well, I hate to repeat a cliché, but . . ."

"It's not your department."

Mark nodded, embarrassed.

Hideo spoke up. "My department. You could've asked me. In fact, you should've asked me. Usually a glacier moves maybe a few feet a year . . ."

"That's . . . all?"

"*But,* it's rare but it happens, but there are records of them surging up to a half-mile in a day. Of course, they run out of gas in a few days."

"All right," said Guzman, "I'll grant you the half-mile. Say even a mile. But not twenty miles an hour."

"Jesus, no."

"Well, Mark, that's the rate at which *your* glacier is moving . . . unless that white patch isn't a glacier but clouds."

Mark looked at the photos, and moaned, nodding weakly.

"Well, it's an easy enough mistake to make, especially with the lousy resolution in those photos."

Mark slumped into his seat.

The silence was broken by Fink's gleeful yell. "Too-o-o bad! There goes fame and fortune for our young genius."

"Had me going a while," said Hideo.

"Great to be back in the heat," said Archaeology.

History bent low and squeezed his shoulder. "I'm sorry, Mark. I'm really, really sorry."

"Nice presentation," said Guzman, patting Mark on the back. "It's a little difficult checking these things out sometime." He waved the papers. "Want these back?"

Mark shook his head.

"See you back on the slave ship tomorrow."

Botany asked if someone could give him a lift downtown. Astronomy grabbed History's arm and asked if she'd like to see the wonders of the stars at the observatory.

Finally, Mark was alone in the room, with a very quiet Danny sitting at the other end.

"Well, still want me for your scout project?"

Danny nodded.

"How come?"

"Guzman hasn't *dis*-proved the premise."

"My one admiring colleague. Wanna get drunk together?"

"Uh . . . I think it'll spoil my dinner."

"Oh. My colleague's mother won't let him. Okay, go on home."

"Maybe if I watched, or . . ."

"Go home, Danny."

"Y'know, I should keep a better log on the . . ."

"Go home, Danny. You see more of me than you do of your mother."

"That's all right. She doesn't care."

"She says she loves you."

Danny shrugged. "I . . . guess . . ."

"C'mon, give her a chance. Let her be a mother to you. And you can start by being a kid."

"I'd rather . . ."

"I'd rather you went home."

"You excluding me from your research?"

"Not only that, I'm kicking you out. Good-bye."

Danny's face tightened. He turned on his heel and walked out.

Mark sat alone in the meeting room a good while, then wearily dragged himself back to his office.

The model of the world's weather system had

run down. The dry ice had evaporated, the dust settled, the currents were stilled. It was the state of the Earth at entropy, at its termination a million, perhaps a billion, years in the future. Mark felt a chill. It was as though he were looking at a corpse.

Almost desperately, he turned on the receiver.

The life of the planet filled the room, governments broadcasting news and music and culture and propaganda, individuals and institutions caught up in their daily commerce and diversions, while the complexities of the world's weather sounded in dit-da-dits, defying any one human to make sense of it.

It was time for the transmission from Mali. Mark turned to Dr. Schumer's frequency, and waited. There was only the hiss of an open channel.

Maybe it was all a joke. The rest of the world went right on functioning, as it had, as it would, until entropy a billion years hence.

There was no need to rush things.

A knock at the open door interrupted his reverie. Mark looked up to see Danny's mother.

"Hi."

Mark nodded.

"Danny told me about your big meeting."

"It was nothing. Just that my theory got shot down."

"Sounds painful."

He shrugged.

"I figured you could use some consolation. Would you like to have dinner with us?"

"I wouldn't want to butt in."

"It's not interference. Believe me, it's not."

He hesitated.

"Please."

Mark switched off the receiver, and followed her out.

Professor Guzman looked long and hard at the papers, the graphs, the news clippings, the satellite photos, then picked up the phone. "John? Guzman here. I know we've discussed this before, but I'm ready to put some of my savings into real estate. Down south, I think."

"Well, the Carolinas are nice . . ."

Guzman looked at the world map. "I was thinking of something more exotic. Southwest Mexico or Guatemala. I'll let you know specifically."

It was late, and Danny was asleep in his room. Mark handled the Eskimo carvings as they talked.

"The worst part is just . . . not knowing, not knowing what happened in Mali, or what's happening with the world. It's just . . . so inexorable."

"Well, it is," said Karen. "Why can't you just accept it?"

"Ac- . . . you mean, just accept whatever nature throws at us? Not just storms and drought, but disease, and death?"

She smiled. "Civilization's accomplished quite a lot."

"Damned right."

"So why am I safer walking the Greenland Ice Cap than your city streets?"

"So all parts of civilization don't always work at their best, but it does work."

She shook her head. "There are other ways to live."

"If you call that living."

"Just how much do you need out of life? To be alive and happy, to live for yourself and those you love. That's really all."

"Pretty short list."

"What more do you need?"

"A lot more."

"Really? Why?"

"Because that's what makes us human."

"I once asked an Eskimo what he wanted out of life. He said he would like to have animals enough to feed and clothe him, and to keep sadness and pain from those near to him." She sighed. "He was human. I thought he was a beautiful human."

"They . . ." he hesitated.

"Say it."

"Okay. They're living like they did a thousand years ago. They haven't moved forward an inch."

"Maybe that's because they like it where they are."

"But where are they? They've done nothing, accomplished nothing."

"You're holding something."

He looked down at the carving in his hand. It was exquisitely wrought, with the detail of a craftsman who had taken infinite pains, carving evidently for the love of the work itself, and for love of nature. But it was alien to Mark all the same. The maker made no attempt to understand nature, decode it, ultimately conquer it. He would merely accept it, and if a storm came that wiped him out, he would accept that too, without knowing the reasons or forces, or caring to know.

Disturbed, Mark set it down. "It doesn't satisfy me."

"Why not learn from it?"

"Learn? I was thinking maybe we could teach them."

"I asked an Eskimo to sing his war song for my tape recorder. He asked me what war meant." She shrugged sadly. "I'm afraid I taught him."

Mark took a deep breath. "Well, I guess we could argue all night. It won't change the world."

"Why do you have to change it?"

"Look," he answered, stirring, reaching for his jacket. "Today I was humiliated, deflated, dehumanized, and I'm in no mood to argue the beautiful ways of mankind."

He paused. "I'm sorry . . . I . . . Thanks for the dinner. Say good night to Danny for me."

She followed him to the door, and put her hand on his shoulder.

"Look, you're still the nice guy who helped Danny, and helped me through the cafeteria line."

"I'm glad that it matters a little."

"It's all that matters," she said and kissed him.

Startled, he responded, kissing her closed lips. Her lips parted, and her tongue sought his, and again he answered, even as he wondered.

His tongue dove under hers, felt the wet silk beneath and stroked it. His right hand reached for the buttons on her dress, as his left pushed them through the buttonholes.

Even though he knew they would soon be in bed, he noted with satisfaction and relief that she wore no bra, and there would be no need to unfasten tiny metal clasps while otherwise pretending nothing was happening.

His hand reached further around, and it seemed he reached through to the very insides of her and felt her trembling. He knew, even as his fingers grasped her close, that all of her was his, not to possess, but to embrace and cherish.

His hand crept down her back, feeling each vertebra as her spine curved inward, then outward as it softened to pliant buttocks. He caressed them, and let his fingers slide into the crevice, and he stroked there. She accepted his hand as she had accepted his lips and his tongue.

There was a flash of doubt, for after all, there were men who were "nice guys." Would she take them all to bed, anthropologists, Eskimos, shadows he couldn't even name?

He reached up, pulled on the hanging flaps of her dress and brought them forward, around her shoulders. She turned her arms, the better to free them, letting the dress drop. She stood before him, naked, vulnerable, and trusting.

It was him she wanted and accepted, he himself, right now, this minute, and the shadows of others had no substance or meaning.

He kissed her as he wrapped his arm about her, cradling her, and lifted her to him. She was light in his arms, and would be loving in her bed.

It was all that mattered.

He awoke slowly, as if arising from the deepest darkness of the bottom of the sea.

He lay next to her, and he realized it was morning, and she was still asleep. Before she awakened, he wanted to think it out, the whole process by which he came to this unfamiliar feeling, of the weakness, and terror, and blissful pleasure of awakening for the first time in his life.

He realized he had always kept sealed some vital part of himself, for fear that a total surrender would be akin to dying. But this time was different.

He remembered that she had led him, that once he had entered her, she had guided him. For a moment he had hesitated, because for all the women he had taken to bed, he now felt strangely innocent, recapturing the sweet fright of the first time.

He had gradually realized he sensed none of the usual remorse or remonstrance. In that deepest of communications of sexual touch, and as deeply as he probed her being, the sense was communicated as clearly as if their minds were as intermingled as their bodies, that nothing he might say or do was unnatural or alien or hostile.

He realized that all of his life it had been otherwise, that there were aspects of the body reminding him he was no more than an animal. His whole society had frantically buried these beneath attitudes and cosmetics, and when they appeared despite those efforts, they were greeted with repugnance, or pretended disregard, or apologies followed by reassurances.

But Karen was different. To her there was nothing unnatural. One's animal nature was faced, welcomed, accepted.

So one taboo after another was faced, and she accepted him totally, so he gave himself to the fullness of his animal being.

Now he watched her go through the same stages, her eyes flickering open, overwhelmed and frightened by the light of the world, withdrawing a brief moment, then plunging forward, seeing him, remembering, and receiving him into her life.

" 'Morning . . ." she said.

" 'Morning yourself."

"What're you smiling about?"

"It was sweet."

"It was, but that's not what you were smiling about."

"I thought . . . Eskimos just rubbed noses."

"For a start."

He rubbed her nose. "It's a good start." He kissed it. "Of course, with all that ice, there's not much else to do."

"Oh . . . it's not just ice." She stroked his hair, and pulled him closer.

"No?" He kissed her eyelids.

"The sky'd be all gray, and then the sun'd come out . . . and it'd be like molten gold just pouring across the ice . . ."

"Molten gold . . ." He nibbled at her earlobe. "M-hm-m."

"And each little crystal'd catch the light and sparkle . . . with every color of the rainbow . . . and it'd be like piles of diamonds."

"Sounds nice." He rolled his tongue in her ear and heard her ecstatic gasp.

"And the ice makes noise when it moves, a splintering, and then a rolling thunder that . . . just seems to echo forever. It'll be quiet for a long time, and it'll fool you . . . then 'poom . . . bowm . . . boom!' and it'll shake you out of bed."

"Pooooom." He rolled his tongue down her neck to her breast, and swirled it about her soft nipple. She clutched his hair tighter.

"And there're ice sculptures that the water carves out . . . Sometimes they're crystal flowers . . . and when the sun catches them . . . there's nothing more beautiful."

"Oh, yes, there is."

". . . Oh? . . ."

"You."

"Thank you." She smiled, and nibbled at his ear.

He felt himself drifting off to sleep, and started to dream of that land where the ice was fire, and the quietness was rolling thunder, and it played games with you, so that you thought it was quiet, when suddenly it said, "Boo!" . . . in her voice . . . Her voice?

He opened his eyes. "What'd you say?"

"I said, 'Boo.' I didn't want you going to sleep on me when you were doing so nicely."

"What'd the ice say?"

"The . . . ice?"

"The sounds."

"Oh. Well, first you hear a kind of splintering noise, and then a thunderclap, and sometimes you'd feel the ground shaking like an earthquake, even though . . ."

"How long's that been happening?"

"More and more lately. When it moves, you can see it creeping. Probably it'd cross a space like this room in a day, but lately it's been . . ."

She stopped. He had already bounced out of bed. "Gotta use your phone."

"Sure, but where . . . ?"

He was already dialing. "Hideo? . . . Mark Haney . . . No, I don't know what time it is, and I'm not sorry I woke you up. Now get your head on straight and listen."

Karen stared as a very naked Mark talked feverishly about a moving glacier, forgetting she was even there.

"Sure it was cloud cover. The question is, what the hell is cloud cover doing over Greenland? It's desert there . . . Yeah, it's ice, but it's desert. It doesn't snow, at least until now . . ."

The conversation grew increasingly technical, until he hung up.

"He buys it! Son of a bitch, he buys it. Plus, he's got a foundation grant he can switch. The only thing is . . ."

"What?"

"You want to go back?"

"Where?"

"Greenland. The glacier. It'd work out perfect. You know the tribe, you can get us guides . . ."

She shook her head, bewildered. "It's pretty sudden . . . How soon . . . ?"

"As soon as we clear it."

"How important . . . ?"

"Damned important."

"What about Danny?"

"He'll see the necessity. He'll know we have to check out the . . ."

"Mark, you're asking me to leave him behind!"

"Well, he'll certainly understand it's no Cub Scout camping trip."

She moaned. "My God, Mark, you know the shocks he's had. How much love has he ever gotten from any of us, and especially from me? Now you're asking me to desert him again."

Mark stared, bewildered. "Am I missing something? I thought he'd even enjoy it. We'll leave him some extra food in the refrigerator . . ."

"Oh no!" She almost laughed as she shook her head. "You're kidding?"

"What's the problem?"

"Do you know how long we'd have to be gone?"

"Well, about two or three days' travel time—to allow for connections and all . . ."

"Which leaves getting around once you're there."

He nodded. "So?"

"Well, it's late summer now. I figure we'd be back mid-winter."

Mark's mouth dropped as he slumped on the bed. "I don't suppose there's any way of . . . flooring the gas pedal, or whatever you do in dog sleds."

"Like goosing the dogs?"

He nodded.

"The Eskimos spent six thousand years learning how to travel. If there was any way of . . ."

He held up his hands in surrender. "All right. We've got problems. Three, to be exact. One, Danny, two, money, and three, convincing my boss."

He brightened. "Actually, we may have only one. If we don't convince Guzman, then we don't even have the other problems."

It seemed to Mark that they would indeed have only one problem. Guzman remained unconvinced, despite the new evidence.

Mark was nearing the end of his emotional and mental tether. Hadn't Guzman himself said that glacier movement was the crucial climate factor?

"Glacier movements are nothing new."

"This glacier's been surging, not just moving. Karen was begging the natives to move their village because it was directly in its path."

"Then why doesn't it show up on the satellite photos?"

"Jesus, sir, you're the one who pointed out the cloud cover. And the cover itself means that area is getting turbulence."

"That could mean anything."

"It means *something*. The only way we'll know exactly is to measure it, density, rate of movement, force . . . Look, that's Hideo's department. He's convinced."

There was a silence.

"Who'll cover your classes?"

"Anyone could do it. It's all elementary stuff this semester."

"I'm not so sure. I think a class could be severely disturbed by a change in teachers."

It suddenly seemed to Mark that Guzman's objections were not well grounded in either fact or logic. He tried another tactic.

"You may be right, sir. There may be nothing happening. If that's the case, of course I'll turn over all my material to you. 'The Impossibility of Long-Range Climate Projection.' That'd look good over your name."

That appealed to him, thought Mark; it was about time.

While Mark was bargaining with Guzman, Karen reached a decision. She described the trip carefully to Danny, who listened so solemnly that she almost felt like grabbing him by the shoulders and shaking him, until the adult mask fell away. Instead, she asked, "Danny, would you like to come?"

"With you?"

"With us, to Greenland." After all, she thought, every child loves an adventure. Facing a new world, one he would have to master, might help make him be a child again.

For an instant she saw that flicker of excitement in his eyes, but it quickly faded.

"It's . . . primitive."

"Yes. It's exciting."

"Months and months of . . . snow and ice. I . . . couldn't cope with that."

"Eskimo children do. You'll meet them."

He turned up his nose. "Primitives. What'll I talk to them about?"

"You'll learn more than at school."

"Oh . . . Oh, I couldn't miss school. Oh no, I couldn't miss school."

She wanted to ask, "Not even for me?", but didn't. She knew what the answer would be.

After Mark left, Guzman shivered, although the room was warm. He picked up the phone, dialed for an outside line, and was soon talking to the bank officer.

The bank officer had made inquiries. There was nothing of value about or under the land. He'd follow orders, of course, but he didn't want to see Guzman lose his shirt on something so transparently useless.

"Let's just say I'm crazy. Look, how fast can you close deals there?"

It would take time, the bank officer said. There were problems of money exchange, working through intermediaries, and so forth. Negotiations would be protracted.

"Forget negotiations. Just grab it, at the first price."

"Forget . . . You're sure you . . . ?"

"I said I'm crazy, didn't I?"

The satellite circled above the city, measuring the changes as summer waned. Masses of sluggish air that had kept the major cities of the Northeast sweltering at last began to break up. The complex spirals about the planet heaved and twisted under pressure. Mountains of air reshaped and reformed. Cold fronts met warm fronts in violent confrontations, and beneath those mountains, people blessed the break in the hot spell.

As the planet continued on its orbit, its relation to the sun altered, and the direct paths of the sun's rays worked their way slowly southward.

For a moment, the center of the sun was suspended over the celestial equator. It was the equinox. Day and night were equal in all parts of the world.

In the northern hemisphere, the days would shorten, and the countless forms of life on the planet would make their instinctive adjustments, withdrawing, shriveling, burrowing deeper, collecting diminishing warmth.

The astronomy professor watched the process occur on his instruments at exactly the right instant. For a moment, he recalled a raucous meeting about a coming ice age, but that faded. Even his usual frustrations of inadequate equipment, the paper he would never write, the fame he would never acquire, were eclipsed by the reassurance of the constancy of the solar system.

At the *Times,* a journalist was given an assignment he did not relish immediately, the editorial on the seasonal change. The news that was fit to print was usually bad news, change was usually for the worse. But not this.

"We thought autumn would never come, but here it is, as always . . ."

Overhead, the satellite circled, gathering information denied the journalist.

HUMBOLDT GLACIER, GREENLAND:

An ancient Greek explorer called it, "A sluggish and congealed sea which could neither be traveled over nor sailed through." It was like a sculpture of a great river, smooth and glassy where a river would run smooth, but where the ground beneath—sometimes as much as a mile—was uneven or rocky, the cataracts were exaggerated to giant crags and peaks.

The ancient explorer who assumed the glacier impassable would have been amazed at the sight of the two dog sleds. The Eskimo driver guided the lead sled expertly through the smooth sections of the ice river, so that all Mark heard was the hissing of runners, and the occasional crunching of small bits of ice crushed beneath.

Once in a while, the dogs would falter and fall out of step, nipping at each other's heels, and the smooth ride would be broken. The Eskimo would curse and lash out with the whip that could reach out thirty feet across the line of dogs.

The lash would come down again and again, stinging, then dancing out of their way as they would attempt to bite it down.

At last, sensing the owner of the whip was their master, they would whimper sullenly and resume their synchronized running.

Sitting close to the ice gave Mark the illusion of great speed. It seemed he was flying on the wings of the wind.

The delight was enhanced by Karen straddling him from behind. He would occasionally reach behind him to stroke her thighs, and she would poke him in remonstrance.

Getting started had been less comfortable, he recalled. Each dog had howled and battled ferociously as it was tied to the team, starting battles among the other dogs down the line. As they finally got moving, the dogs took the opportunity to clear their bowels, and the sled had to pass over the collective droppings. So much for the unsullied Arctic.

Mark looked behind him and saw that Hideo was also enjoying his ride. The Eskimo driver rode in back, at times jumping off and running alongside to adjust a tangle in the leather traces. When Hideo had remarked on his resemblance to the Eskimos, Karen mentioned that to the best of modern knowledge, Eskimos were the descendants of Asians, who had crossed a then-existent land bridge between Siberia and Alaska to North America.

Mark turned forward. The distant ice peaks appeared very close and two-dimensional, like some medieval tapestry. The sun broke through, the grayness of the tips of the peaks catching the light first, seeming to glow from within, the radiance gradually creeping down the peaks like spreading fire.

They traveled on in silence, as if borne by giant birds. Mark felt he was outside time itself. He felt his mind drifting.

The driver let out a scream. Almost magically, part of the solid ice gave way as so much fluff. An abyss opened before them, and the lead dogs disappeared over the edges, howling, while Karen shrieked, "Off, off!" and Mark felt himself flying.

As the world spun, he looked up and saw the sled above him. Instinctively, he pulled back as it came crashing down, missing him by inches.

There was a pandemonium of human curses and animal howls. A dozen huskies pawed pathetically at the ice, strangling as their leather traces tangled into Gordian knots. Immediately the two Eskimos were at the edge of the precipice, pulling hand over hand with all their strength, gradually working the hysterical dogs back to the level ice.

Hideo came running up, his gleeful expression out of all keeping with what had just happened. He gave Mark a hand up.

"What . . . what the hell was that?"

"What we've been looking for."

Hideo led Mark to the edge of the precipice.

"That's the major crevasse. They get covered with loose snow and you can't spot them. It's like an ambush. We'd lose whole tractors that way."

"Jesus . . . You bastard, you let us go first."

"No, Mark, the dogs went first. If we'd used snowmobiles, we would have been dead."

Now that the snow had fallen away, Mark could see it was about forty feet across to the other side. Gathering up his courage, he looked down. The walls were as sharp and jagged as the craggiest of mountainsides, but they seemed illuminated from within, in shades of green and blue. Somewhere from deep below echoed an unexpected sound, the roar of foaming water.

"How deep would you say that is?"

"Well, if you fall, it's a fifteen-story drop. But I don't intend to fall."

"You're going down there?"

"That's what I'm here for. I'll tell you this much right now. If you've got crevasses like this, you've got moving ice."

"How do you know?"

"The ice at the bottom is compressed. Up here it's light and brittle, so when the bottom moves, it cracks up here."

"You call *that* a crack?"

The Eskimos brought up the gear, and Hideo unpacked a series of instruments. One of the Eskimos laughed and made a remark to Karen.

"He said they look like children's toys."

"Like hell they are."

There was another exchange. Karen translated:

"He said he guided some government people up here a few weeks ago, and they had the grown-up versions."

"Ask him if one of the instruments looked like a mirror, broken into crystals."

She translated, and Hideo could see the Eskimo's assent. "Lasers. They're after the same things I am." He sat down glumly on the ice.

"What's the problem?"

"There goes our paper. Whatever I'm gonna find, they already found."

"But they haven't announced anything. So look at it this way: whatever it was they found, you're gonna find."

Hideo looked at him. "That's stupider than anything you said at the meeting." He sprang up. "But let's check it out."

An expert climber, Hideo lowered himself by the rope, shouting commands that had to wait for translation by Karen. Instruments followed as Hideo made himself fast, and he devoted the next hour to chopping parts of the ice away, stringing lines and electrical probes from one point to another, turning a hand drill for core samples. The tapping of the hammer and the crunch of the drill seemed violations of the beautiful desolation.

The dogs were growing uneasy. One of the Eskimos muttered anxiously to Karen, who passed down the word. "He said to come up quick."

Hideo's voice came echoing up. "Almost through."

"He means *now*."

"In a minute."

There was a rumbling that Mark could feel in his gut, so deep and low at first he thought it was a mere sense of unease. It gradually became louder and more ominous.

"That's my cue," yelled Hideo. "Get me out of here."

They all pulled.

"Hurry up, goddamn it!"

The rumbling increased, and Mark felt growing panic.

"We're pulling!"

The dogs were howling in terror as the rumbling became a violent shaking and the mile-thick ice seemed to slip from its moorings. Mark looked across to the far side of the chasm and saw it rumbling closer.

"*C'mon!*"

The chasm started to seal from the bottom, with

Hideo scrambling up just ahead of it. He was pummeled against the ice crags, trying to keep instruments and ice samples out of harm's way.

Mark was sweating profusely despite the cold; keeping his balance was increasingly difficult on the shaking ice, as he pulled hand over hand on the rope.

At last Hideo came up over the edge, scrambling for a handhold as he floundered about like a fish out of water. He was screaming: "The instruments, the goddamn instruments!"

"Forget 'em!"

"No," and he turned to the rope, pulling with the others. "There it comes . . ."

The driver reached across the chasm for a better grip, when the ice cracked open around him, and the chunk slid down into the crevasse. He flailed about helplessly and fell, screaming. He hit bottom with a sickening crunch that silenced his scream, and then the edges of the crevasse came together and he was gone.

Then, as suddenly as they had started, the rumblings quieted, and the ice settled.

A sobbing Karen ran to the crevasse, or what had been a crevasse. There was barely a seam to mark the spot.

Mark put his arm about her, and gently led her away. Hideo stared numbly at the rescued instruments.

The calculations were long and tedious. Hideo analyzed ice samples for density, opacity, electrical and thermal properties, finally translating these statistics to rates of movement.

Mark took the calculations, transforming glacial geophysics to atmospheric physics, measuring the effect of glaciers on weather. Then Hideo retransformed these to the effects of weather on glaciers.

When at last they came to the reasonable approximation of what the government scientists found with the world's most complex satellite and computer, Mark had exactly the same reaction as an anonymous government scientist.

"My God!"

He looked out to see Karen waiting. He went over to her and squeezed her hand. "I'm sorry . . . about your friend."

She nodded thanks.

He was silent a minute, then burst out, "Hell, no I'm not. Maybe I even envy him. He's the one who got it the good way, sharp and sudden. And I was worried about a paper. Jesus, a goddamn paper . . ."

"For God's sake, Mark!"

He took a deep breath. "Civilization generates a lot of heat, which has evaporated ocean water and added considerable cloud cover, which makes it cooler."

"Enough to correct itself?"

He laughed. "We've given Nature a hand in the correction, added dust particles, altered air and water currents . . . We've given her the means to make snow."

Karen swallowed. "How much?"

"Well, when the warm spell breaks, it'll be with a storm. My guess is it'll hit the Northeast with the biggest blizzard since '88."

"It's not the end of the world. It was bad, but New York survived."

"And we'll survive this one, too. Only it's just the beginning. It'll cool things further, and trigger the bigger storm here. That'll feed the glacier."

He paused. "We'd better tell the village."

"Tell them what?"

"To move."

"I've been trying to tell them. But how far will the glacier come?"

He looked at her. "How far?" He slumped against the tent. "Oh, Jesus." He looked up at the mountains that until now had hemmed in the glacier. "The glacier'll grow, and squeeze through the mountain pass. That's the end of the village."

"They'll move."

"So will the glacier. It won't stop till it reaches the sea. But that's not all. It'll send cold air down the globe. That'll start more storms which'll feed more glaciers. Soon you reach a point where the planet doesn't even soak up the sunlight. It just bounces off the ice."

"Where will it stop?"

He drew a rough map of the continent in the snow. "Here's the state of Washington . . . there's New York. It'll be one thick glacier from one to the other, just like the last big Ice Age, except it won't take ten thousand years."

"How . . . long, then?"

"Like Fink said, an hour and a half."

"Mark, be realistic."

"We're almost too late already. If we started home now, we just might meet that first blizzard. After that, it's an accelerating process. I don't know how long it takes to evacuate a country, but I wouldn't give odds on our chances."

"But . . . a glacier can't move that fast."

"Doesn't need to. We'll be dying long before then. The glacier'd just finish off what's left."

"But there'll still be safe places."

"Not too many. Even if they have spring, they won't have summer, and that means they can't grow food."

"Even the tropics?"

"The tropics'll be safe, but then you have to subtract places like the Andes and the Sahara, and of course the oceans, which'll be dead anyway. There's not much land left to live on."

He took a long, sad pause. "Well, what would your noble Eskimos do?"

"Nothing. They'll just accept it."

"We're back to that again. Accepting. Well, this time it means they stand there and get flattened."

She nodded. "They know the rules. They lived by them, they'll die by them. It's just as natural."

"It's not natural. Nobody dies that easily."

"They'll move when the glacier comes, but they'll leave behind the old, the ill, the crippled, just as nature would do. And the old people'll wear their best clothes, and face that death cheerfully. It's the way they've done it for a thousand years."

"That . . . that's sick."

"Oh? Tell me about the way we treat old people."

"A damn sight better than that."

"I'll ask you again when you're old."

"If any of us make it that far."

"Some of us will."

"Most of us won't."

She shrugged.

"Even if it includes you?" he asked.

"Everybody dies."

"When it's their time."

"Well, maybe it's our time."

"And you're not afraid to die?"

She gestured to the village. "They're not."

"Because they're too stupid."

"Or too smart."

"Smart? They'll be wiped out like the dinosaurs."

"And what about us, the 'civilized' people who brought it on?"

That silenced him briefly. Then he said, "Damn it, we're not dinosaurs. Not yet." He shuddered. "Not yet."

The Earth continued its slow revolution about the sun, its tilt bringing the southern hemisphere beneath warming rays as its northern half grew cooler. The seasonal changes worked their way through the system, and a world adjusted in calm, instinctive, familiar ways . . . with increasing exceptions.

The satellite orbited the Earth as the planet orbited the sun, tracing the complexities of currents, noting the departures from the norm that only a very few experts had deciphered. It passed over an African desert where two hundred thousand people had died, following what would ordinarily be the paths of the jet streams to the fertile crescent, the extraordinary area of the Earth that gave birth to Man, and now supported half its population. Here, not the passage of the sun but oceans and winds were the governors of the seasons.

The major streams of air affected the lesser streams. The winds that usually blew out to sea would ordinarily reverse, and carry the moist, cool marine air, bringing autumn and unleashing the monsoon rains.

All through Asia, the farmers watched the sky, and prayed in their temples.

BHANDARA, INDIA:

No one remembered when the giant waterwheel had been built, but the ancient engineers had built knowingly and well. The weight of a single farmer climbing the slats at one end precisely balanced the weight of water lifted at the other end, and so were the fields irrigated.

But the monsoons that had fed the river had been unaccountably late, and the river was turning to mud. The wheel became harder to turn, and the farmer had to use his two eldest sons for added counterweight.

The wood creaked dangerously.

BOMBAY:

The telephone rang earlier than usual, and a sleepy Dr. Singh had to shake himself awake before answering. He knew before he heard that the news wouldn't be good. In a country where the monsoon was a life-and-death matter, the meteorologist was more venerated than the heart surgeon.

And now, as Dr. Singh was brought up to date by the meteorologist on night duty, he reacted as grimly as a surgeon hearing of a patient's reverses.

The reports were coming in from the Indian Ocean, Arabian Sea, Bay of Bengal. There were no changes of wind or pressure. There were no signs of the monsoon's arrival.

Dr. Singh knew that when he reached his office, there would be imploring messages from every governmental official, and he'd have no answer. He worried for his job.

Then he worried for his country.

The satellite traveled on, noting that while certain turbulences had failed to develop as they should, many areas would get precipitation they had not bargained for, and for which they were ill-prepared.

The satellite circled down about the South Pole, noting the shifting of ice masses, and came up the approaches to South America. The graceful whorls of clouds about the Orkneys and Cape Horn were really the savage squalls of the most storm-ridden area on Earth.

Eventually, it came to North America and Cape Hatteras, off the Carolinas. Here, the sensors watched the confusions of conflicting air masses and ocean currents, cold air meeting warm in endless conflict. Here was the spawning ground for the storms that eventually worked their way up the northeast coast, to the most densely populated and industrialized section of the world.

Here, a low-pressure center was being born. It was only one of many, and the satellite had no more interest in this one than in the others. Indeed, human forecasters unaware of such factors as the shifts in jet stream and Gulf Stream, alterations of the storm tracks, the accumulations of dust and pollutants, gave it little more thought. Unfortunately.

The final leg of their flight was uneventful. Mark spent most of the time looking out through the window at the clouds, as if he'd see the first signs of that coming turbulence. All he saw were fair-weather wispy cirrus.

He turned to Karen. The arguments were forgotten, and he knew she was thinking, as he was, of their first night together. If convention allowed—if the seats allowed—he'd make love to her here and now. Instead, they made love through their eyes and their hands. He'd have her always, even with the world coming down around them.

Mark wondered about Hideo. He had been fascinated by the Eskimos, and his own resemblance to them. He insisted on staying behind a while, and so they had left him there.

The filtered voice of the captain cut through Mark's thoughts.

"Ladies and gentlemen, we'll be arriving in New York in approximately two hours. The Weather Service reports we'll be greeted by light snow flurries. There will probably be no accumulation, and I hear the reservoirs can use the run-off."

The passengers murmured. One leaned across the aisle and said to Mark, "Well, things're back to normal."

Mark smiled politely.

Karen pulled him back, and whispered, "Is that the blizzard you were talking about?"

Mark nodded gravely.

Ordinarily, the infant storm would have never reached maturity, speeding up the coast, dusting the Northeast with light snow or rain before scurrying out over the Atlantic and dying young.

This time, however, the growing heat and the increased water vapor were nutrients for the storm. In addition, the shifting jet stream and Gulf Stream combined forces to keep the storm longer in its spawning ground, lengthening its childhood, permitting it to grow larger and more ferocious before sending it on its way.

Even before its full maturity, it would be a force to be reckoned with.

The recorded female voice went on cheerily, even musically, "United States Weather Service forecast for New York City and vicinity," hitting her high note on "City," and then descending to a more businesslike monotone to describe the various readings, and predicting the light snow flurries would end in an hour or two.

That can't be right, thought Danny. He had always presumed the Weather Service's omniscience, using their forecast as the corrective standard for his own. But this time he *knew* they were wrong.

For a moment, he considered calling their office and speaking to the head meteorologist, but he had learned from Mark it would probably be futile. Those people were locked into their twenty-four-hour forecasts, the short-range world. He certainly knew a ten-year-old was not taken seriously.

He would do what he could under the circumstances. He dialed the school office and asked to speak to the principal.

"He isn't in yet. Who, may I ask, is calling?"

"Daniel Magnusson."

"What is this in reference to?"

"The current weather situation."

"Yes?"

"Well, it's rather complicated, and there's really no reason to go into it in detail, but there's going to be a major storm, perhaps the worst of this century."

"Are . . . you with the weather bureau?"

"It's called the Weather Service now."

"Oh, sorry. But we just heard the forecast . . ."

"It's in error."

"But . . . why should . . . ?"

"Rather than spend time talking, you ought to get out an announcement that the school will be closed, and advise people to stay home."

"That has to come from downtown."

"Look, you can speak to downtown with more authority than I can."

"How can . . . ?"

"I know I'm right about the forecast. Now I don't think I should come into school today, and neither should anyone else."

"You . . . what . . . what are you, a student?"

Danny realized his mistake, but it was too late

to go back on it. "Look, I've been tutored by Professor Mark Han . . ."

"Now look here, Daniel Magnusson, you had better be here when that bell rings."

"But I'm telling you . . ."

"You're already in trouble, young man. I'm giving your name to your teacher. Don't add truancy to it."

Just before she clicked off, he heard her say, "Hey, y'wanna hear what a kid just tried to pull?"

He held the dead phone a while before he set it down, sighed, and looked out the window at the gray sky.

It would have been a major storm, one to exasperate a community, but certainly not maim it. This time, the community aided its own destruction.

The northeast coast of the United States is an extensive sprawl. City touches city to form a giant megalopolis, and this huge heat machine gorged the storm, whipping its cyclone to a frenzy.

The water vapor was dispersed through the storm-to-be as droplets so small a million would make a raindrop, and so light they floated to the highest, coldest reaches of the atmosphere. They were cooled to a temperature below freezing, remaining water, needing only a shock to change them to ice. Here, in those atmospheric reaches, waited the sources of that shock, the minute grains of dirt, dust, and pollutants.

It was almost like a meeting of sperm and ova. Each grain of dirt or dust invaded a water droplet. Molecules shuddered, rearranged themselves, and a metamorphosis was almost instantaneous. Water snapped miraculously into ice, but in crystal form, hexagonal stars. The turbulence kept these countless crystals stirred and agitated, while the arms sprouted exquisite designs, baroque and intricate, almost infinite in their variations so that among those trillions of stars, no two were quite alike.

Eventually they grew too heavy for the clouds to

hold. One at a time, then by hundreds, then thousands and hundreds of thousands, they began to fall those seemingly endless miles.

The scenery through the airplane window seemed to flutter as wisps of cloud flew by, and then the wisps grew thicker, and the ride suddenly roughened.

The seat-belt sign flashed and the captain came on. "Those're the flurries we spoke about, ladies and gentlemen. Ride's a little rough up here, but nothing to worry about."

Mark groaned.

Karen shook her head. "There's nothing you can do now."

There was a long silence while they both watched the dervish-like dances of the blowing snow against the window.

"Y'know," said Mark suddenly, "I had a friend who was a meteorologist for the Air Force. I was jealous as hell. In the Air Force, they're the glamour boys, next door to God. They tell the generals when to fly. I was only Coast Guard, and we told nobody.

"Well, one day he missed a guess. That's easy enough to do in our business, except this time four planes never came back. My friend shot himself."

He paused.

"I said I never wanted that. I went into teaching, and I was never responsible for any lives at all."

He sank back into silence, but growing more agitated with each passing moment as the plane dropped lower. Finally, he unstrapped his belt and stood up.

"You'll have to sit down, sir," said the stewardess.

"I have to talk to the captain."

"I'm sorry, sir," she said, much more sharply, "but you'll have to sit down."

Mark hesitated, and sat down. He turned back to Karen. "Yeh, I'll take on the world, all right."

The airport came into view, and they listened in silence to the increasing roar of engines braking, and the whine of the landing gear.

He looked at his watch. "Just about everybody'll be going to work about now."

Karen blanched. "Danny'll be on his way to school. He'll be caught in it."

Mark shook his head. "Danny has sense. He knows what's happening."

Karen shut her eyes, and prayed for everything to speed up, for the wheels to touch down, for the plane to come to a halt, for the passengers to scurry out the doors while the stewardess bade each one good-bye with her usual smile and mechanical phrases.

Instead, each step happened with an awful, interminable slowness, until Mark and Karen found themselves in the terminal, and looking unsuccessfully for an unused phone.

Danny looked out the window at the first few flakes, following their path as they fell below him and melted on contact with the warm asphalt. He watched for several minutes until he realized he was going to be late. He put on his heaviest jacket with a sweater underneath, and ran downstairs, stopping halfway down. He knew they would laugh at him, but when school let out he'd have the last laugh.

He went back up, to his closet and a coat he had never dared wear, a present from his mother. It was a sealskin outfit made for Eskimo children. He had been mortified by the parka, with its fur hood practically hiding his face, the fur pants, mittens, and inner and outer boots.

He hesitated, hearing the taunts of his classmates. It was getting late.

He tried to ignore the ringing of the phone that followed him down the stairs.

"Damn!" said Karen.

"Keep ringing."

Behind them, the line stirred restlessly.

"Hey, lady, c'mon!"

Karen tightened her lips, and hung grimly to the phone.

Mark allowed himself a slight smile. "You've learned something about lines since we first met."

She was about to hang up when she heard a click. "Hello?"

"Oh Jesus, Danny!"

"Oh, hello, Mother. I'm glad you're back," he said dutifully.

"I'm glad to be back with you. Where were you?"

"I was on my way to school. I was down in the street, in fact."

"God, it's a good thing you came back. There's an awful blizzard coming down on us."

"I know, Mother. That's why I came back. There's that Eskimo outfit you brought me . . ."

"Danny, you're not going out again."

"I've got to, Mother. There's school."

"School's not that important, Danny. Stay home; you'll miss a day's school. They won't even have school."

"Mother, I can't stay away from school."

"I'll give you a note . . . I'll say you were sick. For God's sake . . ."

"That'd be dishonest, Mother, but that's beside the point. There's school, and I've got to go."

"I'll put Mark on . . ."

"He knows the importance of school better than I do. I'm sorry, Mother, I'm late already. I'll see you when you get back. Good-bye, and don't worry."

He hung up. Karen looked at the dead receiver, and finally turned to Mark to tell him what happened.

"How can a brilliant kid be so dumb?" said Mark.

"I guess . . . school's been better to him than I have."

One child could scarcely be blamed for his sense of obligation. All over the city, the process was repeated among adults, as workers finished their breakfasts, kissed wives and lovers good-bye, and headed to work. They started their cars, or waited for buses or subways or commuter trains. Most were shivering a little by the time the temperature started dropping, and the snowfall thickened.

It never occurred to any of them not to go. Certainly their bosses would not have sympathized, and none were so independent as to lose a day's pay. After all, they were not primitives out in the forest. The most powerful and industrialized nation on Earth doesn't stop functioning because of a few flakes.

Mark looked out the observation window at the increasing snowfall. The ground was cold now, and as the flakes fell, they no longer melted but began accumulating. It was already obvious that this first snowfall of the season would not vanish as quickly as predicted.

"As a scout, Danny couldn't find his way out of the woods. He's going to be one lost little boy."

"Mark, we've got to find him. I know what a blizzard can do."

"Forget the luggage, and let's get out of here." He grabbed her arm and headed out the doors.

The cabs were lined up, and their only concession to the snowfall was to keep their windshield wipers working. They never considered canceling their shuttle trips to the airport, as it provided their steadiest fares.

When Mark gave the south Manhattan address, it certainly never occurred to the cabbie he might never reach there. Instead, Richie Fuselli did what he usually did, noting the destination on his log, and calling it in on the CB radio.

A moment later, the answering squawk came in, unintelligible to Mark and Karen, but the cabbie was satisfied.

He pulled out of the line and headed toward the Van Wyck Expressway. "Nice to have a little snow for a change."

By the time he had gone three blocks, Danny had decided, he would laugh with the others when they saw him and pretend it was a joke.

He certainly would have seemed an amusing sight to anyone who cared to notice, a little Eskimo with glasses, scurrying down the city streets, his fur outfit bouncing loosely about his skinny frame.

The clothes were too warm, and he was perspiring before he had run another block. His breath and body heat fogged his glasses, so he had to frequently take them off to clear them.

There was little difference in vision when he put them back on. The snow was thick, and the wind kept it swarming.

He looked at a clock in the store. It was very, very late. It would be his first tardy slip.

Young Peggy Bjork looked out the farmhouse window and knew she wouldn't have to go to school.

Nature was not so lightly regarded on an Ohio farm. The elements swept across the flat land with nothing to obstruct them except for the strange haystack boulders. She knew how dangerous a snowstorm could be, and she would stay indoors.

The only thing she would miss in school would be the pioneer stories. She had loved the idea of families sticking together through awful hardships. There was a kind of romance about poverty.

Certainly, as her father's farm grew bigger, he seemed to have less and less time for Peggy or her mother.

There must have been something very special about a family that carried everything it owned in one small wagon. Peggy could read about the troubles of pioneers caught in the Donner Pass, and be grateful she was in her big, warm room, but she would feel a certain wistful twinge just the same.

Mr. Bjork had no such romantic illusions, and no time to indulge them. Animals still had to be fed, and after the loss of his crops in the freak thunderstorm, the animals were more important than ever. Downstairs, he looked out the window, muttered a few curses, and gulped down the last of his morning coffee.

Mrs. Bjork was somewhat better-humored about it. Perhaps, if the storm were severe, she might catch up on some sewing she had been putting off.

In the city the storm clouds blew past the tops of the skyscrapers, water droplets smashed against cold stone and steel. On each projection, each cornice or ornament, a skin of ice formed, in turn grabbing other droplets and transforming them so that, millimeter by millimeter, ice built up.

Hundreds of feet below, the snow caught on store awnings and fire escapes. Cursing, storekeepers poked up at the awnings with poles or broomhandles and dislodged the accumulation. Some rolled up their awnings to prevent it happening again. Others reasoned that pedestrians might seek shelter under the awnings, and might be drawn into the store, so they let the awnings stay.

Projections such as fire escapes presented no problems. The snow built up on the narrow railings until the piles became unstable, and fell over, adding their small bits to the storm.

A theater marquee formed a deep well for snow to accumulate, hiding it from the wind and from the view of passersby beneath.

The expression "light as a snowflake" is misleading. It is not so much light as aerodynamic in its form, so as to be carried in the wind. A cubic foot weighs five to twelve pounds, and if tightly packed as much as fifty pounds.

The theater was built in the late nineteen twenties, in the days of optimism in the movie business, and the marquee was made large, its measurements multiplying to over eleven thousand cubic feet. The supporting brackets and mortar were old, and certainly never intended to support the steadily increasing tonnage of collecting snowflakes, already equal to an automobile.

Pedestrians hurried on their way. Some sought shelter under the marquee.

The Long Island Expressway was growing dangerous as tires compressed the snow, melting it into a slush that hardened again into thin skins of ice.

"Jesus, I need instructions." Richie Fuselli grabbed the microphone. "Office, this is twenty-three . . ."

He let up on the button to listen for an answer, but he heard a stranger's voice. "Hey, buster, get off this channel."

"Who the hell is that?"

"You're crowdin' the channel, mister. I'm stuck in the snow and radioin', so get your ass off."

"Watch your mouth, fella, you're on an open . . ."

"Press another button or press your prick, buddy, I don't care which. Just get offa' this . . ."

"You wanna tell me where you are, loud-mouth . . . ?" Remembering he had customers, he turned apologetically. "Everybody's got CB's, and sometimes some of these loud-mouths . . . the first storm you get . . ." He muttered a curse, and tried driving on, watching the road closely, trying to avoid other vehicles.

Karen bit her lip. "Danny's systematic. He found the best route, and always takes it."

"Fine," said Mark. "He'll make it to school, or we'll find him along the way."

Karen squeezed his arm, grateful for the reassurance.

A little Eskimo with glasses waddled, lurched, slipped on icy patches, and tried to find his way through white swirls despite his fogging glasses. He should have made a left turn on Greene Street, but the street signs were covered with snow. The accumulations seemed to wash out familiar landmarks into shades of white. He passed the turn.

Young Peggy Bjork was excited as she gazed out the window. It was going to be a major storm, all right. Trees would fall down on the lines, and cut out the power. They would have to take out kerosene lamps and candles. No one would venture outside. They would stay about the dinner table, and huddle close together. They would talk and tell stories. They would live like pioneers. It would be a great adventure.

In the city, the wind swept the super-cooled droplets down from the high atmosphere to form skins of ice at street level, setting people and vehicles slipping and sliding dangerously.

Soon, the trees in Central Park glistened in icy sheaths, and their branches bent under the weight.

For the various bridges connecting Manhattan with the other boroughs, however, the beauteous icing made travel quite perilous. It coated cables, walkways, roadways, railings, and solidly sealed the machinery of the drawbridges. A car that slid on such an icy roadway could go plunging over the side, and wary motorists abandoned their cars on the bridges rather than take that chance.

The ice brought another danger, not so immediate but carrying graver implications for the city's survival. Before 1888, utility lines were strung along poles so that the nerves of the city lay exposed. That blizzard had so devastated power and communications that from then on, such lines were put underground. In the more sparsely settled outlying boroughs, however, burying cables was considered economically unfeasible. As the city grew, the economics changed, but far faster than the situation. Cables were still exposed above ground.

Now, the snow built up on them. When the mounds toppled over, that set the wires into vibrations that shook off the rest of the accumulation.

The frost was another matter. As on the buildings, it built up slowly, with each droplet adding its own mass. All over the city, exposed cables began sagging under the weight of tiny ice crystals.

If the task of burying cables was beyond the city's capability, burying the miles of elevated transit lines was barely a dream.

The motorman's cab only had an observation window, smaller than an auto windshield. The single wiper was inadequate for this storm, and the motorman had to follow each swipe of the wiper blade to see anything at all. Even so, he could see only yards ahead, and so he slowed the train to a near crawl.

He reached for the radio-telephone, and let the dispatcher know the situation.

At the dispatcher's office, a series of lights on a schematic map showed where each and every train was at any given moment. He sent out orders that slowed one train, rerouted another. At least, with this system, there was no danger of collision.

Passengers at the station had no such system, of course. More and more people crowded onto the platform, not knowing of the delays. They accidentally bumped and jabbed each other, apologized, and put themselves through contortions trying to read their newspapers. Conversations about the sudden cold snap alternated with gripes about the train service. Some engaged in the particularly dangerous habit of craning over the edge of the platform to watch for the train's approach, as if that would bring it any faster.

As more people crowded onto the platform from the rear, those in front were pushed forward, closer to the edge.

Inevitably, one man fell over the edge. There were screams, and the crowd pushed back. It was only a fall of four feet, and the man was more shaken than injured. He grabbed the first helping hand, and scrambled back up.

"Oh, wow! . . . Close call!" was all he could say. His mind was certainly not on the storm.

By the time Farmer Bjork finished feeding the animals, the drifts were already knee-deep. The wind whipped the snow into tiny whirlwinds and sent it blasting against his face. As he walked against the wind it sucked heat from his body, with every added mile-per-hour equaling a drop of two degrees, making the chill as penetrating as any in the Arctic.

For his daughter back in the house, the romance of the storm vanished as she felt the wind enter through every window frame. The oil heater was straining to its limit, but she could see the temperature on the thermostat continue to fall.

She and her mother frantically stuffed rags into the windows, and then towels. Finally, they stuffed clothing.

Richie Fuselli drove slowly and carefully, gripping the steering wheel tightly as the snow came down.

"Damn heaters." Though he had it turned on full, the defroster control barely deflected warm air onto the windshield, and failed to melt the increasing accumulation.

"Damn cars're death traps." He turned around. "Sorry. Didn't mean that. They're . . . good cars. Nothin' goes wrong in the city. You're always near help."

"Just keep an eye on the road," said Mark.

"Yeah." Fuselli turned forward and saw he was coming to a downgrade. "Uh-oh." He saw some cars stuck at the bottom, and stepped hard on his brakes.

The car swung about beneath him, and continued sailing down the hill, tail first. He frantically pumped the brakes and swung his steering wheel in an effort to gain control.

Mark shoved Karen back against the seat and yelled, "Brace yourself!", as he shoved his legs firmly against the front seat.

They struck the pile with an impact that sent Fuselli against the steering column, and Karen and Mark sprawling sideways.

"You all right?" said Mark.

"Nothing broken."

Mark turned to the cab driver. "You okay?"

"I dunno. Pain in my chest."

"Just stay there. We'll get help."

"The radio . . ."

"Yeah, thank God for that." Mark turned it on, and was immediately deluged in a sea of voices. He pressed the button on the mike.

"Break, break, break!"

"Jesus, another one."

"Get off the fucking line, breaker!"

"I got an emergency here," yelled Mark.

"Well, who hasn't? Get your ass off."

He turned to the emergency channel, with much the same results.

"Look," he said to Fuselli, "we can't stay. We'll get help as soon as we can, unless you want to come with us."

"Oh no, I ain't goin' out in that. It's comfy right here. Got the radio, got the heat. I mean, this ain't the North Pole."

"Okay, good luck."

"Me? You're the one needin' it."

As Mark opened the door, he was almost blown back by a blast of wind and snow.

"You're right." He finally got out, to see a good fifty cars slammed together on the highway, with more cars joining.

"Jesus, what a mess!"

He could see the towers of the Brooklyn Bridge ahead. "We're not so far from home."

"Get a group together," said Karen.

"For that?"

She nodded.

Mark turned back to the cabbie. "You'll be okay?"

"Better'n you'll be."

Mark smiled, and waved good-bye as he shut the door.

Fuselli checked the fuel gauge, saw he had plenty of gas, and turned on the motor. He pulled out his own transistor radio, and turned it on, letting it drown out the hubbub on the CB.

"Hope you're real warm and snug, watching that

bum storm from some cozy fireplace," said the congenial disc jockey, before launching into a dreamy record.

"Makin' do," Fuselli answered. He put the heater control up all the way, and shut the windows tight. He gunned the engine, and as it ignited the gas, it changed one set of complex chemicals into another, some of them toxic. Carbon monoxide was the most prominent of these, colorless, odorless, and deceptively nourishing to red-blood cells so that they readily gave up oxygen for this new gas.

Between driver and engine stood the protection of a so-called firewall. In years of hard driving by various cabbies, extra holes had been worn around brake and gas pedals, and the exhaust seeped in.

With each breath he took, more cells died.

The dreamy music played on, and Richie Fuselli relaxed in the warmth. Civilization lay just outside the door, and he had no worries.

The people who had abandoned their cars milled about, apparently hoping for a leader.

"People," Mark announced, "we've got an ex-Eskimo here for a guide, and she says we ought to stick together."

"Look," protested Karen, "I was the guidee, not the guider. You lead, and if I've got any hints, I'll whisper 'em."

"Okay. Any for starters?"

"Just keep your face away from the wind, even if it means not knowing where you're going, and hold onto each other."

"Pleasure," said someone.

Someone else started singing, "Ninety-nine Bottles of Beer on the Wall," and others joined in.

The mass of cars faded into the swirling snow behind them, while the bridge loomed ahead.

As Mark held Karen's hand he squeezed it tighter. "Whaddaya bet Danny's safe and snug, and we're the ones in trouble."

Danny was thoroughly lost now. Around him, sky, buildings, streets merged into a white blur, and the snow edged down his neck through the loose hood. He tightened it and looked for help. He felt himself crying, and tried to stop when he felt the tears turning into ice on his cheeks.

They hadn't been aware of the roar until it died. Now they realized in the awful silence that the sound had been comforting them all along, and it was Farmer Bjork who put it into words.

"It's the furnace. We're out of fuel."

He reached for the phone, and heard nothing. The lines were down.

In the stillness, the wind outside howled like a triumphant banshee. Then they heard a new sound, weaker but far more frightening. It came from the attic, an ominous creaking as roof timbers strained under tons of snow.

As they climbed the stairs, they could hear the creaking grow louder and yet louder, and by the time they reached the attic, they could even see the timbers bending under the weight, groaning with resistance, straightening, bending again a little further as the weight increased and the wood weakened. Already, some snow was working its way in through little chinks.

Peggy Bjork looked to her parents for strength, and saw only helpless terror.

The first forecast had been for light flurries, and the airlines had made their plans accordingly. The clerks passed along the optimistic words to telephone inquiries, and as a result, thousands of passengers who arrived for flights now found themselves marooned.

They had warmth, but little else.

There were long lines at the restaurants and food stands, and even they were running out of food.

The announcer's voice came over the loudspeaker, cheerful and optimistic. There was no acknowledgement of the earlier mistaken forecast. Instead, the

Weather Service predicted heavy snows, ending in a couple of hours.

There was really nothing to worry about.

The commuter trains, operating at ground level in thinly settled suburbs, were more vulnerable than the subways.

It was an image from some wartime newsreel, the train packed solid with refugees coming into an equally packed station. With groans and curses, the waiting passengers still tried to force their way on. There were cries of, "C'mon, buddy . . ." "There's no room. What's the matter with you?" "Push in there. Gimme a break!" But mostly there were simply cries of protest.

As people inside were crushed even more tightly, some people outside tried hanging on in precarious positions, one or both feet off the steps, gripping handrails for dear life.

Entrance to the city from the north was through a series of open cuts, and here the snow collected in mounds as high as the train itself. The engineer saw them ahead, braked, and the wheels sparked, but continued to slide on the rails until the front car ploughed into the drift.

People were thrown forward in almost a single mass, loudly exchanging curses and apologies, and the conductor yelled for quiet:

"Folks, can I have your attention, please?"

He had to repeat it several times and when he finally had it he told them the railroad would be sending out a snowplow car. They should please be patient.

There was a new round of groans.

"I've been patient for twenty years," said one passenger.

"I'm for walking," said another. "Who's with me?" He squeezed his way to the doorway, shoving people aside with, "Pardon me . . . Pardon me . . ."

Several passengers followed. The wind hit them sharply when they stepped outside.

"God pity the sailors at sea on a day like this," said someone, retreating back inside.

Some people laughed.

It was called an ocean station vessel, maintained by the Coast Guard for weather observation. For the most part, it had been interesting work, and Commanding Officer Manujian had picked up a smattering of meteorology from the civilians aboard, but the lousy part of the job was when the ship had to ride out storms at sea as part of its research.

This one was a hell of a lot worse than the meteorologists had anticipated. Certainly, no one expected them to give up their lives, and now they clung in terror to any available handholds, and learned anew the power and puzzle of nature.

Still, they were better off than the crew and captain, trying to save the ship. Several on deck had to hack away the frost forming on the rigging, setting it groaning with the weight. Snow and icy spray made axes slip in their hands, and one crewman gashed his leg deeply. Stunned, he watched his blood being carried away by the wind.

"Get below!" screamed Manujian, trying to be heard above the storm, but he finally had to push and shove the stunned crewman. As the sailor limped off, a great wave crashed across the ship, and rolled across the deck. The crew hung on, gasping and sputtering, but the dazed sailor was caught at the deck's edge and swept off the side.

"Man overboard!"

"He's a dead man. I've got a ship to save!" Manujian swore to himself if he ever got out of this alive, he was finished with this insane duty.

The pedestrian shook the snow from his coat as he came under the shelter of the theater marquee, joining a dozen others, stomping and blowing on their hands to keep warm.

"Jesus, I was a damn fool to go out in that."

"Y'got company, all under here."

"Well, I ain't so damned a fool as to go out in it again. I'm stayin' right here till it blows over."

In the deep well of the marquee, the snow continued to accumulate, pushing down on the snow at the bottom, squeezing out the air, packing it denser, multiplying the weight of each cubic foot, adding more tons of stress upon rusting steel and ancient mortar.

Already, the first hairline cracks appeared, working their way outward, slowly widening, groping toward weaknesses like tree roots seeking moisture.

Mark caught his breath when he saw the sight. The wind tore unencumbered across the East River, whistling and screeching as it passed through the intricate network of cables on the bridge. Lighter cars were turned about like weathervanes, and jammed up by the dozens. People abandoning their cars were being thrown about against each other, and Mark could imagine the moans of pain and terror that were submerged in the storm.

He turned back to Karen. She was almost in shock. She knew the perils better than he.

"Dear God . . ." Mark thought she was going to faint, but she shoved him forward.

Then the pedestrian behind released his grip. "Forget it. Not me."

"Well, we're crossing," said Mark. "Who else is?"

They all held back, until a housewife came up. "I've got two kids waiting for dinner."

A well-dressed middle-aged man with an attaché case joined them. "I'm the one with the keys to the place."

Karen gestured to the attaché case. "You need that?"

He nodded.

"The case or the contents?"

"The contents."

"Stuff them under your coat, and dump the case. Anyone else?"

There was no one else.

"Keep your side to the wind, work from hand-holds if you can, but not with bare hands."

They clutched arms tightly, and Mark took his first steps out onto the open roadway. He gasped as he felt the blasts, and was almost shoved back against the railing. He reached for a girder.

"Not with your bare hands!"

He pulled out his handkerchief, and used it for a buffer as he edged out further.

The view of the city was awe-inspiring, with the wind blowing the thick snow in eccentric swirls about the skyscrapers, even as it continued to slam the foursome against railings and girders.

They wrapped their coats tightly around themselves, tried crouching down into their collars, kept their eyes averted, and went on.

The housewife was last in line, and she suddenly slipped, bringing the businessman down with her. She shrieked as she was blown against the guide-rail and saw with stunning clarity the river twenty stories below. Terrified, she grabbed the guide-rail, and held fast.

Karen's cry was too late. When the housewife had steadied herself, she tried removing her hand, and found it welded to the metal.

"Don't!" Karen shrieked, as the woman tried pulling it loose. "You'll lose half your hand."

"Oh God . . . Oh God . . . Oh God . . ." she moaned. Her knees buckled under her as she stared at her frozen hand. She knelt in the snow, retching.

"What can we do?" yelled Mark.

Karen turned pale watching. "I . . . I don't know."

"What would they use?"

She almost laughed helplessly. "Seal blood . . . or oil . . ."

"Seal . . ." He stopped. His head down against the wind, he fought his way to an abandoned car, and disappeared beneath it. He reappeared long moments later carrying some empty cans.

"Thank God for litterbugs."

"What's in them?"

"Seal oil, thirty-weight." He worked his way cautiously back toward the railing.

"Let's go slowly." He had to use almost all of one can before her fingers gradually began working loose.

"I think you better go fast, before it freezes too," said Karen.

They bathed her hand with all the cans simultaneously, and at last she was able to work it free.

The housewife grabbed arms again, and they groped their way on.

Mark worked his way from girder to cross-brace and the rest followed, but as they fumbled toward the bridge's center, they could see the snow had piled up against the barriers, so that they would have to climb above barrier height to get across.

The wind shrieked more dangerously here.

"Getting icy . . ."

"Dig in your foot before you move."

The businessman felt the papers sliding out from under his coat, and let go his arms to grab at them.

"Forget them!" yelled Karen.

They flew in every direction, and the man followed after. Some went over the edge, and he reached. He hit the railing, and his outstretched arm provided just enough weight to tip the balance. His feet flew up from under him, and the next instant he was flying through open space, his scream blending into the wind. Then the river swallowed him up.

The housewife began to cry, and Karen yelled, "Forget him! You've got your own to worry about!"

The girl in the bikini lolled under the hot sun, sipping a soft drink, watching the surfers trying to hang ten. A wave rolled up the shore and touched her feet. She wriggled her toes in the warm water.

The passengers in the plane sighed as they watched.

"Looks great. When do we get there?" The passenger lifted the shade over the airplane window. The snow still seethed across the airport outside.

The airline had thrown open some of its grounded planes, even showing movies, usually travelogues of the destinations, more remote now than ever.

In the terminal, even the candy machines were empty. There was still liquor available, however, and that was warm and filling. At first, the passengers bought it by the shot, but soon they were negotiating for whole bottles.

Cheer soon returned as each person's glow extended to a neighbor. Someone started a small fire on the floor, and fed it with newspapers and magazines. People gathered around, put their arms about each other's shoulders, and sang old, nostalgic songs. In the secluded corners of the terminal, some couples wrapped themselves in the blankets from the plane and made love.

The wind piled the snow thicker about some obstructions, sparser about others.

Danny rested in the meager shelter of a lamppost before he spotted the doorway of one store almost completely free of snow. He reasoned the owner must be there, keeping it clear, and with his last bit of strength dragged himself through the drifts.

He tried the door, but it was locked. He turned back, and the snow surged about him, surrounding him.

Most sanitation men were unable to reach their stations, so with inadequate manpower the Department decided to clear the main arteries and let the side streets go. The East River Drive was one of the most crucial, and a number of plows and trucks were deployed there.

Harry Teague felt the truck shake like a toy as it received the tons of snow from the rotary. One of the pleasures of driving a heavy truck was the feeling of stability, even of power, and it was certainly safer in this snowstorm. The bouncing, however, gave him a woeful if temporary insecurity, and he tightened his seat belt, a rare act for him.

"Take 'er to Florida," said the supervisor.

"Florida" was the East River alongside, though the joke had more meaning than they knew. Snow had indeed been loaded onto freightcars heading south when there was no place else to dump it.

The East River would do fine for Teague, however, though other truckers wouldn't even drive the few blocks to the pier, and simply put their loads on the first side street whose tenants seemed least likely to complain. Teague was a little more conscientious. With the truck fully loaded, heavier than ever, his security was restored.

"Get out of the way, world, here comes Harry Teague," and he barreled his way around the tangle of abandoned cars, exulting in the solid traction and the only feeling of power he had in his life.

He was passing beneath the Brooklyn Bridge when he saw a couple desperately flagging him down. Ordinarily, he wouldn't think of picking up hitchhikers, but this was no ordinary time. He pulled up.

"Hi," he said, rolling down the window, "you want some snow delivered?"

"No thanks," laughed Mark, "but we need a lift real bad, up to Houston Street."

"Further than I'm going, but you're welcome's far as I go." He leaned across and opened the door for them.

As they climbed in, Karen sighed in relief. "Heat, Lord, I never thought I'd want heat."

"Yeah, you must really wanna be going somewheres."

"I'm trying to find my son. I think he's gotten caught in the storm."

Harry grunted. "Hell, there's always an open doorway or somethin' to duck into."

Karen nodded.

They rode in silence until Harry passed the pier. "Well, here's my dumping . . ." He paused.

"Yes?"

"Nothin' . . ." He rode on, toward Houston Street, and dropped them off. "You'll find your kid, don't worry. This's New York."

He watched them cross the downtown side and plunge into the drifts, until they disappeared into the whiteness. Then he turned around and looked for a dumping point by the river, not willing to drag his load all the way up to make a U-turn and then all the way back. He finally found an opening, maneuvered about, and backed the truck carefully to the edge, wondering if he'd get some heavenly reward for his small good deed.

"Look out, river. Harry Teague's dumpin' on *you.*"

He threw the lift motor into gear, and felt the truck lighten as the cargo bin tilted. That sense of power seemed to drain away and then insecurity became alarm as the wheels, all weight gone, lost traction completely. They slipped and slid from side to side, and before Teague could reverse the motor the whole truck swayed, and the tons of snow carried the truck backward.

The rear wheels went off the pier as Teague struggled with his seat belt, and then, like a toy slipping off a table, the truck slid into the river, and the next moment icy water stifled his scream.

They started with the table, piling everything upon it that they could find in the attic. When Peggy Bjork stopped for a moment to catch her breath, she marveled at how her family was working together. This must have been like the pioneer days, perhaps just as when the Indians were attacking while wives and children loaded the ammunition and passed the muskets to the fathers. Now they were passing furniture to her father while he stacked them against the ceiling and crammed them in tightly.

At last the roof seemed adequately braced. The creakings diminished, and they all sighed in relief.

"We've beaten it."

They laughed, and threw their arms about each other. They were a family again.

When they went back downstairs, it seemed strangely dark. Farmer Bjork looked out the window, and saw the snow climbing, even pushing drifts up toward the second floor.

"My God, it could cover the whole house."

He raced back up to the second floor and looked out. "I'd have to go for help. There's no other way."

"In . . . that?"

He made a gesture of helplessness.

They huddled in the phone booth as the wind piled snow against the glass. The sound was so loud, and the phone connection so poor, Karen had to hold her hand over her free ear.

"Daniel Magnusson . . ." said the switchboard operator at the school. "Oh no, I was hoping I wouldn't hear that name."

"What . . . what's the matter?"

"Tell me, how does he know more than the weather bureau? What's he got, a direct line to God?"

"Did he come in?"

"No. I said he was smart. Us adults, we're the dummies."

"You're sure he's not there?"

"Ma'am, I know every idiot who came. We're all stuck here together."

Mark could tell by Karen's look as she hung up.

Without another word, they slogged grimly through the drifts, looking into every possible doorway, yelling his name into the wind, stopping strangers, while Karen grew ever more desperate.

Soon, they too were freezing, and looked for shelter.

"Under here!"

They stumbled under the theater marquee to see several pedestrians stomping about, blowing on their hands to keep warm, or looking forlornly through the closed glass doors into the lobby. There were nods of greeting all about, strangers caught in a common predicament.

Mark and Karen looked glumly out at the blowing wind, and the snow piling ever higher. Mark thought he heard a rumbling, strange and apart from the storm. He looked above him. The sound was gone, and he thought no more about it.

"Look," he said at last, "if we can find a place to duck under, so can he. Especially a bright kid like that."

"A bright kid wouldn't have gone out in the first place."

"Most mothers usually boast about their brilliant children."

She only sighed and looked across the street. "Like over there. You'd think the owner'd have brains and roll up the awning. In a few hours, he won't have one."

Indeed, the awning was sagging from the accumulation.

"Well," said Mark, "I think Danny's got enough brains not to stay under an awning."

"Reassure me."

"We didn't find him under one. In fact, since we didn't find him at all, it means he's safe indoors, having a nice hot . . ." Again Mark heard that strange rumbling. He looked above him, and then across to the sagging awning. He thought about the nature of snow, its easy compressibility, its density when so compressed. He thought about the marquee as a giant awning, pictured snow getting caught in the well, made some random estimates of the marquee's size, began multiplying random figures together . . .

There was another rumbling.

"*Get out!*" He shoved Karen, and turned to the others. "*Get out!*"

Even as he pushed, above him metal bolts were working loose, old mortar giving way. Steel struts went flying, and tar and asphalt tore like paper. It was like an earthquake, or cannonade, or the Day of Judgment.

Most of the people did not even see the steel and stone that crushed them. One old man was pinned, and screaming.

Mark grabbed a loosened steel rod, used rubble

for a fulcrum, and managed to pry up the slab a little. Sweating, he looked up to see people leaning out their windows.

"Call for help!"

A woman was talking to her sister in Kansas City. She blurted a few words of what had happened, and hung up to call the emergency number, but now could not even get a dial tone. She gave up, and wrung her hands frantically.

A man across the street, however, got a dial tone almost immediately. He quickly dialed 911. It rang endlessly.

"C'mon, you lazy sons of bitches . . ."

The policemen were seated flanking a conveyor belt. Their job was to keep callers calm as they took down the nature and location of the emergency. The notes were dispatched along the conveyor to the appropriate departments, but it is the irony of disasters that they demand the very services they simultaneously cripple. While phone calls backed up on the switchboard, there were not enough policemen to man the phones. When ambulances, police cars, and other emergency vehicles were most needed, they were stuck in the snow.

At the same time cables were carrying their maximum load of phone calls, they were passing their maximum load of accumulating ice. At the instant one cable finally gave way, dozens of conversations went dead, and the callers cursed the terrible service.

The repairmen had gone almost twenty hours without sleep, and barely rest, when the emergency call came through. With groans, they pulled themselves out of their naps, climbed back onto the equipment truck, and went out to face the storm again.

They soon located the break, and two men gingerly climbed the glazed pole to reach the broken line. With snow and wind tearing at their faces and hands, they managed to winch the broken ends together, and splice them with copper sheathing.

They sighed in relief, and one man said he was going to sleep on the open truck, snow and all, when they saw the line break at two more places, almost simultaneously.

"I can't . . . Jesus, I can't . . ." Karen moaned.

Mark worked some rubble under the heavy slab to lighten its weight on the old man pinned beneath. "How do you feel?" he yelled. "Can you crawl out?"

"I . . . I don't feel a thing."

"You'll have to pull him," he yelled to Karen. "I'll get the boulder up, and you'll pull."

"We'll be here for hours . . ."

"Until the rescue squad comes."

"For hours."

"All right, then, for hours."

"What about Danny?"

"I don't know. For God's sake, Karen, there must be a dozen people pinned under here."

"Where's Danny?"

"We'll find him, but you've gotta help me . . ."

"I . . . I'm sorry . . ." She wept as she tugged desperately at him. "Leave them. We've got to find Danny."

"Leave them? They're dying!"

"They're dying all over. I'm not responsible for the whole fucking city."

She pulled harder at him, until he shook her off, slapped her sharply, took her arms, planted them on the old man's shoulders, and yelled, "When I tell you, pull!" He pried up the boulder. "Pull!"

Sobbing hysterically, she pulled. The old man scrambled and came free. Crying his thanks, he grabbed weakly at Mark's leg.

Mark acknowledged it, gave him a reassuring clasp, and turned to Karen. Cradling her, he said, "I'm sorry. I had to."

She wept. "An old man. Just an old man. In Greenland, they'd've let him die."

Kerosene heaters were illegal, but that was certainly not on the mind of Mrs. Ramirez as she lit it.

She wondered why she had ever left the beautiful Puerto Rican tropics. She remembered her terror the first time she saw the strange white stuff that came down from the sky.

She felt some of that old terror now. The oil truck couldn't make delivery, and the radiator and hot-water pipes were almost as cold as the outdoors. Already she could see her breath.

She cautioned the children not to get near, moved the heater to a secure corner near a window, and went back to the kitchen where she could stay close to the stove.

The vapors were hot even well above the kerosene flame, and warmed the window curtains. They soaked up the heat until they reached their ignition point, and burst into flames that swept up one curtain, then across to the other. It finally fell on the stuffed chair, setting that afire as well.

When Mrs. Ramirez heard her children's screams, the room was already ablaze.

The old saying came back with full force: "Ain't nothing between Ohio and the North Pole but a barbed-wire fence." The flat land was transformed into a series of hills by a wind that seemed indeed to be coming straight down from the Arctic.

Already, Farmer Bjork was regretting his decision to go for help. His feet seemed to weigh a ton as he fought to climb a monumental drift while the wind beat him back.

Somehow, he thought, if he could reach the top, he would survive. It would be downhill after that.

With what he was sure was his last bit of strength, he surmounted the hill and looked about. There were only other, greater hills beyond.

He looked back longingly to the farmhouse, but it had disappeared, enshrouded by the white curtain that seemingly hung just beyond reach.

With a groan, he sank into the softness to almost the full length of his legs. It was a very pleasant sensation, and he thought of such soft things as beds and downy quilts. It was much better to submit than fight, just to lie down in it, just for a minute, just to rest.

He let it cradle him. It felt surprisingly warm, and he had a childlike yearning to be smothered in it. He would rest a moment, shut his eyes briefly, and be on his way again. Only a few moments, he told himself.

In that first moment, he fell fast asleep, and the snow billowed about him.

There had been some talk of installing two-way radios in these trains, but the suburban commuter lines were financially marginal operations, and the expensive installations had been endlessly postponed. It would have meant, after all, another fare increase which commuters would not have tolerated.

Certainly the switch and signal system had served the line well for nearly seventy years. When a train stalled, the conductor would set out a signal flag or flare at a safe distance to warn the train upcoming. Even at night, the flare would be visible for at least a mile.

The storm was too severe for the conductor to wander out, however, so he contented himself with a single flare at the rear of the train. No other train would be coming at any great rush, he reasoned. They'd sensibly be at slowest throttle, if they weren't stopped completely.

But the train coming up behind had no such caution. It, too, was filled with increasingly anxious passengers urging on the engineer who certainly had lost time to make up. He went as fast as he could through the storm.

Then he saw the flare, and pulled the emergency brake. Six hundred passengers went sprawling forward almost as one mass. The brakes emitted showers of sparks as wheels piled up snow, and continued sliding on the rails until the second train slammed into the first, burrowing beneath in an explosion of glass and metal. The engine lifted the rear car and threw it off the tracks, derailed the next car and piled it at an askew angle before finally derailing itself.

Some passengers were crushed on impact. Others were thrown clear, only to be sliced and decapitated by sharp-edged debris. The snow was drenched in blood, and the moans of the hundreds of wounded added to the bitter image, a battlefield massacre.

Hundreds of feet above the downtown streets, accumulating ice on cornices and projections passed their point of stability. More like ice stalactites than icicles, they broke off one by one, accelerating second by second as they plunged to earth, velocity acting on mass, mass on pressure, pressure on sharpened points, in those awesome laws of physics that have driven sheaves of wheat through trees, and now made razor-sharp spears out of ice, penetrating with great ease clothing, skin, flesh, and bone.

The fire that started with a kerosene heater spread from room to room, and one apartment to another while the fire engines struggled through the snow. They would race down one street only to find it impossibly jammed with drifts and abandoned cars, and then have to laboriously back up. When only one or two cars blocked their path, the cars were crushed or thrown aside, but the trip that would have taken minutes now took an hour and a half, and when the engines finally arrived, the whole building was ablaze.

Except they did not quite arrive, for the narrow slum streets were choked, and the engines had to park blocks away.

The firemen raced with hoses, snaking them about cleared areas while they groped for buried hydrants. Their own yells mingled with the screams of those caught in the fire as they frantically shoveled the snow from the hydrants, only to find them encased with ice.

They hacked at the ice again and again, until it turned white, and pieces fell away.

Furiously, they turned valves with heavy wrenches, as others bolted on the hoses and waited for water.

But they were too late. For the past few hours, the

water temperature in the mains had been dropping and, as with all matter in the universe, it had contracted as it cooled. But then, with a property unique to water, as it reached its freezing point it began expanding again. Denied its freedom, it pushed with awesome pressure against its prison, pound mounting on pound as it grew, until it reached a full ton per square inch.

Finally, the weakened pipes burst with explosions barely heard through asphalt and concrete, and above the tumult of the storm.

Now, the firemen who expected cataracts of water heard only a hollow hissing that dropped in pitch to a sigh before it died completely. Finally, a few pitiful drops trickled out, while the flames leaped to the next building.

"Gimme that, you son of a bitch," said the round-faced man, pulling the bottle back from his companion.

"Let's see you take it, fuckface."

The man grabbed for it; his companion hit him with the bottle.

At the other end of the terminal, a girl screamed and kicked as a man grabbed her away from her boyfriend, squeezed her breasts as he tried working his way between her legs, ignoring the boy pummeling him.

The camaraderie had evaporated, and fights erupted everywhere at the terminal. They fought over drinks, over women, over football scores, over anything.

A security guard tried telephoning for reinforcements, but his line was dead.

All across the Northeast, people were frantic over missing family and friends. For the most part, their telephones were useless because of lines that were overloaded or fallen. They could not phone for ambulances, doctors, the police, the fire department, or simple reassurance. In some places, power was gone, which meant there was no electricity for the pumps. Faucets were dry, toilets foul, food in the refrigerators began rotting. Places fueled by oil or coal grew cold.

Planes, trains, trucks, the vital carriers of food, fuel, and supply were not sent out, or were mired in the snow. Milk trains sold their cargo at pennies per gallon to customers with buckets; a few miles away, customers pushed and scrambled for watered-down pints.

Ships were thrown against piers, or battered at sea like bathtub toys.

Like some immense organism, the city shriveled at its extremities and then, little by little, death crept toward its vital communication centers, the nervous system.

There were fitful, if forceful, sparks of life, CB radios in cars and trucks, shouting, jabbering, pleading, already badly overloaded like party lines with too many gossipers. Ham radio operators worked in freer channels, answering or relaying what messages they could.

Most important of all were the radio and television broadcasters, bleary-eyed and short-tempered, and the sleepy, overworked skeleton staffs who occasionally pushed wrong buttons and cut off the news in mid-sentence.

Outside of its communications, the city had been pushed back a century, to a time of local street peddlers, hawking odd amounts of food and fuel at ten and twenty times their normal price.

For some, unable to venture out, the thrust backward was far more severe, to an age when tribes huddled in caves against a fearsome darkness outside. Now, they shivered in tight, lonely places, and wondered if there was a world at all beyond the white blur at their windows.

On the roof of the Weather Service there were the sensors of the various instruments, all frozen, locked solidly, and so even the meteorologists were helpless to know the storm's duration.

One instrument was free, however. In the basement of the Planetary Sciences building of the nearby

university, a miniature witch stood outside a miniature house.

Gradually, however, very gradually, a string of
catgut suspending the witch began twisting as it shrank
from the decreasing moisture. Slowly, she was pulled
back into the house, and out came a little Hansel
and Gretel.

At the airport terminal, with its wide, panoram-
ic windows, someone noticed the first lightening of the
snowfall, and the sky growing brighter.

"Hey, it's over!"

At first, his cry was barely heard above the ruckus, but he yelled it again, louder.

They looked up from their fights, and saw he was
right. They rushed to the observation windows and
watched the clouds thin until they could see the sun's
dim outline. Some wept. Others, who had been fighting
moments before, threw their arms about each other
and laughed.

Other rescuers had come to help Mark and Kar-
en. Mark decided to forget her earlier outburst; he
knew she would not ordinarily have been so appalling-
ly selfish. He ascribed it to emotional distress.

All over the city, people came out of their houses
to bless the sunshine, and dig themselves free.

Passengers stuck in an elevated train let out a
cheer when a huge fire-ladder came to rest against a
car door. They expected a fireman, but got a skinny
pock-marked adolescent who said his name was Herbie, and he was charging them ten dollars apiece admission to the ladder.

"Admission to a ladder? Go to hell!"

Herbie shrugged and climbed back down.

The indignant gentleman climbed out on the ladder, but Herbie shook it from the bottom. The gentleman yelped and scurried back off. Herbie waited until
the man held up a ten-dollar bill, and by the time the

man reached the bottom, quite a few others were lined up at the top, ten-dollar bills in hand.

He looked peacefully asleep when the police reached the cab. They could hear the two radios going inside, the CB and the small transistor.

The door was locked, the windows shut tight. The cop rapped on the window.

"You all right, buddy?"

There was no answer, even when the policeman pounded. At last, he worked a wire lasso through the weather-stripping, and pulled up the doorlock. He gasped from the accumulated gases inside, and Richie Fuselli fell lifeless into the snow.

"Here they come!"

"Thank God, at last."

The passengers ran to the observation window to see their rescuers shoveling through the snow, arms loaded with sandwiches and coffee.

"Oh, brother, are we glad to see you!"

"That's what I figured. Coffee's five dollars, sandwiches ten."

"Are you crazy?"

"That depends. You hungry?"

When the storm died, the silence was total and awful in its own way. Then Mrs. Bjork and her daughter heard the distant drone; they lit a fire, and used dampened clothes to make black smoke.

The signal was seen by the patrolling helicopter. A man came down a ladder to ask if they were all right and what they needed.

"My husband's all right, then?"

The man looked at her blankly.

"Fred Bjork. He reached you, didn't he?"

"Uh . . . no. We were doing a general sweep, and we saw your smoke."

She caught the full implication all at once. "He's out there somewhere!"

The man looked out at the fields, and shook his head. "We won't even be able to find him till it melts."

Mr. Christedes thought he shouldn't wait to open his shoe store. After all, people would need boots, galoshes, and probably new shoes to replace the ones they ruined, so he took a shovel with him without waiting for the sanitation men to do the clearing.

As he worked his way to the door, he was frightened at what seemed a large furry animal curled up in the doorway, and he wondered if he should call the police. Then he saw the glint of eyeglasses, and he realized the animal was human, that it was, in fact, a child.

He shoveled faster now, and when he reached Danny he tried to shake the boy awake.

But Danny didn't stir.

The people who had been marooned in Times Square let out loud hurrahs as the news came flashing along the electric sign about the Times tower. They had lived through a worse blizzard than that of 1888, five inches more snow, eight miles per hour fiercer wind, with drifts two and three stories high.

Then came the sobering statistics on those who had not lived through it, from train wrecks, auto wrecks, asphyxiations, freezing, fire, exposure, starvation.

Business was disrupted, with enormous monetary loss. Riots, gouging, looting, and other crimes were rampant.

Modern society, far from being better able than some primitive culture to resist such catastrophe, was more fragile. Planes were more easily thwarted than cars, cars more than trains, trains more than horses.

Investigations were promised, improvements assured. Emergency systems and procedures would be instituted, and foul-ups would not happen again.

But it was over, and the people who had lived through it would have something to tell their grandchildren.

Danny lay unconscious beneath a plastic tent, looking frail and vulnerable, with nutrients dripping through a tube into a nostril. Karen wept to see him, though the doctor said he was out of danger.

Karen grabbed Mark's hand. "When he's better ... we've got to get out before it hits."

"Of course. Everybody will."

"No ... no, no. Just us."

Mark squeezed her hand, and said nothing.

The snow was already turning black from the soot and fumes, with spots of yellow from animal urine. Children played in the mountainous heaps pushed together by plows, while pedestrians walked warily in the cleared trenches that in some places had to be burrowed into tunnels.

The weather had turned warm again, sending steady trickles of brackish water down into basement apartments, while the sun baked the uncollected mounds of garbage.

"Shut that damn window. The smell's awful," said Fink.

Mark complied, then turned back to the assemblage. "And this was just the beginning, just a taste of what'll happen."

"Ehhh." Fink waved it away.

"Oh Jesus, you mean after all this you're not convinced? This was worse than '88."

"Yeah, we all know about '88, but what about the famous blizzard of '89?"

"What're you talking about? There was no blizzard of '89."

"That, my dear Watson, is the significant fact about the blizzard of '89."

"I don't get you."

"After '88, things went right back to normal. Same here. Your Ice Age has come and gone, Marcus. Just feel, it's warm again. Open the window ... No, don't open the window. Take my word, it's warm again."

Mark turned to his friend. "Hideo, don't you have something to say?"

The geologist's mind was elsewhere, and Mark had to repeat the question. Hideo finally looked up, shrugged, and shook his head no.

Geography picked up the argument. "Fink's right. The storm was disruptive, all right, but it was comparatively localized. And aren't you the one who mentioned there're sixty thousand storms a day on the planet?"

"But this one's significant. It's the A-Bomb that'll trigger the H-Bomb."

"Well, it's your bomb theory versus my burp theory," said Fink. "We had that big gas pain down at Cape Hatteras, it moved up where we burped, and now we all feel better."

Mark shook his head. "I don't feel better."

"Well, even if you're right," said Geography, "what would you expect us to do?"

"Move."

"Where? And what?"

"Everything, to the tropics, where we can survive."

"We'll christen it the Mark Ark. Two of every living thing, right?"

"If you like."

"I like," said Fink, "if you can get me a cute living thing."

The others were already breaking up into their separate cliques, talking about sex and football and getting a paper published. Then they were gone, leaving Mark and Hideo alone.

Mark shook his head in wonder. "I don't believe it. Ostriches, every one of them." He turned to Hideo. "And where the hell were you?"

Hideo said nothing for some moments. "Wouldn't have helped. Want me to tell you about all the houses they build on the San Andreas fault?" He put his feet up on the table, leaned back, and stared at the ceiling.

Mark sighed in exasperation. "Goddamn. I picked you up at the airport myself, but I can't swear you're all back."

Hideo shook his head slowly. "I'm not . . . I'm not." He paused. "Y'know, they lead nice lives, those Eskimos. You appreciate things you never thought about, the warmth of a fire, hunting your own food, children . . . You don't think so much about yesterday or tomorrow, but the now becomes beautiful."

"Well, maybe your 'now' was, but not ours. We had a touch of your beautiful Greenland, just a touch, and it nearly killed us. What happens when it really hits?"

Hideo smiled wanly. "Seemed nice up there."

"Maybe it is, up there, and I don't mind it staying there. But I was down here during the storm, and you weren't, so don't come down when it's melting and moan about truth and beauty. All I see coming is wholesale slaughter. You talked about old Mesopotamia without rice? Shit, this'll be the whole world without a world."

"All right, all right, you convinced me." He got up to leave.

"Where the hell're you going?"

"Putting my head in the sand like everyone else." He paused at the door. "Or in the snow." Then he was gone.

Mark stared at the telephone a while, then he finally called the journalist on the *Times*.

The journalist listened patiently to Mark's entire account, and then finally laughed. "Headline, 'World Coming to End. Football Scores Inside.'"

"I'm glad you think it's funny."

"Look, Haney, we've been getting end-of-the-world stories since they chiseled newspapers on rocks. So far, the world's still here."

Mark kept a check on his rage. "All right, what's it take, what do you need?"

"Corroboration, for one. You got the faculty behind you?"

Mark paused a moment. "They'll . . . uh . . . come around."

"But they're not there yet."

"It's . . . not their department, really, but the fact

is, I'm sticking up for it. I, me, Mark Haney, and I'm putting everything I am on the line."

"Which, face it, Haney, isn't that much."

"Now wait a sec . . ."

"No offense, Haney. I'm low man on this totem pole, too. That's why we're talking. I'd be on the line myself on this one."

"Didn't you once say you were built to take the heat?"

"Not this much. You're giving me a whopper of a story now, and I'm not built that big."

"You mean you're scared of it?"

"Damn right I am."

"I'll bring you the proofs, the photos, the measurements, the math . . ."

"It'll be over my head. Look, show that stuff to some other experts in your field. Go outside the school . . ."

"It'll take too long."

"What's to take? You must have some kind of communication network, a teletype or something."

"Yeah. We meet at conferences once a year, and talk over things in the hallway or a bar."

"Pretty advanced setup."

"A little slow. Even then, we don't trust each other."

"I'm beginning to see why. All right, at least go through your department chairman. Or do you only see him once a year, too?"

Mark hesitated.

"Don't tell me."

"He . . . he's on a leave of absence."

"Oh yeah? Where'd he go?"

"Uh . . . We're not sure. He said he'd be in touch once he was settled."

"Too bad. Sorry."

Even as Mark lied, he worried if poor Guzman was wandering the streets.

There were several reasons for Sr. Avila to be disturbed, as he brought his boat back from the day's fishing. The new fish he had been catching in the Gulf Stream were no longer so abundant. The dropoff had been noticeable and steady, and the old fishes had not returned to make up the difference. Something very strange was happening with the ocean.

Now, as he came closer to the dock, he saw an outsider, looking things over like a tourist. He was an American, obviously, the first of the winter.

Avila was of a mixed mind about these tourists. They brought money, of course, and sometimes they'd hire his boat for a day's fishing. They were demanding, they were arrogant, and if too many of them came, well, one need only look at Tijuana.

But with the fishing so bad, money was money.

Avila figured he would play up to the American, fib a little about the fishing, and perhaps get his boat chartered, with payment in advance. First, he'd get acquainted.

"*Buenas dias,* Senor. You're an American?"

He nodded.

"You've come down early."

"Got cold early," said Guzman.

His voice sounded loud in the 2:00 a.m. quiet. "TL8XNT . . . TL8XNT . . . Hello, TL8XNT. . . Dr. Schumer . . ." Mark paused, and then, taking a slight breath, spoke his own call letters for the first time. "This is W2QRV . . . This is W2QRV . . . Whiskey Two Quebec Romeo Victor, calling TL8XNT and standing by."

He repeated the doctor's call letters and his own several more times, and waited. And waited. There was only hiss.

"Damn!"

He turned around and saw the bed was empty. Karen had gone in to check on Danny.

He turned his gaze to the Eskimo artifacts, to the sharpened bone that was a sewing needle, to the oversized ashtray that was really a whale-oil lamp,

and to the whip with its intricately carved handle and
long lash. We'll be needing that stuff someday right
here, he mused.

He turned back to the radio, and made another
attempt to raise the doctor in Mali.

Finally, he flipped to another frequency, one
crowded with a complex of signals, intermingled with
buzzes, whistles and cracklings of atmospheric interference, all together forming the cacophony of civilization.

He listened until Karen came back into the room,
comfortably naked though the room was cold.

"How's he doing?" Mark asked.

"Sleeping okay. Still weak. It'll take a while."

"Yeah, if we've got a while."

"What were you doing?" She stood behind him,
looking at the radio while she stroked his neck.

"Trying to raise the dead." He laughed.

"You can't. Learn to accept nature."

"We're back to that again."

"Our only disagreement." She slid round him to
sit in his lap, and hugged him.

"Yeah, that and keeping the room so goddamn
cold."

"We keep each other warm."

"Mm-hm." He kissed each breast.

She hugged him tighter, and was silent for a
while.

"Mark?"

"Hm?"

"Why do you listen to that?"

"I like the music."

"Whatever . . ." She hesitated.

"Yeah?"

"Whatever happens to them, I don't want happening to us."

"It needn't happen to any of us. Enough time,
and they'll come round."

She shook her head.

"Meaning which, there's not enough time, or they
won't come round?"

"Meaning don't bother. Meaning, just let it happen."

He nodded to the voices on the radio. "Those're human beings out there."

"They're just voices. We're the only reality, just us and Danny."

"We're a civilization. What we are, what we do . . . You lift out three threads, and the fabric comes with it."

They snuggled closer, and said nothing for a time.

"Mark . . ."

His sigh had a slight edge.

"That teacher . . . from Geography, what's his name?"

"Whatever."

"Yeah, Professor Whatever. Remember about the lions?"

"What lions?"

"Where they saved all those animals, and then deposited them in a safe place?"

"So?"

"You put four lions where only two lived, and you wind up with no lions."

He pushed her away to look at her. "You're calm and controlled, and you know perfectly well what you're saying."

She nodded.

"Okay, say it."

"The government knows, and they're not telling."

"Yeah?"

"They're right."

"They're right? It'll be a bigger slaughter than a nuclear war. Ninety percent of the globe is going to die."

"The other ten percent'll survive. But not if the whole world comes pushing on down to the tropics."

"I can't help that."

"Meaning, it's not your department."

"It's not my department. I have to do what's right for me."

"For us."

"All right, for us."

"Mark, *we* are us."

"Huh?"

"We are the only us."

"I'm losing you."

"No, you have me. You have me." She hugged him again, let her breast fill his mouth, stroked his ears, felt him grow hard. She almost wept, desperately. "Mark . . . let *us* live."

She lifted his head to her and kissed him, opening her mouth to receive his tongue, then closed it about. She gasped in ecstasy. They pulled back for breath.

"You . . . talked about . . . accepting death," he said.

"Eventually . . . when it's right . . . when it's meant. Until then, I want to live . . . I want us to live."

He swept his hand down to her thigh, felt her grow moist with desire. He cradled her as she turned about, dropped one leg and circled it about him as they drew together, and he felt himself entering, sliding in with delicious ease.

The radio signals sounded on, a hundred voices that were not in the room, from remote corners of the globe, at distances beyond comprehension and beyond care.

The air currents still traveled their basic paths, as unchangeable in their way as the basic laws of physics, warmed by the sun about the equator, and then drawn to the coldness at the Poles, but now they were traveling new paths, describing new patterns.

There had been a storm in the Northeast, the worst storm in the memories of most living citizens, but it had passed out of their concern as it had traveled on.

Indeed, the storm would normally have blown itself out at sea, but normality as humanity perceived it was fast-fading. For one thing, the heat that generated water vapor over the Atlantic did the same over the Arctic seas, and so a cloud lay waiting over the great ice sheet of Greenland, moisture to revitalize the storm before it died.

Soon, out of sight of all human eyes, a new blizzard raged. Inch by inch the snow accumulated on the ice, the individual flakes settling lightly, held apart by the branches of each flake. But as more snow fell, as inches grew to feet and then yards, the snow at the bottom was squeezed as one might squeeze a snowball. The branches were snapped off by the pressure, and the crystals were bunched closer into a granular ice.

The fattening glacier in turn chilled the air above, bringing yet new snow, yard after yard, ton atop ton, and that granular ice was compressed further, until the last bits of air were wrung out and it was transformed into a special kind of ice with density beyond belief, an immovable, impenetrable solid by any human reckoning.

Nature, however, operated with forces of grander scale. Millions of tons continued to accumulate on top, but there was nothing more to be squeezed out at the bottom. There was nowhere to go but out, and so this hardest of solids oozed like molasses.

Physically, it was flattening out, spreading under its own immense weight. It behaved like a living thing, an amoeba hundreds of miles across, blindly sending out exploratory extensions of itself, fingers of ice groping among rocks and boulders, thickening as they found passage, and the huge, slow body of the great glacier lumbered after.

Rocks and boulders were swept up, rolled about to become teeth, or giant rasps, so that now the glacier could grind and pulverize as well as swallow whole.

At last it reached the mountain range, and here it was stymied. The fingers seemed to withdraw as more ice joined, and the glacier gathered itself together.

A hundred miles back, the snow continued to feed it, and so its front grew higher, patiently working its way up the mountainside, until it reached the pass, and then overflowed it. Physically, each movement forward, even downhill, was the product not of concord but of turmoil, as countless crystals gave way grudgingly, twisted about, reshaped themselves, finally conformed.

At the glacier's base, the immense pressures kept these conflicts sealed in one gelatinous mass. On top, though, that turmoil was revealed, and the ice split and sundered in a thousand crevasses that grew and diminished, sealed and reformed with each bend in the earth.

Below lay the Eskimo village. The inhabitants had fled, leaving behind one old woman. She sat outside the igloo and waited. She had waited a long time in exactly this position, unmoving, calm and quiet.

She remembered when she herself had left her parents behind. Those times they would have faced the white bear, or simply starved. There were times long ago, spoken of in the ancient stories, when people had faced the great ice itself in its slow march.

Certainly it was far better to die in such a way, to be embraced by the Earth itself, to partake of the Spirit of All Being.

The thunderings were almost deafening as the ice crept down, sweeping all into its maw. It was a spirit of infinite hunger, or infinite love.

It came to the igloos, took them up easily, returning ice to ice. Someday, it would make them anew, igloos, mountains, bears, and people. And who could say which of these the old woman might herself be?

It towered above her. She could not see its top but she could look into it, and she did. She saw its light, all the colors dreamt and undreamt, a dizzying, whirling kaleidoscope, extending to infinity. It was the light of the Spirit itself, and as she looked deeper, she could now see its All Being, the bears and seals and fish her family had killed, now all welcoming her.

She looked deeper and now she saw the other spirits, her husband, her parents, her grandparents, all calling to her, holding out their arms in welcome. She extended her arms, and at the last moment, touched them all, touched eternity.

Twelve thousand miles above, the satellite watched the little village's destruction. It saw the glacier growing more massive by the moment, measured the heat its ice sapped from the atmosphere and the cold it released in its stead, breathing it into the currents that wound about the planet.

As cold air met warm, there would be new convulsions, new storms, new destruction. All this the satellite would watch impassively, observing, recording, transmitting. It mattered little whether there would be an intelligence below to receive that transmission. Fed by its solar batteries, stable in its orbit, it would go on forming its electronic chirpings, whether or not it had an audience.

OWENS VALLEY, CALIFORNIA:

"Mom, it's beautiful."

Peggy Bjork threw her arms around her mother and cried just as she did when, years ago, she found a rocking horse under the Christmas tree, though otherwise it scarcely seemed like Christmas. The day was bright, and the fields were green and growing.

Indeed, she had never felt a sun so warm. Ohio was far away, and so was the snow, and so was her father's death.

Mrs. Bjork wept too, with the same emotions with which one faces a new life, mingled anticipation and fear, along with a strange disbelief. She knew, though, she couldn't live anymore in Zanesville, not on that same farm where her husband had frozen to death, not through another bitter winter.

And so the bank had made the arrangements, a sale of one farm, the lease of another. Perhaps it was Peggy and her pioneer stories who had influenced the choice of California, but it certainly seemed a wise choice in any case.

Mrs. Bjork was a little surprised at the ease and swiftness of it all. The matter of a lease rather than an outright sale was unusual, but Mrs. Bjork's old regard for "land of one's own" had soured, and seemed more like enslavement.

Even more peculiar was the fact the actual owner, at the end of the long list of agents, was the County of Los Angeles, practically at the other end of the state, 350 miles to the south. Strange were the ways of government.

In fact, the ways of government were sometimes crafty and farsighted. A half century before, the County had sent agents to buy up these northern farms just to get the ground-water rights, and then leased them back to the original owners.

This was at most of academic interest to Mrs. Bjork. She recognized a well-run farm, good topsoil, mild climate with consistent sunshine, and a careful balancing between cattle and crops.

There was no worry of rain and hail and snowstorm here. Nature had been managed and tamed. Beneath the stable sky, waters were brought in monitored and measured amounts in irrigation ditches, in turn connected to awesome reservoirs fed by the snows of the Sierra Nevada. And should the aqueducts fail, there were the wells to the seemingly inexhaustible groundwater. When Mrs. Bjork tasted it, she found it pure, fresh, and sweet, unlike the flat-tasting rainwater or polluted riverwater of Ohio.

It was nature bounteous and unending, and both mother and daughter knew they had found their new home.

The television news showed villagers tearing down some religious statue and holding it up to a noose, threatening the god with hanging if the rain was not to come soon.

The newscaster filled in the abstract information, that the United States had no immediate security interests but was closely watching the situation. The imminent collapse of the Indian government, the starving of many millions due to the unaccountably delayed monsoons, and the resultant riots, were not seen as having direct implications, but of course the American government would be rushing aid to the stricken.

There was a brief view of the Indian Meteorological Service facilities, and an interview with a thoroughly inarticulate meteorologist, Dr. L. V. Singh. He seemed in a state of shock, in fact, and the interview was cut short.

Mark recognized the emotion. He had had it himself. He recognized something else, barely noticed in the clutter of instruments, a ham receiver.

The newscast switched to the more immediate local news, but Mark was already riffling through the pages of the ham radio register, looking for Dr. Singh's call letters, and warming up his transmitter. In a few moments more, he was sending out those letters, adding his own.

It took a while to raise the doctor. Soon, they were past the introductory chatter, with the standard abbreviations hams have used to bridge language barriers, and came to deeper talk. In fact, Dr. Singh spoke almost unreally perfect English, the typical product of higher education in a former British colony.

"Thank God you know," said Mark. "I was beginning to think I really must be crazy."

"You may be reassured, my friend, if you will call it reassuring, that it is the world that is crazy. And it will go crazier. The ostriches will have to bury their heads deeper into the sand."

"Look, the problem is in finding safe havens. We have to find places along, or near, the equator. It has to be a functioning society, and still keep the records of . . ."

"You may have to, we don't. Bombay is only eighteen degrees north latitude. The equator is just down the street."

"Then the ice won't touch you. You can survive there . . ."

"Yes, the ice won't touch us; no, we will not survive. We are dying now. The monsoons fed half our rivers. The snows in the Himalayas feed the rest. What happens when they no longer melt? Six hundred million people. We have nowhere to go, nowhere."

Mark fell silent a while. "Look, it's like a burning house. You can't save everything, so you save what you can. Even if a few of us survive, if we stay in contact . . ."

"Then what?"

"We fight."

"Fight? Fight what, the planet, the gods?"

"Then you're just going to lie down and die?"

There was a long pause, and for a moment Mark thought the connection was lost, but at last Dr. Singh spoke up again. "We have a long view, Mr. Haney. Our society was built on the ruins of another, and that on yet another. Someone will build on ours."

"If there's no one and nothing left, it'll finish with you."

"Then it will finish with us."

"Look . . ." said Mark, after a while, "keep the channels open. I'll get others. We can plan . . . something. It's more than one society. It's the whole damned human race that's at stake. We'll be dinosaurs."

"Noble creatures, the dinosaurs. More successful than Man. Their reign was fifty times ours."

"They didn't fight their end. We will."

"Do you know what you're fighting?"

"It's not the planet, and it's not the gods. It's just goddamn ice."

THULE, GREENLAND:

A government that had fought clandestine battles, and even whole Asian wars in secret, found no problem in shrouding its strangest battle. The enemy was remote, and still not near the Air Force base. All necessary radio communications were scrambled, and the scientists who had been flown up from Maryland had received the usual clearances.

They all watched in awed silence as the ice crept down the mountainside like white lava, its countless cracks and fissures widening and resealing, its booming thunder and splintering echoing for miles. At that moment, it seemed a force of God, relentless, magnificent, and they were mere insects in its path.

"Just some lousy ice, that's all," said the artillery

commander. He had, of course, fought grimmer enemies, ones that shifted position readily and unpredictably, that hid beneath clever camouflage, that exhibited intelligence that could match his own, and worst of all, that could shoot back.

He radioed orders to the mobile Howitzers, and they roared into position, their caterpillar treads churning up the snow in fountains.

"Captain," said the glacierologist, "if you want a target, you have your best chance against the blue lines. They mark the seams."

"Best chance?" He almost snorted, but he passed the word down to the section chief.

The M110 Howitzer was the heaviest of field artillery, but mechanized and mobilized far beyond the clumsy cannons of the last great war. It was more like a thirty-ton open tank, self propelled, carrying its own five-man crew. Now, as each wheeled into its best location, and as the section chief passed down the orders, with range and bearings, diesel engines and intricate gears spun seventeen-foot barrels into firing position.

The commander called the order to fire, and in moments the cannons responded with roars that matched that of the approaching glacier.

Each projectile weighed two hundred pounds, but the Howitzer could hurl it over ten miles, and even then it would penetrate eleven inches of solid concrete. The commander had good reason to snort.

Round after round exploded against the ice walls, throwing up geysers of white powder, but when after several minutes the walls had not come crumbling like Jericho, the commander called a halt.

There was some initial chipping, each pit perhaps a few inches deep, such as one might find hacking at some ice block in a home freezer, but beyond that the glacier seemed unbothered.

The commander stared astonished through his binoculars. "What the hell is that?"

The fliers had been waiting their opportunity, and now the jocular voice of one came over the radio.

"Hold onto your martini glasses. We'll be coming back with some ice cubes."

The glacierologist just grunted, but he had to admit as he watched the planes fly in from Thule that the sight was spectacular. The bombs dropped in formation as carefully measured and as beautiful as some precision chorus line. They exploded in sequence like some vast firework display.

In a time when "blockbuster" is applied casually to movie premieres and advertising campaigns, it is difficult to recapture the terror it once created. The same formation of these bombs, each weighing ten thousand pounds, five full tons, leveled whole cities— Berlin, Frankfurt, Essen, and later, Hanoi. Afterward, one might travel mile after mile down the central street and see only mere piles of brick and rubble, with some occasional bare shell, and find difficulty in imagining a great city was there mere days instead of five thousand years ago.

Well placed, each bomb would reduce a full city block—perhaps a half dozen apartment buildings, or a great museum—to a pile of rubble. In the Vietnam jungles, it gouged an instantaneous crater for mass helicopter landings.

"Jesus, what the hell's that stuff made of?" came the stunned flier's voice over the radio.

The glacierologist didn't answer. He was already consulting with the Army Corps of Engineers. These men were cautious and serious. They made plans, studied photos, analyzed stress patterns, tested samples, and concluded that thermite bombs were a waste of time. They knew immediately they had only one good possibility.

It took a special order of the President, clearance with the National Security Council and the Atomic Energy Commission, all given with emergency speed.

The boring was made by a special drill used by oil companies to drill through granite, and which was singularly applicable here. Instead of a diamond bit, it used a series of white-hot jet flames, fed by hydrogen gas under pressure.

Alignments, however, proved extremely difficult because of the constantly shifting ice, but eventually the well was completed and the charge planted.

It created a small earthquake when it was detonated. The ice shook, fragments flew in every direction, and there was a searing, hissing sound like some great boiler. The steam vented to the surface and took the form of the familiar mushroom cloud.

The engineers cheered. This was the device they had longed to put in general use, that could have dug a harbor at a stroke, or the fifty miles of the Panama Canal in a day. But a fearful public unreasonably forbade its use. Perhaps, when they were finally allowed to hear how it had saved an Air Force base and, beyond that, a whole continent, they would change their minds and mankind could fully enter the Atomic Age.

It was a couple of hours before the cloud cleared and they could survey the damage. A crater had been blown in the ice about 150 yards in diameter. Fissures worked their way out in every direction for perhaps a quarter of a mile, and now, even as they watched, the melted waters came flowing back in, sealing the fissures, filling the crater, freezing again. The glacier was healing itself.

"Captain," said the glacierologist, anticipating the officer's question, "remember the Alaska quake in '64?"

"Not easy to forget."

"Not surprising. Worst quake in the history of North America, felt across fifty thousand square miles. Y'know what it did to the glaciers there?"

"Hadn't heard."

"I'm not surprised, wasn't worth mentioning."

"So why're you mentioning it?"

"What I mean, Captain," said the scientist with an edge, "is that a catastrophe equaling twenty thousand H-Bombs did nothing notable to the glaciers. They just rumbled and settled back, and that was all. Now, now it's worth mentioning, I think."

The captain whistled. "Guess it is. But if we concentrate that force . . ."

"Yes, we can. We can use 'em against the glacier all day, or all year, and then what've we done? Melted some ice, maybe, except it travels right up as water vapor, condenses, and it snows again, only this time it's radioactive snow."

"What . . . what do we do, then?"

"Retreat. Evacuate."

"Evacuate what? Retreat to where?"

The glacierologist laughed a bitter laugh. "I was hoping you'd tell me."

Guzman sat on the porch of the hacienda. He should have been enjoying the sweet and indolent life, the retirement dream of any hard-working executive. But he was not enjoying it.

He looked to the north, to the hills, as though he expected something to come swarming down from there. Nervously, he got up, paced the porch, and then wandered inside.

The house was stockpiled with canned and dried foods, enough for a lifetime. There were clothing, blankets, fuel, safely buried beneath the flooring. He was, he knew, secure for the rest of his life.

And yet he wasn't.

The cleaning woman watched him with astonishment. There had been much talk about the crazy American, and she now saw he was crazier than the rumors, and perhaps dangerously so.

He turned on the radio, a strange, complicated one with many switches and dials. He rotated these anxiously, listening. There were peculiar beeps and whistles, and then many voices talking at once in many languages.

He finally fastened on one, and she could see his face harden.

Then he did a truly frightening thing. He opened a locked strongbox with a key. Inside were rifles, pistols, a submachine gun, grenades. He checked them, seemed satisfied, and slammed the box shut.

Then he wandered out again and looked to the hills, leaving the radio so loud it echoed about the house.

She decided then and there she wouldn't stay here any longer, regardless of the money.

"Dit-dit, da-da-dit."

"Dit-dit, da-da-dit."

"Dit-dit-da, dit-da-dit-da, dit-dit-da-da-dit-dit."

"Dit-dit-da, dit-da-dit-da, dit-da-da-da-dit-dit."

It was all Danny could do to keep from breaking up in giggles, but he knew there was a serious business to the game. "More, more," he said, hitting his lap as he leaned forward in bed, watching Mark carefully.

"Okay," said Mark. "Dit-dit-dit-da-da-da-dit-da, dit-dit-da-da-dit-da-dit-dit."

"Dit-dit-dit-da-da-da-dit . . ."

"What're you doing?" asked Karen, coming in with Danny's medicine.

"Just a game," said Mark.

"Don't tell me Danny's actually playing a game."

"Well, with serious intent," said Danny, resuming his serious mein, and looking old again. "I'm learning the radio. It's a lot to learn, Mother. It's a whole language." He turned to Mark. "Try me on vocabulary. Go ahead."

"QNP."

"QNP, unable to copy you."

"QTU."

"QTU . . . uh . . . What hours is your station open?" Danny caught Mark's beaming look, and turned to get similar approval from his mother, but met only a frown.

"I think you could be learning a real language," said Karen, "something you'd have use of. Spanish, for instance, if we wind up in South America."

"Spanish? Mother, this is a real language, and it's beautiful. It's so concise. The same three letters, you can ask as a question, and it's also an answer. 'QSL?' Do you acknowledge? 'QSL.' Yes, I acknowledge. See? And it's international. I can talk to someone in China, or India, or . . ."

"Only up to a point, I imagine. If I'm talking to someone in China, I'd like to know what their life is

like, their family, their feelings, their hopes, things that
don't go by number."

"You're not supposed to. This is so precise, there's
no room for misunderstanding. You don't appreciate
science, Mother, that's your problem."

"I guess it is. Look up, here's your medicine."
She was about to feed him, but he took it away indig-
nantly. He caught the look his mother gave Mark.

"I suppose now you want to go outside so you
can talk about me."

"QNX, a minute?" asked Mark as he took Karen
to the door.

"Huh, QNX . . . A minute!" answered Danny as
Mark shut the door behind them.

Outside the room, Mark was about to explain the
abbreviation to Karen when her lips were suddenly
upon his, her tongue stroking, coaxing entrance. He
sighed appreciatively, felt himself grow hard, then
pulled away.

"You're surprising sometimes."

"How?"

"Just when I thought we weren't getting along."

"We get along fine, just fine," said Karen.

"Horizontally, yeah. Not always vertically."

"Almost always."

"Except Danny?"

"A few slight things about Danny."

"Like teaching him the radio?"

"There're more important things, Mark."

"Like?"

"The world's coming to an end for example. Little things like that."

"I'm doing what I can," said Mark.

"All the wrong things."

"We've got a civilization to save."

"We've got ourselves to save. Danny'll be well
enough to travel soon. Why aren't you getting pass-
ports? Why aren't you getting us packed, buying up
land someplace . . . ?"

"How do I pack a civilization, Karen? What do I
do, call Mayflower Moving?"

"One thing I learned from the Eskimos. They learned to travel light. They packed everything onto a sled or two, they moved on, and they survived. Now, what is it you really, really need? Get it down to the barest things, pack up, and let's get out of here."

"And then what?"

"What do you mean, and then what? We live, whatever, wherever, however we live."

"Without art, without culture, without science?"

"If it costs too much to take, then we leave it behind . . ."

"I suppose that includes the radio."

"Especially. I don't understand your obsession with that goddamn noise box."

"Well, somebody does," said Mark, pulling himself away, re-entering Danny's room. "Okay," he said to Danny. "Where were we? Dit-dit-da-da-dit-dit-da."

"Dit-dit-da-da-dit-dit-da," said Danny, giggling.

Karen watched a while, then turned away.

The great glacier pushed and groped blindly on a front a half-mile wide, until it reached the sea. It crept out into the water like a hesitant bather, and the grinding rubble fell away beneath in a shower of rocks.

The rising and falling tide now worked at the unsupported ledge, pushing and pulling until the surface cracked in a thousand places. The sea continued, forcing the cracks further into the ice until they found the blue lines, the seams. Here the cracks joined together into one fracture until finally the sea accomplished what no man-made weapon could.

With a roar of thunder that carried for miles, the glacier gave birth to a child of a mere million and a half tons.

It sank beneath the surface, then bobbed up, the seawater cascading down its face in giant waterfalls. Down it went again, spinning and turning, struggling to find its balance, and each bob and turn sent out an undersea wave that would travel twenty to thirty miles, eventually to crash upon a shore with the height of a tidal wave.

Eventually, the newly born iceberg found its balance, its crown catching the light in countless sparkling crystals, its form sculpted into fantastic crags and spires, a white gothic cathedral in complexity and size. Some of its siblings would stand as tall as skyscrapers, but even so, this only represented a tenth of its total bulk.

As huge as it was, the iceberg would still be pushed by wind and carried by current, eventually floating out to the open sea, crossing the world's most heavily trafficked shipping lanes.

Behind it, the glacier groaned again, pushing another tongue of great ice floating above the sea.

"Doesn't look like much now, does it? Kind of tame, almost like a sleeping pet. But it was once the monster that conquered the world."

The park guide had told his story so often he could almost feel himself switching on like a tape recorder. He waited, as he waited three times a day, for the tourists to pull out their cameras and start clicking. They were surrounded by the wondrous beauties of nature around Mt. Ranier, but their attention was fixed on the frozen rivers of ice sprinkled about the mountain range like so many gemstones.

The guide continued his talk, comparing the dying glaciers to the dying dinosaurs, an endangered species growing extinct even as they watched.

"Hey," a tourist broke in, "if it's dyin', how come it's doin' this?"

"Doing what?" It took a moment for the guide to switch off his mental tape. He followed the tourist's pointing finger to the glacier's edge where a rock had been uprooted by the ice. The glacier was growing.

There was no coverup this time. Calcutta and Bombay were not remote African villages. The news teams were there to record—sometimes at great danger to themselves—the breakdown of a whole society, of millions dying of thirst, of cattle rotting in the streets with their skins cracked open like the dried mud of the river.

The flies were everywhere, swarming equally upon human and animal.

The camera followed a water truck as it was stopped in the middle of the street by a crowd that attacked it, then attacked each other. There was a blur, as the announcer explained the cameraman was swept into the riot. Only the film survived in its well-shielded camera.

"Jesus," said Mark.

Hideo shrugged.

The government of India had collapsed, said the newscaster. The ancient border dispute with China had erupted again as hundreds of thousands tried crossing over the mountain border, and were stopped.

"It's staggering," said Mark. "You'd think it'd shake us up here, that we'd get something going. There'll be a hundred million dead in a few weeks. A hundred million, and the guy on the *Times* won't even talk to me."

"Big deal, a hundred million. Half the planet's always starved to death anyway. The cyclone in Pakistan, in 1970, half a million dead. The Peking earthquake killed even more. You going to tell me it made one bit of difference in your life?"

Mark was stopped for a moment. "Maybe not, but now it'll happen here."

"Then I'll worry."

"Then it'll be too late."

"Mark, did it ever occur to you that one day, no matter what you do, you're going to die anyway?"

"Sure, but I don't think about it."

"The defense rests. Fatalism is a really worthwhile philosophy when there's nothing else around."

Hideo's wife was bringing out coffee and cake just as Mark was putting on his hat and coat.

"Where you going?" she asked.

"Sorry, Wendy, it's getting late."

"You're getting to be very unsociable lately."

Mark looked at them both. "I'm running out of words."

"V3TAD, this is W2QRV . . . Whiskey Two Quebec Romeo Victor . . . Dr. Singh . . . Dr. Singh, this is Mark Haney in New York . . . V3TAD . . . Victor Three Tango Alpha Delta . . ."

For long hours there was only hissing. Finally Dr. Singh answered, his signal weak and bathed in static, his voice hoarse.

"This is a long way to go for conversation, Mr. Haney."

"There's no one else to talk to."

There was a silence. "Dr. Singh, over."

"I'm here, Mr. Haney . . . I was at a concert. Six hours."

"Six hours? How the hell is there time for a six-hour concert?"

"There's time for nothing else. We could go to a concert, or we could watch each other die."

"You called nature your friend. How do you like your friend now?"

"How much of a friend have *we* been?"

Mark sighed. "All right, wherever the blame lies, we can still do something."

"For example?"

"We don't know yet, but at least keep the channels open so we can work together."

Now it was Dr. Singh who sighed. "Well, Mr. Haney, I suggest for that you send out a CQ and talk to anyone who answers. It's a little late for me."

"Dr. Singh . . ."

"I'll probably be dead the next time you try and reach me."

Mark tried to laugh.

"W2QRV, from V3TAD, out and closing switches permanently."

"Dr. Singh!"

Mark tried a few more times to raise him, then he sent out a call he had last heard from a lonely physician in Africa. "CQ . . . CQ . . . This is W2QRV in

New York . . . Will talk to anyone on this frequency . . . CQ, CQ . . ."

BAFFIN BAY, 75° N. LAT.:

An army of great white ghosts moved in stately formation. Some came crashing together, mountain meeting mountain in great thunderbursts, knocking away huge chunks that tumbled down the sides to fall into the sea.

There, balance altered, the bergs shifted, or even rolled over in lumbering somersaults.

There were thousands of them, birthed by the Humboldt Glacier, in turn fed by the unending Greenland blizzard.

As they continued south, into the Davis Straits, some were snagged in the convolutions of the Greenland shoreline on the one side, or Canada's Baffin Island on the other. They might eventually diminish and die as compressed gases exploded with the melting ice. Or perhaps the wind and current would free them again in time.

Eventually the armada came out of the Straits into the open sea to be caught up in either of two currents. The North Atlantic Current carried some to the east, to brush past the British Isles and Scandinavia. The Gulf Stream carried the others into the body of the Atlantic, as far south as Bermuda, eventually to melt, rejoining the seawater, evaporating to be carried back to the Arctic as water vapor, renewing the cycle. They would not, however, melt all that quickly.

There have been schemes to tow bergs to desert countries ever since there were ships conceivably powerful enough. The slow, careful journey through the Mediterranean to an African port, with six tugboats, would take half a year, but the diamond-hard ice would have scarcely diminished, providing fresh water for a needful desert for another two years.

While a single iceberg in the right place might be quite beneficial, now there were thousands of them in very wrong places.

"My God, where has the water gone?"

Mrs. Bjork watched the cattle moan heartbreakingly as they nibbled at the ever diminishing grain. The irrigation ditches had dropped to trickles, and even now the crops were turning brown and shriveling. When she tried to divert the well water into the ditches, the pipes sputtered with air and mud.

It had all happened so suddenly. The water in the mountains had dried up, and now the groundwater seemed to have just fallen away.

In fact, the waters were being drained away by a thirsty Los Angeles County a full 350 miles south. Its nearby reservoirs were emptied by the continuing drought, and so it reached further and further north until it began drawing the groundwaters beneath the Owens Valley.

Even as the local politicians began frantically printing up circulars for water conservation ("Don't flush . . . Don't run water while shaving . . . Water your fields with washing-machine runoffs . . ."), Los Angelenos went blithely on, washing down their cars, sprinkling their lawns, running water while shaving, no more involved with the growing crisis in the north than they were with the collapse of India.

Danny pointed out the changing patterns of cloud cover in the satellite photo, the advancing ice in one section, the increasing dryness in another, and explained some of the process. Then he stopped.

"Mother, this sort of thing really interest you?"

"Why not?"

"I just thought you liked, well, primitive people, and carvings, and weird music, things like that."

Karen pursed her lips momentarily. "I love you, so I'm interested in what interests you. And of course, besides, it's the most important subject in the world right now."

"It sure is."

"All right, can you figure something for me?"

Danny groaned. "I sure hope so."

"Where will it be warmest?"

"You mean after the ice? I figure the Sahara."

"Oh? That's not very encouraging."

"Yeah, and it'll be even drier than before. Y'see, all the waters'll get drained a lot by the ice."

"All right, what'll the best place be?"

"You mean for us?"

"Just us."

"Well, Mom . . . I mean . . . just us?" He looked at her. "All alone?"

"We don't have much choice, Danny. If there's one Eskimo too many, just one, the whole tribe dies. They know that, and they sacrifice themselves if they have to, for the benefit of the tribe."

"Is . . . is that going to happen to us? Will I . . . will somebody have to die?"

She laughed, and hugged him. "No, Danny, but we would have to do another kind of sacrifice . . . just things."

Danny gulped. "What . . . would I have to give up?"

"Danny, wherever we go, we'll probably have to live simply. You know, not burning up the environment like we do now."

"You mean . . . like primitives?"

"They're very happy people, Danny. If we'd've taken you with us, you'd've seen that."

Danny flinched. "The . . . the instruments . . . my weather station . . . the books and maps . . ."

"Danny, I'll be leaving behind all the things I love, all the artwork . . ."

"But . . . that's different . . . That's just . . . things."

"What are these, then?"

He clutched at the weather map, looking anxiously at the instruments about him. "We'll need the radio, and . . . these things. We've got to *know*. We've got to be smart."

"Danny, if we take the radio, what'll we plug it into?"

"You can always plug it into something. There's electricity all over the world. The plugs're just different."

"Danny . . ."

"Or there's batteries . . . or something with windmills. Or sun power."

"Danny."

"The satellite. The satellite that took this picture, that works on sun power."

"Danny, we're not dealing in fantasies. We're talking about surviving."

"Mom, what'll we . . . do? I mean . . . what'll we *do?*"

"Just live, Danny. And be happy, like the Eskimos."

Danny was rocking back and forth in bed, holding onto his legs.

"Danny, learn to accept, like they do."

"Mom . . . Mom, we're going to save the world. Mark and me, we're going to save the world . . ."

Karen shook her head and grabbed him by the shoulders. "Danny, stop it!"

He shook her away, and buried his head between his legs, cradling himself into a foetal position, shutting her out, shutting the world out, as he went on rocking himself and weeping.

Manujian stared anxiously from the bridge, listening for the slightest change in sound.

"Bad as the Grand Banks," he said to his executive officer. Indeed, like Newfoundland, the fog hung low and strangely cold on these southern waters.

Manujian thought he'd be avoiding troubles on his new tour of duty. After his stint of weather observation, he had put in for command of a buoy tender, one of the dullest possible ships in the Coast Guard. It set a relatively simple course, maintaining, setting, or pulling buoys in Atlantic channels. It seldom ventured far out to sea, and he certainly never had to take it out to observe storms. That made his pregnant wife happier, and he couldn't care if he never met another meteorologist.

At least that *had* been true. Something certainly seemed wrong with the weather, and he could have used an expert opinion. Trouble seemed to be following him.

He turned to his executive officer. "We off-course?"

The X.O. looked down at the gyro compass. "Half a degree. Maybe a mile."

"Feels more like two thousand."

"Yes, sir," agreed the X.O. automatically.

Ever since men first ventured out onto the seas, the fog carried its own peculiar dread. The accustomed loneliness suddenly became desperation, for now they were cut off from humanity by a curtain that hung all about them, just outside reach, holding fast with them as they traveled. Behind it lay any number of terrors, some the products of fearful imaginations, but others only too real that could, and sometimes did, snuff out whole ships and their crews in moments.

With all its far-ranging electronic eyes and ears, the modern ship still sounded its deafeningly loud horn as a warning of its approach, and the sailor on watch still stood nervous, absolutely alone, detached from the world, taking reassurance from the foghorn that at least he and his ship were alive.

Both men jumped at the excited cry from the pilothouse.

"Radar reports a contact, sir! Fifteen hundred yards, at bearing two seven zero!"

That was almost dead ahead. Both men gasped and strained their eyes to see that distance, though they knew visibility barely carried beyond the bridge.

Further word was not long in coming. The radarman's voice showed some measure of disappointment.

"Soft contact, sir. Probably floating jetsam."

The executive officer relaxed. There need be none of the elaborate plottings and procedures to avoid collisions, no testings of the latest sea rulings on right of way.

Manujian did not relax, but grew increasingly uneasy about the strange weather.

He turned on the spotlight, and the fog drank up the beam.

The X.O. said, "You suppose, Captain, that jetsam could be the . . .?"

Manujian shushed him. The situation carried an air of déjà vu. There was something about the pattern of sensations, pieces in a puzzle slowing coming together.

He strained his ears, and then he heard a sound he would not have believed, that of waves breaking as if on a shore. Then, moments later, the cries of birds.

It wasn't possible. It was as if an island had suddenly popped up in the middle of the sea, and Manujian felt the sense of physical shock that comes with total disorientation.

His logic could no longer deny what his senses told him. All of a sudden, he *knew*. All the clues suddenly coalesced into a vivid, and terrifying, realization.

In an instant he was at the engine order telegraph, pulling the handle to stop all engines, while yelling at the top of his lungs to the helmsman.

"Hard right rudder! Hard right rudder!"

". . . what? . . ."

"Son of a bitch! *Hard right rudder, Seaman!*"

The helmsman gulped. "Hard right rudder, sir!"

He spun the wheel with both hands at once, grunting with the effort, even as he wondered if the C.O. had gone crazy.

"Bearing, two eight zero, turning right, sir," he called out.

"Radar, where's that contact?"

"Twelve hundred yards, closing distance, sir."

Manujian wondered about how it would look in the ship's log if he were wrong.

Then he wondered how it would look if he were right.

"Bearing, two nine zero, turning right, sir," called the helmsman.

The whole crew heard the engines quit, felt the sharp turning and came out on deck. The buzz of their consternation reached Manujian on the bridge, and he felt his predicament magnified, as if the world were looking over his shoulder.

"Contact at one thousand yards, closing distance, sir."

He had never felt so powerless. The ship was acting under laws other than his own, making its maximum possible turn, drifting under its own inertia. The slower the speed, the tighter the turning circle, but if he reversed engines to slow it further, the prop would swing her to port, and to certain collision. All he could do was pray.

"Bearing, three zero zero, turning right, sir."

He remembered his tour on an icebreaker, six months of despairing isolation, and the weariness of the constant battering as the ship hammered its way through frozen channels to open them to shipping.

"Contact at five hundred yards, closing distance, sir."

Small wonder that icebreaker duty was the most hated in the Coast Guard. It wore away friendships, exposed raw hatreds, and fistfights broke out over disputes that would have been trivial on some other ship in some other ocean.

"Bearing, three one zero, turning right, sir."

And yet one fear eclipsed all others. That icebreaker had been heavily reinforced with double-thick plating, extra heavy beams, and a specially shaped hull, all to withstand the thickest ice, but even so it was a mere paper boat against the fragments of the glacier in any of its floating forms.

"Contact at three hundred yards, closing distance, sir."

When the fog grew thick, or newfallen snow hid the varying ice floes beneath a common blanket, the crew lived wary hours. Any one of them might be an iceberg.

"Bearing, three two zero, turning right, sir."

Not enough. They had come about a full fifty

degrees, and it was still not enough. A cautious skipper would steer a mile from a berg to be safe, and would still not feel safe.

"Contact at two hundred yards, closing distance, sir."

Any arrogance about modern shipbuilding, ice patrols, or radar would be as misplaced as the vanity that called the *Titanic* unsinkable. The peculiar shapes of icebergs could deflect and confuse radar waves. Far harder than any ship's steel, they usually floated in thick fog such as this, hiding as effectively as any mine, and as treacherous.

"Bearing, three three zero, turning right, sir."

The largest of these would dwarf any ocean liner, but the smaller ones, the so-called growlers and bergy bits, were even more dangerous. Floating low in the water, they might totally escape notice, but the greater mass would be submerged out of sight, with some jagged edge protruding, waiting to cut open a ship's hull as easily as one might filet a fish.

"Bearing, three three zero, turning right, sir!"

"Contact at one hundred yards, closing distance, sir!"

Not enough . . . Not enough . . .

The cry came up from a seaman on the bow. "My God, there it is!"

"Holy shit!"

The crewmen jumped back at the sight.

It was like a specter, half as large as the ship, coming at them through the mist as if in vengeance to strike them down for their sins.

They watched in stunned silence. With engines dead, they could hear every creak and groan in the ship's beams as it strained to execute its maximum possible turn.

"Bearing, three four zero, turning right, sir!"

Manujian's knuckles were almost as white as the ice as he gripped the railing.

"We missed it!" his X.O. called. "Holy Mother of God, we missed it!"

Slowly, ever so slowly, the white form passed

them on the port side, and some men ran with it along the deck to keep it in sight. It had suddenly lost its horror and had become a mere curiosity.

The helmsman was about to ease up on the wheel.

"Keep it hard right!"

"Sir, we . . ."

It was like an explosion. The helmsman was suddenly sent sprawling off his feet, and the wheel spun crazily before Manujian could reach it.

The ship heaved and yawed, and the crew could actually feel steel beams come apart.

The next moment, there was a confusion of shouts, commands, and alarm bells.

Then the confusion subsided as discipline was reasserted. The procedures impressed in endlessly repeated collision drills took effect. Under the direction of the damage controlman, and with each crewman knowing his proper role, the hull was soon braced, and the excess water pumped out.

When the immediate danger passed, Manujian again wondered how it would look in the ship's log. Collisions with other ships were a danger, but not with icebergs two thousand miles off their course.

He remembered how little he once cared if he never met another meteorologist. But that was twenty minutes ago. He'd have some pointed questions now.

WOODS HOLE, MASSACHUSETTS:

The distress call went the usual route through the efficient Coast Guard system. After reassurances that the buoy tender had the situation well in hand, and could make port on its own, a nearby patrol cutter was dispatched to the scene and told to stand by.

Simultaneously, a radio report on the iceberg was sent to the CG Ice Patrol operations office at Woods Hole.

Radioman Pete Stojka whistled as he took the report. He passed it on to the plotting officer, who stood at a large chart with a triangular pin marking each ice-

berg. Each carried its own number, with relevant data
of size and direction of drift. There were over a thousand.

Around the peripheral pins wound a cord indicating the boundaries of the iceberg territory.

Stojka watched silently as the officer unwound the
thread and passed it about this new pin, 31° N. latitude, not far from Bermuda. He felt a sudden fear, a
sense of things closing in. Something was going crazy.
He waited for his officer to say something.

"I need some more pins."

Danny was so adept now at Morse code, that he
could follow the various telegraph communications between the buoy tender, its home base, and the cutter
coming to its rescue. It was like following an exciting
adventure story. He bit his fingernails, giggled, and
finally cheered like a child at a Saturday movie mati-
nee, telling Mark of each new development. Little by
little, step by step under the guidance of Captain Manujian, the situation was being stabilized.

But Mark didn't share Danny's excitement. In
fact, he grew more grave with each new bit of good
news Danny reported.

"Mark, why don't you tell him?"

"You mean tell Manujian that the iceberg was
no freak, and what'll be happening afterward?"

"If anyone'll listen, I'll bet he will."

"He will, and he'll probably believe me."

"So why not tell him?"

"Because we were friends once."

Danny stared. "And now you don't like him anymore?"

"I liked him very much, Danny. We rode out a
few storms together, and you sure get to know who
your friends are."

"Were you in the Coast Guard?"

"Sort of."

"Were you a hero?"

"You want me to tell you what a hero I was, or
do you want the truth?"

Danny hesitated. "The truth."

Mark chuckled. "You're the oldest ten-year-old I know. All right, I was a civilian aboard a Coast Guard cutter, along with a few others from the Weather Service. They called it an ocean station vessel, and part of our job was to observe storms from the inside. We had to ride 'em out, and I guess it got pretty hairy at times."

"I'll bet you were a hero."

Mark smiled. "The hero was the guy who had to handle the ship. That was Manujian."

Danny's eyes shone. "Then you oughta tell him."

"I wouldn't be doing him a favor."

"How do you mean?"

Mark sighed.

"I'll be telling him to throw his rulebook out the window, and giving him nothing to replace it."

Danny was silent.

The radioman was hesitant when Manujian answered him on the intercom. "Uh . . . sir . . . I . . . I've got a call from a man named Mark Haney . . . New York City . . ."

"Oh Jesus! Give him my regards. Tell him I'll call him when I don't have my hands full."

"Sir, he was awfully insistent."

"He was always insistent. Scare him off." He hung up and returned to his task, but in moments the intercom buzzed again.

"Sir . . . uh . . . he didn't scare, and he's jamming the frequency. Maybe it'd be easier . . ."

Manujian sighed. "Put him through."

He greeted Mark warmly. "Haney, you son of a bitch, we've got an emergency going, and if you don't get off this frequency, so help me, I'll find you and put a gun to your goddamn head. Now get off."

Manujian listened a moment.

"That's right, you don't scare easy . . . So what's on your mind that's worth a Federal bust? . . . No, Haney, you *are* crazy, and this proves it, but you're not stupid. So tell me in a hurry."

Mark told him, and suddenly Manujian was no longer in a hurry.

"All right, Mark, you did me a favor. What can I do for you?"

Mark laughed. "You might bring me an ice-breaker."

"An ice . . ." Manujian stopped. He pictured his buoy-tender with its curved, reinforced hull and snubbed bow. He pictured an icebreaker, its curved hull riding atop the ice, its flattened bow crushing down. With the exception of the bow design, they were really quite similar.

"Hold on, Mark." He buzzed below for the damage controlman. "Where's most of that damage?"

"In the bow, sir, just below the waterline. We're getting it welded, but the real work'll have to be done at Curtis Bay."

"Could it be reshaped flat?"

"Like an icebreaker?"

Manujian's breath caught. "Yes."

"Well, sir . . . I guess they'll understand if we ask 'em."

Manujian came back to Mark. "I think we may get you your gift, Haney."

"Okay, now can you get me onboard?"

"A meteorologist? I think you'll be needed."

"I don't think you understand, Larry."

"Then explain."

"This line secure?"

"Secure? Onboard it's secure. Out there, it's an open broadcast."

"That's all right. To anyone out there, we're just two crackpots. Look, I'll be working out a safe haven for some people. Get us there, and you're all welcome to stay."

"You know what you're asking, Mark?"

"There are no rules anymore, Larry."

"Not yet."

"The chain's already breaking down. That's why you haven't heard anything, and you won't. You'll be a ship without orders."

Manujian took a deep, long breath. "I'm promising nothing, Mark."

"Well, at least let's keep in contact."

"Yeah . . ." Manujian's voice trailed off. He had a lot of thinking to do. He worried for his wife and child. Then he worried for his job. Then he worried for his country.

Manujian's radio line was indeed secure. His radioman respected confidentiality, and the transferred call was kept private and intact.

There was, however, another listener on that frequency who had been forgotten, nor did he remind them of his presence. Indeed he was just about to respect that confidentiality and remove himself from the line, but the call had held him intrigued just a few seconds too long, and then he didn't dare cut himself off.

Radioman Pete Stojka at Wood's Hole had just heard a ship's C.O. agree with a professional meteorologist that the world as they knew it was coming to an end.

He felt the room heaving beneath him as if it were a ship in a storm, felt his knees grow weak, his mouth dry, and a nausea in the deep of his stomach.

Stojka took a few deep breaths as he looked across the room.

"Ever see a berg that far south?" he finally asked.

"Can't say that I have," said the plotting officer.

"Something odd's going on, then, don't you think, sir?"

The plotting officer shrugged. "Pretty busy, yeah."

"You never seen it this bad, have you, sir?"

"Not since I've been here, no." He played with the pins. "Pretty bad in '29, they say. Thirteen hundred bergs. Couple of years later, though, hardly any. It comes and goes, Seaman."

"Yes, sir, thank you, sir."

After duty Stojka went out with his mates to a bar and got roaring drunk. He tried to pick up one of the town girls, picked a fight with her boyfriend, and got punched out pretty well for his trouble.

By the next day he had forgotten about the overheard conversation completely.

"WB2XQR . . . This is W2QRV . . ."

As Mark leafed through old issues of the *Journal*, he remembered how the bylines once concerned him more than the subject matter. Now he was desperately interested in anything relevant to the coming calamity, diminishing temperatures, shifting storm tracks, climatic instability.

"Whiskey Two Quebec Romeo Victor . . ."

From there he went to the ham radio register. It seemed a fair number of meteorologists had been tuning to the satellite, and gradually discovered the other bands on their receivers. Eventually they too had become avid hams, and Mark was able to talk to colleagues he would have only caught by chance in the hallways at the yearly conventions.

"Hello, W2QRV, this is WB2XQR, calling and answering . . ."

Introductions and small talk about reception quickly gave way to discussion about survival.

"Yeah, Mr. Haney, I've been aware of it, but I talked to one of our graduates who's in the W.S. down at the Maryland computer. He said there's nothing to it. It's all hysterical rumor."

"You believe him?"

"Well, he's on the inside. He'd know."

"Suppose it's true, and he does know? Think of the implications and then tell me if he'd tell you."

There was a pause.

"All right, let's say I believe you instead of the rest of the world. Now what?"

"We need a base of operations, and other disciplines with whom we can cross-fertilize."

"Any bases in mind?"

"That's one of the things we have to figure out, and I think someone in geography can help out there. Best climate, best land use and resources. And of course it doesn't have to be one base. The important thing is that we're all in touch."

"So we also need a good radio man, and somebody on power sources, which means somebody on fuel production . . . I see what you mean, Mr. Haney. It becomes increasingly complicated."

"Exactly, Professor Kaplan. Which is why we need communication most of all."

"I can't even talk to people down the hall?"

"Where've I heard that before?"

"Terminal jealousy is the occupational hazard."

"We're in for terminal everything if you don't push."

A pause. "I see."

"Look, Professor Kaplan, now we're only a few mavericks, but we have the potential for exponential growth, a world-wide think tank. We'd survive."

A pause. "Then there's hope."

"Damned right."

"Okay. We'll QSO again in forty-eight hours. WB2XQR, out and leaving the air."

"Wilco. W2QRV, out and clear."

Mark's closing words indicated he welcomed calls from anyone who overheard. He didn't have to wait long. An engineer with some experience on solar power called. He asked what was happening with the weather, and if there really was an Ice Age coming.

"The pioneers had it worse in Death Valley," said Peggy Bjork to her mother.

Peggy knew the reality of their situation was far more serious. The pioneers needed only to traverse Death Valley. Now, Death Valley was slowly reaching out to ensnare the Bjorks.

Each day they tuned to the radio to hear another new gloomy report, another 10 percent cut in water rations, another plea for conservation. Until now, neither had been quite aware of how much water they used, ninety-five gallons a day, in drinking, showering, cooking, washing.

But the demands of the farm were far greater. One acre of crops took enough water for three families.

The cattle moaned, pulling up isolated tufts of

what was once range grass, but now shriveled into powder in their mouths. Their skins grew dry as parchment, and began to crack. The cattle were too weak to slap with their tails the flies that were drawn to their open sores.

Peggy brushed away the flies, gave the steers water in a tray from her own rations. She had gone without a bath for a week, but then so did the pioneers, she told herself, and no one ever complained about their body odor.

At last, hearing there was ample water to the south, Mrs. Bjork had the hired hand load up everything in the pickup truck that could hold water, pails, buckets, garbage cans. They drove along Highway 395, paralleling the aqueduct that carried their groundwater all the way to Los Angeles.

After two hundred miles, they had to stop for gas. The storeowner was hosing down his car, and let the water run when he came up to the Bjorks.

Peggy gave him a piece of her mind.

He was quite peeved. "What water shortage? Look, kid, in case you ain't heard, the Earth's three-fourths water."

It was hot, very hot on the roof as he worked. He felt dizzy with the heat, and when he looked up, he saw the sun grow larger and hotter, gradually filling the sky.

He realized it was plummeting down to earth.

He tried to run, but his feet were trapped in the tar. He looked up to see the collision, sun destroying earth in a shattering explosion.

A million lights fell about him, the pieces of the sun glittering in the myriad colors of the spectrum. Gradually they congealed into a new whiteness, a cold whiteness that drained heat instead of emitting it.

It was the coming of the ice, the great glacier rending the city, crushing all civilization beneath a moving mountain, awesome, magnificent, implacable.

Buildings came crashing down about him, mere toothpicks to be swept aside.

He looked at the glacier's face, the icefall, and he saw the gleaming crags, the blinding reflections, the dizzying colors, the face of his death.

He tried to run, but his legs were still stuck. He struggled, but his body was weak. He felt like an old man, a hundred years old. His bones were brittle, his eyes dim, his teeth rotted, and while he lacked even the strength to put his hand to his face, it must have been as lined and furrowed as the ancient Eskimo he had seen in that village.

He called out . . . to Karen . . .

"I'm here, Mark . . . here . . ."

He sprang awake. ". . . What? . . ."

"I'm here, Mark, right beside you."

"Where?" He needed her so very desperately now.

"Here . . ." She kissed him. "Here . . ." She reached for his penis, stroked it till it grew hard. "Here . . ." She guided him in, further and further. "Here . . . Here . . . Here . . . Here . . ."

The dream, the awful whiteness and cold, faded in the warmth and wetness of her being.

There was only the gentle darkness now, soothing, reassuring within her, surrounded by her as he emptied himself into her, at last totally surrendering.

The blackness came up and washed over him, and his existence vanished.

Slowly, he awoke to light. It was morning. He turned to watch her come alive.

"Hello," he said.

"Hello."

She smiled. They kissed, and sighed pleasantly. And now he knew why he stayed with her, because in the awesome emptiness of the world, there was only her, the sun of her face in the dark cold, the touch of her body a mooring in the icy sea.

He thought of the radio. It was only distant voices, non-bodies when hers was here, to be touched and savored. Here was his reason for living, because he was in all senses a man, and those senses lay with a woman.

He saw it in her eyes as she looked at him, and he knew that when his nightmare came true, when the city would be coming down about them, there would always be her, and he would never be alone.

From that beginning, then, from the original man and woman, would come forth civilization anew.

"Mark."

"Mm?"

"How's about the Amazon?"

"The what?"

"The Amazon jungle. The ice'll never hit there, and hardly anybody'll find their way in. I don't know what the tribes are like, but the department's probably got some field work on them. I hear some of them are practically pure Stone Age cultures, and that'd be beautiful for us . . ."

He was alone again.

MAR DE GLACE, HAUTE-SAVOIE, FRANCE:

The European remnants of the last Ice Age were scattered across the tops of the Alps, and among the most beautiful of these was the one called "The Sea of Ice" on the northern slope of Mont Blanc. Mountaineers would start their climb from the town of Chamonix below, while less hardy tourists would admire the beauty from the highest aerial cable cars in the world, twelve thousand feet.

The "Sea" was more properly a river, three miles long, its motion apparently frozen for eternity, though it was actually inching down the mountainside, fed by snows at the crest, and melting just enough at its foot to appear stilled.

Mountaineers, however, were aware of its motion. They would lose climbing gear at one point in the ice, only to recover them next season a few hundred feet further down. Once, some climbers were thought lost forever when they fell into a crevasse near its top. Thirty years later the glacier disgorged their remains at its foot.

For years the glacier had been receding, melting

faster than it formed, and this in turn had adversely affected the mountaineering and tourist trade. Lately, though, the Chamonix townspeople had noticed the new advance of the glacier, so there was considerable optimism for the coming season.

Climbers who reached the mountaintop of the Alps' tallest peak, reported unusually severe storms there, obviously feeding the glacier. Those few climbers who attempted the top were cautioned.

Naturally, the townspeople never made the connection from Mont Blanc to the cold currents that came down thousands of miles from the great Humboldt Glacier in Greenland. The greatest interest was taken of the ice which now dangled awesomely over an escarpment, and the little cracks that were working their way slowly through to the blue seams.

On Greenland's shore, the process would have calved an iceberg. Here, the results were different.

Passengers in the cable car saw it first. It looked like a little puff of smoke, or a skier sending snow flying as he made some sharp turn short of the edge.

Then the puff began to grow like a rose unfolding in a nature movie. Still seemingly small and harmless, it grew faster, gathering rocks and rubble into itself.

The friction of its hundred-mile-per-hour descent, rubbing against the cliff walls, melted huge quantities of ice, saturating the rocks as it crushed them to rubble, all together forming an abrasive kind of mud. The few climbers at this altitude were engulfed before they were aware of the slide and swept into the torrent, changed in an instant to more raw matter.

On it went, gaining speed and mass, a complex of ice, water, mud, gravel and, most destructive of all, air.

A truck roaring down a highway pushes a column of air ahead of itself so that someone down the road is cooled by the breeze. But the wind generated by the avalanche was overwhelming. It came in waves.

First, the wind carried the fiber particles of the rubble, dust and powdered snow that were rammed down mouths, throats, lungs, so that people choked and strangled to death, even before the second wave reached them.

This wave was the massive force of the air itself, unable to find its way around the mile-wide slide, and bunched into an awesome mass, nearly the density of a solid. It leveled houses and humans as if they were paper cutouts.

Then came the body of the avalanche, growing as it took into itself living and non-living matter. Even those houses free of its direct path did not escape its destruction, for the same force that pushed compressed air ahead also pulled air after itself, creating a vacuum that sucked first the windows out of houses, and then the inhabitants.

Dangling in space, the tourists in the cable car could only watch in helpless horror as the slide swept away the cable station then the cables themselves, as if pulling threads from a fabric, bringing down the steel towers. The whole cableway came collapsing, with the car and its inhabitants sent screaming in a two-mile fall.

The pressure wave fell full upon the town of Chamonix in the bowl of the valley, crushing houses and populace beneath an invisible forge press.

Then a remarkable thing happened. The pressure wave provided a cushion for the avalanche, so that at first it swept over the town without touching it, inertia then carrying it a full mile up the opposite cliff, giving time for the air to disperse. Only then, after that reverse avalanche swept away many more climbers, did it settle back to finally bury the town, and the people it had already killed.

When the awesome roar had finished echoing across the valley, it was followed by a deathly quiet, as if nothing had ever disturbed the valley's beauty since Earth's beginning.

"My God, oh my God."

Karen rubbed her hands together nervously as she watched the TV news. She saw the rescuers poking through the rubble with long sticks, probing for bodies or, on some infinitesimal chance, survivors. All the while, they cast nervous glances up toward the mountain, worrying about the chance vibration that might set off a second slide.

It was more a matter of cultural closeness than mathematics. The thousands killed in the Mont Blanc avalanche were a bigger news story than the millions dying in the Indian famine.

"Mark, it's getting closer."

She expected some answer, and turned around to see why there was none. Mark was busy with an excited Danny at the radio.

"Wait until he says 'Out and clear.' That means he'll talk to anyone listening in," said Mark, placing his headset on Danny's ears.

Danny waited, nodding with the conversation he was overhearing, growing more and more nervous.

"He won't listen," said Danny.

"He'll listen."

"My school didn't listen."

"They can't take it all at once. They'll choke on the truth. It's like a thick steak, take it one small piece at a time."

Danny nodded. "He's coming to an end."

Mark gave Danny a wait sign.

"He's saying it, 'Out and clear . . .' "

"Go ahead."

Danny flipped the switch and spoke. "Hello, VE3NLW. This is W2QRV, Whiskey Two Quebec Romeo Victor, calling. Over . . ."

Danny started rocking in his chair with excitement as he heard the answer.

"You're only a three-five here, readable with difficulty. Over . . . Yeah, signals have been deteriorating lately. I've got some answers, you want to hear? Over . . ."

Mark gave Danny a stage whisper. "One piece at a time."

He listened as Danny got involved in energetic but careful discussion, and was startled by Karen's hand on his shoulder.

"Did you hear me? I said, it's coming closer."

"I know. We're trying to establish a radio net. If only the ham register catalogued 'em by profession instead of call letters, we'd have . . ."

"Look," said Karen, a little more loudly, "it's coming closer. We're going to get caught."

"By the time we get things together, get a miniature society functioning, oh yeah, you can bet we'll get caught."

"Jesus, Mark, what are you doing? You're talking about toy radios, and toy weather maps. I'm talking about saving ourselves."

"So'm I, Karen, so'm I."

"So why aren't we on a plane and out of here?"

"You're the anthropologist. You know what's involved in a functioning society."

"A family, an igloo, and a dog sled."

"There's a hell of a lot more. Look out the window. Hell, look at the bookcase."

"Okay, we'll take some books."

"I'm also talking about fighting this thing."

"You're dreaming."

"That's where it always starts, with somebody dreaming. But look what we've got. There are experts in solar technology in the Netherlands, there's oceanography in Japan, agronomy in Venezuela, weather manipulation in Russia, a whole variety of skills, and we can cross-pollinate with this . . ." He nodded toward the receiver.

"With that?"

"You know why your Eskimos are still stuck in the last Ice Age? Lack of communication. We can't find how they survive the ice, they can't find how we do everything else. Somebody invents the wheel in Africa. Somebody in Asia invents gasoline. Somebody in Europe invents the engine. But there's no automobile until they get together. This gets 'em together."

"And what good'll an automobile be in the ice?"

"A snowmobile, then, or a machine to make heat, and another to change the ocean currents, and another to seed the clouds so it snows only where we want it to."

"It's not Buck Rogers time. We're living in the here and now."

"Like your Eskimos, and that's all they'll ever have, the here and now."

"At least they survived in the here and now."

"Not when the glacier hit."

"Our society breaks a lot easier."

"No, we survive and we build, through our technology, our culture, our communications."

"Quite a lot to pack in a valise."

"It'll take a ship."

"Which you've got, of course, one that'll go through the ice."

"Which I will have."

Karen looked at him. "And I'm supposed to believe that?"

"It's here," he said, tapping the radio. "It's all with this."

Karen grimaced in disbelief. An excited Danny poked at Mark.

"Mark, he's listening. VE3NLW, he believes us."

Mark nuzzled Danny's head. "Tell him what we'll be doing, and ask what he can contribute."

"You do it."

Mark picked up the mike, put on the headphones, and in a moment was lost in conversation.

CURTIS BAY, MARYLAND:

Even at this distance, inside the office, the noise was unbearable. Manujian wondered how the construction workers stood the noise of welding and hammering. Perhaps they had grown mercifully deaf.

He watched as they tore away the damaged bow and prepared the new sections, riveting the cross-ribbing, bracing the double-thick steel sheeting in the characteristic flat-bow shape of the icebreaker.

He didn't hear the chief engineer come up behind him.

"Hey, y'know, you don't have to get paranoid about it."

"What're you talking about?"

"This is what I'm talking about," and the engineer unrolled the blueprints across the drafting table. "The boys here think you've gone off the deep end."

"You mean you can't do it? Or is there static upstairs?"

"Look, we'll do it. One thing you learn on the job's how to work regulations. Otherwise we'd need one dock for ships, and another for the paperwork . . ."

"But?"

"But why? I mean, that one berg was a freak. They ain't gonna come chasing after you, y'know."

"What's the matter, it giving you problems?"

"Well, no. It's an easy enough modification, but what's up?"

Manujian studied the chief engineer. "You're not going to believe me. There's an Ice Age coming."

"A what?"

"The Atlantic's going to freeze over, snowstorms will bury half the country, and a glacier's going to flatten New York."

Now the engineer studied Manujian. "I take it Godzilla'll be tilting the North Pole."

"That's the word," said Manujian.

The engineer shrugged in exasperation and shoved a procurement order under Manujian's nose. "All right. Sorry I asked. Just sign where it says."

Twenty miles above, the jet stream weaved about the planet, sweeping up moisture or cold from one place, depositing it in another, its churnings affected by every mountain and lowland, every body of water, every smokestack and automobile, indeed every beat of a bird's wings.

The satellite watched it all with its unchanging calm, snapped and transmitted new pictures. To most watchers below, the pictures proved ever more baffling, the pattern—if there was one—ever more elusive. A weather forecast was a self-contradiction. The freak became the norm.

Some wondered if the laws of physics had been canceled. Others suspected there must be some pattern nonetheless, and trusted the giant computer would make sense of it all. They waited for word, but the government only made further excuses.

And of course a few knew the truth. With each new revelation, each new so-called freakish catastrophe only providing confirmation, they only argued anew over policy. But there was no computer to answer the riddles of society. There were no answers at all.

"There's a nice place," said Peggy, and Mrs. Bjork agreed. She turned the car into the rest area.

"Maybe we could eat here," said Peggy.

"Guess so," said her mother, trying to appear cheerful.

SCENIC VIEW, said the sign, and Mrs. Bjork took the opportunity to look, while Peggy used the rest room.

They were almost two miles up, heading into Kings Canyon National Park, part of the Sierra Nevadas. Mrs. Bjork had looked forward to this little car trip and picnic as a means of forgetting the shocks she had been getting lately, the ever more oppressive water bills, the cattle dying despite their valiant efforts at trucking water.

But now she was reminded of that water shortage all over again. Above her stood the mountains, bare and bald without the snowcaps that were supposed to provide the spring runoff.

But it was when Mrs. Bjork looked back, down into the Owens Valley, that the full impact fell on her. She could see the geometric patterns, like a quilted bedspread, of the farms and ranches below, once shades of muted green but now brown and dry.

There was some haziness to the southeast, which was surprising because of the supposedly dry air. Could it be fog or clouds, signaling the end of the drought? She was afraid it might be a fire.

Hurriedly she put a dime in the pay-telescope.

What she saw was far more horrifying than any mere fire, the same sight that had shocked the African Bambara farmers, that had wiped out their farms, and then their country.

To the southeast lay the Mojave, the central desert of the state, fifteen thousand square miles, quite puny beside the Sahara's vastness of three million square miles, but it was growing, even as Mrs. Bjork watched. At its edge, new earth was turning totally dry, withering to sand that the wind picked up in miniature dust storms. The desert was creeping straight toward her ranch.

Mrs. Bjork felt ill.

Peggy came up behind her. "Something pretty out there?"

The great drought affected a wide crescent from Oregon, down through California and Nevada, all the way into Texas. Within that belt, farmers were facing the coming spring with almost no water for irrigation, losing not only the crops but the plantings as well. The only water available was from a private company at eighteen times the price, a third of the farmer's total income.

The drought took other tolls. All along the great rivers, the Columbia, the Colorado, the Snake, industries had grown up, dependent on them for raw water, hydroelectric power, and waste disposal.

The hydroelectric companies supplied most of the Pacific Northwest's energy needs, and now they began cutting back the supplies to factories, homes, and finally to other power companies. When the Bonneville Power Administration cut its power, it was felt deeply by Pacific Gas and Electric, eight hundred miles to the south.

Like toppling dominoes, the shocks multiplied as they worked their way through the system. The aluminum plants along the Columbia River had to shut down, laying off workers who now could not pay their bills at the town stores, which in turn could not pay their wholesalers and manufacturers—while with the simultaneous scarcities, the prices for commodities multiplied.

Still the drought went on. A fish flapped in death throes in muddy riverbeds, the roots of trees protruded above ground like entrails, and the very air grew parched.

Obeying the immutable physical laws that govern the weather, the warmed dry air rose, and new, cooler air was pulled down from the north to fill the vacuum.

These north winds picked up the grains of newly formed sand and dust. The same dust storms that had devastated Oklahoma in the 1930's now spread through the wide crescent of states, tearing out five full tons of topsoil from every acre, hurling it miles upward, carrying away the richest farmland in the world.

Practically overnight, the deserts crept out of their confines, the Mojave, the Arizona, the Colorado, the Great Salt Lake, snatching new acres, slowly reaching out toward each other.

Los Angelenos who awoke at dawn were amazed to see the sun disappear almost as soon as it came up. The clouds came sweeping over the San Gabriel mountains with a roaring like a giant vacuum cleaner, then it swept down upon them with full force, whipping in through open windows, chimneys, vents, pulling people out of their sleep as they coughed and hacked for breath. They ran to shut windows and turn on air conditioners.

They were totally disoriented. Some vandals had unloosed vacuum-cleaner dustbags over their houses, or the Communists had declared war with some kind of germ bomb. They called the police, or the Fire Department, or their radio stations.

Those out on the freeways heading to early-starting jobs had a better view, and a worse fate. They saw the clouds come down over the city like swarms of locusts, blackening the sky, churning sand and dust through the streets and houses, heading toward the freeways.

Suddenly the clouds were inside the cars, choking drivers and passengers, pitting the windows and blasting the paint down to the raw steel.

All over the city, cars smashed blindly into other cars in pileups of ten, twenty, fifty. Some, caught on overpasses, went through the barriers to go plummeting to the roadways below.

Others who could bring their cars to safe stops before accidents, or before sand caught in the engines, huddled in terror, waiting for a fate they could not understand.

Some people knew what was upon them. A couple named Wilson had lived through it once in Arizona. A number of Oklahoma farmers had migrated here to escape just such devastation. They did not wonder if the world had gone mad. They already knew.

Then as quickly as it had come, it was gone, leaving behind wreckage, some deaths, many injuries, a chilling feeling of vulnerability, and a blanketing of sand that would take weeks to clean out of machinery, closets, beds, carpets, cars, food.

Still, it was over, and the sky was clear. It was a freak, they said, and freaks by their nature only happen once.

In truth, though, the dust had been merely gathered out of sight, twenty thousand feet up, and then carried north along the rivers of air that flow to the Arctic.

Again, dust particles invaded droplets, formed ice crystals, ammunition for a new storm.

The process fed itself, doubling and redoubling, spreading from Greenland to Canada, ever more voracious, gobbling more dust and water, shifting the zones, breaking the bonds that had kept it tied to the great glacier, making ready to carry the Arctic south.

"*Bonjour,* Paul."
"*Bonjour,* Therese, *comment allez-vous?*"

"Tres bien, et vous?"

"Let's speak French. *Radiodiffusion-Television Francaise* presents Lesson Four in our easy conversation course. Today, Paul and Therese discuss the adjective . . ."

Mark flipped the dial.

"The overseas service of the BBC presents *The Light Programme,* honoring first a request from a listener in Brisbane, Australia, who would like to hear 'Journey into Melody' by Robert Farnon . . ."

Mark flipped the dial.

"In the structure of the *raga,* there is first a brief survey in the *auchar,* a solo for the *sitar* without rhythmic pattern, in which the musician explores . . ."

Mark flipped the dial again, to another language lesson on Radio Japan, to a jazz group on Radio Sweden, to a documentary on salmon canneries on Radio Kiev, to opera, folk music, travelogues, news programs with certain news conspicuously missing, to a globe with its head in the sand—or ice.

He turned off the receiver and stared at the telephone. After a while he called the *Times* and asked to speak to the one reporter he knew. A secretary took the call.

"Oh yes. He'll call you when he can."

"He hasn't yet."

"Well, he's been very busy."

"Yeah, I can believe it." He hung up, and turned to see Danny looking at him. "Why aren't you in bed?"

"I wanna practice my code transmission, and I've gotta take my weather observations. Don't they know you're right?"

"It's easier to believe I'm crazy. You gonna go back to bed?"

"Eventually. You know who you oughta talk to?"

"No. When're you going back . . . ?"

"The teachers at the college."

"Ha. You saw what they were like the first time."

"Yeah, but they've already had their first time, so they're already different."

Mark looked at him. "You're supposed to be in bed."

"If I go back to bed, can I come to the meeting?"

"Meeting? You think those idiots'll come to a meeting I call?"

"I'm not supposed to know. I'm only a kid."

"All right, kid, get back to bed. I'll call, and if they come, so can you."

Danny clapped his hands together. "I thought of it."

Mark sighed. Danny could be delightfully child-like at times, and it would be a shame to disillusion him. Mark knew nobody would come, but he picked up the phone anyway, and called Fink first.

Fink looked up from the newspaper with its head-line on the L.A. sandstorm. "So this boy says to his fa-ther. 'Daddy, why'd they put Los Angeles in the middle of a desert?' And the father answers, "Don't bother me, son, or we'll miss the next Hollywood camel.' "

When nobody laughed, he put down his paper and looked hurt. "Well, I thought it was pretty funny."

"Maybe it's just a little too true to be funny," said Mark.

"No such thing. Real trouble is, you've got no sense of humor."

"It's just in shorter supply these days . . ."—he looked about the room—". . . along with everything else."

There were indeed fewer participants at this meet-ing. "History, Archaeology, Geology, and another Meteorology. Just the sciences we need to save the world."

"Cheer up, Mark," said Fink. "At least I'm buy-ing it this time. Now if you had Guzman on your side . . ."

"Speaking of which," said Helen. "Any news, Mark?"

"The cops know one thing. He didn't *want* to be found."

"Ah, a girl in the case."

Fink said, "Mark, if you can find a girl in a case, put me down for several cases."

"I'll see what I can do. What I want to know right now is, do you all believe me?"

The teachers glanced at each other. Hideo smiled slightly. The others shrugged or nodded.

Fink smirked. "We five are going to change the world."

"Six," said Danny. "Seven, counting my mother."

"Oh. Jesus! Okay, my Teddy bear makes eight, and my horsey makes nine. Hey look, Mark, I don't mind you baby-sitting, but can't you keep the kid . . . ?"

"I can speak for myself," said Danny testily. "I just might have something of value to contribute."

Fink sighed. "Sorry. I forgot you're a midget." He turned back to Mark. "Okay, we got a few more people than I thought, but you add up the families, house pets, and even the germs we carry, it's still not enough for a good Saturday night party. So what've we got?"

"I'll tell you what we've got, a smattering of experts linked by radio . . ."

"Like us?" asked Helen, deprecatingly.

"Yeah, we're smattered all right," said Fink. "Smatterest bunch I've ever seen."

"And an icebreaker, or at least something that'll serve for one."

"That sounds pretty weird. What's it do meanwhile, crush ice cubes for drinks?"

"It's a Coast Guard buoy-tender, laid up in port right now, being converted to an icebreaker."

"The Coast Guard? What makes you think we'll be on their shipping orders?"

"We won't be."

"So how're we going to get picked up?"

"I know," said Fink, "we go out there in a rowboat. Helen here pulls the plug, I whip off my shirt and wave it frantically . . . No, strike that. I'll pull the plug, Helen here rips off her shirt . . ."

"The captain's an old friend, and he'll do everything he can."

Ice!

The Archaeology teacher coughed. "Pardon me for talking about the past . . ."

"It's your field."

"This's shortly after Babylon. I carried a rifle in our nation's defense, so I know a little about the military. The dirtiest crime, dirtier than murder, was desertion."

"Who said anything about desertion? I just said he'd be . . ."

"Picking us up, I know. Vice Admirals, Fleet Admirals, Rear Admirals'll all be in line, but he'll be picking *us* up?"

Mark nodded.

"He'll be disobeying orders and deserting his post."

"Disobeying whose orders? Deserting what post? We're talking about the total collapse of society. Maybe he'll have his orders, maybe not. My guess is he's going to be forgotten in the ruckus. They'll be looking for icebreakers, not some pipsqueak buoy-tender."

"Let me get this straight, Mark. You're not telling us to get out now, grab a plane ticket to the equator. Instead, you're telling us, hang around, wait for the ice to hit . . ."

"Not just hang around. No, there's a hell of a lot to be done . . ."

Fink said, "Mark, you're talking to a nice Jewish boy whose parents were in Germany in the 1930's. They didn't wait around when things started closing in. They packed their bags and split, and I'm a very scared chip off that block."

"The difference is, there was still a place to go to. Now it's the whole world coming down. Where does the globe go to when it dies?"

"Uh . . . Philadelphia?"

Helen said, "You're telling us we're doomed, Mark?"

"I'm offering you the one hope. Look, you can take an airplane out now, but where do you go, how do you live? It's not forty pounds of luggage for a European vacation. There won't even be a Europe."

Fink said, "Yes there will. We'll just name it different: the Riviera Icecap, the Eiffel Pancake . . ."

"We're talking about a responsibility to Mankind, to preserve what we can of civilization for the generations that follow. It's not only our best chance at survival, but our one chance to fight back."

"Who, us? When the whole government hasn't?"

"They're locked in, unwieldy. Right now, they're probably running around like chickens without heads."

Said Helen, "Unlike us, efficient, well-oiled machines . . ."

Mark said, "It's not just us in this room. We'll be hooked in on a ham radio network."

"Ham radio? For a Jewish boy?"

"It's all we've got. Without it, we'll be just a bunch of parasites dying when the canned foods give out. But with the radio, we've got our one chance, our cell hooked into other cells around the globe, cross-fertilizing ideas and actions. That way we keep civilization alive."

They all looked at each other.

"Hey look, Mark, I'd just like to come out alive. I don't need this white man's burden bullshit."

"It's the only way you'll come out alive, that's what I'm trying to tell you. We'll need a whole Ice Age technology, even to grow things. Government won't be doing it for us. They never have before, and there's no sign they're doing it now. They're looking out for their own necks. But we here . . ."

"Yeah, Mark, we charitable, loving, selfless colleagues, who've never known a moment's jealousy . . ."

"Whatever we were, when you see what the alternative is . . . well, we'll do it."

Hideo had been quiet up to this point. Now he spoke up. "Mark . . ."

"Yeah."

"You're making it so complicated . . . and it's simple, really."

All eyes turned to him, as his easy tone seemed to say he had found the secret. They waited for more, and continued to wait.

"No hurry. Take your time."

"There is no hurry. While you were scurrying

around, making all those phone calls, stopping people on street corners, kicking up dust, what do you suppose the Eskimos were doing?"

"Dying, probably."

"And what do you suppose, with all that energy, the world'll be doing when the ice hits?"

"Getting killed, killing each other, God knows."

Hideo nodded. "Why'd you go into meteorology, Mark?"

"Oh, for God's sake . . ."

"I mean it."

"Because nature was a mystery, and it looked like fun trying to find the answers."

"Same for me. Well, you got your answers?"

"You kidding? I didn't get much of anything."

"Except fun."

Mark shrugged.

"C'mon. Some?"

Mark half-nodded. "So what're you getting at?"

"It's the game. You got more going out than you had going in, so be grateful. So've I, and so've we all here. We all came out ahead."

"So?"

"So that's it. It's been fun, but the game's over, and that was always part of the rules."

"Are you telling us we're just supposed to lay down and die?"

"Everybody dies."

"The whole human race?"

When Hideo finally spoke, he seemed more remote than ever.

"Y'know, we go digging through the rocks, and we find thousands upon thousands of species, all extinct. Not just dinosaurs and dodos, but little apes, great apes, early Man, late Man, and now final Man. We had quite a few Ice Ages, you know. And I don't doubt whoever, whatever was around was thinking, 'Wow, the world ends with us . . .' Well, now it's down to us. Somebody, something'll come after . . ."

"You're talking like Karen talked. Even she changed her mind . . ."

Hideo shrugged. "We've all got our own paths to Nirvana, or Philadelphia, or whatever you call it."

"Oh Jesus . . ."

"Cheer up, Mark," boomed Fink. "We've still got the midget here on our side. He'll save the world all by himself if he has to."

"If I have to," said Danny.

The journalist had taken a liking to the task. The last editorial, he felt, had been stiff, even pompous, but as he gained confidence he relaxed in the writing, and even let his tongue glide slowly to his cheek:

"Six months ago, some of you may recall, at the time of the autumnal equinox, we wrote about the coming of fall and winter. We hadn't anticipated one as bad as we had, but at least it did come on schedule. Now, six months later, it is a pleasure to report that the sun has again crossed the Celestial Equator, this time on its return. We never thought it would be here, perhaps, but spring has indeed arrived and is keeping to schedule, we are glad to report.

"At the moment, day and night are equal, but that will change, is even changing as you read this. Now the days will grow longer, the nights shorter. For those of you who managed to stick it out and who thought, through our worst blizzard, that Nature had deserted you, be comforted. She may be harsh, but she obeys her own laws. Spring is here."

The journalist was not quite right. The drama of the heavens indeed played itself out as usual. The sun had indeed begun its climb northward from the equator and would soon begin warming the northern hemisphere again, but other participants in the drama had more important roles now. The jet stream, the shifting currents, the growing ice fields, the dust storms had taken over.

Just as the autumnal monsoon had not come to India, North America would not see spring. In fact, the seasons as the world had defined them were to be no more.

The checkout girl stared at the shopping carts Mark and Karen had filled.

"Wow, what're you, opening your own store?"

Mark looked at the girl. She was probably just out of high school, living with her parents, possibly saving up for college, and most likely to go to a tuition-free school, the very college at which Mark taught. Soon she would be dead, along with her family, her boyfriend, her graduating class.

"No, just a big family," said Mark finally. He filled out a check for the amount, knowing they would never collect on it. He even felt guilty.

Next he called the offices of the Morton Street pier and asked to rent a large block of space. His final task was to purchase a snowmobile. It was the last one, the floor demonstrator.

"You going to drive it home?" smiled the clerk.

"There's going to be lots of snow here soon enough."

"Don't blame you for thinking that, after the winter we had. Actually, you're pretty smart, sir. You get it cheaper now and store it. I'll bet you'll wait for winter to buy your air conditioner."

"Yeah," said Mark, "you got me dead to rights."

The We Came Through Club held its party around an outdoor pool, to a rock band playing full-blast. Since the entire living population of the Northeast was eligible, exclusivity could not have been the club's primary attraction. And it wasn't.

"Hi. Well, what's your story?" yelled one young man above the noise.

"About what?"

"The blizzard."

"Oh yeah . . . uh . . . Me and a friend . . ." The girl stopped. "We kept each other warm."

She laughed, and the man smiled and edged closer. "Uh-huh. Well, you might want some more warming."

"What makes you think so?"

"Well, you can never tell when it'll get cold again."

"Now that you mention it . . ." She started to shiver. There was a breeze coming up. "I think I better . . ."

"Hey, don't go. I'll lend you my jacket."

The breeze had now become a wind, and the others at the poolside were setting down their drinks, putting on jackets, heading inside.

The sky darkened appreciably, and now some snowflakes drifted down, melting as they touched the ground.

"Oh no," he said, as the flakes fell more thickly and began sticking. ". . . not again . . ."

People sensed immediately this snowstorm would be different. It was not the blustery, raging storm of the winter. This was the spring snow, slow and gentle, quiet, almost comfortable, like the slow drift into death.

The air was clear, and the city seemed to grow suddenly quiet, as if its inhabitants by the millions had stopped what they were doing and looked up to the sky to await the Second Coming.

"Is . . . that it?" asked Karen as she stared from the window.

Mark stopped his packing and followed her gaze. "That's it. Look familiar?"

"Like . . . like Greenland."

"Then it should make you feel comfortable."

She shook her head. "That old story where the parents wish for their dead son to come back, and he comes back a living corpse . . ." She stuck her fingers against the window pane. "The cold comes straight through. Not like igloos . . ."

She turned around to watch Mark, then said, "Let's drop this and get on a plane before it's too late."

"It is too late. Look, we're set up to ride it out. Take it easy."

"We'll be submerged. Let's forget the stuff and get out now."

"We couldn't anyway. You remember how the city gets jammed up. There's going to be hysteria out there. Wait till it dies."

"Which, the hysteria or the city?"

"C'mon, Karen, keep your head. The city'll be overloading all its circuits . . . We'll just have to wait till the fuse blows."

"And how'll we know?"

"The receiver."

They both looked to the radio to see Danny listening with his headphones on.

"Gee, it's something. Wanna hear?" He switched it to the speaker.

On the Citizen's Band, one channel after another began filling with the aggravations of motorists caught in traffic jams and accidents, truckers unable to deliver loads, and threats as callers began interfering with each other and refused to give way.

It became a cacophony, and Karen held her ears. "When does it stop?"

"It will," said Mark grimly. "It will."

In the Bronx Zoo, the moose snorted in relief, trampled down the snow in its wide yard, and felt very much at home.

The otter pawed and brushed at the snow, gradually burrowing a network of tunnels, and then punched little vertical holes to the surface for air and light.

The deer pawed away the snow as it fell, reaching the grass beneath, and nibbled comfortably.

In the great bird cage, the eagle huddled in a corner, flapped its oily wings to brush off the snow, and drew its neck down as far as it could beneath its wings.

In the lion house, the great cats roared in anger and resentment as the keeper failed to show at the appointed time.

An increasingly nervous plotting officer handed Seaman Pete Stojka the new data. Stojka gulped, opened the key, and sent out the first of the two daily ice bulletins:

". . . Southernmost bergs estimated at 46°10′ N., 51°05′ W . . ."

At sea, a hundred ships received the news and adjusted their courses in a southward arc. They would be arriving rather late.

Rivers throughout the Northeast began freezing. On the Ohio, the ice halted shipments of coal and oil to the electric generators. On the Susquehanna, the ice blocked intakes to cooling systems, overheating the machinery. On the Niagara, the cataracts slowed and grew sluggish, and the water-powered turbines began winding down like an old phonograph.

All through the Northeast, lights flickered and grew dim. Exasperated and frightened customers went about their houses, turning on one lamp after another to compensate. Then they plugged in their electric heaters as their radiators grew cold, multiplying the loads on the increasingly strained lines.

Radio and television stations switched to their emergency power systems to broadcast reassurances, urgings for conservation, for avoidance of panic, for pleas to stay home.

There were hints on keeping batteries fresh, on conserving body heat, warnings to keep dry as well as warm, to avoid liquor: A single candle in an enclosed space can provide enough warmth to stay alive. Several layers of light clothing provide better warmth than one heavy coat.

Above all, people were warned to stay calm, avoid listening to or spreading wild rumors, call in neighbors to hear these news broadcasts.

Indeed, those with battery-powered radios and TV's were calmed by the sights and sounds of familiar voices whose very associations were of authority and compassion. They were believed when they said the emergency was serious, but would pass.

Then the mayor came on with his own assessment

of the situation, especially with regard to the panic-buying at the supermarkets.

"There is no cause for concern," he said, avoiding words such as "grave" or "crisis," which might provoke panic. "The greatest food distribution and production machine in the world is still doing its job. Spot shortages may mean a minor inconvenience for a few hours, but the city's snow-removal and road-salting machines are on the job, and deliveries are being made. The National Guard has been mobilized, and is aiding in the task . . ."

No mention was made of how the Guardsmen were to get to their posts, but people were by and large calmed by the reassurances, and the panic-buying leveled off for the time being.

LAKE OROVILLE, CALIFORNIA:

Lake Oroville lay one hundred fifty miles north-east of San Francisco, the heart of California's water supply. It had so diminished during the drought that much of the lake bottom lay exposed for the first time.

The lake had fed a number of reservoirs about the San Joaquin valley, their names redolent of the state's frontier heritage, Sly Creek, Lost Creek, Camp Far West, Little Grass Valley. All of them were drastically depleted.

Now a new danger threatened the remaining supply. As the water levels dropped, San Francisco Bay began encroaching, creeping upstream mile after mile. Visitors along the riverbank could see the strange progression, the salty, brackish, oily waters of the port city advancing up the Feather and Yuba rivers to the lake, there in turn to poison the myriad reservoirs.

There would be no water for people, industries, farms—or for fires.

The forests and parks were as dry as tinder. The sparks from one fire flew to set off others, and they in turn yet others, working their way down the state, from Trinity Forest to Shasta to Lassen to Plumas to Eldorado, a great green belt extending down into Baja

California, and in various leaps and jumps through the Southwest.

The air above Los Angeles was saturated now with smoke and sand, so that people choked and wheezed and ran to faucets that sputtered more air than water.

There was a new phenomenon. The displaced people from the north, the farmers and ranchers, arrived in town with their trucks and vans, looking for water, food, and jobs. There was precious little of any, and the streets and beaches were crowded with dazed people. They were unused to being refugees.

Mrs. Bjork bought new roadmaps, counted the gallons remaining in her tank, and watched the meager water sputtering from the faucet.

"How'd your pioneers handle this?" she asked her daughter.

"They just kept right on, till they found what they were looking for."

Mrs. Bjork studied the map. San Diego was a hundred and twenty miles to the south, and the border was shortly beyond. She wondered what Mexico might be like.

A dazed Seaman Stojka tapped out the new data.

"Present southernmost bergs estimated at 33°10′ N., 61°19′ W . . ." It was practically on a line with his home town of Savannah, Georgia. He turned back to his plotting officer, hoping for reassurance.

"It's never been this bad . . ."

The plotting officer bit his lip. "No, never has."

"What's happening, sir?"

"I . . . don't know. Just follow the orders as we get 'em."

Pete Stojka kept the receiver open and waiting. He had never been so hopeful that there would be orders.

MID-ATLANTIC: 33°10′ N., 61°17′ W.

"My God."

The radioman had just buzzed Captain Dlugatch

with the new berg locations. He looked out from the bridge and could see, just at the horizon, the top of what must be a massive berg, right where the dispatch indicated, and he was headed in a straight-line collision course.

He looked behind him to the other ships of the convoy. They had already made one cautious turn to a new southern circle route, and that had surely been a hazardous maneuver. This would be far worse.

Freighters had taken to traveling in packs, huddling together against the ocean's perils much as they did in World War II, but this provided perils of its own.

Dlugatch was thinking of his own ship now. He sounded the alarm, and ordered a 90° turn in as tight a space as possible. There was no time to waste, not when the ship would take miles to complete its turn. He reasoned the others had received the same data, and would take the same action.

But they did not do so as rapidly, and their turning circles were even wider. It was like a pileup on a highway as the second ship piled into Dlugatch's freighter, cleaving it directly amidships, and getting thrown askew itself.

The chain reaction grew as ships plowed into each other, steel splintering steel with roars that drowned out the screams of the men as they were thrown into the icy waters. Their clothes were soon soaked through, and the water drained heat from their bodies many times faster than air. They were all dead within six minutes.

The old saying went, "Ain't nothing between Ohio and the North Pole but a barbed-wire fence." Indeed, across America there was not one east-west mountain range to protect it from the Arctic winds that now swept down a virtually open country, burying cars, swamping trains, crushing farmhouses. Rescue equipment, rotary plows and bulldozers, were themselves pinioned. Power and phone lines snapped under the weight of their frost sheathings.

Citrus and deciduous crops needed only to be

touched with frost to wither and die. Wheat, tea, rye, corn, oats, rice, millet, cane sugar, beet sugar, soybeans, cotton, hemp, species and sub-species in endless variety, all dependent on the intricate balance between soil and water and air, all shriveled as the balance came undone. Sub-surface crops like carrots and potatoes were safely insulated, but the ground was frozen solid, and they could only be dug out with pneumatic drills.

Fish in lakes and streams were soon wedged between growing banks of ice, fluttering in ever tighter space until they died.

Birds foraged endlessly until they felt the warmth coming through windows. They beat their wings frantically against the glass, terrifying the inhabitants. After a while, the people would open their doors cautiously, and find piles of dead and frozen birds. Those who could suppress their revulsion would have food a while longer.

Cattle would only eat grain in immediate reach, and ignored the food drops made by courageous pilots. Instead, they would merely turn their backs to the wind, their fattened carcasses protecting them for a while, but about the unpadded areas, the knee-joints and hooves, they were vulnerable. These were soon too raw and frostbitten for them to move even the few feet to some meager shelter, but they were also too afraid to simply lie down in the insulating blanket of the snow itself, nor would they drink from it. Their running noses froze into bleeding icicles, and so they stood, bearing their pain and thirst until they dropped and died.

Pigs are the most intelligent of barnyard animals. They clustered together as close as they could, gathering their body heat, even mounting each other for the greatest area of contact. It delayed their deaths as long as several days.

The horses struggled, jumping up and over the snow, only to have their narrow hooves sink right through again. Over and over they jumped, fighting fruitlessly to stay above until they tired. Gradually, their straight legs drew closer, digging out small spaces, until their torsos formed arcs or bows, until they could no longer hold their balance, and their stiff carcasses fell sideways into the drifts.

The voice was absolutely cheery. "You're coming in fine business here in Miami, four-eight reception, which is pretty good, all things considered. Weather's cool, but definitely not cold. The beautiful birds aren't wearing their bikinis, which is a shame, but count your blessings. We're sitting things out in high style here. Over."

Mark glanced out the window, and shook his head. "Unbelievable, Pat, unbelievable. Guess you know the messy details up here."

"Yeah, and it's unbelievable for us, too. I don't know about all those communication foulups. Somebody's sure getting the news. We got people pouring in here by car, bicycle, motorcycle, rollerskates, rickshaw, you name it. Too bad I'm not in the hotel business. They're the ones making a killing here, and they're starting to stack 'em three high in the lobbies."

"Not surprised. Whoever can get out is getting out, and it won't get any better. Don't worry about the hotel owners. They'll soon have too much of a good thing."

Professor Patrick Keegan paused a moment before answering, and his easy joviality quieted a bit. "Look, Mark, if you can make it out, you're welcome down here. We'll put you and your family somewheres. The house has a back end we can clear out, and the college can sure use any guy who was bright enough to've seen this coming."

"You make it tempting, Pat, but I'd better pass."

"What the hell for? You missed springtime up there, maybe, but it's fine down here."

"It's the summer that worries me."

"Comes June 21, in case you haven't heard."

"Beg to differ, Pat. We didn't get spring, and you won't get summer."

"So? Still the better deal down here."

"Not by much. If there's no summer, what do you grow?"

There was a silence for some moments, and Mark added, "Over, Pat."

"Yeah, Mark, I heard you. Well, look, it's outside my department, but we have an Agronomy Department here with some smart guys. Give 'em time, and they'll work up some food grains that won't need summer. And you guys must have some seeds of something up there to get us started, winter wheat or whatever they call it."

"Outside my department too, but I imagine all that stuff's been destroyed. I don't think it's going to work anyway. Miami is land's end, and the people pouring in'll just pile up there. Maybe they'll get boats out, maybe not, but with no food coming out of the ground it sounds like a no-win situation. Let me offer you a counter-proposal. You come in with us. An oceanographer'll fit in fine with our think-tank."

Pat Keegan swallowed before answering. "I think your think-tank's got bubbles, Haney. We're offering you joy and comfort, and you're offering us a one-way ticket on a tramp *Titanic*."

Mark paused, and finally said, "Okay, Pat, maybe you're right. Give my regards to the Miami birds, and stay in touch."

"Wilco, Mark."

Mark gave the customary closing, switched off, and turned to Karen. "Unbelievable," he said.

At the other end, Professor Keegan turned to his wife. "Unbelievable," he said.

The poodle had always been pampered. For all of her life, the highest grades of meat had been served at precise times. Her bed was an ornate basket with satin cushions. Barbering was attended to by professionals, her nails clipped, her fur shaved neatly to the skin leaving tufts in attractive patterns. She was walked regularly, either by servants or professional dog-walkers, held gingerly on a leash attached to a rhinestone-studded collar.

The rhinestones mattered less to her than the meals, of course, but now, for reasons she couldn't comprehend but somehow felt to be her own fault, all that was gone.

Instead, she was on the street by herself, in the middle of snow drifts, and hunger seemed to bore through her insides. Worse was the cold. Those bare parts of her skin stung with each snowflake.

Hunger, cold, and abandonment were new and terrifying. She gave three yelps, in the past the signal that would bring owner or servant running with a round of pampering and sweet and soothing words. But no one answered.

There was neither home, nor warmth, nor bed, nor food. There was only the whiteness and the cold.

Some dim survival instinct now tugged at her, a meager remnant of the wolf supposedly bred out completely. She pawed at the snow as her ancestors had done, searching for some kind of food beneath, but her clipped nails left her only the softened frostbitten flesh of her toes. Nor could she even know for what to hunt.

Her heart was racing now, adding to her terror. The best she could do, she felt, was to stand and yelp. They would surely come soon. She had been merely temporarily overlooked.

She barked again, and waited, while the snowflakes began covering her feet.

The Great Lakes-St. Lawrence Seaway System was a network of what had once been 95,000 square miles of waterway. Eight states bordered the lakes, and another adjacent eleven were equally dependent on that ship traffic. Now those lakes began freezing over, trapping barges carrying iron ore, coal, limestone, gypsum, one-fourth of the nation's cargo.

In his radio room, Pete Stojka was handed new orders to transmit. Every listed and known icebreaker in the Coast Guard fleet was ordered to proceed to Cabot Strait, through the Gulf of St. Lawrence and the St. Lawrence Seaway, to enter the Great Lakes and clear new passageways.

Communication was getting increasingly tangled, but despite the static and crosstalk, Lieutenant Commander Manujian heard the orders come through. There was no mention of the Briarwood, there being little need to tend to buoys when the transatlantic routes were being shifted almost daily by far huger markers.

In light of the grave and volatile nature of the current emergency, all other ships were to engage in search and rescue as needed, and at the C.O.'s discretion.

"At my discretion . . ."

He took a deep breath, signed the orders, had them entered into the log with his new course setting, toward New York City. Nobody questioned him. They saw he had a lot on his mind, which was not surprising.

The dog had waited for days in the empty house. At times he would howl, other times chew at the rug or furniture in loneliness, and to punish the master through his possessions for this desertion. He was large, over two feet high at the shoulder, powerfully built, thick gray and white fur. One could surely still see the wolf within the dog.

He carried his head high, and his slightly domed skull spoke of a developed brain beneath, an uncommon craftiness which now told the dog the master would not ever come back.

Through the bottom of the door he could sniff the strange scent. It evoked a memory he could not immediately place, but he associated it with something deeply pleasurable.

Looking for an exit, he tried all the doors and windows, but their operation baffled him. At last he descended to the basement, dark with its window blocked. Blindly, he groped at the spring-lock and attached pull-chain of the window.

After long minutes of manipulation, of frustrated chewing and pulling until the chain began cutting into his paws and mouth, he suddenly hit on the right combination of force and angle, and the window fell inward, throwing him back to the basement floor amid a shower of snow.

He was stunned for some moments, but as he rolled about to right himself, he caught at the soft substance. He knew immediately he could slake his thirst with it, and licked it ravenously.

Then he climbed back up to the window, and dug vigorously at the packed snow with his strong thick paws, panting desperately until he suddenly broke through into daylight, into sharp, stinging cold air.

He howled with delight, rolled and tumbled in the soft blanket, kicked his heels in the air while he twisted his spine back and forth as if to shake off the years of civilizing. This would have brought him a sharp slap from his master, but there was no one now to do so.

He barked as loud as he dared, then louder, and louder yet.

He carried two coats of fur, a dense, soft undercoat, and a long, straight, coarse top coat. These had long plagued him in the hot New York summers, itching unbearably, but now the snow seemed like gentle, cooling eiderdown against his body.

Here, he knew, was his home.

The master, the disciplines, the civilizing, all faded away as he padded through the snow. On occasion he tossed his head high for his tongue to catch at the falling flakes.

He dug into the drifts and soon turned up mounds of garbage, kept from rotting by the cold, and satisfied his hunger with these. Then, without fear, he turned north, where he sensed lay his ancestral home. His dark almond eyes sparkled with the deliciousness of this white world, anticipating new challenge, new adventure, untethered by any leash or restraint.

The sound of crashing glass broke the silence first, followed by a chorus of gleeful yells.

Snow poured into the supermarket, and the people followed, some sliding down the drift as if children on a slide-upon. Then, once inside, they went wild, indulging fancies long held in check by locks, by police, by simple deprivation. Now was their chance, when the rest of the city was as hungry as they had always been, when the police and even militia were paralyzed, and all their desires were within easy grasp.

They piled up foods, the exotic as well as familiar, the caviar and pâté that they had never tasted (and would soon spit out, wondering what the hell rich people saw in it), the meat they so desperately needed and was nicely preserved in the cold, and certainly the liquor.

Then someone discovered charcoal and firestarter. Soon a bonfire roared in the aisle. They gathered around, got drunk, made love. There were some jealous fights, but there was enough of everything for everybody.

Next door was an appliance store, and of course they broke into that next, again carting away all they never had, always just out of reach behind that glass.

They didn't think, or didn't realize, or didn't care that there was no electricity to operate the TV's and stereos. Craftier looters carried off battery-run CB radios and walkie-talkies.

For all, though, the law would never come. With luck, it would never come again.

The patients staggered, stumbled, were dragged or carried, and sometimes were miraculously found by attendants ready to collapse themselves.

Frostbite was, of course, the most common, but most had passed beyond first- and second-degree, with blisters and peeling, to third-degree, with hands and feet swollen with fluids and deep tissue destroyed. The patients needed antibiotics and antitetanus shots to ward off infection, anticoagulants to prevent clots in the blood vessels, and surgery to remove dead tissue or even whole limbs before gangrene spread.

There were also heart attacks from over-exertion against the snow; hypothermia, in which body temperature falls below normal, slowing all the body functions; fractures from slips and falls, sometimes complicated by suffocation if they had remained unconscious or immobile for any length of time; and finally burn cases from the fires that now began breaking out.

But medicines could not be brought in, nor ambulances go out. The medical staffs that were stranded grew weary with the endless hours, their vision blurred, their senses dulled, their thought processes confused.

There was one saving grace. For all the breakdowns of power, refrigeration, sanitation, there were none of the epidemics that would have devastated the community in moderate weather. Dysentery, cholera, diphtheria, and the like never materialized. The cold kept water, food, even sewage and garbage, all sterile. The community, for all the deaths, was disease-free, the healthiest climate in the world.

The man had learned his lesson from the last blizzard. He now knew, for example, to leave the window open a bit to let foul air escape, especially the poisonous carbon monoxide that could build up inside the car. He also knew to run the engine only occasionally to save gas.

Most of all, he had installed a CB radio, a marvelous instrument not only to while away the loneliness, but now to tell others of his emergency.

For a good while, all the channels were crowded with pleas for help and the confusions of catastrophe. Still, he had made contact. Someone had answered, asked his location, and assured him they would soon be there to help.

At last he saw them, a group of youths crawling through the snow. They were not quite what he expected, but he figured they were volunteer rescuers. As they came closer, he felt an unease. They seemed in need of rescue themselves.

He opened the window to greet them, and then he saw the guns.

"Okay, motherfucker, out!"

He gasped. "I warn you, the cops're coming. I sent in a call."

"Yeah," said the youth, holding up his own mobile CB, "we answered it."

The next moment was a blur, and he only saw the handle of the gun come down toward him.

When he awoke, his head hurt. When he put his hand to it, it came back bloody. His coat was gone, and everything of value stripped from the car, including the CB radio. He felt the blood grow cold in his hand, and then saw it crystallize. The man knew he was going to die.

As the wetness penetrated his clothes and sapped the heat from his body, he shivered. This was the body's attempt to keep warm by motion.

So-called goose bumps formed next, in part a vestigial reaction of that ancient time when Man was a fur-bearer, and this would have fluffed out his coat for insulation. Lacking that, however, the reaction at least expanded the surface area of his skin so that it could take maximum advantage of whatever little warmth existed.

As the cold penetrated further, the body mobilized to preserve the heat in the vital central organs, necessarily shutting down blood flow to the extremities.

The fingers and toes went numb first, for which the man was grateful as he felt the pain lessening. In fact, the frost was now destroying layer after layer of skin. The slightest touch, and the skin would crumble and fall away.

The body fluids that had been held in balance by intricate mechanisms now went badly awry. Fluids rushed in to fill those crevices in the skin, and his feet and hands grew swollen.

The frost now sought to enter the body by the man's mouth. He had some cavities in his teeth, with metal fillings that contracted in the cold and fell out, leaving exposed nerves and unbearable pain.

The steaming breath was moisture leaving the body that would never be replaced, but the cold was even sucking moisture out from the eyeballs.

Soon, however, the body visited a mercy upon him. As the blood grew colder and congealed, the circulation to the brain slowed. The state of shock came as a pleasant dreaminess. He even hallucinated, and thought he saw his child right beside him, asking him to please get up because he had promised to take the boy to the museum to see the dinosaurs.

They were standing before the great creatures, and the man thought it was damned hot. Didn't they know when to turn off the radiators?

The child was crying for some mysterious reason, because the dinosaur died, as if he'd rather they stayed alive. The man thought he argued his son out of that one, but then the boy asked unexpectedly, "Dad, are *we* gonna die?"

It was a hell of a question to be asking, and for moments the man didn't know what to say. Do you tell your son about death or not? Either way you've got troubles.

"Nobody's gonna die," the man said finally. "Not like them, anyway."

Then the vision faded and a gentle black ocean seemed to buoy the man up. He relaxed and submitted.

The heart struggled a few last beats with the thickened blood, then stopped.

The snow soon covered him.

"This is the news . . ."

He was tired and haggard, seemingly having aged years in just these few days. His suit was badly rumpled, his face unshaven, combining to give him a shocking hobo appearance. The reassurances that had always carried weight now seemed hollow, and as weak as the TV image itself.

Lest the nation think that it alone was affected, the news, insofar as it could be received, told of other global crises. The ancient border dispute between India and China, exacerbated by the Indian refugees swarming across the border, was rapidly deteriorating into a full war. The commentator noted drily that since both nations had diverted their resources from food production to atomic weapons, the pattern of events had pretty well been decided quite a while ago.

There were, however, other crises, ancient disputes fanned to full flame by the climate crisis. Israel was rumored planning raids into Saudi Arabian oil fields after their Iranian source had been cut off. Several black African states had made crossings into white South Africa, practically pursued by a growing Sahara desert. Russian refugees had come down through Hungary, and were being stopped at the Yugoslav border. Troops of all three countries were being rushed to the scene. And on and on.

Even as he spoke, frost outside was building on the steel latticework of the transmitter, inch by inch until steel beams began bending under the awesome weight.

On the screen, his image grew ever more gray and pallid. Dancing grains of interference seemed to clump themselves together and grow larger. Simultaneously, the background noise grew more noticeable, and viewers across the country saw the commentator gradually disappear behind a snowstorm of his own.

Our own country, he went on to say, had been entering into thoroughly peaceful negotiations with Mexico and Central American countries to accept some small measure of immigration from displaced Americans. No real trouble need be expected from our friendly neighbors. Other information would be forthcoming.

Outside, the transmitting tower finally sagged under the weight of the frost. The commentator's image was snuffed out like a candle.

Suddenly, each home knew nothing beyond its walls. Inside, families huddled close for warmth and courage as they watched their stockpiles diminish. Soon, even the ties to immediate neighbors would vanish in mutual suspicion.

In some homes, however, there were still tielines to the twentieth century. Those radio hams with battery power and mobile units could still communicate, could even work themselves into their own network. These remained feeble sparks in the growing darkness.

Usually, at times of great catastrophe, they transmitted news, distinguished fact from rumor, allocated emergency services and supplies, minimized panic until the emergency eased as the intact society outside re-established full access.

But this time there was no outside.

"Mayday! . . . Mayday! . . . Mayday! . . . This is K2XAN with distress traffic for south Manhattan . . . I have emergency traffic for south Manhattan . . . Stations in or near south Manhattan, please respond . . ."

Mark had kept the radio for last, packing away everything else of value, food, clothes, books, notes, and necessary records into the snowmobile trailer. He had intended to communicate instructions between the buoy-tender and his own group, and the rest of the world was pretty much forgotten. Now, however, it intruded, blaring in on the open frequency.

"Mayday! . . . Mayday! . . . Mayday! . . ." The caller repeated his call sign and message, this time more desperately.

Mark stiffened, and hesitated.

"Stations in or near south Manhattan, please go ahead . . . Please go ahead . . . Mayday! . . . Mayday! . . ."

Mark was about to reach for the switch when Karen interrupted. "It's not your business."

"Karen, for God's sake, somebody needs help."

"Everybody needs help."

"I saved one man from under that marquee . . ."

"Fine. He's dead now anyway."

The call continued. "I have *emergency* traffic for south Manhattan! Stations in or near south Manhattan, please go ahead. Please go ahead! . . ."

Mark turned the switch. "K2XAN, this is W2QRV . . . Whiskey Two Quebec Romeo Victor . . . go ahead."

"W2QRV, thank God . . . Look, we've got emergencies backed up a mile here . . . There's a tenement burning, corner First Avenue and Houston. Fire's spreading, and nothing's checking it. No water, no phone, no electricity. Get the Fire Department. Got an old man with a heart attack, needs an ambulance. We've got frostbite and exposure victims here, need medical aid . . ."

The list went on, with calls for medical supplies, food, water, heat, help of any and every sort.

Mark turned around to stare at his own boxful of supplies.

"No," said Karen. "Don't let them. You've already said too much."

"I haven't said a thing."

"Yes, you did. Your call letters. That registry will tell them where you live. How long you think before they come up here to get you?"

"Get me? What're you talking about?"

"Survival, Mark. You answered the call, which means you *can* answer, which means everything else they can figure, including that . . ." and she nodded to the supplies.

"But they don't know about that."

"No, not yet."

Mark swallowed.

The dog soon lost his exhilaration. Freedom had become a constant hunt for ever more elusive scraps. Even so, there was a sense of challenge, the mixture of pain and the thrill of rediscovery in working with atrophied powers. He would sniff, track, paw, grab, pull, so that when he finally crushed the morsel in his jaws, there was the pleasurable sense of reward for work done. It was surely more just than his arrangement with the master, where food and affection was given or withheld by some incomprehensible caprice.

Yet, being alone had its disadvantages. One time the Husky encountered a single forlorn squirrel. For all the pounding of blood, the thrill at the chase, he wound up baffled, and more tired and hungry than ever.

At that moment he realized the need for others, a team that could track, surround, then trap.

Now, as he pawed through the snow to get at a scrap, he heard a low growl. He looked up to face a German shepherd, equally hungry, equally determined.

The Husky drew back his lips, bared his fangs in threat and declaration of possession, but the shepherd answered in kind. It would not back down.

The Husky was the more naturally aggressive of the two, and struck first, his fangs digging beneath the short fur of the shepherd's flank and tearing a gash inches long.

The Shepherd howled, and dug into the Husky's withers, but could not quite get beneath that double-thick fur. As the dogs rolled in frenzy in the snow, the shepherd sought desperately for a vital center and bare skin. More by luck than intent, its sharp nails swiped past the Husky's right eye.

The Husky screamed in pain and partial blindness, but his instincts drove him on until his fangs caught the shepherd square by the neck. Instantly, threatened with death, the shepherd submitted, fell flat on its back, its throat bare, and offered the pose of surrender.

The Husky sniffed at the shepherd, licked at him, and waited while the shepherd rolled over, stood up, and gave deference.

That former exhilaration returned, the feeling of mastery eclipsing the awful pain.

He took the major share now of the bare scrap while the Shepherd waited obediently. Then, when he felt ready, the Husky rose up and trotted on, the Shepherd following.

The Husky knew he was meant to be leader, just as he knew they would find others, that he would defeat them in battle, that they would join him and follow.

The world of white spread out before him, his own world, ready for conquest.

"W2QRV, this is Cutter Briarwood. Over."

"Cutter Briarwood, W2QRV. Over."

"Mr. Haney, I have a message from the skipper. Quote, ETA 1500, so get your ass down here, unquote. Do you copy?"

"Wilco. Tell him my ass is on the line if his is."

He signed off and switched to the CB band.

"W2QRV to Mobile One, acknowledge."

There was some static and incomprehensible squeals, and finally Fink's voice came on. "How the hell you work this goddamn thing, Haney?"

"You're doing all right. Listen, rendezvous's at three. Pass the word. Over."

"Ah, our ship's in. Three o'clock, Morton Street pier, right?"

Mark groaned. "Thanks. Maybe you won't even have to pass the word now."

"What're you talking about?"

"Survival, Fink, survival." He looked up to see Karen smirking.

"Maybe there's no one to hear anyway," she said.

Mark grunted uncomfortably, and turned back to the receiver. "I'll be late. I'll have things to pack."

"Things to pack? Why the hell didn't you pack until now?"

"I have to pack this radio, remember?"

There was a silence. "Oh . . . For a moment I was hoping I wasn't the only idiot. Okay, Mark, over and out."

"Hey Fink, 'over and out' is a contradiction. You can't . . ." But Fink had already switched off.

Mark sighed. Had Noah had these problems with the ark?

He had a great deal of work ahead. He dragged the snowmobile and its trailer carryall out into the hallway, and returned to begin breaking down the radio.

Because he had tried to receive signals the entire width of the radio spectrum, he had innumerable antennas, each of different length, each tuned to a different band. There were short wires, long wires, insulators, connectors, and all of them had to be carefully folded and packed.

Karen watched worriedly. "That'll take forever."

"Not quite."

"The glacier'll beat you here."

"Hope not." He smiled.

"You sure the ship'll wait?"

"What is sure anymore?"

She moaned, paced the floor, walked out to the hallway to the snowmobile and, as she saw the pile of possessions mounting in the carryall, she shook her head.

"Lord, we accumulate. The Eskimos get it all in one sled. We're prisoners of our possessions, Mark."

"Moving-day blues. Don't forget the real stuff I stored at the pier."

"Lord . . . How'll they get it aboard?"

"The same way they get buoys aboard. Don't worry about it."

Karen worried. She watched Mark continue to load his intricate gear. She had weeded down her Eskimo artifacts to the fewest possible, even taking pride in the smallness of the intricately fit package.

Then she noticed Danny's voluminous weather instruments, their odd shapes precluding compact packing.

"Oh lord, Danny, you really need that?"

Danny sighed. "Mom, at this stage you really shouldn't be asking foolish questions."

He gingerly prodded them into available spaces, shoving aside some of Karen's artifacts.

"We can fit it in if you let go of some of this stuff. I mean, Mother, what're we gonna do with a stone carving?"

"Look, Danny, I'm not arguing with you. I once told you you'd have to let go of some things you'd like, and one of them's your toys."

"Toys! Jesus, Mother, these aren't toys. Toys are for children. These are working instruments. They tell you what the weather's going to be . . ."

"Fine, but Mark already has those. You don't need these . . ." She reached for them.

"Mother . . ." He got louder, and began pulling at them. "I built these. I made these . . . I mean, your Eskimos, they built those, but I built these!"

"Look, Danny, when you're an adult, I'll argue the meaning of art with you, but we're saving what's important." She reached again for them, and he pulled harder.

"Mom, this is important! It's mine . . . It works. It . . . It's important!"

He began crying, and in moments more was hitting the wall.

"Danny, a temper tantrum is not going to help you. We've got decisions to make, and it's hard for everybody. Now learn to accept what you've got to. It's not a picnic we're going on . . ."

Mark interrupted. "Hey, can I talk to you?" He pulled Karen down the hallway, out of Danny's hearing. "Look, I don't want to subvert your authority with Danny."

"Good. Don't."

"But this is important."

"We're agreed on that."

"It's certainly important to him."

"No, it's not. It's a spoiled attachment to a toy, that's all."

"Not to him."

"We're talking about survival, Mark, and what's important to the group."

"So how do you justify those Eskimo artifacts?"

She sighed. "Anthropology in twelve seconds . . . They are the summation of a culture in as tight a package as possible. The Eskimos traveled light, but they traveled with this . . ." She stopped a moment. "They're probably all dead now, and this is what's left. It's what they've left me . . ."

Mark paused carefully before answering. "All right. Your Eskimos meant something to you like the weather station means something to . . ."

"Damn it, Mark. Objectively, and I mean dispassionately and objectively, you've got your scientific instruments, and you'll need them. Fine. Danny's only got some toy versions . . ."

"Call 'em models."

"Doesn't matter what I call them."

"All right, but they're not the valuable resource . . ."

"So then why . . . ?"

"Danny is. Some day, if we all come out of this alive, he'll be taking over. I don't want his growth stunted, physical or mental. That weather station's a toy to you, maybe even to me, but it's school for him, and he loves it."

"But it'll take up . . ."

"We're wasting time."

He turned back to Danny. "Okay, we decided. Finish loading."

Danny suddenly brightened. "Hurray!"

Mark couldn't help smiling as he watched the little bundle of fur busily scrambling onto the carryall and crawl over the boxes like some busy caterpillar.

Karen muttered, "Thanks for not subverting my authority."

"I'm sorry. It was too important."

The silence fell on both of them. He reached for her shoulders, and she turned away. He reached again.

"I'm sorry . . . Karen, I'm really sorry. Look, I love you, I love him . . . Don't ask me to choose."

Troubled, she still let Mark kiss her. "I hope you don't ever have to."

Danny called out, "Hey, are we ready?"

They looked up to see him atop the pile.

"You want to ride there?"

Danny nodded. "I'm guarding it."

Mark murmured to Karen, "We'll make him a kid yet."

He shoved open the fire-escape door and looked out at the city. The snow came to his feet at the second floor, as he had expected, but with all his foreknowledge he couldn't have predicted the city's appearance, buried in its deepest snow in ten thousand years. The streets were eradicated, and the buildings protruded out of the snow like wood pickets on a white-sand beach.

It was not frozen still, however, for fires could be seen burning, and their smoke hung low in the overcast sky. Many buildings had already been gutted, and their empty shells were filled with snow.

Winds had interacted in capricious ways with street layouts and building contours, so that the sides of some buildings were completely bare, while others were banked with drifts a half-dozen stories high.

Mark stared a long while, and as Karen and Danny looked out, they fell silent too.

"Where're all the people, you suppose?" Danny asked at last.

"Dead," said Karen.

Mark shot her a look. "People don't die off that easy. They're around."

A sound welled up through the silence, the howls and pained barkings of countless dogs.

"That shows there're people," said Mark.

"That shows there aren't."

Mark grimaced, and turned the ignition key. The snowmobile didn't start at once, and he had to pump it a little, but then it came to life with an astonishingly loud and piercing roar, a good deal more so than Mark had expected.

"Christ!"

The sound reverberated sharp and clear in the silence of the city, bouncing off bare stone walls, muffled by deep snows.

"It's no dogsled."

He knew the sound was carrying dozens of blocks. If there were anyone alive, he or she certainly knew about Mark now.

Cautiously, he put the gears into low. He didn't dare go too fast with the delicate instruments in the carryall, and Danny atop. The tread spun freely for moments until it bit into the snow, tossing mounds behind it like a rotary plow until finally it got its purchase on the snow and moved forward.

"At least there're no dog droppings."

As he turned west along Bleecker Street, he had to get his bearings from some recognizable tall buildings. Street signs, and indeed the streets themselves, had disappeared.

As they passed their first tall building, Danny looked anxiously toward the high floors.

"Mark, do you think we're being watched?"

"Well, we sure as hell can be heard."

Karen said, "It's all right, Danny. There's no one there."

"They're there," said Mark, testily.

"Oh yes, frozen, or starved to death, or maybe dead of thirst because the water pipes burst. Any number of possibilities, but all dead."

Mark sighed. "Let's just say we don't know, Danny."

Danny clutched uneasily at his weather instruments.

At Seventh Avenue, a theater marquee lay dangling from one end by twisted struts as its other end rested in the snowbank.

"You suppose, Mark, that old man you saved is still alive?"

"I wouldn't know, but I'm glad I saved him."

"Too bad you missed all these."

He turned south at the next block, with a clear view to the south, and the tall buildings of the Wall Street district.

"I'll bet quite a few got out of the city, and are heading south now," said Mark.

"Yes, all those with snowshoes around the house."

Mark glared at her. "This isn't the only snowmobile in the world, you know."

"It's the only one I hear."

"How about skis? There were enough weekend skiers in the city."

"I don't see any trails, do you?"

"For God's sake, Karen, civilization just doesn't lay down and die. It fights back, like we're doing."

"I thought what we're doing is running."

"I think they'd call it a strategic withdrawal, a regrouping of forces the better to fight back later."

"Who's around to call it anything?"

They passed the grimy gray towers of a prison.

"Mark," asked Danny, "what happened to prisoners?"

Mark shrugged. "I don't know. I guess they transported them south."

Said Karen, "Last I heard in a Soc class, we had over three hundred thousand prisoners. I suppose they packed 'em in one big snowmobile with bars."

"Well, they didn't just lock 'em up and leave 'em."

"So what did they do, just let them go?"

"I don't know, Karen, I don't know."

"Well, weather's your department. Human behavior's mine." She looked up at the barred windows. "They probably were pounding on their cages till they died." She looked back to Mark. "In a civilized way, of course."

Danny shuddered. "If there *are* people around, they'll be watching us now."

No one said anything further as the piers came within view. The Hudson River was icing in from the banks, but still moved sluggishly in the middle, carrying ice floes three hundred miles from the Adirondack Mountains. Ships lay on their sides or tossed atop the piers. Many had their hulls crushed, their decks broken. All wore ghostly shrouds of varying thickness.

Then they saw the buoy-tender, almost two hundred feet long, its black hull standing stark against the white environment, the slanting red stripe near the bow like a chevron on a sleeve, and on it the Coast Guard crest. Its most prominent feature was its loading boom, sticking up like an anachronistic sailing mast.

Already, on the foredeck, Mark could make out a dozen people, anxiously moving about, perhaps keeping warm, or performing their tasks, or perhaps active out of sheer nervousness.

Danny tried standing atop the carryall to wave.

"For Christ's sake, sit down." Mark grabbed for him. As he turned forward, he could see a few figures on deck waving back.

He nudged Karen. "There's our civilization."

He revved up the engine. The pitch and volume rose as the snowmobile's tread spun faster.

Mark didn't notice the figures until he was almost

upon them. They must have come out from behind a building, and had been waiting for him.

Now they stood there forming a loose phalanx between him and the ship, and they were advancing upon him. He looked behind him. Others had come out there.

To the left was the building wall, the edge of the pier at the right. He was totally hemmed in.

"Christ!"

He spun to the right until he saw the drop down to the frozen river. Danny screamed, almost getting thrown from the carryall as it spun about. Mark looked to see the men closing rank about him. Their faces were covered with cloth like desert Arabs, but the rest of their clothes were tightly bundled collections of rags, of odds and ends of clothing. He could see in some spots the deadened and discolored flesh of severe frostbite, but something more frightening was the quality of the feral about them, as if they were no longer men but ravenous animals.

He spun back, straight toward them, expecting to see them scatter, but instead they kept coming, their hands more like open claws shivering with expectation.

The next moment, he heard Karen yell as one of the figures pulled her off. He kicked at another who was suddenly all over him with swinging arms. He rammed the snowmobile straight into a third, and the whole craft shuddered and rolled sideways.

Danny yelled in terror as the trailer fell over on its side, hurling him into the snow, and spilling instruments and supplies upon him.

With yells of glee, the other figures came at the pile in a rush, stepping on Danny as they went tearing through boxes. At least three were fighting over the gasoline in the tank, trying to catch the spillage with anything that might serve for a vessel.

Danny shrieked, and tried to stop them. One of them slapped Danny with the back of his hand with such force the child went flying backward several feet. He screamed as blood came pouring out of his mouth.

Mark was trying to reach behind him to grasp

at a figure that seemed as elusive as the snow itself. The figure tore at Mark's coat until the fasteners came apart. Mark hurled the sharp edge of his right elbow in a sweep behind him and felt it strike bone. He continued his spin, using the full force of his body for the flattened palm of his left hand, slamming the figure in the jaw.

The figure gasped, released his hold as he flew back into the snow, but now a second was upon Mark's back, his arms around Mark's neck. Mark fell backward into the snow atop the new assailant, and felt the snow cold and wet against his skin as his coat was pulled off. Struggling about, he freed his arms and kicked as he tried to grab his coat back.

Then another arm reached about him, strong and firm, pulling him back and up to his feet. He whirled around, his fists clenched, but two arms held him at bay. He suddenly noticed a sleeve carrying a double stripe.

"Leave 'em and let's get out of here," said the seaman.

"I need the supplies!"

"Fuck the supplies. Let's get outa here . . . 'Scuse me, sir."

Mark looked about. Karen lay in the snow, nearly unconscious, her coat gone. He ran to her, picked her up.

She moaned. "Danny?"

Mark looked there. Danny was like a tiny tiger, moaning, screaming, punching as the figures went through the overturned trailer, hurling his weather instruments about, breaking Karen's carvings, kicking the radio.

"The boy . . ." yelled Mark.

"I see him."

The Guardsman grabbed the boy and gestured toward the distant gangway, where others waited to pull it up.

Mark slogged through the snow, puffing with Karen in his arms. He looked behind him to see figures pursuing, clawing their way through the drifts with the same ferocity with which they tore through the supplies.

The p.a. sounded. "Haney, get your ass up here!"

He looked up to the bridge to see Manujian at the microphone.

"Whyn't you use your guns, for Christ's sake?" Mark yelled.

"This's the Coast Guard, not the Mafia."

In a few steps more, Mark reached the gangway. It rolled dizzyingly on casters with each motion of the ship.

"I'll make it . . ." murmured Karen as he set her down, and she reached for the guide-rail.

At that same moment, a tattered sleeve reached around Mark's neck and pulled him back to the dock. He kicked behind him as hard as he could, and the figure went crumpling.

He crawled more than he ran up the gangway, pulling and heaving all the way, almost losing his balance with its movement.

"All right, stand clear . . ." came Manujian's voice. The gangway rolled up and folded onto the deck as the engines started up and Mark felt their throbbing through the flooring.

Then he was looking into the grim face of Lieutenant Commander Manujian.

"Thanks for nothing," said Mark.

"Don't bug me. You're alive."

"What the hell you got against me all of a sudden?"

"I just told you. If you'll excuse me, I've got a ship to run." He turned on his heels and climbed back up to the bridge.

Mark stared after him a moment, then looked back to the dock. The figures were fighting and clawing over the supplies, smashing the snowmobile, struggling for the gasoline.

Beyond them lay the white-shrouded city. Palls of black smoke rose in the air from fires controlled and uncontrolled, as the city cannibalized itself to keep warm.

He turned to the north, upstream the Hudson. The river ice came floating down in ever thickening clumps. The ship swept them aside with dull thumpings that carried through the hull, leaving them behind to turn and roll in the ship's wake.

He looked to the south, dead ahead, where the river emptied into New York Bay, eventually opening out into the Atlantic. There was ice of a different sort here, salt water ice, newly formed and thin, shifting with the wind, much like oil streaks on the water.

Soon, the ship crossed ice several days old, a few inches thick, pulled into innumerable tiny clumps.

When the ship entered the body of the Gulf Stream, Mark knew they would cross ice ever older, ever thicker and stronger, weeks old, years old, even centuries old, from the ancient icecaps of the Arctic. If they were unfortunate, they would confront the absolutely impenetrable ice from the great glacier itself.

Then the executive officer was there. "Sir, your group's in the galley."

"It's been a while, Mr. . . ." He looked at the X.O.'s name tag. ". . . Redfield. You'll have to show me."

As Lieutenant Redfield led the way along the passageway, they had to squeeze past the cartons of food and supplies that were tightly stacked along every conceivable space.

"Pretty tight here."

"Way I hear, we're set for a long haul."

Mark hesitated a moment. "Mr. Redfield, can I ask you something? What's Manujian got against me?"

Redfield looked at him. "None of us're too happy about the situation."

"He's not happy against me in particular."

The X.O. nodded. "Galley's just ahead, sir. Watch out for the cartons." He found an alcove to step into to let Mark pass. Then he was gone.

Mark sighed, and entered the galley to find his group gathered around the table, forlornly drinking coffee.

Fink nodded a weak greeting. "Haven't seen you in an ice age."

"Where's . . . ?"

Hideo smiled. "Karen's baby-sitting in the wardroom."

Mark blinked. "Baby-sitting?"

"She told my kids they looked like little Eskimos, and that started them off."

Mark shook his head in wonder. "Danny's there?"

"Fat chance. He discovered the chart room and the radio room."

"Yeah," said Fink. "When he discovers the pilothouse, I'm getting off."

"But we're all present and accounted for?"

There was silence for a moment.

"Our archaeologist is missing."

"Yeah," said Fink. "Just the skill we needed to dig us out."

"Y'know," said Helen angrily, "you're pretty callous and nasty about someone who's probably dead."

"Given the choice between nasty and dead, I'll take nasty."

"All right, stop that," snapped Mark. "What about the crates. They safe in the hold?"

"Crates? Jesus, Mark, *we're* lucky to be here."

"You mean they're still back on . . . ?"

"In your captain's words, we got our asses up here, and that's all. You saw what was going on at the dock."

Mark moaned, and collapsed into a chair. "So our stuff's all back there, and this whole thing was a waste." He shook his head. "I'll bet Karen got a laugh out of that."

They looked at each other. "She didn't say anything."

"My God, she should've. One more royal fuckup. All of the things to save civilization." He looked out the porthole in despair.

The ice was growing thicker, now forming a rind like the surface of an orange. The ship cleaved it cleanly, leaving a sharply marked canal behind, as far back as Mark could see, a dark ribbon unrolled across the whiteness. He strained his eyes to follow it back to the distant city.

"I'll bet someone's sure having a high time with that stuff."

The one-eyed Husky had added three more dogs to his pack, all large and well-furred, all ignored, ill-treated, or even brutalized in the past, so they had learned to survive without dependence on humans.

Other dogs, the small, the shaven, the pampered and petted, all languished and died in the snows, pining for masters that never came.

After the German shepherd came the bull mastiff, its square bulldog head atop a massive and powerful body. Then the schipperke, a smaller black without a tail, and a fox-like head. Bred by a barge captain as both watchdog and ratcatcher, it found larger game much to its liking.

Then the mongrel, black with a white band about its neck, it was short-tempered, even unstable, protective of the pup forming within her.

They had all deferred and submitted to the one-eyed Husky, and as they wandered the city, they had gradually refined their hunting. Each learned its function and place in the group, to chase or to corner, to make the initial attack or the secondary, indeed all the techniques of the wolf pack.

So far they had subsisted on the small game of the city, rats, cats, crippled pigeons, and the occasional squirrel. Garbage and scraps were getting harder to find, and were surely less exhilarating than the pleasure of live game. Also, that ran more risk of contact with the hated humans.

Beyond food, they needed a lair for the mongrel to give birth. In their wanderings, they came to the pier. The building was cavernous and dark, like the caves that had protected their ancestors. Packing crates lay upended, their contents scattered, and these seemed much like rock crannies.

The mongrel immediately claimed one and settled there, pulling objects about her for a barricade.

A low moan suddenly made them stand taut and tense.

The man was in rags, crawling dangerously close to the lair as he sought cover from the snow.

The Husky dug its paws into the snow, bared its teeth, and growled.

The man gave a cry, reached through the snow and came up with a book, one of many left strewn about, and hurled it.

The Husky howled more in rage than pain, backed away, and emitted a low, charged snort. The next moment, the man was surrounded by a threat far more terrifying than mere starvation, a pack of great, fierce dogs, circling warily, fangs bared, mouths salivating, throats emitting low, ominous growls.

Cowering, the man groped again through the snow and came up with something heavier, a strange stone carving, making a heavier missile.

He hurled it, and it caught the schipperke. The dog went sprawling and howling in the snow, but picked itself up again.

The pack was galvanized, and now they all came charging in rapid sequence, taking sharp, quick bites and darting back before the man could strike. No sooner did one dog retreat than another came charging from a new direction.

The man groped frantically and came up with another oddity from the packing crate, a whip with a thirty-foot lash. It was an impossible object to use properly, especially in such close quarters. Finally, he wielded it from the top end, using the handle as a club.

The dogs ducked, howled ferociously as the handle came down on heads or flanks, but it only enraged them further, and their attacks came faster. Each successive slash of claw or fang opened more of the man's rags until suddenly the Husky cut through a vein in the man's thigh.

The dog felt a warm, delicious syrup in his mouth,

giving his tongue the same exhilaration the snow had given his skin.

So the hated and feared human was no more than the squirrel or cat, mere meat and blood. The Husky was freed. His vocal cords responded to the sensation, gave voice to his feeling. He jerked his neck back and uttered the cry of his ancestors. Then, maddened with the totality of sensations, he dove for the human.

The man managed one last swipe with the whip before it fell from his grasp.

Danny barely looked up when Mark entered the chart room. "It's exciting."

He sat huddled by a small radio receiver blaring static and squeals.

"The radio man said I could listen in here, where he's got this little extra one."

The receiver suddenly squawked, "Cape May, this is One-Four-Zero-Eight, setting down at four-two after hour . . ."

"That's one of their rescue helicopters. They're supposed to pick up some emergency cases."

After a pause, the radio squawked again. "Cape May, One-Four-Zero-Eight, at rescue point. Heavy crowd there, will not disperse. Please advise. Over."

"Zero-Eight, this is Cape May. Hospital facilities overloaded. Choose only most obvious emergencies, tell others to wait. Over."

"Roger, Cape May. I'm down, but . . ." His voice grew conspicuously nervous. "Hey . . . they're not backing off . . ."

A new noise came through as the copter motor died, the sounds of a yelling crowd.

"They're just swarming all over . . . They're shoving, and . . ." Then his voice echoed as he switched on the public address. "Stand clear . . . Please stand clear . . . We have emergency cases to be picked up . . . Please stand clear . . ."

"Zero-Eight, use sidearms if necessary. Keep crowds from the ship . . ."

The pilot was yelling now. "They're turning over stretchers . . . They're trampling 'em . . . Hey . . ."

The next few moments were a Babel of glass smashing, of yells, screams, splinterings and thuds. There were two gunshots, and suddenly the signal vanished.

"Zero-Eight, this is Cape May. Over . . . Zero-Eight, come in . . . Zero-Eight . . ."

But the hiss was the only answer.

Danny sat stone-still, staring at the receiver, visibly shocked. Then, holding back tears, he turned to Mark. "Mark, why do they do that?"

"Everybody's afraid to die, Danny. This time, they look around and they see the whole world dying."

"Mark . . . is the world worth saving?"

"You know it is, Danny."

"Mark . . . what'd they do with my weather station?"

Mark didn't answer.

"It's probably in a million pieces . . ." The tears came. "They're not worth saving . . ." He sobbed. "They oughta die . . ."

Mark put his arms around Danny, hugged him gently, but said nothing.

Finally, after long minutes, the tears subsided.

". . . Mark . . ." he sniffled.

"Yes, Danny?"

"Mark, where're we going?"

"We don't know that yet. We have to work it out."

"You suppose . . . wherever it is . . . they've got kitchens?"

"Kitchens? I guess most places do. Why?"

"Then they'll have funnels . . . and broomstick handles . . . I can make an anemometer from them."

Mark stroked his hair. "I'm sure you'll be able to, Danny." He released the boy and rose up.

"Where're you going?"

"To use their radio room."

"For what?"

"For somebody who's worth saving."

Out in the passageway, he again had to squeeze past the boxes of food and supplies. When he came out on deck, he saw yet a new and strange ice formation, the next step in its gradual thickening.

The ice had broken into countless individual pieces that came striking and rubbing against each other, thickening their rims as they were simultaneously rounded off, so that they resembled stacks of gray and white pancakes heaped out to the horizon.

The ship was now encountering resistance from the ice, and it battered more than cleaved its way.

When Mark entered the pilothouse, the atmosphere was subdued despite the number of crewmen crowding the room. They were engaged tensely at their separate tasks; at the charts, the wheel, the radar, or scanning the horizon with binoculars.

A loudspeaker crackled with the same hissing and static that Mark had just heard below.

"I guess you heard it for yourself," said Mark.

Manujian nodded. "It's been happening. So what do we do, Mark, save people or shoot 'em?" He elbowed Mark out of the way as he reached for the intercom.

"Radio room."

"This is the captain. You got comms yet?"

"Negative, sir."

Manujian grunted, and turned to Mark. "Haney, where're we going?"

"South, I hope."

"A little more specific."

"Not that easy. I have to consult some people."

"What people, where?"

"Miami, Cleveland, London, all over."

"What the hell're you talking about?"

"Your radio room. I've got comms of my own."

Manujian stared. "I can't turn over the radio to you."

"I'm sorry, Larry, I didn't bring my FCC license with me. I'm taking up space, so let me justify it. There's a bunch of experts scattered around the globe, and ham radio's our tie-in."

Manujian thought a long moment. "Kind of crowding the facilities, aren't we?" He picked up the intercom again.

"Radio room."

"This's the captain. I'm sending down a civilian named Mark Haney."

"Oh . . . him."

Manujian cast an amused look to Mark. "You left an impression." He turned back to the phone. "He is authorized to use the radio for . . ." He turned back to Mark.

"More the better. A lot of calculations to work out."

Manujian winced. "One hour out of every watch."

"I need . . ."

"You're wasting your hour, Mark."

Mark cursed, bounded out of the room, down the steps, again squeezed past the boxes in the passageway, and greeted the radioman opening the door.

"Don't wreck the thing, Haney. We need it."

"So do I."

The radioman grunted, and watched Mark set the dials and switches, until he was satisfied that Mark seemed to know what he was doing.

Eventually, Mark reestablished his connections.

It was fortunate that English was the international language of scientists, for once beyond the "Q" abbreviations of the radio ham, they had to discuss climatic belts, ocean current shifts, energy concentrations, landforms, precipitation patterns, vegetation belts, soil groups, mineral concentrations.

The geographer's news was not encouraging. Even before the climatic shifts, only ten percent of the planet was ever suitable for cultivation. Agriculture would have to be precisely managed on such land that would remain, and only the most energy-efficient crop could be grown.

Corn, Agronomy noted, converted and stored more recoverable energy than any other staple.

Chemistry could produce commercial alcohol

from corn, and Engineering could convert internal combustion engines to alcohol.

"Time's up, Mr. Haney."

The radioman was there, and Mark had to remove himself from the net.

Three hours later, at the next watch, he reestablished contact. The needed combinations of climate and soil for corn cultivation had been worked out, but with climatic shifts there would be new balances of sunlight and precipitation. Calculations had to be reworked, and the hour was up entirely too quickly.

When he stumbled wearily out on deck, Mark saw the ice had again changed. The pancakes had disappeared, and they were crossing ice several months old, with light tints of green.

The ship could no longer batter the ice readily. With its flattened bow, it rode ever so slightly atop, using the ship's weight to crush down, shooting up mixtures of water and ice above the bow. The ship rode up and down as if riding great waves in extreme slow motion, and Mark had to hold onto the railing as he made his way back to his room.

His sleep was fitful, and his dreams were of riding atop the shuddering glacier, of falling through crevasses that opened beneath him, and of being crushed as the ice closed in again.

By the time of his next session, the new combinations of climate and soil had been worked out, and now Political Science had a say. Governments were heading toward collapse. New patterns of migrations had to be anticipated, with resultant border clashes and wars. The fields were narrowed further.

In North America, the only reasonable possibility was a province in Mexico, part of the peninsula jutting into the Gulf of Mexico.

Mark rolled the name around in his mind. Campeche. Now mainly sparsely settled fishing villages, it would be the center of survival technology.

The last Ice Age had wiped out the dinosaurs, and perhaps Man would retreat and retreat, but at Campeche he would make his last stand. He would survive, and perhaps prevail. He would defeat Nature at her own game and turn back the ice.

Mark told Karen first. She wanted to know about the people and their culture.

Mark looked at her blankly. "I figured to teach them ours."

She paused. "Perhaps we could learn from theirs."

He knew, of course, he could speak more easily to Danny, and found him in the chart room, still listening glumly to the little receiver.

Danny perked up when Mark gave him the news, and became especially excited when Mark pulled down charts and showed him the exact place.

"And I think they'll have kitchens, too."

"Yeah. And maybe your captain friend'll let us have this extra radio."

"Maybe. Or maybe there'll be someone down there who already has one. Or maybe . . ."

"What?"

"Well, if his orders don't come through, we'll all be going to this place. Y'know, this ship is a whole technology center by itself."

Danny's eyes danced behind his glasses as he thought of the ship's resources. Then a cloud crossed his face. "But why shouldn't he get his orders?"

Mark grunted, and they both fell silent.

The receiver came alive again, crackling with a new emergency, a riot in Los Angeles around a water truck. The shoving crowd had provoked fistfights, and the growing melee was beyond the control of the local police. Federal troops were being requested. There was no acknowledgment.

"It's breaking down, Danny, the whole government. He won't get any orders."

The ship was climbing alarmingly now as it began hitting older and thicker ice. Mark was not surprised when he looked out the porthole to see blue streaks through the green. The ice floes were becoming a patchwork of colors and thicknesses, different floes intermingled and jammed together by the current. Every once in a while, the bow would strike a particularly resistant floe, and the ship would shudder as if hit by an explosive.

Then the p.a. sounded, requesting Mark's presence in the captain's cabin.

"I've got comms," were Manujian's first words when Mark entered. He said it without discernible emotion, and for a moment Mark didn't understand.

Then he did. "Your orders?"

Manujian nodded.

Mark felt a stab of fear. "What'd they say?"

"Guantanamo."

"Guantanamo? What the hell've we got in Guantanamo?"

"Pretty damned big military base, in case you haven't heard."

"But . . . but it's not viable. It's dependent on the outside, and there's nothing outside except a country that doesn't want us there in the first place."

"Those're the orders."

"You know what's going to happen, don't you, Lar? It'll get so crowded, you'll be standing on each other's shoulders. And you can't produce, just stockpile, so it's a parasite society. You'll have to push into Cuba to survive, and they won't be pushed. You'll be at war in a week, and dead the week after."

"Quite a scenario you built from one word."

Mark hesitated. "Larry, you once said there was a word too dirty to say."

Manujian looked at him silently.

"What I promised would happen has happened. The chain's broken down. The military's in its death throes, and so's the whole government. Those orders prove it."

"So you're getting to the word."

"Listen to me. Campeche Province in Mexico. We've worked it out. It'll be a functioning colony. This ship has the resources to make it work, especially the radio. Believe me, and if you won't, I'll put you on to the experts themselves. Larry, I'm just one part of a whole functioning net, the only thing left that seems to be functioning. We've got the one chance of coming out alive and saving something."

"You're hitting on the word."

"I'll say it. Desertion. But you're the one deserting. You're deserting civilization. Go to Guantanamo, and you join the dinosaurs."

"The rules say we go out. They don't say we have to come back."

"Then why follow the rules?"

"Because there's nothing else."

"There must be, or you'd've been up in the ranks now. You held back because there was something that meant a hell of a lot more than rules or rank."

There was a long, long silence.

"Yeah . . ." said Manujian finally, "but there's nothing else now."

The words hit Mark squarely.

"Oh my God, I'm sorry. Your family." Mark felt the strength go out of him. "I . . . I was thinking of other things. I'm sorry, Larry. What did happen?"

"Trouble is, I don't know." He took a breath, the closest he came to showing his emotion. "Phones were out. There was no way of getting through." He looked out the porthole back toward the city. "No one on the crew got through."

Suddenly the ship seemed to screech as steel collided with hardened ice, then it went tilting up at a steep angle, throwing both men against the wall.

"Jesus . . ."

The next instant the intercom buzzed.

Manujian picked it up. "Yeah, I know. I'll be right up." He turned to Mark. "It all just might be academic anyway."

As Mark followed him out on deck, he could see the reason. The ship had run solidly aground, its bow thrust above the ice at an incredible angle. With half the ship's weight bearing down, the ice was holding firm.

The stairway to the bridge was almost vertical, and Mark felt he was mountain-climbing.

The executive officer greeted them tremulously. "We were steering it through the white ice. I don't know what the hell happened."

"What happened, Mr. Redfield, is you hit blue ice with snow on top."

The X.O. winced. "Can't make too many mistakes."

"Can't make any. All right, give me full speed astern."

The engine order telegraph changed, engines responded.

The ship backed down from the ice ever so slightly.

Almost before the motion died, Manujian set full speed ahead, putting the rudder back and forth. Behind them, the stern swung wide, and the bow shifted a tiny bit.

"Full ahead."

Again, crew and engine responded.

Again, he backed it down, twisting the rudder, as if working loose an embedded knife. Again forward, again back.

Finally the ship came free, falling through the ice to the sea beneath, and sending ice and water up in a great shower.

The crew cheered their first victory, but then the lookout reported new floes coming down from the north. The ice was closing in.

Even as they watched, floes collided with floes in loud splinterings and thunder. The level ice erupted in ridges and small mountains at the points of collision.

"Like I said, Mark, it may all be academic."

They watched in silence as the floes seemed to close in around them.

"Sir," said the X.O., "shouldn't we try and break through before we're hemmed in?"

"All right, Mr. Redfield, you want to point us toward the thinnest ice?"

"Well, sir, I . . . I don't want to make the same mistake twice."

"That makes two of us."

"Well, what do we do?"

"Wait."

The X.O. blinked, but said nothing. They waited, while Mark fidgeted and worried, and floes collided and new ridges built up, until the formerly flat ice seemed more a moonscape.

Then the lookout called, "Open lead, sir, off starboard beam."

It seemed almost miraculous, God parting the Red Sea for Moses. The ice seemed to clear away, falling back to reveal an open river with jagged banks, stretching directly south, apparently open all the way to warmer seas, and easily wide enough to accommodate the ship.

The helmsman awaited Manujian's orders, but the captain hesitated.

"It's like traveling a maze," he said to Mark. "Except this one keeps shifting as you go through it. We can go down that river, and . . ." He studied it a good while through his binoculars. "Looks all right . . ."

He scanned the horizon one last moment.

"There's another."

It was distinctly less promising, a smaller lead, opening to the northwest.

"Bearing, zero six zero."

"Sir, the lead's . . ."

"Zero six zero, seaman!"

Slowly the ship turned northwest, and for the next several minutes Manujian fed the helmsman the bearings to guide him up that very narrow river.

Then they saw it happen, the ice parting, seeming to give way before them, opening to the south, while the other river narrowed, and the ice came together, sealing it shut.

"Jesus . . ."

"Yeah," said Manujian. "Now all I need's another hundred good guesses in a row."

The rest of the day was a nightmare, of following cul-de-sacs and blind alleys, of leads that opened into flowing water, and then suddenly sealed shut.

The *Briarwood* would go crashing up on the ice as if running aground, and the shock would reverberate as if it were struck by a giant hammer. Crewmen would be thrown off balance, and all unsecured objects would go flying.

With luck, the weight of the ship would be enough to break down the ice. It would then settle back down into the water, rocking and tossing up sprays of icy debris, then the process would begin anew, backing off and ramming—or waiting—until they found a new lead opening up.

Once in a while, the ship would be held fast, and Manujian would send crewmen out with crowbars to pry the ice apart at the seams. If that didn't work, he would use explosives, planted with a giant corkscrew drill.

Its gasoline motor would howl above the rumble of the ice. Then the explosives would send up geysers of steam and ice, and then Manujian would try anew, edging back, rocking the boat by the rudder, and coming forward again.

Progress was soon measured in yards. Beams weakened, rivets and welds worked loose, and leaks constantly erupted. Unburnt oil began collecting like so much sludge around the stack, and was constantly igniting. In the midst of sea and ice, the ship's greatest danger was fire. All operations would then have to be suspended while an assembled firefighting crew trained their hoses at the stack, building up layers of frost until the deck was encased in a thick white shroud.

In the chart room, Danny held his ears, screamed at the noise, tried to concentrate on the charts, the radio, or any textbook he could find.

In the wardroom, Karen tried to distract the frightened children with more stories of other peoples, other societies.

In the galley, a particularly bad collision sent food flying across the room.

"Oh, shit . . ."

Fink scraped food off his clothes, then waited patiently through the series of new rockings, straining engines, and explosions. But this time the ship was holding fast.

"I think they need my help," he said finally, and made his way out the galley, and up the stairs to the pilothouse.

His mouth dropped at the sight.

"Christ, I come up here for reassurance, and I see the captain reading the book of directions."

"I have news for you, Mr. Fink. I'm only a lieutenant."

Fink swallowed, and looked to Mark. "That's the rank they used to give you when you got out of R.O.T.C. He's kidding, isn't he?"

Mark shook his head. "It's a little higher. Lieutenant Commander."

"Hey Mark, what kind of trip'd you get us on?"

"The only one I could get."

"Well, can we trade this guy in for a real captain?"

"He is a real captain."

Fink grunted. "Probably just a taller Cub Scout. All right, what's the scout manual say?"

"It tells me how to pump water between the ballast tanks to rock the boat," said a remarkably calm Manujian.

"So what's keeping you?"

"It's a manual for an icebreaker, Mr. Fink. We don't have ballast tanks."

". . . Oh."

"That all, Mr. Fink?"

A discouraged Fink nodded, and was about to leave when he saw an opportunity for one last wisecrack. "We could all go running from one side to the other."

"Thanks."

Fink shook his head. "No sense of humor." And he left.

Manujian's eyes gradually fell on the loading boom. He pictured the ship rocking, and the boom swinging like a pendulum.

He was on the intercom in an instant. "This is the captain. What've we got down in the hold?"

"Lots of food, fuel tanks . . ."

"Any buoys you forgot to get rid of?"

There was a hesitation.

"C'mon, Mister."

"Yeah, well, one . . ."

"Hook it up."

The operations crew wondered if Manujian had gone mad, but they followed orders.

The buoy was lifted out of the hold like a huge red fish on a line, as large as a room, as heavy as a truck. Under Manujian's directions, the boom swung it over the starboard side as if to cast it overboard.

Down below, the children squealed as they felt the ship rock ever so slightly.

Back swung the boom, heaving the buoy to port, and the ship creaked back. To and fro the buoy swung, a huge pendulum, until the ship began rocking in synchronism, ten degrees each way.

Suddenly it began sliding back into the sea with a loud creaking of steel, bobbing and weaving as it settled.

The cheers from below deck did not raise Manujian's spirits. He stared out to the edge of the horizon, the grim set of his jaw evident beneath the binoculars.

"You've beaten it," said Mark.

"Like hell we have." He handed the glasses to Mark, pointing to the horizon. "That's what we've got to beat."

Mark looked. "Oh, lord . . ."

Mark saw the great, slow procession of the icebergs, pushed by wind and pulled by current, their funereal march still outracing the constantly impeded buoy-tender. They were coming slowly together, occasionally colliding with thunderings that sounded across the icescape like a summer storm. Were they to become welded together, they would be an impregnable barrier.

"Hate to get caught between 'em," said Mark, handing back the binoculars.

"It may all be academic . . ." muttered Manujian, scanning the ice for a new lead.

He yelled new bearings to the helmsman, pushed the engine telegraph for slow speed ahead, and the ship turned about to an infinitesimally small opening, a rivulet rather than a river, too small for the ship.

The ice was of the most intense blue Mark had ever seen. Perhaps the earliest Eskimos had stepped upon it on their migration to Greenland.

Slowly, carefully, the ship edged its way through the seams, and the floes gave way grudgingly.

Then it happened, a slight turn of direction in the wind, a subtle shifting in some distant floes. It was like a trap closing. The clear water disappeared, and the floes snapped shut like the closing of giant jaws.

The next instant, there was a shattering sound, of steel splintering, and the ship shook as if caught in some giant vibrator. Then suddenly it stopped, and the ship seemed free—almost too free.

Manujian was on the intercom to the engine room in an instant. "What the hell was that?"

"We felt it through the shafts. The prop's gone. The blades sheared right off."

He switched to the damage controlman to ask about repair.

"Even if we had a new prop, we'd need an insulated diving suit in that water."

Manujian exhaled. "We'll have to send a distress call."

"You sure it'll be answered?" Mark asked.

"When they can, when they can. Everybody's in trouble."

"So what's your manual advise in this case?"

Manujian looked, and grunted. "It says be patient. The ice'll melt eventually. After all, it always has when spring came."

"I hope they come, Larry, because spring won't."

The crew came out on deck to silently watch the ice begin shoving against the hull. They heard new grinding sounds and thumpings, and the ship began to list slightly.

Across the Atlantic, other ships similarly caught were crushed like so many paper boats, but here the ice pushed against a curved surface, squeezing it upward as one might squeeze an orange seed. The ship was lifted bodily out of the ice, settling in a list to starboard as the ice sealed irrevocably beneath it.

Then the crew made ready for their long wait for rescue. They set out the orange and black distress ensign on the deck so they might be easily spotted by the helicopter. Freezable liquids were drained, and machinery sealed. Ports and weather openings were closed tight. Deck gear was stored, machinery secured. The ship followed the manual in closing down for a long hard Arctic winter—except that this was spring outside New York.

The children grew quickly bored, and Karen spent more and more time with them in the wardroom, telling them of Greenland, of Eskimos who lived quite comfortably in just such surroundings, without even any of the comforts of the ship. Instead, they made their houses out of ice and snow. They were never cold. Indeed, Eskimo children sometimes played naked in the snow.

"Oooh . . ."

They thought their own world quite the most beautiful of any, and they pitied the rest of us. At night there was the thundering of the glacier as it moved. The aurora borealis filled the sky with colored lights, a more vivid display than any television screen.

"Oooh . . ."

They would go riding on dog sleds, swift as the wind, with a ghostly silence as if flying through the air on great eagle wings.

"Where did they do their shopping? How far was it to the supermarket?"

"There was no supermarket, nor even a store at all. Everything they ate, they had to hunt for."

"Oh, we wouldn't like that."

"And what's so exciting about opening a can? Can't you just imagine living your own action-adventure movie every day, watching, waiting, outsmarting, then pouncing? Haven't you ever imagined yourselves tigers, prowling the jungle on the hunt? This time you'd be, really be, the tigers."

"Oooh . . ."

The crew went on functioning, performed their chores, kept up maintenance, stood watch, and observed the ever stricter rationing of food and water.

They even looked forward to the excitement of drills that seemed less and less relevant, fire drills, collision drills, rescue and assistance drills, fog-navigation drills.

Each morning they raised the colors, and then the various departments gathered under their supervisors to discuss the day's duties. At sunset, colors were lowered, and the seamen took their respective turns at the night watch.

The distress banner was flown by day, the lights at night, but they knew they had to wait their turn, that civilian ships came first.

Upstairs in the chart room, Danny listened ever more stonily to the receiver, to signals that seemed to be fading even as he listened.

"Mayday, Mayday, Mayday . . . This is the vessel *Oleander*. This is the vessel *Oleander*. We are 36°16′ North, 41°29′ West. Trapped in ice. Food supplies gone . . . Fifteen crew members dead . . . Twenty-two others need medical aid . . ."

"Mayday, Mayday, Mayday . . . We are the Congo Star. We are the Congo Star . . . Two hundred miles southwest Faial Island on a heading of Two-two-six . . . We have struck a berg and are foundering . . ."

"Mayday, Mayday, Mayday . . . This is the passenger ship *Huron* . . . This is the . . . We are 42° . . . hull crushed . . . water . . . desperately need . . . May . . ."

At last, out of sheer despair, he joined the other children in the wardroom. He listened to the tales of the Eskimos, skeptically, but he listened.

In the galley, Hideo taught his wife meditation, and tried to teach the others, but they would have no part of it.

While Fink thought the situation ready-made for getting Helen into bed, they only bickered.

"Gee, it's too bad, these poor American refugees, wandering the roadways, their color TV's on their backs."

"It's not funny. People're dying back there."

"Oh. Well, pardon me for surviving."

Mark, meanwhile, was granted more time on the radio, and took advantage of it.

". . . You were right about one thing, Pat. Right now this sure as hell looks like a one-way ticket on a tramp *Titanic*. How goes it with the beautiful Miami birds? Over."

"You called it here, Mark. A no-win situation. One overnight frost killed off the whole Florida crop. Well, the loss is bad enough, but now there's two hundred thousand migrant workers suddenly with no jobs, and no way out. They're starving, and they're stranded here. They're walking the streets, getting hungrier, and other people're still pouring in. Something's gotta explode."

"Can you get out?"

"As you said, it's land's end. It's all one-way traffic, piling up. I've heard of people going out in anything that floats, leaky rowboats, bathtubs, inner-tubes. So the Gulf Stream picks 'em up, and floats 'em back north. A no-win situation, Mark."

"As long as you're alive, you can win. Stay in touch."

"Wilco. WB2XQR, out and leaving the air."

"W2QRV, out and clear . . ."

Mark flipped the switch and waited for another caller. It didn't take long.

The voice was old and tired. "Hello, Mark. I'm sorry for your troubles."

Mark blinked. "Hello, this is W2QRV. Please identify yourself. Over."

"Yes, Mark, I'm really, really sorry . . . I was half hoping you'd make it down here. You were the least dumb of the bunch."

Mark's mouth dropped. ". . . Professor Guzman?"

"Y'know, Mark, you keep dreaming about something, the way it's going to be, and it never is . . . I thought I could get away from it all, but . . . I forgot I was taking Henry Guzman with me."

"Professor Guzman, where are you?"

"Y'know, other guys my age . . . they get a little money or a divorce, and they flip out. The old sugar daddies, they dress up in young clothes, they come up to the girls, and say . . . 'Let's screw for a thousand dollars' . . . or a car . . . or whatever . . ." He paused, and sighed. "I wish I could flip out, Mark. Y'know, when you're starving, food's worth more than a car. 'Let's screw for a couple of sweet potatoes.' Hell, they'd screw for one."

He paused again, and Mark broke in.

"Professor Guzman, where the hell are you?"

Guzman snickered. "Well, where do you think, Professor Haney? In Eden, where you wanted to be. Only don't bother coming down. I've got the Garden fenced in."

"Campeche?"

Guzman laughed. "Sorry. Of course you can't. "You're not going anywhere. Just as well. I don't particularly trust anybody any more, not even Guzman's Army . . . I'm wondering if I should've given 'em guns, but then it wouldn't be much of an army, would it?"

"Who . . . who's down there with you?"

"With me? . . . Nobody's with me . . . Everybody's against me, that's the trouble. When you've got the only game in town, the food, the fuel, the guns . . . No, nobody's with me, Mark."

"Professor Guzman, you can't turn your back on other human beings. You've got to share."

"Share? Share what? Share the credit? Share the wealth? Share the research? Fuck 'em. You shared your paper, and you're up shit's creek . . . Ha, a frozen creek . . . I'll keep it all, thank you, including the senoritas."

"Professor Guzman . . ."

"Sorry for your troubles, Mark. Over and out."

"Professor Guzman . . ."

But there was only silence.

Shaken, Mark switched off the radio, and stumbled down the passageway. Progress was easier now that the boxes of supplies had been consumed.

About him, the ship's crew went on with their usual duties. Then he saw the radioman.

"Yours if you want it."

The radioman nodded thanks, and returned to monitor the Coast Guard frequency for the coming rescue.

Outside, the weather was clear, and to the east he could see the great icebergs welding themselves in place amidst the ice floes.

To the west, back toward the mainland, the ice was sealed solid.

"No win," he muttered.

He knocked on the wardroom door. Karen was entertaining the children with another story of happy Eskimos when he walked in. He listened a while to their tale, and finally interrupted.

"Really that good a life?"

She nodded.

"Let's talk outside."

The children moaned as she apologetically left them.

"You really meant that?"

"Eskimos don't lie."

"Did you learn other things, like just plain simple survival?"

"Well, I watched them . . ."

"Not quite the same thing."

"If it were, I'd've been an Eskimo instead of an anthropologist. Why do you ask?"

"Because we've lost our chance at Eden. They'll be dying down there, and they'll be dying on this ship."

She stared. "So what's left?"

He nodded to the west.

She looked at him in amazement. "You mean, go back to the city?"

"There's no other place."

"But we're comfortable. Rescue's coming. They say it."

"They don't know what else to say. Nobody's coming, and there's no place to take us."

She turned angry. "You got us into this. We could've taken a plane a month, two months ago . . . And you had to tell the world on your goddamn radio. So now we're fucked."

"All right, Karen, I'm sorry. I didn't want humanity to die, and I didn't know how else to save it. Now I'm just asking you to do what we both want, to stay alive."

She stared out at the ice. "I don't even know if the ice is safe."

"It's holding up the ship."

She nodded slowly and looked across the endless stretch of ice and said, "Look at the pattern, the way the blue lines run. There's a solid path there."

"Fine. We'll follow you."

"Follow . . . But I might be wrong."

He held her round the shoulders and kissed her gently. "But you might be right."

She began shaking, and he held her closer.

Then they were interrupted by giggling. The Kashihara children had opened the wardroom door. Karen embarrassedly released herself and turned to them.

"Children, how'd you like to live like Eskimos?"

"Ooooh!" they said, their eyes wide.

Danny said, "Mark, what's my mother talking about?"

Mark pulled him aside and told him.

"But . . . we'll be primitives . . . I mean, what'll we *do?*"

"We're not primitives, Danny, we're shipwrecks. We're civilized people using all our wits to survive."

"But . . . what'll we do? *Hunt?*" He screwed up his face with revulsion.

"Danny, think of it as the most awesome, mysterious, and important scientific problem we've ever faced."

Danny thought for long moments. "Maybe they didn't break up my weather station . . ."

"Or maybe you can rebuild it."

Slowly, ever so slowly, he began to brighten. "We'll be rebuilding . . ."

Mark nodded.

"We're not primitives, Mark."

"Not at all."

"We'll still be saving the world, you and me."

Mark nodded, watching a light seem to come into Danny's eyes.

Afterward, Mark brought the others together in the galley and told them.

Fink was stupefied. "Mark, why is it you seem to get crazier with each new idea you get?"

"Everything's getting crazier."

"Yeah, I remember how we thought Guzman was crazy. So if he's crazy, stashing it all away down in Mexico, I guess we're sane, going back to freeze our asses."

Hideo smiled. "Seems to be a return in more ways than one." He looked out the porthole. "It's coming full circle. It's very right . . . quite perfect."

"Oh lord," groaned Fink. "Is this some more of that one-hand-clapping bullshit?"

Hideo regarded him tolerantly. "You Occidentals are so . . . scrutable. What I'm saying is, we'll be returning to our roots, to our true nature, casting off the accoutrements of civilization."

"Yeah, well, I like those accoutrements. What'd we call 'em, three square meals, a warm bed, sexual access?"

"They had 'em better than we had, Fink. An Eskimo would give you his bed, his meal, and his wife for the night." Hideo felt his own wife's eyes on him, and he turned to her. "Well, if the food was blubber, you can imagine what the wife would've been like."

Helen spoke up. "Then why bother, Mark. If it's all dying, why bother?"

"Because it's not. There're other little Edens around the globe we worked out, places in Indonesia,

New Zealand, South Africa . . . Other people'll reach
'em. We'll hang on, we'll keep in touch, and we'll survive."

"What about our captain?"

"I'm sure he'll give us supplies to get back."

"Like what?" asked Fink. "An ice-breaking rowboat?"

"Food, blankets, sleeping bags, some chemical
handwarmers . . . Whatever he can."

"But he wouldn't come with us?"

"No," said Fink. "He'll stay here where it's comfy
and warm, where he has food and fuel, and radio
communication, and a chance of being rescued. Who
wants an idiot like that along?"

Despite Fink's wisecrack, they saw the hopeless-
ness of the situation somewhat better than the captain
did.

"You're crazy," said Manujian, when Mark told
him. "We're supplied, R.C.C.'s got us spotted . . .
Y'know, this isn't the first time a ship's been icebound.
We wait it out, and we get rescued."

"You've been on the bridge, Larry, but I've been
at the radio. Nobody's coming. You're doomed here."

Manujian slammed his hand down on the table in
a sudden rage. "That's enough, Haney!"

There was a stunned silence, and Mark saw Manujian's mouth quivering.

"I think you really wanted to hit me instead."

Manujian nodded slowly. "You don't question
everything a man's lived by. If the service can rescue
us, they will. If not, well, then not. But I knew that
going in."

"That's fine for you, but my group can't be
bound by that."

"You know, rescuing you also means I can restrain you from suicidal action."

"You're not going to stop us."

"I could for your own good." Manujian took out
a set of keys, and opened a steel cabinet.

"You won't," said Mark, stepping to the door. "I

was hoping you'd let us have some supplies, but either way you won't stop us." Then he saw the .45 in Manujian's hand.

There was a long silence.

Manujian pressed the gun into Mark's hand. "You'll probably need this back there."

Mark nodded gratefully.

"Take what you need from storage. If you tear out the stuffing from the lifejackets, they'd make handy backpacks."

"Thanks, Larry." He hesitated. "Everything I need? You meant that?"

"Sure."

"I . . . uh . . . saw the storage room. It'd be just enough for us to get back."

"Oh, don't worry about us. There's tons more in the hold. I'll have 'em bring it up later."

Mark nodded, turned to go, then turned back at the door. "Larry, I hope they come for you."

"They will."

They shook hands.

The sun broke above the horizon and touched the tops of the great icebergs with pale gold, until they glowed like beacons atop the mountains.

The children were chattering with excitement, the adults with dread, as they climbed down the ladder and set foot on the ice. Each of them tested it in turn for footing and firmness, as if refusing to believe the evidence of the person before, or indeed of the ship itself so easily supported.

The sun came higher, and the gold brightened. The incandescence crept down the icebergs like molten lava. With the ship berthed high on its frozen drydock, the deck was far above them. They craned their necks and saw the railing lined with crewmen looking down, watching.

The children waved, and the men waved back, a scene much like the beginning of any ocean voyage, but now in strange reversal.

"All right, everybody . . ."

Mimicked Fink, "I suppose you're wondering why I called you here today."

"You starting again?"

"If you are."

Mark sighed. "This is goddamn dangerous, Fink. We're playing with our lives here. Look, everybody . . . Karen's in charge. She led a group of us through that big winter's blizzard, and she can get us back now. But we follow her absolutely. She guides our lives."

Karen looked at the group, adults and children, all waiting upon her next words. She looked up to the ship, to fifty crewmen also watching. She shivered, hesitated until the group grew restless.

Mark squeezed her shoulder and whispered, "I love you."

She gave a half-smile, and spoke up.

"First of all, the most important thing is a positive outlook, the power of your mind upon your body."

Fink muttered, "My God, we're getting Norman Vincent Peale on this trip."

"The Eskimo survives because he doesn't know he's not supposed to. The children play naked in the snow because they don't know you're supposed to freeze. If the Eskimo gets caught in a blizzard, he simply turns his back, sits, and waits for days until it stops. These are what you can do, the children even better than the adults, if you believe you can do it. An entire race has survived for thousands of years in this climate, and so will we."

Fink muttered, "I believe I'm gonna throw up, is what I believe." The others shushed him.

"The first thing to learn is how to walk on the ice. It's this way . . ." She demonstrated a slow, odd, flat-footed gait, then had everyone practice.

"Looka me," said Fink. "I'm walking on water."

Helen asked, "How do we know where we're going?"

"Sun's rising in the east, over there, so that's west . . ." She stretched her hands. "You line up landmarks. That ridge, miles out there, that's our goal for the day. Tomorrow, we use that to line up new marks."

"Darn clever, these Eskimos."

"They had six thousand years to learn. We'll have to speed it up a little."

"So let's walk fast."

"No, we walk slow . . . Follow me, single file. We go along the bluest part of the ice . . . There's lots more to learn, but we'll learn it."

She adjusted her improvised backpack and, after a nervous breath, took her first flat-footed step of the journey.

Mark looked back to see Manujian on the bridge. Mark held up his hand in a tentative wave, and Manujian waved firmly back.

"Hey, Mark," Fink interrupted, "I suddenly remembered what happened to the last guy who walked on water."

Mark looked at Danny. The boy kept his face down, as if crying.

"You all right, Danny?"

"Oh yeah. I was studying the ice. Here you can see it's cloudy, and there it's clear with cloudy lines. Why is that?"

"That's Hideo's department."

Hideo obliged, and told the boy of the differences in ice, the processes by which salt is gradually forced out of sea ice. The older, the fresher.

"The sun'll melt little pools of water. You use the pools from the blue ice, and it'll be the freshest, clearest water you ever drank."

"That's interesting," said Danny. "Tell me more." He soon seemed to forget the cold.

When they had gone about a thousand yards, a thin, piercing voice sounded from the ship's p.a., echoing across the floes.

"Now first call to colors. First call to colors."

They looked back to the *Briarwood*. It looked almost like a model, incongruously perched, a black toy atop a white sea. Then the men began assembling on deck, and the model came to life.

"Jesus, Mark, what're we doing out here in the

cold?" Fink moaned. "They're in a heated fortress, and all we've got's what's on our backs."

"That's all there is, Lew."

"What're you talking about?"

"I cleaned out the shelves because he told me he had tons of stuff down in the hold."

"So?"

"I looked. There's nothing down in the hold except a red buoy."

Fink took a breath. "Pretty dumb of him."

"Yeah, Lew, pretty dumb."

Just then, the national ensign caught the sunlight as it rose up the staff on the aft deck. Someone blew a whistle, and fifty men stood at attention and saluted.

Then there were three whistles. The men dropped their salutes, and returned to their tasks of the day.

Mark muttered, "Good luck, Larry." Then he turned to follow Karen, and the others fell into line after him.

Blue floes lightened into pale blue, and then into green as they crossed ever younger ice.

At night, they gathered close together in the shelter of the highest ridges, multiplying their body heat. The children giggled. The couples enjoyed the arrangement quietly, with one exception.

"This is the way pigs stay warm," said Fink.

"You would know about that," said Helen.

Fink grimaced, and turned to Mark. "Hey, wasn't this society supposed to provide me with sex?"

"Sexual access, not success."

The next day they awoke stiff and cold, but they did awake. The process was repeated. As the sun came above the horizon, accentuating the ridges in long shadows, Karen managed to pick out yet a new promontory to the west, another day's march.

The cold seemed less bothersome, either through their adjusting, or simple numbness. The packs were less burdensome, either because the people were stronger, or the packs lighter. The flat-footed gait seemed more natural. They walked longer distances with fewer rests.

They came to discern, and appreciate, the subtle differences in the ice of color, clarity, and shape.

"Eskimos have over a hundred different words for ice," said Karen. "I think you're beginning to see how."

"Still sounds like a limited conversation," Mark answered.

By the third day, the cold was not only no longer bothersome, but even bracing. The older adults remarked to one another about annoying nose and throat infections that seemed to subside. Karen told them that the Arctic provided a sterile environment.

"So does Helen," Fink grumbled.

The group might have sworn their skin had grown thicker those few days. In fact, slow, subtle changes were taking place in their bodies. Each individual cell, perhaps sentient in its primitive way, or under control of some higher process, made its myriad adjustments, adapting to its new condition. Blood vessels congealed, fat cells multiplied, mucus thickened, all too minutely to be measured as yet, but a process had begun.

By the end of the fourth day, distant spires of the city became their new landmark. As they reentered Lower New York Bay, they saw ships trapped and half buried, hulls crushed, stacks barely protruding.

The city was upon them with amazing swiftness. The distance was an illusion. The skyscrapers had seemed far out on the horizon, but that horizon was really the snowline.

As they came closer, they saw now the skyscrapers emerging directly out of the drifts without their customary base, tombstones without graves, fingers unattached to hands.

They had difficulty getting their bearings. The entire geography of the city had apparently altered. Lower Brooklyn was almost completely eradicated, and the few downtown buildings that poked above the snow were unrecognizable in their new context.

Instead, the Verrazzano Narrows Bridge marked their entrance into Upper New York Bay. Its towers still stood stark and tall as ever, though sheathed in thick frost like some monumental crystal formations, seventy stories high.

The roadway, however, had fallen in several places under the added weight, and dangled two hundred feet to the ice, grotesquely twisted like giant crepe-paper streamers, while above, the steel suspension cables hung uselessly, their ends splayed, looking like so many threadbare tassels.

The smooth snow drifts grew ruffled with intricate swirls and ripples. Even at this distance, seven miles from Manhattan, the city towers had altered the paths of the winds, much as rocks in a stream introduce lingering turbulence into the flow.

Closer to the city, grooves became trenches, ridges became walls, and all of these gradually converged and intermingled until the patterns lost all coherence.

They could see now the seeming capriciousness of the drifts. Small buildings that should have been totally buried remained comparatively free. Skyscrapers that would have ordinarily stood clear, carried snow well up their sides. Most wore great cones like nightcaps.

The winds that came down from the north had swept snow from the open Hudson River and the docks alongside, so that the group could easily discern the various piers, and retrace their steps to the one on Morton Street.

Karen gestured for silence, and they complied. They listened, as if expecting the assailants were still waiting for them, hiding behind the half-buried shed.

There was only quiet, awesome and unending. The snow had snuffed out the sounds of the city as thoroughly as its streets and inhabitants.

It was suddenly interrupted by a distant boom, followed by an incredible clattering, and then silence again.

"What the hell!"

About a mile to the northwest, a cloud of white smoke rose, and then settled.

"Someone alive out there?"

Mark shook his head. "A building collapsing."

"Why only now?"

He shrugged. "They're all built different, the accumulation's different . . ."

"As you once said," Hideo interrupted, "Greenland's nice when it stays up in Greenland."

"It's not Greenland yet."

They fell silent as they climbed a snowbank up to street level. On the protected south side of the shed there were isolated planks from broken crates, torn pages of some books, gears and wires from instruments, and the badly dented and rusted snowmobile.

"Looka this," said Fink, pulling it out of the snow. "We could fill it up at any corner gas station—if we could only find a corner."

"Something more important," said Mark, shoveling snow away with a plank, and unearthing a black metal box. "The radio."

"Oh. I thought it was something useful, like a refrigerator."

"Get your priorities in order, Fink. Food we'll dig up. We'll stay alive, but this gives us the reason to live."

"A goddamn fucking *radio?*"

"People, Fink, people. Our tie-in to the net."

"And what do we do, melt some frozen electricity for it?"

"If the radio's here, the generator's here."

"Which we fuel at the same corner station."

"We've got something else, and lots of it."

"Y'mean this funny white stuff? Y'want regular or premium?"

"I mean wind."

"Oh, well, that we do have a lot of, and all from your direction."

"All right, Fink, just drop it."

"Hell no! *You're* telling *us* about priorities?"

"Drop it!"

Fink fumed in silence, and watched the others prodding the snow listlessly, looking for the remnants of their own belongings. He watched a while with wonder. Then he kicked at the snow.

"We're dead, only we don't know it. Why don't we bury ourselves now, and save ourselves a lot of trouble?"

"We're alive," said Karen.

He turned to see her holding an Eskimo carving, and smiling. "We're alive, and we'll live."

The others stopped what they were doing, and looked at her.

"I suppose a little stone walrus told you."

She nodded.

"Another loon."

"We're alive, Lew, because a whole race lived this way, and they bequeathed us these." She ran her hands over it lovingly. "We'll live, I know we will."

Fink shrugged in exasperation, but the others gathered around her as if the carving were magical. They took it, handled it admiringly, passed it around as they muttered lame words such as ". . . Beautiful . . ."

"Maybe beautiful, but not edible," muttered Fink.

Danny was still disconsolate and wandered away from the group, into the entrance to the shed. Then he saw something shiny. He brushed away the snow, and let out a yell. It was a funnel.

He dug it out with his hands until it emerged fully, a wheel with funnels at the end of the spokes.

"The anemometer!"

Now he too could feel some of that same magic, that he too would survive, and save civilization.

As he dug deeper, pulling up other instruments, he didn't notice the shadows emerging from the greater shadow.

Then he heard a sound that was distinctly not human, a low soft growl.

He looked up and gasped. There stood a dog that was almost a wolf, over one hundred pounds, a mass of welts and scars, its mouth open, powerful jaws salivating. It showed its teeth, snarled again, and now began warily circling.

"*Ma* . . ." It was a moan of total terror. He looked around for an escape, and saw instead other dogs emerge, all with scars and torn fur, all huge and hungry.

One by one they fell in line behind their leader, until there were fully ten of them. Their eyes gleamed with anticipation, and fixed firmly on the child as the pack followed in that circle.

"Ma . . ."

Karen saw them first.

"Danny, don't move!"

The pack were unconcerned about the other humans. They had singled out Danny, and cut him off effectively. Tighter and tighter they circled, until the Husky stepped out, made a tentative feint toward the boy, and drew back, satisfied he offered no resistance.

"Ma . . ."

Mark raised the pistol and took careful aim.

"No!" Karen practically knocked it out of his hand.

"What the hell're you doing?"

"You couldn't kill them fast enough. Use it, and Danny's dead. Besides, we need them."

"Need? . . . You crazy?"

"Get me some meat, quick," she said, as she picked up a broken plank.

The Husky made a second feint, yet closer, and the other dogs stirred, howled with expectation, then they began stepping out of their circle.

The group dug into their knapsacks, came up with whatever morsels were left, handed these to Karen, even as they wondered. She set the food within reach, keeping her eye fixed on the Husky.

She reached down for a good-sized rock and hurled it at the dog. He howled, distracted, and snarled at her. For a moment, he hesitated, choosing between prey. A second rock caught him, and now he turned, came charging full at Karen, and the other dogs followed.

Mark followed with his gun, and his finger tightened.

"Don't!"

She kept the plank between her and the Husky,

jabbing as the dog came closer, circling as the dog circled.

Then she threw a small chunk of beef in the dog's path. He ignored it, and charged again toward her. Again he caught the plank in his withers.

She backed off, let him come closer, prodded him in the direction of the meat.

He hesitated. Behind him, the other dogs waited.

Finally, ignoring the morsel in the snow, he came lunging again, and again met the plank. He hesitated, backed off, regarded the meat hungrily, chomped at it, then came charging again.

This time, the sight of the plank was enough. He growled, stepped back, took a second bite, tore at it, while pulling and holding it with his paws.

The pack growled, then barked with challenge to his leadership.

He turned and barked back, baring his fangs. The others retreated.

"Give him more," yelled Karen.

"There's almost nothing left."

"Give it to him."

They were about to throw it at the pack.

"To him! He's the leader."

They followed orders, tossing the supplies gingerly toward the Husky.

The Husky at last ate his fill, and growled, backed off, then let the other dogs have at the remains. They fought, scrambled, clawed at each other while he stood by and watched.

Mark said, "What happens when they finish that, and they're still hungry?"

"They'll kill us." Still keeping her eye on the Husky, she took off her lifejacket, taking out a pocketknife and cutting off the straps.

"Then why not kill them now?"

"That's a Husky, Mark, a Greenland Husky . . . and he's the leader." She was almost joyous.

The group watched, unbelieving, as Karen approached the dog, knotting the straps together into one long cord. She muttered strange words to the dog in a modal singsong. Perhaps it was the chant, one ancient heritage reaching out to another through mystic paths, or perhaps merely the general soothing sound, but wondrously, the Husky relaxed and let her work the strap through his collar.

Only then did she herself relax. Her knees seemed to wobble beneath her, and Mark had to catch her before she fell.

"You all right?"

She nodded weakly, clutching the strap. "They'll . . . they'll follow him . . . We can tie them."

"Tie them? Tie them to what, and for what?"

"To the snowmobile. We've got a dog team."

"To the . . . Karen, have you gone . . . ?"

"Don't argue, Mark. There's no time. Hideo . . ." She held out the strap to him. "Hold on, but stay out of his jaw's reach . . . and don't let go." She turned to the others. "The rest of you, get that machine dug out, and over here." She was giving orders like a master sergeant now. "Gut the insides as much as you can. All we really need's the frame and the runners, and if they're rusted, pour water on 'em and let it freeze."

They stared.

"C'mon! We've got tigers by the tails here. We can't let go, and we can't stop. Let's move, or we're dead."

They rushed to follow orders.

Fink stood apart from the group, shaking his head in wonder.

"Lew, you'll help me on the second dog."

"Hey, I'm just a tourist here," he said, backing away.

"There are no more tourists here," said Mark. "We need you."

"Why don't I feel warm all over when you say that?"

"It's not just for you yourself, Fink. We're carrying civilization on our backs."

Fink laughed. "Sorry, Marcus. I've got a slipped disc."

Mark grabbed Fink by the collar with his left

hand. His right held the gun, and he pointed it straight at Fink's head. "Look, Lew, there are no more cripples, no tourists, no freeloaders. If we have to live the way the Eskimos lived, we'll do it down the line, all the way, till we get things functioning again."

A stunned Fink looked down the barrel of the gun. "You're not kidding, are you, Mark?"

He shook his head. "Neither is this, Lew. The Coast Guard loaded it, and they showed me how to use it."

"You . . . you wouldn't kill a colleague."

"Even if he had tenure."

"I . . . I'm impressed, Mark. I'll . . . help tie the dogs."

The bull mastiff growled and showed its teeth when Fink approached, and he backed away. "You did say the gun's loaded."

"We need the dogs," said Karen. "Don't make us choose between you." She took the second strap and approached the dog. "There are two important things to remember. One is to remind yourself they are basically vulnerable and frightened, like little puppies." She murmured soothingly to the bull mastiff, touching its flank respectfully. It growled softly.

"And the other?"

"Is to never forget they're killers." She ignored its growl, and started to slip the strap round its neck. The dog shook its head, bared its teeth, and snapped at her.

With a stunning move, Karen slapped the dog hard across the muzzle. The dog howled, attempted a slash, and Karen slammed him again, harder. The dog whimpered, and drooped its head a moment. Karen neatly and quickly slipped the loop over its face, and tightened it round the neck.

"Jesus," exclaimed Fink.

"They're killers, plain and simple. That's how they survived this long."

"But you'll show us how to tame 'em."

"No, we'll never get 'em tamed. Controlled, maybe, barely . . ."

The bull mastiff was pulling on its rope now, twisting to get back at Karen as if suddenly discovering it had been trapped. The other dogs grew restive watching, and Karen eyed them warily.

"Lew . . ." She held the end of the strap to Fink, who took it gingerly. "Keep its jaws away."

"I . . . uh . . . hope he agrees."

"That snowmobile ready?" she called to the group.

They pulled it to her. There wasn't much left, beyond the sled runners and the connecting frame. The rest lay in a heap of rusted metal and components.

Guardedly, she took the Husky from a shaky Hideo, and, working the strap to stay clear of its reach, she got the dog to the snowmobile and tied him in front with an intricate knot.

Then she repeated the process, taking the bullmastiff from Fink and tying it next to the Husky. Suddenly, they were fighting, snarling and snapping at each other.

Karen picked up a plank and slammed them both. They whimpered and fell silent.

"We better work fast. They're catching on."

With the schipperke, a frisky smaller dog, she had to hold onto its fur as well as the strap to keep it controlled. Again, alternating soothing murmurs with slaps, she managed to bring that dog to the sled, but when she attempted to tie it in place, all three broke into a fight, and now the free dogs began snarling and pawing the snow.

"Use the whip, Lew!"

"The . . . what?"

"The whip, goddamn it!" She pointed to the whip with the thirty-foot lash lying in the snow.

He picked it up. "What'll I do with it?"

"At them!" She pointed at the pack. "For Christ's sake, hurry!"

"I . . . I never handled . . ." He struck at the pack with almost comic ineffectualness. "I mean, what do you think I did for a living?"

"Oh, Christ . . ." She grabbed the whip, and handed the plank to him. "This is easier."

She brought the lash down on the dogs, approaching dangerously close to do so. The lash rolled and thudded on their flanks, wrapping around them, and she had to pull back quickly before its windings got too entangled. She cursed her own incompetence.

At last, between whip and plank, Karen managed to work the rope around yet another dog's neck. Now four dogs fought as she tied them together.

"Lordy," cried Fink, "how long does this go on?"

"We can't stop, not if we want to get out of this alive."

"C'mon," said Mark, grabbing a strap, and trying with the fifth dog himself. "I think we got the idea."

"So've they, Mark," Fink moaned.

At last, with the exhausted help of all hands, the entire pack were tethered together, and comparatively quiet.

Helen gasped, "Karen, do we go through this every time?"

" 'Fraid so."

"It's like having a backyard of tigers."

"That's the point. They're hunters. We let 'em go, and hang on for the ride."

"I thought all we do is say, 'Mush,' and they go where we want."

"Not 'mush,' Helen," said Fink. "What you say is, 'Please . . .' "

"You don't let them choose, Lew," said Karen. "You just have to be scarier than the animals we'll hunt."

"Uh huh. Such as?"

"Rabbits . . ."

"Okay, if they're not too vicious."

"Cats."

"Cats? We gonna be eating cats?"

"People on this earth have eaten anything that swims, crawls, or flies. And most of 'em would retch at T-bone. It's all in what you tell yourself."

Fink swallowed hard. "All right, what others?"

"Wolves, foxes, lemmings, bears, seals . . ."

"Bears? Y'mean polar bears?"

"Whatever comes by, Lew."

"Polar bears, oh Jesus, polar bears . . ." He looked out across the city, to streets that had disappeared, to buildings barely protruding above the snow, to the snowcones atop famous landmarks, to towers and rectangles reshaped into hills and curves by the drifts.

Karen turned to the group. "We've hardly any time. We're out of food, and we've got to start hunting right away."

"Oh no, Karen, we gotta rest."

"We'll only get weaker from hunger, and then we'll really be sunk. First we've got to direct the dogs, if we can't control 'em. Mark, remember how the Eskimos used the whip to . . ."

She realized Mark wasn't there, nor Danny. She turned around to see them both at the radio.

She swallowed, and handed Hideo the whip. "You saw how the Eskimos used this. Try and show 'em how."

"I saw, but . . ."

"Well, I couldn't do it any better." She left him, and headed over to Mark.

Hideo watched her for a few moments, then turned back to the group, and tried demonstrating the whip. The lash tangled behind him, caught him round the neck and nearly choked him. He cursed, and untangled it.

The group was undecided between compassion and laughter.

Hideo tried again. This time, he managed at least to keep it straight, and the lash rolled and thudded.

"They've got a way of cracking it . . ."

"Which you haven't."

"Which Karen hasn't either. The Eskimos were marvelous with it. They could control all the dogs from the sled. It'd just zing and crack, right to the exact troublemaker, and the dogs would quiet right down."

"Well," said Helen, "you haven't got it, Karen hasn't, so it's fair to say we won't. So what do we do?"

Hideo shrugged. "Whatever we can."

By the shed, Karen watched Mark and Danny cleaning out the radio.

"Mark," she said finally, "we've got the dogs together."

"Good," said Mark, looking up from his work to smile at her. "I knew you'd justify my . . ."

"We can't be certain what we'll find, and you've got the gun."

"Yeah." His smile faded.

"Well, either you give it to us . . ."

"Uh . . . no, I'm the only one with any military training."

". . . or you come along."

"This is too important."

"The radio? We're talking about survival."

"So'm I, Karen, our whole reason for survival."

"And what do we plug it into?"

Danny spoke up. "Mom, when I told you, you said it was fantasy. But it isn't fantasy. We've got a generator."

"And what for fuel?"

"The wind, Mom. Mark'll hook up a windmill."

Karen nodded skeptically. "All in good time. Right now we need you, with the gun."

"Karen, I've only a few bullets anyway. What happens when we run out?"

"By that time, I hope, I'll've found my other Eskimo weapons, and we'll've learned how to use 'em. Meanwhile . . ."

Mark sighed in annoyance, with a glance toward the radio and the tasks remaining on it.

"Mark." She pulled him back with a surprising bluntness. "You put survival in my hands. I didn't like it, I didn't want it, but it's in my hands. Right now, I'm asking you—or, if you like, I'm ordering you."

Danny looked at his mother astonished, then across to Mark, waiting to see what he would do.

Mark was equally astonished for a moment. He was about to make a wisecrack about creating a Frankenstein, but thought better of it. Instead, he nodded quietly, and turned to Danny.

"Well, I'd better help your mother. Whyn't you stay here and wait?"

"Wait?" He looked lost a moment. "Maybe it'll be something I'll have to know about."

Karen said, "I don't think you should come along, Danny. It could be dangerous."

"*Rabbits*, mother?"

"The dogs, Danny."

The color seemed to go out of his face. He shook, took several breaths, and forced a smile. "They'll be tied, won't they? And Mark has the gun."

Karen sighed. "All right, Danny."

Mark pulled her aside. "Why do you let *him* decide?"

"It's the way of the Eskimos."

"What the hell's that mean?"

"The only way we'll survive is by following the Eskimos, and that means all the way, everything they do. And Eskimos let the children boss themselves."

"I don't see why, if something's obviously dangerous . . ."

"No, Mark. Their society had six thousand years to develop. Everything in it had its reason, and it all worked."

"But what's survival got to do with a child . . . ?"

"I don't know, Mark. It wasn't part of my paper. But if Eskimos didn't tell their children what to do, neither will we. Danny'll have to choose his own actions."

"But he doesn't know the dangers."

"Neither do we, so who's to say who decides better?"

Mark took a breath. "Karen, you know what Danny means to me."

"He means something to me, too, Mark. He's my son."

When they returned to the team, the dogs were sniffing the air and barking as they pulled at their ropes. They had evidently picked up a scent, and Hideo was trying to restrain them, whipping at them from as close as he dared get.

Danny blanched at the sight, swallowed hard, and put on his bravest face.

"They're sure onto something big," said Hideo.

"How big can it be?" Karen turned to Danny, concerned. "Wouldn't you rather stay?"

"Mother, stop treating me like a child."

She nodded slowly, and gestured Mark and Danny onto the sled. She told Hideo to run alongside, cracking the whip at any disruptive dogs.

"Cracking? Let's say thudding," said Hideo with a wan smile.

She smiled back and then, carefully, she loosened the anchoring rope.

The Husky pulled at his traces, almost strangling himself when the inertia held him back. After a few prods with the plank, he seemed to catch a kind of rhythm, and now all the dogs pulled together, following him, barking and howling. The sled creaked, and took off.

"Hold 'em back . . . Drag your feet . . ."

They did so, and Karen began getting some measure of control over the balancing and steering.

"Wow . . ." exclaimed Danny in elation, as the cold wind began whipping his face, and the buildings began to fly by. Then his elation was dampened as the dogs moved their bowels simultaneously, and the sled passed over their droppings.

Hideo ran alongside the pack, trying to whip those dogs that nipped at each other, or disrupted the line in various ways, back into place.

In this erratic fashion, the team made a sharp turn down a side street, nearly spilling the sled before Karen could right the balance.

Then they came upon the first of a series of huge paw prints. The dogs clustered around sniffing, and went wild. Karen had to throw stones at them from the sled, while Hideo whipped at them frantically.

"That's no rabbit," said Mark. "What is it?"

"You wouldn't believe it."

"After all that's happened?"

The dogs pulled and tugged frantically after the prints, and Karen had to toss out ropes beneath the runners to add further friction to the sled.

Then they saw it.

"Jesus . . . You're right, I don't believe it!"

It turned to face them, howling frightfully. Indeed, it seemed like something out of a dream at first, a white bear against a white background so that it was almost invisible, despite its terrifying half-ton weight. When it stood and roared its defiance, however, it towered over them, only too vivid against the dark stone of the office building.

"Where the hell'd that come from?"

"From the zoo, I should imagine. Probably the Arctic animals were the only ones to survive."

The dogs pulled and strained at their rope, and Karen reached for the knots.

"What're you doing?"

"Letting them go!"

Before Mark could stop her, she had pulled out the knots. Immediately, the frenzied dogs went charging after the bear, surrounding it, leaping and snapping at it as they had after other creatures.

The Husky, following its usual pattern, attacked first. The bear howled, and with a swipe of its paw sent the Husky reeling back into the snow. Now the other dogs attacked, jabbing, feinting, attacking, retreating. Again they were sent tumbling back in showers of snow, only to right themselves and attack again, until they seemed one rolling, howling mass.

The bear began advancing through them, slashing and swiping, drawing blood, advancing straight for the sled.

"Mark!"

Mark took aim at the bear's head and fired. The bear reared back, and went berserk, writhing hysterically in the snow. The dogs attacked again, in full force.

Mark fired again, and a third time, and suddenly the bear was quiet.

Now Karen and Hideo beat the dogs off, bringing down whip and plank until the dogs whimpered and lay quiet.

Danny's eyes were absolutely dancing with excitement.

"Wow!" was all he could say. " . . . Wow . . ."

Mark did not like the look.

They made a fire inside the shed, and Hideo's wife did most of the cooking. The bear steaks were gamy and tough, but the group was hungry and they didn't quibble. The children even liked it. They felt full and warm afterward, and they could easily see something appealing about this life, almost like a camping trip to some northern woods.

"Trouble is," said Mark, "it's only a vacation when you can end it."

"There's another trouble," said Karen. "We'd have to catch a bear every day for the rest of our lives. How many do you think the zoos had?"

"You said there're other animals around."

"Probably. Some wild deer, maybe some birds, a few foxes, anything from the country that'll accidentally come wandering by here." She sighed. "Not too many that're filling."

There was a silence, long and gloomy, as they watched the fire burn down.

Mark was about to throw some more planks into the fire, and Karen stopped him. "We'll need those to build more sleds."

"More sleds? Isn't one enough?"

She shook her head. "Every family'll have to hunt for itself."

They gulped. "What about dog teams?"

"There'll be other dogs, don't worry."

Fink grunted. "If you don't mind, Karen, I'll worry."

Again a silence.

"Martens and lemmings," blurted Mark, bewildering the group.

"What?"

"They were migrating, one of the first signs I found of it getting colder. So if martens and lemmings, why not caribou and seals, and polar bears, and I don't mean from the zoo."

"But even with the cold, they didn't migrate that far."

He nodded. "Something'll be chasing 'em."

"What's that?" asked Helen.

"Something a hell of a lot worse than the cold."

"For God's sake, what?"

"The ice. All the little glaciers, from Greenland to Mt. Ranier, gathering together."

"Well, Jesus, how long before . . . ?"

Hideo interrupted, smiling. "Don't worry about it, Helen."

"Don't worry?"

"It'll be irrelevant anyway, so just relax."

"Irrelevant! What the hell're you . . . ?"

"If we're around, we'll have beaten our predicament. And if not, well, it'll certainly be irrelevant then."

He got up, stoked the fire and revived the embers briefly. "Just think. Whoever, whatever follows us, those future professors, they'll dig through, they'll find our remains here . . . 'Interesting, interesting,' they'll say. 'Maybe there's a paper in this.' "

They did not find any more bears the next day, polar or otherwise, but on Eighth Street, the dogs did catch one rabbit and two cats. The group, hungry as they were, could not bring themselves to eat cats, so they let the dogs take those. Then Karen dug up her old Eskimo spear.

Mark remained behind to dig further, and do more work on his windmill. Danny helped for a while, but talked more about the polar bear hunt than the work at hand.

The third day, the dogs reached Twelfth Street before the team came apart and they tangled themselves in the traces. A block later, they found a starving deer, and again the group had to fight the dogs, beating them back before Karen could spear it. With the deer weak and confused, it was an easy shot.

Mark, meanwhile, had assembled metal blades into a windmill configuration, but the spinning was halting and erratic. Danny was interested, but scarcely excited. Instead, he watched the group practicing with the spear, and wandered over to suggest they make a game of it. In fact, he selected targets and formulated some rules.

Mark had to gently remind Danny of just what was important.

Under Karen's direction, the group cannibalized wood and nails from other packing crates, and built themselves a second sled. It was crude and crooked, but it ran smoothly enough when water was rubbed on the runners.

When the Kashihara twins saw it standing useless, they assumed it was meant as a toy, so they played with it pretending to be hunter and dog, clumsily using the whip. It looked as if they might hurt each other, and Wendy scolded them, but Hideo reminded her of the Eskimo mores they had to follow. The children were to be let alone to find their own way.

The twins invited Danny to join, but he said he was no child, and the sled was no toy.

"Then what's it for?"

"For real dogs."

They laughed, but other strays indeed began showing up, large, well-furred, and savage. Each was caught, slapped or whipped until it submitted long enough to be tied, and soon there was a second functional dog team.

But now there were also twice as many dogs to be fed, twice as many "tigers in the backyard" to try and keep under control. The fights among the dogs occurred ever more often, they grew increasingly unruly, and they even took occasional nips at their human masters.

The group found other animals now, otters, martens, foxes, and rats, hardy burrowers that seemed to survive in dark corners of half-buried buildings. Those were left to the dogs.

Skinning the animals was a nauseating sight that only Karen and Wendy could stand at first. For Wendy, the step from her accustomed raw fish to raw animals was not too great. Danny would watch from a distance. He threw up at first, yet he could not pull himself away. He would swallow hard, come closer as an animal was cut up, and ask about the resemblances of animal anatomy to his own.

He was certainly less interested in helping Mark on the windmill.

Then suddenly it all changed. Mark got the gearings in place, and the generator sparked and crackled. For a while it ran erratically, alternately overfeeding and underfeeding current, but Mark improvised a flywheel and a regulator to steady the flow, and now Danny was excited all over again. He prowled through empty buildings until he had dug out a light bulb and wiring, and helped hook these up.

By now everyone was watching. The rotor squealed, the drive train scraped and clanked, sparks flew, and then the light bulb came on, flickering and flashing until Mark made the right adjustments.

Finally, it glowed steadily, a strange miniature sun. For a while, the group regarded it in awed silence.

"Strange god. White-devil magic," muttered Fink, dancing about it while chanting, and sprinkling snow at it before satisfying himself it would not strike him dead on the spot. Then he even dared approach, and spoke to it. "Hello? Hello?"

"Civilization," said Helen in wonder. "I thought it was history."

Hideo patted Mark on the back. "Well, I guess you better stay here and leave us to do the hunting. You've got a miracle to take care of."

Mark smiled, and looked across at Danny.

"I wanna stay too," said Danny. "We gotta hook up the radio. That'll be the real miracle."

Mark knew what the results would be before he even tried, but it had to be his first message.

"Hello, CGC Briarwood, this is W2QRV, Whiskey Two Quebec Romeo Victor calling. Over."

There was only hiss.

He tried over and over, sometimes asking for Commanding Officer Manujian, but there was no answer.

Danny began to fidget, and wandered back to his weather station. He took his readings, clocked the wind with his anemometer, and noted it was boringly perpetual, just fine for windmill generators.

It was the same old forecast, conditions bleak and unending. He stared gloomily at his instruments, and then he heard a voice on Mark's radio.

It was distant, and nearly drowned in static.

"Bright Flare, this is Dark Errand. That is a negative on the move. Will contact you with new coordinates in about two zero minutes. Do you roger? Over."

There was an affirmative answer, and a sign-off from Bright Flare.

"What's that mean?"

Mark sighed. "Guantanamo Base in Cuba . . . Maybe maneuvers, maybe for real." He looked around him. "Need a better antenna. You wanna help?"

"Sure." Then Danny looked to the city. He could hear the distant cries of the dog teams fighting and snarling, and the yelling of the hunters. "Wonder what they've found."

Karen was wide-eyed. "They've come!"

"Jesus, what the hell are they?" yelled Fink.

They looked like overlarge, clumsy deer, with white shaggy fur on their backs and hanging down from their necks. But quite the most prominent features were the overlarge antlers that curved forward in great semicircles.

"It's amazing. They've come," she said again.

There were flocks of them, wandering confusedly in the streets, padding down the snow with their large hooves, stymied by the buildings, frightened by their reflections in the glass windows, and backing off only to collide with others in the flock, producing pandemonium.

Now the dogs were frantic, barking ferociously, totally out of control as they fought against each other, trying to chase the herd in different directions.

The sled flipped about and sent Fink flying into the snow. He rolled out of the way as the overturned sled came bearing down on him, dragged by dogs in their own state of hysteria.

Karen took aim against one of the animals with her spear, only to be nearly trampled by a second coming from behind.

In moments more, hysteria had become riot, the dogs barking, dragging their overturned sled, the herd bolting in several directions at once, and the humans screaming as they tried to alternately capture and then get out of the way of both the herd and the dogs.

The herd scattered, disappearing down several streets and avenues, leaving behind some well-padded snow and thorough chaos.

The dogs were at last dragged to a halt by their overturned sled, their barkings diminishing to wails as they tugged and strained uselessly against the dead weight.

The group helped each other to their feet groaning, and set about the huge, and dangerous, task of untangling the dogs' traces.

Karen still wore her look of bewilderment, only now it gradually merged with a dazed smile. "They've come."

"Yeah?" said Fink, "Well, I just wish they'd go, whatever they are."

"They're caribou, Lew."

"So?"

"They're migrating."

"Fine. I won't stop 'em."

She smiled. "We will, Lew. Just like the Eskimos did."

"My God, Mark Haney. Where've you been? Over."

The signal was weak, the voice intelligible only with difficulty.

"Nowhere, Pat," Mark sighed. "Right back where we started. How do you read me? Over."

"You're only a three-two, Mark. Can you give me any more?"

"Negative for now, Pat. I need a better antenna. Everything else is jerry-built, including our lives here. How goes Miami?"

There was a pause before Pat Keegan answered. "It's going, Mark. It's all going . . . I've got the house barricaded, but . . . Well, hell, you can hear what's happening out there . . ."

There was a jumble of sounds, mainly yells of a crowd, all almost submerged in the general static, but Mark could guess the situation.

"Sorry I didn't make it down to Campeche, Mark. Would've liked to've met you and everybody else in the net. Guess you'll have to keep it up without me."

Now it was Mark who hesitated. "Pat, we've got to stay in touch, no matter what. Look, we've got to cut down ocean evaporation to break this cycle. Any suggestions?"

"Cut evaporation? . . ."

His voice faded for some moments, and Mark had to summon him up again, manipulating both radio and generator controls.

"Well . . . film of oil cuts evaporation . . ."

"Fine. How much, what kind, and where're the optimum places for the currents to spread it?"

"Uh . . . I dunno. Seems a little faraway now."

"Jesus, Pat, we're talking about survival."

"Survival . . . Oh yeah . . . I was trying to get through to Los Angeles . . . Guess the sandstorms're interfering . . . Hey Mark, I don't want to keep water from evaporating. They need rain there."

"All right, Pat, we've got to be selective. Get me the data, and I'll work it up."

Pat's voice came to life. "Hey Mark, you have a computer there? Great, we've got a chance then."

Mark swallowed. "Uh . . . yeah . . . That's what I'm trying to tell you. We've got a great chance."

"Well, we've sure got a chance," said Karen, making a diagram in the snow floor. "The caribou are moving south, along the wide avenues. North of the Village, the streets are parallel, but at Thirteenth there's another street at an angle . . . uh . . . What was it?"

She looked at Mark. He shrugged, bored.

"Sorry, other things on my mind."

They all had to stop and think before Helen offered, "Greenwich Avenue."

"Yeah," said Fink. "It's history now, your department."

"All right. Greenwich Avenue finishes into snowbanks. It's a dead-end. We detour the herds down that street."

"Aha," said Fink. "Someone stands at that turn-off and directs traffic. I understand Hideo here comes from an ancient and noble suicide tradition."

"No," said Karen, "we need something that'll actually frighten them, something unusual, bizarre, totally outside their experience."

"Well, Helen here's been totally outside my experience . . ."

"With good reason, schmuck," said Helen.

"We're talking about our lives!" said Karen, cutting off the argument with a tone so curt and commanding the two were stunned into silence. She looked across at Mark. "Your windmill, right at that intersection . . ."

He shook his head.

"It's no game, Mark. It's for our survival."

"That's what I'm using it for. Sorry."

There was a silence, until Danny spoke up. "My anemometer."

"Your what?"

"It spins like a windmill. It's a little smaller . . ."

Mark stared. "Danny, have you gone out of your mind?"

Danny shrugged. "Should be interesting."

Mark moaned, and shook his head. "I just hope this doesn't lead to anything."

Mark had ample reason to regret Danny's absence. He was stuck with some hard work, made all the harder and lonelier without Danny's help.

Each band on his radio receiver had different characteristics and use, and each functioned best with a separate antenna, placed as high as possible. He had to reach the roof of a sufficiently tall building, clear tons of snow, and string wires back down to the receiver. All those wires, in turn, had to be cannibalized from electrical circuits in the building. If he were lucky, he might get one band operating by the day's end. It was exhausting (and he had to be careful about perspiring, since his sweat would freeze). Worse, it was boring, damned boring.

Even Danny might have been bored.

"Here they come!"

It was an amazing sight, a forest on the move, a parade of antlers down the avenue, the steam from their breaths and bodies like some mysterious mist that moved with them.

"Wow!" exclaimed Danny, his blood pounding, feeling he might almost die from the excitement. He looked first toward his anemometer, spinning on a pole right in the herd's path, and then down the length of Greenwich Avenue where his friends waited, spaced a half block apart, equally tense, equally excited.

For one heart-stopping moment, it seemed the herd would not stop, would charge right through the spinning wheel, and go on trampling down Eighth Avenue and be gone forever, leaving only some crushed fragments of wood and kitchen funnels.

Then it happened. The lead animal stopped,

reared its head back with a frightened yelp, and those magnificent antlers swung about.

The panic spread and other antlers turned about in successive waves, and caribou collided as the leaders fought their way back.

Across the street, Karen jumped out, her fur coat over her head, waving her arms and howling like a wolf.

Terrified, the caribou retreated, and turned to the only free route, down Greenwich Avenue.

The other hunters jumped up, similarly dressed, similarly howling, speeding the caribou on their way.

And now Danny leaped up, howling at the top of his lungs. It was intoxicating. He ran among the herd, whirling his arms and chasing the animals before him.

The avenue came to its end two blocks later, and the caribou were stopped. The hunters ran after them, howling all the while, closing the circle.

The panicked caribou ran into each other. Some fell, only to be trampled and kicked by the others as they tried fighting their way out.

The hunters charged in with their meager clubs and lances to finish off the wounded.

As Danny watched, he was surprised at his own lack of fear, his exhilaration sweeping aside all other emotions. There was a sense of rightness, as if he were meant to be here and behaving in this way. It was almost as if he had come home.

He wondered how he would feel if he were actually killing.

"Hello, Mark, how're you doing?"

The signal was clear, the voice unmistakable, and despite Mark's feelings he couldn't help using the full, respectful title when he answered.

"Fine, Professor Guzman. How are you?"

"Eating well, eating well. All my appetites, if I want . . . if I want." He paused. "Met a New Yorker here." He waited for some audible reaction from Mark, even a grunt, but Mark did not give him any, and he went on. "Name's Herbie, and a born hustler. He'd've done great in our department. Kept me laughing about the money he hustled during the snowstorm, charging people to get down a ladder. Well, he's grown up in a hurry. Offered me a girl for the night, just for some food, and I'm sure he'll be hustling the food somewhere else." He snickered. "He sure figured who's short of what."

Mark could hear that he had bent closer to the microphone, and his tone was indeed suddenly furtive.

"Mark, what do I do about guns? I'm in over my head here."

Mark felt his skin crawl. "Why're you talking to me, Professor Guzman?"

"Because you're the only one I can talk to."

"Well, I'm sorry, Professor, but I've got other people to . . ."

"Hold on, hold on," said Guzman in a rush. "I've been thinking, thinking a lot about the ice . . . how to turn it back."

Mark sat bolt upright. "Whatever you've got to share, for God's sake, share it."

Guzman almost sighed in relief. "It's a pleasure to talk to you, Mark. God, no one else wants to listen."

"Fine, I'm listening. What do we do?"

"Nothing."

Mark almost switched him off in disgust, a move that Guzman must have sensed, because he spoke again in something of a rush.

"I mean that, Mark. I'd let it alone. It's a self-correcting process. The water vapor drops off, the particulates too, and there are no storm triggers. When the cycle's broken, it'll reverse. Just sit back, and hold out a while."

"How long's a while?"

"Well, it'll be after I'm dead, so I didn't bother figuring. It'll be after you're dead too, so you shouldn't bother either. My chairman-of-the-department advice is to forget all that aggravation about saving the world. Nature'll work it better than you ever will, so just sit back, relax, and enjoy life. And be glad you don't have flies up there."

"Good-bye, Professor."

Mark flipped him off, and rotated the dial to a new frequency. He felt queasy for quite a while afterward.

The blood ran out across the snow in a warm, sticky stream, and then out spilled the greenish intestines in a steaming mass. Before, the group would have been revolted, but now they stared, fascinated.

The dogs were hysterical, snapping at their badly frayed straps.

Karen looked at them worriedly, and finally tossed some parts to the Husky. The other dogs tried to out-grab him, but he bared his fangs, snapped at them, and they retreated sullenly.

"I hope that calms them down a while."

She turned back to her lesson, rolling back the fur and skin and fat. "The fur makes the warmest and lightest clothing, a lot better than what we're wearing. Not to mention that with the antlers, we make perfect decoys . . . If we need tents, we can make 'em from the skin."

She cut deeper, into bone. "They carved tools from this, and toggles for the clothes. Maybe we'll get good at that, too."

She came to sinew. "When we dry that, it'll be stronger than rope. We can string bows with it, make better traces for the dog team, thread for our clothes. For needles we use bone splinters. Nothing goes to waste."

Said Danny, "So one caribou helps us catch others."

Karen nodded. "It was as close a relationship with nature as humans ever had."

Danny squatted next to her. "Let me have the knife, Mom. I wanna try cutting."

"Hello, Mark, we had fun, and we learned a lot."

All Mark could do at first was stare in horror.

Danny's coat was caked with fragments of flesh and gore.

"My God, Danny, what the hell happened to you?"

"Happened?" Danny wiped his nose with his sleeve, leaving a wide smear of blood on his face.

Mark was nauseated. He grabbed the boy. "Danny, you're staying with me tomorrow."

"Tomorrow? . . . But we're gonna hunt tomorrow. This time we can wear a skin, and use the antlers . . . I'll handle a spear and get to kill a . . ."

"Stop that!" he yelled, shaking Danny.

The boy gasped, and he swung his arms up to protect himself.

"I'm sorry! . . . Don't hit me, please, Mark, don't hit me . . . Please don't hit me!" he cried, throwing himself down into the snow.

"Jesus, Danny . . ." Mark bent low over him. "Danny, I've never hit you . . . I never will, never . . . Danny, I love you . . ."

At last the boy quieted.

"Danny, look, I've got something really exciting happening here. I've got most of the antennas up, and I'm getting signals from all over. There's a whole world of people out there, Danny, and I'm in touch with them."

Danny looked at him wide-eyed. For some moments he didn't seem to know what Mark was talking about.

"The radio, Danny. I'm talking to experts in Indonesia, and South Africa, and England . . . Danny, we're going to save the world, you and I . . ."

". . . Oh . . . yeah . . . We're going to save the world." He didn't sound so sure.

"Hello, Whiskey Two, you're four-four here in Pretoria. We think we can hold the line against the desert, but it's touch and go. We're trying to fence the Kalihari with a green belt . . . We're planting Aleppo pine, at least twenty miles wide, but we've got to back it up with irrigation, and the water's disappearing."

"TL8, this is Whiskey Two. You're losing water to the ice sheets. Have you tried oil film to cut evaporation?"

The South African gave a grim laugh. "Oil? What oil? Whatever's left, the military has. They're protecting the borders . . . Must be blacks by the millions there, and the desert coming up behind them . . . Well, we've got the arms and the oil and the food. They've got the desperation. Who'll win, do you suppose? . . . So with all that, go tell the government you want to protect some pine trees."

"Roger, TL8. You've closed the borders, but what about our science group? Is there a way in for them?"

"Sorry, Whiskey Two, I'm not in government, I don't make the rules. All I know is, we've pulled into our shell and shut it tight . . . Right now, I can see smoke drifting in from the west. Somebody's burning something, maybe the fields . . ."

There was a silence before he spoke again, his weariness finally overtaking him. "TL8-Zed-Y, out and leaving the air."

"TL8, when can we continue the QSO?"

But there was only hiss.

Mark looked across at Danny. "I'll try and raise 'em again. We've got quite a few places still to go, even my old boss Guzman. We're all pulling together."

Mark tried Pretoria again, to no result. Danny was losing interest, and an exasperated Mark switched to another band. Voices came in a rush as he rotated the dial.

"Bright Flare, this is Dark Errand . . . You are to commence firing on coordinates Four Zebra Three. Do you roger? Over."

"Mayday . . . Mayday . . . Mayday . . . OUA23, Oscar Uniform Alpha Two Three. Kobenhavn, Denmark. Ice mountain closing in . . . Need helicopter rescue . . . All resources gone. Coordinates follow . . ."

"Mayday. Mayday. Mayday. This is Beechcraft Three Two Two, near Sedalia Airport, Missouri. Failed Takeoff . . . Ribs broken, I think . . . Snow piling up. I'm getting buried alive. Mayday. Please, Mayday . . ."

There were sounds of explosions. "CLA *Tres Quatro*, Antilla, Cuba. . . . *Socorro! Los Americanos nos estan atacando! . . . Socorro! Socorro, por fav- . . ."*

Danny held his hands up to his ears and moaned. "I don't wanna hear any more . . . No more, Mark, no more . . ."

Mark gently pulled his hands away. "Look, Danny, we're the ones who've got to keep what's left of civilization together."

Danny moaned. "We can't, Mark."

"We can, Danny . . ."

"The ice is all over, Mark . . . It's coming all over . . . It's the whole world. We can't save the whole world."

"Danny, listen to me. We blacken the ice . . ."

"Blacken . . . ?"

"Carbon black, when you hold an object in a candle flame, and it blackens. We spread it on the ice, and it absorbs sunlight and melts."

"All over?"

"It's one possibility. Here's another, the Bering Strait. The ocean level is dropping, right? The Strait will narrow to a point where it's easily dammed. We can cut off the whole Arctic Current . . . Here's another. We can spray oil, just a thin film, on the deserts to keep the sand down. We can even plant trees in the desert because the oil film'll keep in the water."

Danny looked at Mark in wonder.

"There's more, Danny, there's lots more, but when you've learned it all, you'll think of new things yourself."

"But how'll I . . . I mean, that's the whole planet, Mark."

Mark took Danny's hand and placed it on the radio. "With this, Danny. Yes, there're people dying, but there're people hanging on, like us. We're going to save the world, all of us together."

Danny nodded slowly. "I'll have to listen, then."

"Not only listen, but you'll have to maintain it. Remember I said we're like shipwrecks? This is the signal fire. We keep it burning day and night for the world to find us, or us to find them. Shipwrecked people sacrifice everything to keep the fire going, because without it they know they'll die. The fire counts more than anything."

Danny nodded, slowly and weakly.

They heard the distant sound of the dogs barking, and the shouts of the hunters.

Danny looked out there. "Something's sure going on," he said, his eyes flickering with excitement. Then the look faded, and he turned back to Mark.

"Yeah, I guess we've got to," he said flatly.

Mark was struggling with his mathematical calculations by the light of his electric bulb, munching absently on a caribou bone when Karen spoke up.

"We saw a seal on the ice, out on the Hudson. We couldn't catch it in time. It went back down its hole."

"They edible?"

"They're everything. Their blubber burns steady in the lamp . . ."

"My lamp's better."

"Bulb won't last forever."

"I'll scrounge a new one."

"We won't make it if we're just parasites, Mark."

"Well, I'm not being a parasite. I'm . . ." He was suddenly aware of the caribou bone in his hand. He looked at her, and there was an uncomfortable moment. "You telling me I'm a burden?"

Karen didn't answer.

Mark looked straight across at Danny, and saw the child eyeing him intently.

"I thought we'd agreed on the importance of . . ."

"Try to understand, Mark. We're living marginally, and right now we're on the wrong side of the margin. If we all don't pull our own weight . . ."

"Meaning I'm eating someone else's caribou. All right, Karen, do I join you on the sled?"

"That's all we need. One mistake on the sled, and we've got some crippled dogs. No, that seal's our great break. You can handle it all alone."

He smiled. "My department."

She nodded.

"Yeah, well, I don't want anyone dying on my account, Karen."

"I know."

He looked to Danny. "Whatever's necessary to keep the group alive, I promise."

Danny smiled, obviously proud of Mark.

"A seal did that?"

She nodded.

Perhaps an icebreaker could not have penetrated the ice at its present thickness, but a miraculous hole pierced it all the way down to the still flowing river beneath.

"Must've done a lot of work boring that."

"Had to. It's his air hole."

"What do I do, cast a fishing line down that?"

She laughed. "Anything out of the ordinary'd scare him right off. No, you have to wait, and spear him when he comes up for air."

"When'll that be?"

"Sooner or later."

"When's later?"

She shrugged. "All day, maybe."

"And what do I do meanwhile?"

"Nothing."

"Well, I can work on my calculations, or get some reading done . . ."

"Nothing means nothing, Mark. Seals are both smart and skittish. They have acute hearing, they can feel the smallest vibrations through the water. He'll see you as a shadow on the ice, and that'll make him nervous to begin with. He'll want to make sure you're a rock before he comes up, so you have to be a rock."

Mark looked at her, and then at the hole. "I just sit . . ."

"Rock-steady. The Eskimos did it all the time. As you once said, they haven't moved an inch in six thousand years."

He took a breath. "I take it, it's that important."

"For all of us, Mark.", She kissed him lightly. "Good luck."

He watched her cross back to the bank in the flat-footed gait that now came so natural to her, and it seemed to him he scarcely knew her anymore.

With no other use for his books, he propped them up for a seat, and waited.

He sat, almost motionless, for what seemed hours. He felt proud of himself, but gradually he wondered why he should. While he was sitting here, the world spun on, stirring up the currents of air that were his enemies.

His mind tried grappling with the intricate equations. He saw figures, signs, symbols, tried to keep one formula in his head while working another, returning to the first while trying to retain the second, reworking each in light of the other, then reworking those in light of a third.

He fumbled, lost track, told himself to hold still while trying to pick up the mental threads all over again.

He felt an itch underneath the parka, and ignored it.

Hold still, he said, while the world dies, while civilization flounders and grasps for bits of warmth.

The itch would not be ignored. It grew worse, more demanding.

Hold still, he said again. He thought of the radio, of voices calling out forlornly for help, for his help, while he tried to hold still.

The itch was maddening. Surely, one tiny movement, one small scratch . . .

Slowly, ever so slowly, he reached beneath his parka . . .

It happened so fast he could scarcely follow the sequence, a splash, a brief sight of a flattened black nose with whiskers beneath, a soft, almost human moan . . . and then it was gone, and he saw its shadow scurrying away beneath the ice, growing dimmer until it disappeared.

"It's a matter of meditation," said Hideo.

"And how do you do that?"

"Essentially, it's a matter of thinking of nothing."

Mark grunted at the humor of it. "Talk about going against the grain . . ."

"It takes a while," said Karen. "You didn't become a professor all in one day."

"I'm stuck with it now. Look, Hideo can meditate, let him do it. I'm the one on the radio, the official civilization-preserver. As a hunter, I'm one royal fuck-up, and I admit it. I have to be useful in the one way I'm useful."

Karen sighed. "Guess you did your best."

"At being a primitive, yes. My old best was a lot better . . . for everybody."

He looked toward Danny. The boy had a faraway look that Mark could not interpret. He aimed his next remark partially at him.

"It's not going to pay off tomorrow, but it will pay off, and if not with me, then with Danny."

Karen looked to her son. "Danny, which do you want?"

"Huh?" It took a few moments before he seemed to return to earth. He looked about, to see everyone looking at him. Self-consciously, he seemed to avoid catching Mark's eye when he answered.

"We gotta save the world, Mom. Mark and me, we gotta try."

There was a silence.

"Look," said Mark, "we will. We're not dinosaurs. We're the most ingenious, resilient, adaptable species the world has ever seen. We've survived every adversity nature has thrown at us, and we'll survive this one. It's not the gods we're fighting. It's just goddamn ice."

He waited for an answer. There was none.

"Just goddamn ice, that's all."

Fed by the dust and waters of the world, the glaciers grew, creeping down from their mountain aeries, from the Coast Mountains, the Rockies, the Himalayas, the Alps, the Andes, the Pyrenees, reaching blindly but inexorably. They sent great fingers of ice groping through mountain passes, and followed full upon them, spreading as they entered the valleys, slow floodwaters pushed endlessly on by the weight of the blizzards in the mountains.

Each carried its own personality. One would insinuate its way silently, snaking down a smooth mountain decline, thus staying sleek and beautifully glistening, and ambush the unwary at its foot.

Another announced its coming miles ahead with deafening splinterings and cannonades, its ice-smooth surface soon broken into innumerable fissures and spires as it strained itself to bridge craggy terrain.

Another acted as a giant chisel, gouging out bedrock beneath it and mountain rock on its banks, littering itself with an accumulation of rubble from giant boulders down to the finest sand. Some of this poured down its face, rolling ahead in a continual avalanche so that cities were buried in rock well ahead of the ice.

For another, the great frictions generated fierce heat in its core, melting a part of itself so that water surged into streams that in turn carved out tunnels, finally exploding at its face, sending torrents down into the valley with as great a force as any collapsing dam.

For another, the well-watered earth at its top had given birth to a full forest. In perfect symbiosis, the glacier gave the forest moisture, while it protected the glacier from the sun. And so they moved on together.

Eventually the valleys were inundated, like cups filling to the brim, adding trillions of tons of new debris, the ground-up remains of Tacoma, Seattle, Vancouver, Bern, Andorra, La Paz, Santiago.

The process multiplied itself by yet a new factor, covering areas of the earth with ice that reflected the sunlight back into space, and so the planet grew still colder in the midst of its summer.

With increasing rapidity, the ice came upon the great plains and spread wide, eventually joining, keeping their separate appearances and personalities a while as they flowed in parallel, but eventually sealing themselves together to form vast, thick sheets.

There were isolated pockets of life struggling to survive on some higher ground, squeezed ever tighter, helpless islands in a rising flood, until finally the ice came higher and snuffed them out.

To feed these vast sheets, the ice drank up water from oceans, and all about the globe. Underground wells fell away, lakes and rivers evaporated, and deserts advanced until they too met, forming whole seas of sand. Much like the pyramids, city skyscrapers soon were dominating only desert.

As the scythes of ice and sand cut their swaths across the planet, people fled to the remaining verdant places. There they collided, pillaged, made war, and died.

The signal was weak, and it magnified the weakness in Guzman's voice. His wheezes and pauses for breath merged with the fading of the signal, and it was difficult to tell the difference.

"I . . . I never saw anything like it . . . Children . . . little old people . . . eyes bulging, skins just wrinkled up . . . And they don't even cry, Mark. They just stare at you, eyes bulging, and then they're dead . . . slip over so quietly, you . . . It's the human race dying . . . The dinosaur eggs devoured . . . We've joined the dinosaurs, Mark."

"We're still alive, Professor, and if we are, there're others."

"There's nobody else . . . The radio's dead . . . the children're dead . . . we're dead."

"No, we're not. There're a thousand possible reasons why there's nothing coming through, but there're people out there!"

"Why do you fight it, Mark? . . . You've been given the greatest gift a mortal can have . . . When you die, the world dies with you." He laughed. "I'm enjoying it." Then he wheezed, as if fighting for a final breath. "Ohh, shit . . ." he moaned, and then there was quiet.

"Professor Guzman!"

There was no answer.

"Professor Guzman, please come in."

Mark looked across at Danny. The boy was looking up from his book. Mark hoped he hadn't heard the conversation.

"Do you remember what you read?"

Danny shrugged.

"All right, Danny, what's gradient wind?"

"Gradient wind . . . wind flowing along pressure isobars where the pressure force . . . pressure force, then something else . . . It's not fun, Mark." He looked longingly across to the shed. Mark followed his gaze.

The little Kashihara twins were giggling as they played their hunting game, where one was the dog and the other the driver, brandishing a whip improvised out of some caribou bone and sinew.

Mark shuddered. "Look, maybe it isn't 'fun' anymore, but being a man, being grown-up, sometimes isn't. This is going to be your responsibility someday. You know what's around us?"

Danny shrugged. "Snow."

"Under the snow, all out there?"

"Streets."

"Civilization, Danny, ten thousand years of it, everything we've built up since the last Ice Age. And this? . . ." He put his hand on the receiver.

"Static, mostly."

"The little, fragile threads that're holding the survivors together. If we survive, they survive. But we've got to stay in touch."

"There's nobody out there, Mark. He said so."

"Guzman's a lonely, bitter old man. He'd just as soon see it all die with him, but I want it to live, and I want you to live . . . C'mon, let's see you do it." He handed Danny the microphone, and Danny took it, dumbly.

"C'mon, Professor Kaplan first . . . WB2QXR."

"WB2QXR . . ." repeated Danny into the microphone.

"This is . . ."

"This is W2QRV, W2 . . ."

"Whiskey Two Que . . ."

"Whiskey Two Quebec Romeo Victor calling. Over." He turned to Mark. "There's no one there."

"Try it again."

"Nobody."

"Keep after it a while."

"Mark, this is *boring!*"

"Only until someone answers."

"He won't answer."

"He's probably in his lab, or working on the generator."

"He's dead. Everybody's dead out there."

"If we're alive, they're alive! Okay, he's busy for the moment. Let's go on, Pat Keegan in Miami . . . the twenty-meter band."

Mark looked across at the Kashihara children, still giggling, still playing their inane game. Inside the shed, Helen and Wendy were sewing, cooking, even chewing fur to soften it. It was distressing to contemplate, especially Helen, whose well-schooled brain seemed to degenerate as she settled into Eskimo domesticity.

The others, Karen, Hideo, and Fink, were in the city, or on the frozen river, hunting one animal or another. They were certainly lost.

That left only Danny to carry on, and even he was succumbing.

"Pat Keegan . . . Pat Leegan . . . Pat Zeegan . . . Pat Shmeegan . . ." said Danny, giggling.

"Danny!"

"I know . . . I know . . ." Danny turned back to the radio. "W2QRV . . ."

Other animals were passing through the city, Arctic hares, lemmings, polar foxes, ermines, birds. Some of the birds roosted briefly in the upper stories of skyscrapers before migrating on. Others hovered near the ground, and were easier to catch.

Karen was teaching Fink how to catch the Arctic terns, using a net made of caribou sinew, at the end of a long wood pole. She would hide behind a mound, and wait until the bird came within distance, then jump out and snag it. It was like swatting an elusive fly with a long-handled swatter, and Fink kept missing. The bird would fly off, but eventually a new bird would come near, and Fink would try again, with his usual wisecracks about taking turns at terns.

She watched him improve slowly, attacking the task with a single-minded intensity she knew Mark would never have.

She reflected on the others, the women with their home tasks, the men hunting, the children playing their games. As they learned the ways of Eskimo survival, they fell automatically into their roles in the Eskimo family.

It was not ideal, or perhaps even agreeable, certainly not for Helen who chafed in the role and resented the waste of her education. It made her life with Fink one filled with constant bickering. But they had survived.

Karen thought wistfully if there were ever a university again, she might do a thesis on it.

"Got one!" He practically jumped with glee, and proudly presented the entangled bird to Karen.

She reached in, wrapped her hands around its fluttering wings, and it slowly grew calm. Then, without a flicker of emotion, she pressed her thumb against its head and pushed hard, breaking its neck.

Fink winced. "Can't get used to that."

"I did, Lew."

He nodded, took a breath, and said, "Let's get another one."

Again he turned to watch and wait. He would wait all day if need be.

None of the rules applied to her own family. The unit broke down as Mark held onto the old ways, keeping Danny at the books and the radio, preparing for something that would never happen.

She was worried. Their rations had been stretched thinner as the animals moved on, and they had to range ever further to hunt them.

The pups had grown so rapidly, they now had three dog teams to work with once they had built yet another crude sled, but that also meant more mouths to feed.

There were some critical decisions to be made soon.

"Hey, look at that," Fink interrupted, pointing to the top of one of the skyscrapers.

It looked like a little puff of smoke, perhaps some strange condensation of water vapor turning into visible steam.

Instead of rising, however, the puff came rolling down the side of the building, enveloping cornices and projections.

Then Karen heard the roar, a sound she remembered only too well, bolts and mortar giving way, steel struts flying, tar and asphalt tearing like paper.

"Run!" she screamed. "Run!"

Fink stood frozen, unable to comprehend what was happening.

"It's an avalanche! Get out of here!"

Fink jumped onto the sled, grabbed the whip, and brought it down on the dogs, yelling. The whip thudded and rolled, but could not reach to the lead dog. Instead, the rear dogs ran on in their excitement, colliding with dogs in front, and in a moment the dogs collided, snapping at each other, their traces quickly forming an impossibly tangled web.

"Shit!"

Karen ran up, and cut the lines loose. The dogs ran off howling in different directions, some still tied together. The approaching thunder echoed from building to building.

"Leave 'em. Just run, and keep running!"

Their feet dragged in the snow. Sweat rolled down their foreheads, burning their eyes.

The avalanche unrolled along the street like some great ocean wave, coming up behind Fink, swirling around him.

"Lew, swim!"

"What?"

"Swim! Swim for your life!"

Bewildered and panicked, he made wide swimming motions, paddling and kicking as the snow came around and covered him, then came toward Karen.

She fought, kicked, and swam, digging out an air pocket for herself as the snow submerged her.

Then all was quiet.

She burst through to the surface, pulled herself free, and saw the mound nearby.

"Lew!"

Desperately, she dragged herself there, pushing snow and rubble aside in butterfly strokes, dug furiously with her hands, and at last broke through to an air pocket beneath.

Fink breathed in the fresh air that rushed in, took several deep breaths, and nodded his thanks.

"Wow! . . . That was one hell of a bird-dropping."

When you're hungry, any food tastes better, Mark admitted to himself as he ate the bird. He had been slow at getting used to the increasing undercooking. Karen had even urged they eat the meat absolutely raw. It had apparently been vital in a land where there were no fruits or vegetables, and indeed Eskimos had actually become ill on their animal protein diets when civilization had introduced cooking.

Well, thought Mark, he was certainly getting less squeamish as he got hungrier. Then his attention returned to Karen's account of the avalanche.

"Mark, what's happening? Everything seems to be getting worse. It's getting colder, the animals're disappearing . . ."

He nodded. "The glacier's coming. The cold air comes flowing down off the ice, and when it gets down here, it triggers ice accumulations on the tall buildings."

There was a pause.

"The animals are retreating, then. We'll have to follow them."

He smiled wanly. "I only wish we had Mayflower Moving right now."

She didn't laugh, or even smile.

"Hey, c'mon, it's not that bad. You've got three sleds, and enough dogs . . ."

"We lost some in the avalanche."

"Still enough, right?"

She shrugged, and fell quiet, watching Mark as he finished off the bird and licked his fingers.

"Still hungry. Anything else?"

She shook her head.

He grunted. "Okay, I don't want to be a pig about it."

"You're not, Mark. I'm hungry, too."

There was a silence.

"All right, Karen, we'll do better. We'll catch up wherever the animals've gone."

"Mark . . . this isn't working."

"What do you mean?"

"I mean . . . we're not Eskimos. Catch up with the animals? We go only a few blocks, and the team falls apart. Then it's a terror trying to separate them . . ."

"That's the same story I heard when we started. Seems after all this time . . ."

"I didn't have six thousand years. My God, Mark, none of us can even work that whip right, and that's our main survival tool. It keeps the dogs in line . . ."

"Okay, there're more important things . . ."

"No, there aren't. I'm . . . I'm stultified. I'm too old."

"Too old. At thirty those wrinkles sure . . ."

"Mark, a ballet dancer starts at age seven."

"Okay, so what's the right age for starting as an Eskimo?"

"Who knows? Whatever it is, I'm past it. Now we're at a crucial step. We've got to become nomads."

"Nomads. It's just moving day, that's all. It'll take a day to get the radio knocked down, the antenna systems, the generator . . ."

"Mark, we can't take that with us."

"Sure, we could."

"There's no room, we'd never get . . ."

"We will, that's all. I'm giving you back your own

words, what we tell ourselves to do, we'll do. Positive outlook."

He reached for her shoulder. She pulled away.

They sat in silence.

Then they heard it in the night stillness, distant but unmistakable, a sound far more chilling than any cold wind, echoing across a vast emptiness, a series of splinterings, but pitched so deeply they could feel it in the pit of their stomachs. Then came a series of gunshots and splinterings, sometimes alternating, and sometimes combining into rolling thunder that was answered before the echoes died.

At last Mark said, "We've got to, so we will." He pulled the bearskin over him, rolled away, and was soon asleep.

Karen lay awake, trembling.

The weather was changing. Mark could feel the cold wind from the north, sweeping down from the distant glacier. He pictured the alterations in the currents, and couldn't help struggling again with calculations on fighting back, spreading carbon black on the ice, an oil film across the water, damming up this strait, opening up that channel . . .

He looked up to see Danny again distracted by the twins at their hunting game. For some moments, Mark was stricken with remorse. Danny had never been a child, and now there just wasn't time.

"Danny . . ."

"Hm?"

"Coriolis force."

"Coriolis force . . . That's . . . uh . . . something to do with winds."

"Jesus, Danny, that's elementary stuff."

Danny looked at him blankly.

Mark groaned. "All right, Danny, what would you like? You want to go back to the radio?"

"I just wanna play."

"It's a waste of time, Danny."

"How's about hunting? That's not a waste of time."

"They'll do the hunting. What we're doing is more important. Now, I'll go over the maintenance of the windmill generator, okay?"

"Sure," he said without enthusiasm.

"Then we'll work radio transmission, send out CQ's a while if nobody answers, and then back to the books."

Danny sighed.

As Mark looked up to the windmill generator, he saw the group several blocks off, gathered near the sleds, gesturing, drawing in the snow. Perhaps they were mapping the animal migrations, or planning the hunt. He hoped they were working out some manner of transporting the radio and generator. It was crucial they take these with them, but he was sure they understood that by now.

Fink erased his doodlings with his foot.

"It's not going to work, Karen. It's a marginal chance at best, and we're on the wrong side of the margin."

She said nothing.

"Look, you know the facts as well as we do, and you're the captain of this lifeboat."

"How would you do it, Lew?"

"Not my department."

"Thanks."

He shrugged.

Karen took a breath, paced about with her head down, folding and unfolding her arms nervously. "Y'know, it really shouldn't be me. I'm the one who's emotionally involved."

Hideo spoke up. "That's why it has to be you. Karen, it's really that circle coming full. We've survived by following you, and you followed the Eskimos. Now you have to take the next step. It's the hardest one, maybe the hardest we'll ever take, but it's inevitable . . . and if we don't take it . . ."

" . . . we don't survive." She looked at the dog team, and at the pups, subtly closer to the Husky strain, already part of the team, pulling their own weight.

She looked out across the city, and felt those new sharp winds. The glacier was quiet . . . for the moment.

It was already dark when the group returned. Mark figured they had spent so much time talking, they must have been set behind on their hunt.

Sure enough, the day's catch was meager, some lemmings, some birds, a hare. He watched the ritual, the tying of the dogs with the almost constant slaps and clubbings to keep them in bounds.

When they had finally been subdued, Karen turned to him. When her face came into clear view beneath his light bulb, he was amazed. He couldn't remember when he had last seen her smile so warmly. How good could the news have been? He felt a vague unease.

"Hello," she said.

"Hi," he answered automatically. "Did you . . .?" She cut him off with a long tender kiss. "Wow!"

"Mm-hm."

Memories came flooding back, of that first time, when they made love because she was grateful for all he had done, because he had been nice to her and kind to Danny. She was grateful now, but for what?

Then, along with memory, there came back all the emotions as he felt her body quiver, even through the thick, clumsy furs.

He reached down, gripped her around her legs, lifted her to him. She was lighter than ever, more fragile, more vulnerable. He knew, even as he wondered why, that she loved him, trusted him, was giving herself to him, and despite the estrangement that had grown between them, they were lovers. Despite the cold, they were feverish with an excitement so intense that he felt he would go mad if it were not satisfied this very moment.

When he took her to their makeshift bed, and reached beneath the furs, he felt her flesh warm, trembling with a desire that matched his. As his hand swept down, he had to grapple clumsily with primitive toggles and clasps, and he dreaded for a moment that excitement might fade, that he might grow soft, but then he felt her wet, and he knew he could enter her easily.

Even in the coldness, he was sweltering, and the sun was blazing, hotter and hotter. It was midsummer, and he was on the roof of the science building, setting up his antenna. He relived each step, studying it carefully, knowing he would have to reverse the procedure when the glacier came.

The black flooring burned through his shoes, and when he tried to lift his feet, he couldn't. He looked down, and saw them sticking to the melting tar.

He looked up to the sun, and it hung huge and white in the sky. Hotter and hotter it became, seeming to plummet to the earth, growing larger until it filled the sky.

He tried to run, but his feet were trapped in the tar. He looked up to see the sun colliding with the earth in a shattering explosion. He screamed—or was it her screaming?

He felt himself dying, drained, emptied. The light faded, gradually cooled, then going beyond coldness to entropy, to absolute zero, absolute death. The planets were dead, icy shells now.

The whiteness no longer emitted heat, but devoured it, drained it from the universe. It was the great glacier, and it was rending the city, crushing all civilization beneath a moving mountain, awesome, magnificent, implacable.

Buildings came crashing down about him, mere toothpick models to be swept aside.

He looked at the glacier's face, and he saw the gleaming crags, the blinding reflections, the dizzying colors, the face of his death.

He tried to run, but his legs were still stuck. He struggled, but his body was weak. He felt like an old man, a hundred years old. His bones were brittle, his eyes dim, his teeth rotted, and while he lacked even the strength to put his hand to his face, it must have been as lined and furrowed as the ancient Eskimo he had seen in that village.

He called out . . . called Karen . . . called the one woman he loved.

But there was no answer.

He called again, and yet again, but there was only the hiss, the empty static of a dead planet.

She was no longer by his side, and would never be again. He would no longer know her touch, her soft sweet body, her simple presence.

And in her stead, only the obscene death embrace of the ice.

He was so old, so very old. Life was only deep pain, and perhaps death could now be welcomed. Perhaps he could submit gladly to his fate, the ice as his final lover.

Then he realized he himself was that Eskimo, awaiting death, and he ought to be happy because he would soon be released from this pain. He was alone because they had been merciful. They had left him behind to bring him to death, and to save themselves.

The ice surrounded him, and as he turned to face it he knew. In that last instant, before it crushed out his life and mind, he *knew*.

Suddenly he was awake.

He was beneath a bearskin in a shed near the frozen river, and outside a cold gray dawn was breaking. The light entered the shed dimly, but he could see Karen alongside. For a moment he was reassured. It was only a dream, and she loved him.

Then he saw the tears still on her face. She had fallen asleep crying. She did indeed love him, and she had cried because she knew they would never make love again.

He heard sounds outside, the dogs stirring uneasily as people moved about nearby. He struggled his way up and looked out through a slat in the wood. He saw them loading food, fur, weapons onto the sled.

"Karen!" He shook her awake.

"Mm-hm?" For moments, she was still under the spell of their night together, and she reached toward him drowsily and pleasantly.

"You're leaving me behind!"

She didn't answer but he could see the change in her eyes, and the sickness tore at him, pulled apart his insides until he had to open his mouth and take several breaths to keep from gagging.

"There was no choice," she said finally.

"What do you mean, no choice? There's no choice except to carry on just as we have."

"We can't, Mark. We're nomads now. We have to follow the animal migrations, and we can barely do that as it is. If we take you, we'll all die."

". . . Oh Jesus . . ." he moaned at last. "All right, I'll hunt. I'll join the group. I'll kill, I'll butcher . . ."

She shook her head. "You could never make it. You've said so yourself. You're too . . . civilized."

"Oh, Jesus . . ."

"Mark, you're the best of what we were, what we might become again, but now you're a burden who'll drag us all down."

"I could force you." His voice was hard.

"You made me leader, Mark."

"Hell, I wasn't expecting something like this."

"Nobody was. Mark, help me to be leader."

"Are you crazy? You're asking me to commit suicide."

"Then why did you care about the radio, or about Danny?"

"Danny! That's what this is all about, it's Danny."

"You know that's not true."

"I know nothing of the kind." He yelled, "Danny!"

There was no answer. He struggled into his parka, and as he stumbled toward the entrance, he tripped. "The hygrometer . . . He wouldn't leave without his weather station."

He looked out to the sled. Danny was helping load hunting weapons.

"My God!" Mark came back, and tore through a

pile of gears and electronic parts until he found the buried gun.

"Mark!"

She hurriedly got on her own clothes, and followed him out.

"All right," he said to the group, "everything goes back!"

"I'm sorry, Mark, we can't do it," said Fink.

He pointed the gun at Fink, and saw the others circling about him.

"It's an automatic. I could get you all fast enough."

"And then what," said Karen. "You couldn't survive on your own."

"I'm a dead man anyway. Are you telling me there's a difference?"

"You know there is, Mark."

"Not to me. If I'm dead, what's it matter?"

"Who do you sound like now?"

"Who . . ." Then he realized. "Guzman."

"You know it's what we leave after us that counts."

There was a long pause.

At last he nodded. "What we leave after us." He

"You were destroying him, but he'll be all right with me."

"No."

"You were destroying him, but he'll be all right with me."

He reached for him. Danny backed away.

"No . . . Please don't make me die, Mark."

"Danny, how can you say that? I love you!"

"You're going to die, Mark. Please let me go. I don't want to die!"

A stunned Mark turned to the others. "You did this."

He kept the gun trained on the group, reached out with his other hand for Danny, and dragged him from the sled.

"He's my child, Mark!"

"Not any more."

Danny was screaming now, struggling in Mark's grip.

"I'm sorry, Danny. You don't like it now, but you will. You will again, when they're gone." He turned to them. "Now go."

Karen shook her head. "Not without Danny."

"I'm sorry."

"Mark, if you can't survive, how will he?"

They were all rooted in place, immobile, and then they all heard it, the splintering and thunder echoing down from the north.

"Oh Jesus . . ."

Mark released Danny. The child stood paralyzed with terror and bewilderment.

"Go to your mother, Danny."

The boy ran back crying into Karen's arms. She looked up toward Mark, then, before the tears could come, she turned back to the dogs, let out an animal yell, and lashed out as far as she could with the whip.

The sled jerked and took off. The others followed her lead as she ran it down an embankment onto the frozen Hudson.

She looked back. Mark stood on the pier watching them go, a picture of lone defiance, his radio, windmill, and single light bulb all against the immensity of a half-buried city.

The dogs again began falling out of step, nipping at each other's heels, running in and out of their proper positions, getting traces tangled. She tried whipping them, but the lash fell short of the lead dogs, until finally she had to toss a rope under the runners to brake the sled, then get out, cuffing them while struggling to avoid getting bitten herself.

At last, the dogs fell back into place, and she was able to take off again.

Mark watched them disappear down the Hudson, three little boats, traveling erratically.

They had left enough food for a couple of days. After that, who knew? He'd dig up something.

First things had to come first, though.

"WB2QXR, this is W2QRV. Whiskey Two Quebec Romeo Victor calling. Over."

He tried again, then one by one he went through all his friends and correspondents, all the members of the radio net, the people who would save civilization.

"CQ, CQ, CQ," he said at last. "This is W2QRV, standing by for a call. Will talk to anyone on this frequency. CQ, CQ, CQ . . ." He worked his way up through every band, every possible channel.

The wind blew colder, and he felt a chill creeping in through the sloppily sewn seams of his parka.

The thunder was closer than ever.

Until now, slowness was for dawdlers, loiterers, laggards. It connoted hesitation, weakness, weariness, stupidity. In nature, speed was for the horse, the tiger, the hurricane. Slowness was for the snail, the turtle, the worm.

The slowly advancing army is incompetently led, signals its unsureness, gives its opponent time to regroup, rebuild, and launch new attacks.

But against the glacier there was no possible attack nor defense, not by the combined might of all the arms and armies of history. Its awful slowness, then, was its greatest horror. Its creep was absolutely predictable, and absolutely inexorable.

It has already rolled over some mountains, sheared the tops off others, gouged out great river beds, obliterated others, scraped earth down to bedrock in some places, redeposited it in others. Now it came to a mere city.

At first it oozed through streets and about buildings, extending pseudopods like a great amoeba, seeking the paths of least resistance.

Then the fingers thickened and swelled as more ice gathered. Its pressure mounted, from pounds per square inch to tons, the hypothetical irresistible force made terrifyingly real.

Different materials reacted differently. Bricks held firm, and then would suddenly blast apart. Steel girders bent slowly, giving way gracefully, but eventually they too were ground under. Glass shattered simultaneously along its entire surface, and its shards were eventually milled back to sand.

Parts of taller buildings were scooped up, lifted along the creeping outline until they rode atop the glacier. It slid easily on the convenient snow base, pressing its flakes into new glacier ice.

As it traveled south, neighborhood by neighborhood, Inwood, Fort George, Washington Heights, Harlem, lost their identities. It came at last to the college.

The library of over a million volumes was at the northern end of the campus. Many books had already been ruined by seepage and snow that had broken through the roof. The glacier pushed the wall down, sending great showers of rubble through the stacks, and then the ice itself fell upon them, reducing paper to pulp.

It moved on to other buildings, to Business Administration with its computer, to Engineering, Music, Art, Law. Disciplines, occupations, departments that had kept themselves carefully separate, were all finally fused.

There was a mural in the main conference room portraying the history of the Earth. There were dinosaurs on one panel, stiffly posed as if for a royal portrait. Indeed, their reign was far longer than any human dynasty, fifty million years, but now the ice decimated them a second time.

On the ice went, a tireless juggernaut, hour after hour, destroying landmarks and obscurities, ancient buildings and modern, great art and total trash, all with equal ignorance.

It was like a continual roar, pounding waves heard from inside a cave, and Mark had to hold his headphones tight to hear the radio signals.

Except there was nothing to hear.

He changed his call to Mayday, relating the emergency, begging anyone to answer, but from one end of the spectrum to the other, through every frequency of the Broadcast Band, Amateur Band, Citizen Band,

Public Safety, Maritime, Aeronautical, Industrial, Military, there was only empty noise.

Was it all a waste, then? Should he at least now abandon it all and try to save himself?

And then he heard it, dimly at first, but growing stronger until it completely supplanted the hiss of the radio. It was the signal of the weather satellite, as strong as it had ever been, a complex of whistles and chirps, like electronic music. After three minutes, it faded finally, and only the hiss remained.

But it had been there, and Mark knew it would come again, and yet again, day after day for thousands of years, as long as the satellite remained in orbit.

Something of Man was left. If Mark had survived, then why not others? They couldn't run their radios for the time being, but someday they would. They would hear that signal, and even if they had forgotten its purpose, they would be obsessed with its puzzle, and inevitably find each other's signals. Thread by thread the network would be built again, from one isolated camp to another, until learning and civilization were restored.

He couldn't run away from that. He had to take the radio with him, no matter the hindrance.

He dismantled the prop, governor, cowling, carriage, alternator, regulator. He wound up antenna wires, each band with its own separate length and assembly, with their insulators, lead-ins, standoffs, grounds. Then the transmitter and receiver, microphone, headphones, hand key, log books.

He dragged an armload for a block, then returned time and again for more. Then on for another block, and back again for another armload. He wished for a snowmobile, a dog sled, even some flat-bottom conveyance he might pull himself, but he had less than the primitive.

The glacier was slow, but he was slower.

Showers of rubble roared down the snow-filled streets, an onslaught as wide as the eye could see. Still, he could escape if he dropped it all and ran, even if he walked.

The glacier was not advancing in a straight line. It was further south on Eighth Avenue than on Ninth, and a toppling building nearly caught him there. He watched a moment in awe as it came down upon the streets in a tidal wave of steel and stone. He retreated, gasping for breath, and set the radio down a moment.

He looked back. One more armload. He hesitated. These were components, each useless without all.

He thought a moment, calculated. He could make it. What he willed, he'd do. He ran back for it, scooped it up, and turned around.

The ice had tricked him. The rubble was already piling up ahead of him, flowing into every side street and sealing every crevice. He was trapped. Ahead, the rubble. Behind him, the ice.

He turned to confront it, and saw a moving mountain, fissured and furrowed like an incredibly ancient Eskimo face. He looked up. It towered far above the tallest buildings. He could not even see the summit.

Its face changed even as it moved, one feature dissolving into another. Some parts were caked with accumulated rubble, but elsewhere it washed itself clean with friction-melted waters. There it glistened astoundingly, passing through all the colors of the spectrum, seemingly opening into endlessly winding caverns of sparkling crystal.

It held him transfixed. He was looking into infinity, into complexities greater than any weather system, mysteries deeper than those of his own life and death. If he let himself travel down that cavern, he knew he would be given the answers. He would close the circle of all existence, be part of nature, at one with life's beginning and end. The colors whirled about him, inviting him to submit.

Then he caught himself. He had transcended nature, and would again. He would fight, to the very last moment.

But with what?

He had the gun. He raised it and fired the last

bullets. The sound was absorbed in the roar, and the ice seemed to swallow the bullets without a trace.

And then he had nothing except himself, and his voice yelling defiance to the last.

The glacier went on, flattening the crowded towers of the financial center before its slow sweep across the Battery, and then out to the frozen bay.

Finally, like a pendulum at the extremity of its swing, counterforces began to reassert themselves. The jet stream, the mysterious stratospheric wind that had wandered off its normal course, reached the limit of its deviation.

As more water became locked away in ice sheets, there was less left for new storms. The man-made particulates of combustion and pollution were finally swept from the atmosphere. The snows grew sparse, and the awesome weight at the glacier's head finally lightened.

The processes of the Ice Age wound down, and the glacier came to rest.

Eventually, someday, the pendulum would begin its swing back, and the processes would reverse. The ice would retreat, leaving behind a great line of rubble to mark the line of its furthest advance.

The largest of these were called "haystack boulders," once regarded with some awe by an Ohio farmer who wondered how they got there. Perhaps there would be others in the future to again wonder. Perhaps not.

For now, there was only a great silence.

"First the sun'll melt the water on top, and the water'll eat its way down, right into the heart of the glacier. It'll become a whole underground river that'll dig and dig, until it's carved out one tunnel after another, and then that whole great mountain'll just fall down. The water'll break free, and gush out like a mighty fountain that'll get bigger as the ice melts away. It'll wash clean the rocks and rubble, and nothing'll happen for a long while, and just when you think nothing'll ever happen, suddenly it will."

"Oooh, what?"

"It's a little flower called an avalanche lily, and it'll struggle up right between the rocks. And then the grass'll grow, and trees and bushes. Soon after, all the animals that went away will return, and then the people too."

"Other people? Are there other people?"

Hideo hesitated, and looked across to Karen. "You want to handle that one?"

Karen took a breath. "Somewhere, over the ice, there are other people, just like us, living as best they can. And some of them are boys and girls just like you."

"Then why don't we go visit them?" asked Danny.

"We don't know where they are, and we can't travel too far, not with the way the dogs fight."

"Then we'll wait until the ice melts."

"That'll take a long time, many, many years," said Hideo.

"How many?"

"I'm afraid you won't ever see it."

"Oh."

They were visibly disappointed. Finally one of the twins said, "Let's go out and play." Her sister nodded, and the two crawled out the little tunnel.

Danny looked after them a moment, and turned back, his eyes bright with excitement. "We'll go there. I'll drive the dogs all the way, and I'll take the twins with me, and my kid brother when he's born. We'll go there and meet the other people. They'll tell us their stories, and we'll tell 'em ours."

"Yes," said Karen, "of course you will."

He smiled. "I'm gonna go play," and he crawled out after them.

There was a silence for a moment. They were suddenly aware the room had gotten darker. The setting sun cast a reddish glow through the caribou membrane that served as a window. Karen lit the oil lamp.

It flickered and smoked a little, and the smoke rose up to escape out the little vent atop the igloo. Eventually the flame settled, and its clear, bright light cleared the gloom.

Then Fink said, "Why didn't you tell him the truth?"

"Well, what's truth anyway? The best truth is what he wants to hear, what makes him happy."

"Huh? More Eskimo philosophy?"

"Well, even Mark's philosophy. If we're alive, then there must be others alive somewhere."

"All right, now the philosophy according to Fink: We're dead, and therefore so is everyone else."

"How are we dead?"

"Mathematics, Karen. The highest truth. You may know your Eskimos, but I know my calculus. Well, I used to know it." He looked up with a momentary, faraway gaze. "I feel parts of my brain rusting away lately . . ." He came back to earth. "But I still remember my long-division."

"Well?"

"Your term, the Eskimo unit—father, mother, children, dog team, maybe an anthropologist—together they need four hundred caribou a year or the equivalent. That's one caribou every day, day in and day out, plus an extra one three times a month. That's month after month, day after day, for the rest of our lives, unless we fall behind, then we have to get two the next day."

"We've been doing it. It's been hard, but we've been doing it."

"Face the mathematics, Karen. We've been getting our one a day, but not the extra ones. Just catching one soaks up all our energies, and there's nothing left. We're incurring a debt that's slowly mounting, and little by little it's destroying us."

"We're not all complete units, Lew. You and Helen, for instance . . ."

"Yeah, well who knows? Someday we just might shake hands, and that'll get her pregnant right there.

Which brings up you. You're seven months along. How much longer can you hunt?"

"I'll be up and around pretty quick after that. The Eskimo women always were."

"Yeah, fine, except you'll have all those lost days to make up, which we haven't done yet. Plus you'll have an extra mouth to feed."

"Who'll be a hunter someday too."

"Uh huh, if we make it that far. Throw this into the equation: as we get weaker, it gets harder to hunt, so we'll fall further and further behind until we're dead. Worse than dead, extinct."

There was a silence. Karen felt for her growing protuberance through the fur. Ever since its first kicks, it had seemed like Mark living on inside her, and she felt comforted by the sense of life's continuity.

Wendy watched her. "When I had the twins, the school paid for it all, doctor, nurses, anesthetist . . ." She sighed.

"Eskimos managed without any of that."

"How'd they do it?"

"The woman goes into her igloo alone. There's no one to help. She stands, holds onto something, and lets the baby just drop down into the snow."

Wendy winced. "You'll do that? All alone?"

"Not much choice. Don't worry, Wendy, it's time-tested."

She laughed, then shuddered. "I couldn't do it."

"Yes you can. And you will."

Wendy looked at Karen, her eyes lighting up with some hope, some faith in the future.

"I can't believe this," said Fink, "two dinosaurs talking Dr. Spock baby care."

Hideo had remained silent all this while, his eyes closed, and the others had forgotten about him, thinking him asleep. Now they almost jumped when he entered the conversation.

"What do you think'll replace us, Fink?"

"What?"

"Us, the dinosaurs, like we replaced the originals?"

"That's a rather grisly thing to be thinking about, isn't it?"

"Not any more. I've accepted it, and now I even like speculating. All the puzzles of our life, and we come now to the ultimate one. Who'd have said, once upon a time, that of all the powerful and beautiful creatures roaming the planet, that some middle-sized, indifferent ape was going to take the heavyweight crown from tyrannosaurus rex? Who's the next runt warming up right now?"

"Well, I'm sure as hell not warming up," said Fink. "If you ask me, the polar bear's got the edge. He sure seems boss of the berg."

"But not when it melts, Lew. He'll be on his way back to the Pole then."

"All right, apes then, one of them. They're closest to Man, if they care to admit it."

"Well, assuming there are any left. But I think Man blew it for the whole ape family. If they had his advantages, they'd also have his liabilities, so they'd be out too."

"Do sea creatures count?" asked Wendy.

"Hadn't occurred to me, but the game's open, and there's probably some life down there. Who've you got?"

"Dolphins. They're supposed to be very intelligent."

"All right, but where are the dolphin books, or cities, or even simple tools? You need an opposable thumb to hold a club, or write, or accomplish anything on which to build a culture. Once you've got that, the brain'll grow to meet the demands."

"Or shrink from the lack," muttered Fink. "All right, Karen, who's your candidate?"

There was a pause. "I'm sorry, Lew, I'd rather not play the game."

"C'mon, why be a spoilsport?"

"I just don't want to think about it." She looked down at her protuberance, and was suddenly quiet.

After a while, Hideo spoke up. "Well, I had a head start. I accepted things a long time ago."

They waited for him.

"I think it'll be a burrowing creature."

"Why?"

"A burrowing creature is protected from the elements. It's warmer under the snow, cooler under the desert, so he survives. Then later he digs down further, and what does he come upon? The Library of Congress, the Hall of Records, the Smithsonian."

"So what good's that to him? You ask him about Shakespeare, and he'll say, 'Oh yeah, *Hamlet*. Tasted great.'"

"Eventually he'll learn what to make of it. His brain will develop under the stress, and he'll learn that Shakespeare not only tastes different from Einstein, it also looks different. Eventually he'll decode it, and then all the rest will follow."

"So you've got someone in mind?"

Hideo nodded.

"We need a ceremony," said Fink. "May I have the envelope, please? . . . And the winner is . . ."

Hideo paused for effect, and finally said, "The hairy-nose wombat."

Fink stared. "You're making that up."

"No, I'm not. It's a little bear-like creature, carries its young in a pouch, and . . ."

"The hairy-nose wombat?"

"Oh yes. I'm telling you, I'm right. It's got fur, but light fur, so it's adaptable to different climates. It has a rudimentary opposable thumb which could evolve . . ."

"The hairy-nose wombat?"

"It's not very big or imposing, but who ever said we were? I'm sure right now this creature is surviving down in its hole, and has come upon the first . . ."

"THE HAIRY-NOSE WOMBAT?"

"He's come upon some of our buildings, or tools, or whatever, and is puzzling over it. Eventually, little by little . . ."

"Good Lord, Kashihara, that is *disgusting!*"

Hideo looked hurt. "Well, to you, maybe, but to a female hairy-nose . . ."

"Do you realize what you've done, you sadistic pervert? The Louvre, the Empire State Building, the Pyramids, the Sistine Chapel, Beethoven, Rembrandt, Newton, the laws of thermodynamics, man on the moon, ten thousand years of accumulated humanity . . . and you've turned that over to the *hairy-nose wombat!*"

"Look, Lew, I don't like it any better than you do, but I've . . ."

For a moment, Fink looked ready to hit Hideo, then as if he were ready to laugh the longest, loudest laugh of his life, but, astonishingly, he broke down weeping.

"Oh God, oh God, oh God . . ."

The other watched, paralyzed, embarrassed. They waited for a joke, a wisecrack, a punchline, but Lew Fink only continued to weep. "Oh God, oh God . . ."

Finally it subsided.

Wendy broke the silence.

"No!"

They all turned to look at her. She had always been so shy and self-effacing, her imperative tone was a jolt.

"No," she repeated, a good deal quieter, as if discomforted by their sudden and full attention. "It'll be the dogs. Just listen."

Through the snow walls came the ominous sounds of over thirty dogs, growls, snarls, and occasional wolf-like howls.

"They know. They know we're growing weaker, and that all they have to do is wait. Someday soon we'll die, and then there'll be only the children . . . just the children to face the dogs."

There was a long, stunned pause.

Fink took a breath. "I'm gonna talk to Helen about adopting a wombat. Maybe he'll support us in our old age." He nodded good-bye, and crawled out of the tunnel.

Karen took that as her signal to leave, and Wendy stopped her. "I'm sorry. I don't know why I said that."

"It's all right. It's what we were all thinking. Maybe I could be resigned to it like Hideo . . . but you're right, it's the children."

Wendy swallowed. "About your baby . . ."

"I'll be all right." She kissed Wendy on the cheek, crawled outside, and stood up.

The setting sun lit the snow in red and gold, emphasizing every mound and ridge in deep, long shade.

Already she could see the glow of the oil lamp in Fink's igloo, and shadows moving about. Their voices were raised as undoubtedly he argued with Helen about one thing or another. Suddenly, a section of the igloo collapsed in a shower of snow.

There was a loud cry of, "Oh shit!" and moments later they emerged and struggled together to try and rebuild it, arguing all the while.

Karen looked on in concern until the commotion of the dogs caught her attention. Only the leader, the great Greenland Husky, regarded her quietly, his eyes catching the gleam of the darkening light. It seemed to her a moment of understanding was passing between them. She was indeed dying, and he needed only to bide his time.

She felt the infant kick inside her.

The Eskimos did not even think of the future, and perhaps that was best. What will happen, will happen.

The children were still at their noisy hunting game.

One of the twins tried cracking the whip at Danny, who had taken the role of sled-dog.

"C'mon, dog!"

The lash rolled erratically, and fell to the snow in a limp heap like a dead snake.

Karen was about to caution them, but she stopped herself. The Eskimos never disciplined their children, never spoke a harsh word, nor even told them when to go to bed or come in for dinner. They were given much love and affection, but otherwise were left to find their own way. Karen and her group had survived thus far by following the Eskimo traditions, and she had to continue, no matter where the road led.

If they survived, so must have others, and some-day the children would indeed travel there and meet them. If . . .

"Let me . . ." shrieked the other twin, grabbing for the whip.

"No, me!" yelled Danny, trying to outreach the both of them.

Karen saw he had become a child at last, but for what? She felt like weeping.

Instead, without a further word, she turned and crawled into her igloo.

"Me, me, me," yelled Danny, grabbing for the whip.

"No."

"You're the dog. C'mon, dog." He jerked the whip ineffectually at her.

"Ha, told you. You're better as the dog."

"No, I want another chance."

"C'mon."

He backed away. "Stay back. I'm the big hunter." Again he tried. It rolled about and thudded, tracing a curlecued line in the snow.

"C'mon, Danny."

He backed further away, and tried again. This time the whip made a slight sound it had not made be-fore.

"There, y'see? I'm getting it."

"You're not getting anything except a punch in the eye."

"Stay back, I'm warning you. I'm the big hunter."

Again he tried. The sound grew louder until it was a distinctive, sharp report.

One of the girls screamed, "Hey, that hurt!"

Again and again he tried, and now the girls re-treated fearfully.

"I'm the hunter!" he yelled. The whip rolled, and the tip of that great long lash snapped with a sound like a gunshot. Exhilarated, he ran to the dogs.

"Danny, stay away, they'll eat you!"

The dogs stood up as he approached, their ominous growls turning to frantic barking. They strained at their traces, fangs bared.

For a moment, Danny retreated, shaking as his old fears came rushing back.

"I'm the hunter!" he said aloud.

He lashed at them again, and yet again, his aim growing surer with each whipping.

Now the dogs turned their rage upon the lash itself. They snapped at it, jumped after it, tried to bring it down. Each time it would strike a dog, then seem to dance out of the way, nimbler and fiercer than they, its bite sharp and unerring.

At last their howls subsided. They cowered, whimpered, and hunkered down into the snow in quiet submission.

They had found their master.

The last of the weather satellites was by far the most complex—and the most successful—of a series that began in 1960 with Tiros I. It orbited from Pole to Pole at right angles to the Earth's rotation, so timed as to daily scan the whole of the planet as it passed beneath.

It tracked the currents of air and water working their slow, sinuous paths from equator to Poles, but watched with eyes far more varied and subtle than human ones. Certain senses were attuned to invisible segments of the spectrum. Others were turned toward space, and noted the emissions of sun and stars and space itself. All the known influences upon weather and climate were recorded and transmitted openly and freely to any receivers about the Earth.

With its solar batteries supplying unending power and its orbit perfectly balanced, it would function in the protective vacuum of outer space for thousands of years, endlessly transmitting its complexity of data without worry or wonder if it had an audience.

At night, it shone by intercepted sunlight, a seeming star except for its great speed, and a path clearly different from other stars. A primitive tribesman contemplating the night sky might eventually take note of this curious light, and ponder.

ABOUT THE AUTHOR

ARNOLD FEDERBUSH was born in New York City in 1935. He received a B.A. from Washington Square College of New York University and an M.A. in Theatre Arts from the University of California at Los Angeles. He is a film writer and film editor and now lives in Los Angeles.

A SPECIAL PREVIEW OF THE
RIVETING OPENING PAGES FROM
THE NEW SUPERSONIC SUPERTHRILLER

FIREFOX
BY CRAIG THOMAS

"Virtually in a class by itself—a chilling,
superbly researched thriller."
Jack Higgins, author of THE EAGLE HAS LANDED

"A marvelous read—a gripping, believable
thriller that flies at Mach-5 speed."
Ira Levin, author of THE BOYS FROM BRAZIL

The man lay on the bed in his hotel room, his hands raised like claws above his chest, as if reaching for his eyes. His body was stretched out, rigid with tension. A heavy perspiration shone on his brow and darkened the shirt beneath his arms. His eyes were wide open, and he was dreaming.

The nightmare did not come often now; it was like a fading malaria. He had made it that way—he had, not Buckholz or the psychiatrists at Langley. He despised them. He had done it himself. Yet, when the dream did come, it returned with all its old force, the fossilisation of all memory and all conscience. It was all that was left of Vietnam. Even as he suffered, sweated within its toils, a cold part of his mind observed its images and effects—charting the ravages of the disease.

In his dream he had become a Vietnamese, Viet-Cong or peasant it did not matter—and he was burning to death, slowly and horribly; the napalm that the searching Phantom had dropped was devouring him. The roar of the retreating jets was drowned in the roar of the flames as he singed, burned, began to melt. . . .

In the flames, too, other times and other images flickered; flying sparks. Even as his muscles withered, shrivelled in the appalling heat, he saw himself, as if from a point far at the back of his brain, flying the old Mig-21 and frozen in the moment of catching the USAF Phantom in his sights . . . then the drugs in Saigon, the dope that had led to the time when he had been caught in the sights of a Mig . . . then there was the breakdown, the months in the Veterans' Hospital and the crying, bleeding minds all around him until he teetered on the verge of madness and wanted to sink into the new darkness where he would not hear the cries of other minds or the new shrieks of his own brain.

Then there was the work in the hospital, the classic atonement that had turned to a vile taste at the back of his throat. Then there was the Mig, and learning to fly Russian, think Russian, be Russian . . . Lebedev, the defector with the Georgian accent, they had brought in to coach him, thoroughly—because he had to be fluent. . . .

Then the training on the American-copied Mig-25,

and the study of Belenko's debriefing, Belenko who had flown a Foxbat to Japan years before . . . and the days and weeks in the simulator, flying a plane he had never seen, that did not exist.

The napalm and the flames and Saigon. . . .

The smell of his own burning was heavy in his nostrils, vividly clear, the bluish flame from the melting fat . . . Mitchell Gant, in his hotel room, burned to death in agony. . .

HEAD OF SIS TO PM—EYES ONLY   4/2/76

Dear Prime Minister,

You asked for fuller information concerning the Mikoyan project at Bilyarsk. I therefore enclose the report I received last Autumn from Aubrey, who is controller of the espionage effort there. You will see he has a rather radical suggestion to make! Your comments would be illuminating.

> Sincerely,
> Richard Cunningham

      ●   ●   ●   ●

EYES ONLY—HEAD OF SIS   18/9/75

My dear Cunningham,

You have received the usual digests of my full reports with regard to the espionage effort being made against the secret Mikoyan project at Bilyarsk, which has received the NATO codename 'Firefox'. In asking for my recommendations, I wonder whether you are sufficiently prepared for what I propose.

You do not need me to outline Soviet hopes of this new aircraft. Something amounting to a defence contingency fund has been set aside, we believe, to cope with eventual mass-production of this aircraft. Work on the two scheduled successors to the current Mig-25, the 'Foxbat', has or is being run down; the Foxbat will remain the principal strike plane of the Soviet Air Force until that service is re-equipped with the Mig-31, the 'Firefox'. At least three new factory-complexes are planned or under construction in European Russia solely, one suspects, to facilitate the production of the Mig-31.

As to the aircraft itself, I do not need to reiterate its potency. If it fulfils Soviet hopes, then we will have nothing like it before the end of the eighties, if at all. Air supremacy will pass entirely to the Soviet Union. We all know the reasons for SALT talks and defence cuts, and it is too late for recriminations. Suffice it to say that an unacceptable balance of power would result from Russian possession of the production interceptor and strike versions of this aircraft.

With regard to our own espionage effort, we are fortunate in having acquired the services of Pyotr Baranovich, who is engaged on the design and development of the weapons-system itself. He has recruited, as you are aware, two other highly-qualified technicians, and David Edgecliffe has supplied the Moscow end of the pipeline—Pavel Upenskoy, his best native Russian agent. However impressive it all sounds—and we both know that it is—it is not sufficient! What we have learned, or are likely to learn will be insufficient to reproduce or neutralise the threat of the Mig-31. Baranovich and his team know little of the aircraft outside their own specialisations, so compartmented is the secrecy of the research.

Therefore, we must mount, or be preparing to mount within the next five years, an operation against the Bilyarsk project. I am suggesting nothing less than that we should *steal* one of the aircraft, preferably a full production prototype around the time of its final trials.

I can conceive your surprise! However, I think it feasible, providing a pilot can be found. I would think it necessary to employ an American, since our own RAF pilots no longer train in aerial combat (I am considering *all* the possibilities), and an American with combat experience in Vietnam might be best of all. We have the network in Moscow and Bilyarsk which could place pilot and the plane in successful proximity.

Your thoughts on the above should prove enlightening. I look forward to receiving them.

Sincerely,
Kenneth Aubrey

* * * *

My dear Sir Richard,
    I am grateful for your prompt reply to my request.
I really wished to know more about the aircraft itself
—perhaps you could forward a digest of Aubrey's reports over the past three years? As to his suggestion
—I presume he is not in earnest? It is, of course, ridiculous to talk of piracy against the Soviet Union!
    My regards to your wife.

                        Sincerely,
                        Andrew Gresham

'C'/KA   13/2/76

Kenneth—
    I enclose a copy of the P.M.'s letter of yesterday.
You will see what he thinks of your budding criminal-
ity! At least as far as aircraft are concerned. His opinion is also mine—officially. Privately, I'll admit this
Bilyarsk thing is scaring the pants off me! Therefore,
do what you can to find a pilot, and work up a scenario for this proposed operation—just in case! You
might try making enquiries of our friend Buckholz in
the CIA, who has just got himself promoted Head of
the Covert Action Staff—or is his title Director over
there? Anyway, the Americans have as much to lose
as Europe in this, and are just as interested in Bilyarsk.
    Good hunting. On this, don't call me, I'll call you—
if and when!

                        Sincerely,
                        Richard

                    •   •   •   •

My dear Prime Minister,
    You requested Sir Richard Cunningham to supply
you with clarification of certain technical matters aris-

ing in connection with the aircraft we have code-named the 'Firefox' (Mikoyan Mig-31). I suppose that this letter is an opportunity to further plead my cause, but I think it important that you understand the gravity of Russian development in certain fields of military aviation, all of which are to meet in the focal point of this aircraft.

Our information comes principally from the man Baranovich, who has been responsible for the electronics that make practical the theoretical work of others on a thought-guided weapons system for use in high-technology aircraft. Baranovich cannot supply us with all the information we require even on this area of the Bilyarsk project, and we would be unlikely to successfully remove him from Russia, guarded as they all are in Bilyarsk. Hence my suggestion that we steal one of the later series of production prototypes, which will contain everything the Russians intend to put in the front-line versions.

Perhaps I should cite at this point an interesting civil development of the idea of thought-guidance—the latest type of invalid chair being studied in the United States. This is intended to enable a completely paralysed and/or immobilised person to control the movements of an invalid carriage by positive thought activity. The chair would be electronically rigged so that sensors attached to the brain (via a 'cap' or headrest of some kind) would transmit the commands of the brain, as electronic impulses, to the mechanics of the wheelchair or invalid carriage. A mental command to move ahead, turn round, to move left or right, shall we say, would come direct from the brain—instead of the command being transmitted to wasted or useless muscles, it would go into the artificial 'limbs' of the wheelchair. Theer is no projected military development of any such system; whereas the Soviets, it would appear, are close to perfecting just such a system for military use. (And the West has not yet built the wheelchair.)

The system which we are convinced Baranovich is developing seems designed to couple radar and infra-red, those two standard forms of detection and guidance in modern aircraft—with a thought-guided and -controlled arsenal aboard the plane. Radar, as you are aware, bounces a signal off a solid object, and a screen reveals what is actually there: infra-red reveals on a screen what heat-sources are in the vicinity of the detection equipment. For guidance purposes, either or both these methods can be used to direct missiles and to aim them. The missiles themselves contain one or both of these systems themselves. However, the principal advantage of the thought-guided system is that the pilot retains command of his missiles after firing, as well as having a speeded-up command of their actual release, because his mental commands become translated directly to the firing-system, without his physical interference.

It must be said that we do not have, nor do the Russians we understand, weapons that will exploit such a sophisticated system—such as new kinds of missile or cannon. However, unless we quickly nullify the time advantage of the Russian programme, we will be left too far behind by the undoubted acceleration of missile and cannon technology ever to catch up.

Therefore, we must possess this system. We must steal a Mig-31, at some time.

Sincerely,
Kenneth Aubrey

* * * *

Alone in his office, the smell of fresh paint still strong in his nostrils, KGB Colonel Mihail Yurievich Kontarsky, Head of the 'M' Department assigned to security of the Mikoyan project at Bilyarsk, was again a prey to lurid doubts. He had been left alone by his assistant, Dmitri Priabin, and the sense of reassurance he had drawn from the work they had done that afternoon had dissipated in the large room. He sat behind the big, new desk, and willed himself to remain calm.

It had been going on too long, he realised—this need for the sedative of work. He had lost, he knew, the sense of perspective, now that the date for the final weapons trials on the Mig-31 was so close. It was nothing, it seemed, but a last-minute panic—grabbing up the bits and pieces of his job like scattered luggage. All the time afraid that he had forgotten something.

He was afraid to leave his office at that moment, because he knew his body could not yet assume its characteristic arrogance of posture. He would be recognised in the corridors of the Centre as a worried man; and that might prove an irretrievable error on his part.

He had known about the security leaks at Bilyarsk for years—about Baranovich, Kreshin and Semelovsky —and their courier, Dherkov the grocer. Over such a period of time as the Mig had taken to be developed and built, it was impossible that he should not have known.

But, he and his department had done nothing about them, nothing more than reduce the flow of information to a trickle by tightening surveillance, preventing meetings, drops, and the like. Because—he suddenly dropped his head into his hands, pressing his palms against his closed eyelids—he had gambled, out of fear. He had been afraid to recommend the removal of vital human components from the project, and afraid that even if he did then the British or the CIA would suborn others whose existence would be unknown to him, or put in new agents and contacts he did not know. Better the devil you know, he had told Priabin when he made the decision, trying to smile; and the young man had gone along with him. Now it seemed an eminently foolish remark.

The price of failure had been absolute, even then. Disgrace, even execution. He tried to comfort himself by thinking that whatever the British and Americans knew, it was far less than they might have known. . . .

His narrow, dark features were wan and tired, his grey eyes fearful. He had had to let them continue working, even if they were spies. The words sounded hollowly, as if he were already reciting them to an unbelieving audience, even to Andropov himself . . .

1
THE
MURDER

The walk from the British Airways BAC-111 across the tarmac of Cheremetievo Airport seemed interminable to the slightly-built man at the end of the file of passengers. The wind whipped at his trilby, which he held in place, jamming it firmly down with one hand while in the other he held a travel bag bearing the legend of the airline. He was an undistinguished individual —he wore spectacles, heavy-rimmed, and his top lip was decorated with a feeble growth of moustache. His nose was reddened, and his cheeks blanched, by the chill wind. He wore a dark topcoat and dark trousers, and anonymous shoes. Only the churning of his stomach, the bilious fear, placed and defined him. . .

He knew that the men who stood behind the customs officials were probably security men—KGB. He placed his airline bag between the screens of the detector, and his other luggage came sliding towards him on the conveyor belt. The man did not move—he had already anticipated what would happen next. One of the two men standing with apparent indifference behind the customs men, stepped forward and lifted the two suitcases clear of the belt.

The man watched the customs officer fixedly, seeming to ignore the security man as he opened each of the suitcases, and urgently, thoroughly, ruffled through the clothing they contained. The customs official checked his papers, and then passed them to the controller at the end of the long counter. The ruffling of the clothes became more urgent, and the smile on the face of the KGB man disappeared, replaced by an intent, baffled stare into the well of each suitcase.

The official said: 'Mr. Alexander Thomas Orton? What is your business in Moscow?'

The man coughed, and replied: 'As you can see from my papers, I am an export agent of the Excelsior Plastics Company, of Welwyn Garden City.'

'Yes, indeed.' The man's eyes kept flickering to the frustrated mime of the security officer. 'You—have been to the Soviet Union several times during the past two years, Mr. Orton?'

'Again, yes—and nothing like this has happened to me before!' The man was not annoyed, merely surprised. He seemed determined to be pleasant, a seasoned, knowledgeable visitor to Russia, and not to regard the insults being levied at his possessions.

'I apologise,' the official said. The KGB man was now in muttered conversation with the customs officer. The remainder of the passengers had already passed through the gate, and spilled into the concourse of the passenger lounge. They were gone, and Mr. Alexander Thomas Orton was feeling rather alone.

'I have all the correct papers, you know,' he said. 'Signed by your Trade Attaché at the Soviet Embassy in London.' There was a trace of nervousness in his voice, as if some practical joke which he did not understand were being perpetrated against him. 'As you say, I've been here a number of times—there's never been any trouble of this kind before. Does he really have to make such a mess of my belongings—what is he looking for?'

The KGB man approached. Alexander Thomas Orton brushed a hand across his oiled hair, and tried to smile. The Russian was a big man, with flattened Mongol features and an unpleasant aura of minor, frustrated, power about him. He took the passport and the visas from the official, and made a business of their scrutiny.

When he appeared satisfied, he stared hard into Orton's face and said: 'Why do you come to Moscow, Mr.—Orton?'

'Orton—yes. I am a businessman, an exporter, to be exact.'

'What do you hope to export to the Soviet Union, from your country?' There was a sneer in the Russian's voice, a curl of the lip to emphasise it. There was something unreal about the whole business. The man brushed his oiled hair again, and seemed more nervous than previously, as if caught out in some prank.

'Plastic goods—toys, games, that sort of thing.'

'Where are your samples—the rubbish you sell, Mr. Orton?'

'Rubbish? Look here!'

'You are English, Mr. Orton? Your voice . . . it does not sound very English.'

'I am Canadian by birth.'

'You do not look Canadian, Mr. Orton.'

'I—try to appear as English as possible. It helps, in sales abroad, you understand?' Suddenly, he remembered the vocal training, with a flick of irritation like the sting of a wet towel; it had seemed amidst his other tasks absurd in its slightness. Now, he was thankful for it.

'I do not understand.'

'Why did you search my luggage?'

The KGB man was baffled for a moment. 'There—is no need for you to know that. You are a visitor to the Soviet Union. Remember that, Mr. Orton!' As if to express his anger, he held up the small transistor radio as a last resort, looked into Orton's face, then tugged open the back of the set. Orton clenched his hands in his pockets, and waited.

The Russian, evidently disappointed, closed the back and said: 'Why do you bring this? You cannot receive your ridiculous programmes in Moscow!' The man shrugged, and the set and the passport were thrust at him. He took them, trying to control the shaking of his hands.

Then he stooped, picked up his hand grip, and waited as the KGB man closed his suitcases, and then dropped them at his feet. The lock of one burst, and shirts and socks brimmed over. The KGB man laughed as Orton scrabbled after two pairs of rolling grey socks, on his knees. When he finally closed the lid, his hair was hanging limply over his brow, interfering with his vision. He flicked the lock away, adjusted his spectacles, and hoisted his cases at his sides. Then, mustering as much offended dignity as he could, he walked slowly away, into the concourse, towards the huge glass doors which would let him into the air, and relief. He did not need to look behind him to understand that the KGB man was already consulting with his colleague who had not moved from his slouched, assured stance against the wall behind the customs desk, and who had obviously been the superior in rank. That second man had watched him intently throughout his time at the desk—customs, passport and KGB. . .

He called for a taxi from the rank outside the main doors of the passenger lounge, setting down his suitcases, and cramming his trilby on his head once more against the fierce wind, little abated by the shelter of the terminal building.

A black taxi drew up, and he said: 'Hotel Moskva, please,' in as pleasant, innocuous a voice as he could muster.

The driver opened the door for him, loaded his suitcases, jumped back in the cab, and then waited, engine idling. Gant knew he was waiting for the KGB tail-car to collect him. Gant had seen the signal from the KGB man who had bullied him, a shadowy, bulking figure. He took off his hat and leaned sideways, so that he saw the long, sleek, vividly-chromed saloon in the driver's mirror. Then the driver of the taxi engaged the gears and they pulled out of the airport, onto the motorway that would take him south-east into the centre of Moscow—the wide, prestigious Leningrad Avenue. He settled back in his seat, being careful not to glance behind him through the tinted rear window. The black saloon would be behind him, he knew. . .

As he considered his success, and was thankful for the solid lack of imagination and insight of his interrogator, he acknowledged the brilliance of Aubrey's mind. The little plump Englishman had been developing Gant's cover as Orton, a cover merely to get him unobtrusively into Russia, for a long time. For almost two years, a man looking very much as Gant did now, had been passing through customs at Cheremetievo. An exporter, touting with some success a range of plastic toys. Apparently, they sold rather well in GUM, in Red Square. A fact that had amused Aubrey a great deal.

There was, naturally, more; Alexander Thomas Orton was a smuggler. The KGB's suspicions had been carefully aroused concerning Orton's possible activities in the drug-smuggling line a little more than a year before. Orton had been watched carefully, closely—yet never harried so openly before. Gant wondered whether Aubrey had not turned the screw on him. The big, dumb KGB man had expected to find something in his luggage, that was certain. And, now that his suspicions, aroused and then frustrated, had remained unfulfilled, Gant was being tailed to his hotel.

The taxi passed the Khimky Reservoir on the right, the expanse of grey water looking cold and final under the cloudy, rushing sky. Soon, they were into the built-up, urban mass of the city, and Gant watched the Dynamo Stadium sliding past the window to his left.

Aubrey, Gant knew, had been unimpressed by him. Not that he cared. Gant, for all his involvement in the part he was playing, had never intended to impress. He was at the beginning of his journey and, if he felt any emotion at all, it was one of impatience. Only one thing had mattered to him, ever since Buckholz had found him, in that dead-beat pizza palace in Los Angeles during his lunch-break, when he had been working as a garage-hand—it had been the first, and only time, he had left the Apache group, the tame Mig-squadron belonging to the USAF, and only one thing had ever mattered. He would get to fly the greatest airplane in history. If Gant possessed a soul any longer, which he doubted, it would be in that idea, enshrined perhaps, even embalmed therein. Buckholz had got him to fly again, on the Mig-21, and then the Foxbat; then he had left, tried to run away. Then Buckholz had found him again, and the idea had been broached ... the Firefox. ...

He wiped the sweat from his forehead on the leg of his dark trousers. He closed his eyes, and tried not to think about the past. It had been the dream, he thought. That damned dream had started this. That, and his nettled, irritated pride because smug, patronising Aubrey had looked down his nose at him. Gant's hands bunched into fists on the plastic seat. Like a child, all he wanted to do now was to show them, show them all, just as he had wanted to show them in Clarkville, that dead town of dead people. There was only one way to show Aubrey. He had to bring back his airplane —the Firefox.

Kontarsky was on the telephone, the extension that linked him with his superior officer within the Industrial Security Section of the 2nd Chief Directorate, of which the 'M' department formed a small, but vital, part. Dmitri Priabin watched his chief carefully, almost like a prompter following an actor, script open on his knees. Kontarsky seemed much more at ease than during their interview the previous day, as if action had soothed him during the last twenty-four hours.

During that elapsed period, Kontarsky had received an up-to-date report from the KGB unit at Bilyarsk, and surveillance of the underground cell had been increased. There had been no unaccountable arrivals in Bilyarsk during the past forty-eight hours, and only the courier, Dherkov, had left the small town. His grocery van had been thoroughly searched on his return from Moscow. Kontarsky had ordered searches of all vehicles arriving in the town, and a thorough scrutiny of all personnel passing inside the security fence of the factory. Dog patrols had been intensified around the perimeter fence, and the number of armed guards in the hangars had been trebled.

Once those things had been done, Kontarsky and Priabin had both begun to feel more at ease. Priabin himself was to leave for Bilyarsk that night by KGB helicopter, and take over effective command of the security forces from the officer on the spot. Effectively, within hours, he could seal Bilyarsk tight. Kontarsky had decided not to travel with the First Secretary and his party, but to impress by being on the spot himself twenty-four hours before the test-flight. They would arrest the members of the underground only a matter of hours before the flight, and at the time of arrival of the First Secretary, they would already be undergoing interrogation. It would, he calculated, be sure to impress the First Secretary and Andropov who would be part of the entourage. Both Priabin and Kontarsky anticipated extracting the maximum satisfaction from the interrogations. Baranovich, Kreshin, Semelovsky. Dherkov and his wife, would be snatched out of their false sense of security in a theatrical and impressive display of ruthless KGBM efficiency. . .

Once in his room, Gant removed the clear-glass spectacles, ruffled his hair deliberately, and pulled off his tie. It was as if he had released himself from a straitjacket. He opened his suitcases, then slipped off his shoes. The room was a small suite, with the tall windows looking out over the windswept expanse of Red Square. Gant ignored the window, and helped himself to a Scotch from the drinks trolley placed in one corner of the room. He seated himself on a low sofa, put his feet up, and tried to relax. He had begun to realise that his attempted indifference would not work, not even in the apparent, luxurious safety of his centrally-heated, double-glazed hotel room. He had been instructed not to look for bugs, since he couldn't be sure that he was not being observed through some two-way mirror device. . .

The Scotch, as he swallowed another mouthful, no longer warmed him. Already his thoughts were reaching into the immediate future, towards the meeting with three men he did not know on the embankment of the Moskva, near the Krasnokholmskiy Bridge. He was to leave the hotel after dinner, and behave as a tourist, no matter who tailed him. All he had to do was to be certain to arrive at ten-thirty. He was to be sure to take his hat and overcoat—no, to wear them—and he had to take the transistor radio. That told him that he would not be returning to the hotel; it would be the beginning of his journey to Bilyarsk.

The moment Gant steps out of the Moscow hotel, the KGB is in pursuit as he begins his daring mission to penetrate Bilyarsk and steal FIREFOX, the deadliest warplane ever built. Taut, compelling and brilliantly researched, this novel moves to a climax of explosive, nerve-shredding intensity.

Read the complete Bantam Book, available November 29, wherever paperbacks are sold.

WHAT IF . . .

Fires, floods, air disasters, political intrigue. Events that could happen . . . and do in these exciting best-sellers. Guaranteed to keep you on the edge of your seat.

☐ 10476	AIRPORT	*Arthur Hailey*	$1.95
☐ 10940	BLACK SUNDAY *Thomas Harris*		$2.25
☐ 11708	JAWS 2	*Hank Searls*	$2.25
☐ 12600	JAWS	*Peter Benchley*	$2.50
☐ 10888	RAISE THE TITANIC! *Clive Cussler*		$2.25
☐ 11766	DELUGE	*Richard Doyle*	$2.25
☐ 11767	IMPERIAL 109	*Richard Doyle*	$2.50
☐ 12679	RUNWAY ZERO-EIGHT *Arthur Hailey*		$2.25
☐ 10048	SEVEN DAYS IN MAY *Knebel & Bailey*		$1.95
☐ 11631	22 FIRES	*Agel & Boe*	$1.95
☐ 12520	ICEBERG	*Clive Cussler*	$2.25
☐ 12302	AVALANCHE *Robert Weverka*		$1.95
☐ 12151	ICE!	*Arnold Federbush*	$2.25

Buy them at your local bookstore or use this handy coupon for ordering:

DON'T MISS
THESE CURRENT
Bantam Bestsellers

☐ 11708	**JAWS 2** Hank Searls	$2.25
☐ 11150	**THE BOOK OF LISTS** Wallechinsky & Wallace	$2.50
☐ 11001	**DR. ATKINS DIET REVOLUTION**	$2.25
☐ 11161	**CHANGING** Liv Ullmann	$2.25
☐ 10116	**EVEN COWGIRLS GET THE BLUES** Tom Robbins	$2.25
☐ 10077	**TRINITY** Leon Uris	$2.75
☐ 12250	**ALL CREATURES GREAT AND SMALL** James Herriot	$2.50
☐ 12256	**ALL THINGS BRIGHT AND BEAUTIFUL** James Herriot	$2.50
☐ 11770	**ONCE IS NOT ENOUGH** Jacqueline Susann	$2.25
☐ 11470	**DELTA OF VENUS** Anais Nin	$2.50
☐ 10150	**FUTURE SHOCK** Alvin Toffler	$2.25
☐ 12196	**PASSAGES** Gail Sheehy	$2.75
☐ 11255	**THE GUINNESS BOOK OF WORLD RECORDS** 16th Ed. The McWhirters	$2.25
☐ 12220	**LIFE AFTER LIFE** Raymond Moody, Jr.	$2.25
☐ 11917	**LINDA GOODMAN'S SUN SIGNS**	$2.50
☐ 10310	**ZEN AND THE ART OF MOTORCYCLE MAINTENANCE** Pirsig	$2.50
☐ 10888	**RAISE THE TITANIC!** Clive Cussler	$2.25
☐ 11267	**AQUARIUS MISSION** Martin Caidin	$2.25
☐ 11897	**FLESH AND BLOOD** Pete Hamill	$2.50

Buy them at your local bookstore or use this handy coupon for ordering:

RELAX!
SIT DOWN
and Catch Up On Your Reading!

Bantam Book Catalog

Here's your up-to-the-minute listing of over 1,400 titles by your favorite authors.

This illustrated, large format catalog gives a description of each title. For your convenience, it is divided into categories in fiction and non-fiction—gothics, science fiction, westerns, mysteries, cookbooks, mysticism and occult, biographies, history, family living, health, psychology, art.

So don't delay—take advantage of this special opportunity to increase your reading pleasure.

Just send us your name and address and 50¢ (to help defray postage and handling costs).